Revenant Sun

A novel by Eric Danhoff

ShadowArt Publishing

ISBN-13: 978-0692600948
ISBN-10: 0692600949

For Annie.
For our baby.

Revenant Sun

Part one:

Abnormal End

ONE

The screen of the computer reflected white lights against open eyes. Sirens were in full scream from the outside. Distant shades of crimson and ocean coated dilated pupils. Glass shattered loud enough to elicit movement from the man barely awake. The hotel room was a small, dark cube; littered with enough trash and wires to resemble the inside of a failed machine. His body was an apt comparison. A cocktail of drugs weaved through a bloodstream squeezed of oxygen. Gunshots were faded, but loud enough to raise the tempo of his heartbeat. The windows near him shattered. Hands moved across the table and swept away half eaten food for the device. Liquid had pooled out from his eyes and mouth, dripping slowly. They were coming for him.

A metal surface came into contact with an anxious hand. His fingers scrambled for the activator on the top of the device. Sounds of storms pushed their way through weak walls. A clicking noise began to emanate from the metal sphere near the center of the table. The man slowly got to his feet and reached in his pockets. A gun was left in the corner on the kitchen counter. Tripping over spare parts, he grabbed the pistol and left.

The hallway went in two directions. He made a decision. Blue lines followed each turn of his head. Movements were exaggerated. The air was heavy, it forced him to struggle. Behind him, wood splintered underneath a steel battering ram. They did not take time to shout his name, or to announce his arrest. The goal was blood. Within the darkness of the room, the sphere ignited littered paper and old wood. Equipment burned within seconds, along with several cops. Boots melted, powder blue uniforms seared with a sound that was buried by their own screams.

A window cracked open led to the fire escape. The stairs were rusted brown and made too much noise as he descended. Garbage piled up near a dumpster looked like a safe landing. There were still five levels. In minutes, cruisers would find their way around to the alley below. The gun almost slipped from his hand with each jump to the next scaffold. He decided to try it and poured himself over the railing. His body smashed into the pile, no feelings of pain. He thanked the drugs, shaking off what could have been a broken rib. The hand holding his gun felt an extra spur of bone pressing underneath the skin. At the end of the road past the intersection was the entrance to an old aqueduct. Lights ripped away comfortable dark. They moved faster than usual tonight. He hopped over the fence, tearing holes in his jeans on barbed wire decades old.

The hotel was further away now, covered in all sirens and lights. Swift footsteps marked the night with percussive beats. He still knew how to move despite the handicap of chemicals in his system. Step after step through emptied alleys. That was all he knew, really; systems and how to break them down. All a hacker really did in his mind was knock down an existing wall to help build a better one. Step by step, the beats increased in speed. Systems he knew, and also chemicals. He loved those. Just like a body, in that when one is pushed to its maximum potential, it will soon falter. The process of breaking down can take years. Even as the functions of a machine continue without flaw, better ones will be formed and pushed out to the audience. Knowledge of the turns and twists leads to manipulation by curious minds. The entrance to the aqueduct was an open tunnel down a slope of beaten concrete. Cool air from flowing water coated him with a certain comfort. Lights behind him grew bright. The voices telling him to stop were more vicious.

Once a system is figured out by said minds, it can be stretched into something else. It becomes a weapon in an arsenal. People were ignorant to the real movement behind their own technology. Countless names became a currency at a young age. His legs pumped new blood, less enamored with the drugs. He climbed to an overhead slum, tucked away from the main roads. Platforms held makeshift houses for those unable to live in townhouses and compacted apartments high above the storm that followed him. Cops would not interrogate the homeless. No need to ask questions. They knew exactly who he was, and where he was going. Kids began to follow him across the platform when bullets found their way through the metal. Screaming interrupted the tempo as some of the children found themselves targets in the blind fire. Little bodies hit the platform hard, but he smiled. No need for sorrow. Life was temporary as it was.

Beneath the slum was a garden of dead grass. Faded flowers struggled along in private corners. Looking down, he saw through chain link fence to see dirty toys and old tools. There must have been a switch. Uniforms of blue finally bashed their way into the slum from the streets below. He stopped and counted the seconds while stomping his foot along the poles of the fence. Soon, the pressure point triggered and the fence disconnected from the platform. He hit the ground hard enough to elicit a laugh. Cops shined flashlights down into the garden before descending. His hood ripped open, shredded even more on brambles and weeds. He hoped for an opening out to the road. A hole, small even for a child, was there. His body was thin enough to slide through. The main road was more than 30 feet away. Freedom was, too.

Once that new wall is built, the hacker is tasked with starting over that same process; studying the target, adaptation to its pattern, discovery of any anomalies, exploitation of said advantages. Once the new weapon is added to the arsenal, the prize claimed in the meantime is open to the world of commerce. The supply and demand of private information was always a business of risk. It was the only reason for the bullets behind him. He could see the aqueduct entrance dip down behind the street. The legs of this machine were tired. His fingers traced the bone sticking out from the others, wondering when he would find time to get it looked a…

The sound of his body smashing into metal and glass was sickening. His limp body was thrown off into the distance. The black car did not take a moment to slow down. Unseen, the driver knocked a bigger hole into the windshield before disappearing into black. Sirens returned in broken echoes. Blood and blue sea washed over his eyes. Both legs felt different. Something must have broken in each of them. Steps were made carefully. He could put his weight down. It was enough to try running again. Weapons were pointed. Those same voices were now hoarse. They promised death if he took the chance to run for water. The buildings all around him were filled shadows hidden behind glass as yellow poured out into the street from each square. Unknown faces looked into him.

His lips curled into a smile. There were just enough chemicals in the system to keep him from fear. Life was temporary, wasn't it? One hand moved from the bone in his side to the pistol in his pocket. The screams became louder. It was a surprise to him that they did not fire right away. Maybe if he took it out and started shooting it? Once the gun came out, his face became stone. The clip was missing. It had been left in the hotel room. Every other weapon in a one block radius emptied enough bullets to rip him apart. It was not fast enough to keep his face from changing back to a smile. He hit the ground hard. His legs peeled back as if the bones were removed from the skin. The back of his head smashed into the pavement. It created a haze that distracted him from overwhelming pain. His eyes stayed open, staring into the night sky. Medical teams arrived within a minute. Two men burst through the back door of the transport unit, items in hand to grab the body in the middle of the street. A hand grabs each of them at the arm. A few feet away sat a black car, a hole in the windshield. Two new men stood in black suits behind them. Their holsters were exposed from the folds of their tailored jackets. Each held a large gun that poured out with each step from the shadows.

The world went black for a second. The medic stood frozen. His eyes were stone. Darkness and light repeated over and over as if someone were toying with a light switch. The picture returned and disappeared again just as quickly. Existence was suspended. The film had fallen off the reel. Everything stopped for a few awkward seconds. The colors of the image came and went with the whirring sounds of a broken projector. Somewhere in that same dark, there was a voice that spoke calmly.

"It felt real, didn't it? With a resolution so clear, it's as if these moments were happening right in front of you."

There was someone else in here. The others in the room were on edge. They could hear the voice speaking all around them. The sound was warm.

"But I know that some of you still have doubts about the capabilities of the program."

His robotic tone vibrated their eardrums. Something changed in his inflections. The words became closer, his volume lowered. It was meant to recreate the feeling of someone whispering. Tension was building. Each of them could almost feel a small burst of air. Invisible breath created waves of electricity, reflected by the hair on the back of their necks. They all wanted to know; who was this speaking?

"Let's continue, then…"

The picture moved in rewind, from the hacker's death, to the chase past the hotel and through the slum. Small short films repeated the series of events from behind the cops themselves like old memories. Lines resembling white noise cut through the pixels of color. Some said that it resembled tracking from old VHS tapes. They all moved their fingers and toes restlessly. There was a feeling of warmth, and weightlessness. The others in the room were frozen, no way to tell how many, or what size the room itself had been. No lights except for the screen that consumed our eyes in a flood of information.

The unknown host called out to phantom engineers to stop the feed.

"Let's have some fun…Try channel seventeen."

A new voice echoed through their ears.

"Police chased the man through a series of alleys until a hit and run knocked his body high into the air."

She was a newscaster. Each word was spoken with poise. She over-enunciated every word with no sign of emotion. Soon, her words faded into the sea of sound as the host continued.

"Her voice is as clear and as warm as my own. She sounds as if she is speaking directly into your own ears. Thirteen."

The cameras cut to different angles of the alleys.

"What's most beautiful about this observation is that it is true. Eighteen."

A ripple of white noise took them to a new perspective. New voices broke their silence with each change in viewpoint. Each reporter continued the report given to the public regarding the incident.

"The bones in your ear are stimulated by small electrical shocks, vibrating your eardrums to create the sensation that your brain recognizes as someone speaking directly into your ears. This way, the audience feels completely at home. The reporters are reading to you in the comfort of your own home; a quiet room, unaffected by the outside."

Helicopter lights flashed over brown concrete revealing pools of blood. Different lenses moved back and forth between shocked bystanders. The red ran down from the platform and into the dead garden.

"Once surrounded, the gunman, attempted to fire his weapon upon the officers, but was thankfully gunned down before any more innocents could be claimed."

The voices of different reporters began to loop and combine into a mess of sounds. It became a pool of static that continued even as the host called out to lower the volume. All heads in the audience moved in unison. To them, this could not be real. They wanted to see more, see what other news stories could be opened up and pulled apart completely. Some of them wanted to unplug and go back home to their empty beds. But the host did not cease, instead calling out for the lights to return. Soon, the audience could see their surroundings. There was no soundstage, or theater screen. Each of them had been sitting in the chairs of a waiting room. The room was an empty, dead white. Without warning, a man with clear skin in a neatly tailored suit appeared in their field of vision. He existed only through their eyes. A simulation. This was the initial demonstration that greeted a newDawn user. This was demonstration number two million, three hundred thousand, ninety four.

"Now, you can see me. It may seem jarring at first, but try not to be alarmed. Remember that I am not in your head, but rather, I am merely a piece of the information flowing through it."

The host took a bow amidst ever changing skin.

"My name is Adam, and I am here to introduce you to the future."

The audience was captivated. They always were.

"It matters not what I look like, for you have created what is here before you. Residual imagery based on centuries of personality and preference data fills this empty space occupied by my voice. To everyone viewing me, my features will be unique to your own subconscious specifications. The colors I wear, the skin covering my shell, are every shade that has ever been."

The host was right. Each took a moment to fumble with their interface. There was an option to change to the perspectives of the other users. After 30 seconds, the option disappeared. Their reactions were always forms of awe and disbelief. Some had waited to see if Artificial Intelligence would ever take a moment to be lazy, to only show two or three color schemes. It would have been enough, considering the strength of the current software. But every time, every perspective was different, unique to the very person viewing the shell.

"What if I told you that your entire life was being built up to a specific moment in time?"

By and large, this was the best part, according to general opinion of first time users.

"Imagine growing into an adult never being able to control your own life, shape your own destiny. The world moved on its own, and you were a spectator to history."

Adam disappeared into lines of code, slowly forming an eternal ocean of text that spread over their eyes.

"Imagine being left behind, as bigotry and negativity pierce every image and sound produced at large. This was the world before the fall."

The ocean of text began to form lines and gain colors, bringing forth images of the past.

There was footage of fires, natural disasters taking place in real time. It was interesting to see what he showed to each audience. Depending on the people connected, he moved in sync with their own tastes. The few times that apathy registered with some of the viewers, the slideshow changed to garner more visceral reactions. There were still frames of expired humans but those too began to move. Some were piled into large mounds. Bodies were raped, engulfed in flames that soon consumed entire cities. Soldiers were mutilated with slow precision. These were products of the old wars. It was hard to watch at times. Most often, they would close their eyes and let those cruel realities be relived with new eyes. Those who did not react to said images were reported to the authorities. Adam was constantly evolving. It knew how to influence you, make you feel what needed to be felt. It could make you understand.

"Can you recall the hatred and ignorance of the last century? History books may paint better pictures than the actual truth; that society reveled in its improving technology."
Games and cell phones appeared between the old footage of trash being dropped, crushed and discarded by old machines into any place not lived in. These were artifacts, just like the film that produced the images themselves.

"Society found a way to use up as much energy as possible, every resource available. They found a space for every piece of its own garbage. Soon, you ate and drank off your own poisons until it nearly made you extinct. You were too afraid to invest in new ways of life. It took losing everything to realize that you were nothing."

A logo began to emerge in countless pixels that formed behind Adam, breaking the stream of data pouring into those new minds. The pixels became letters, forming newDawn.

"Decades later, in this year of 2045, you are here as part of an advanced, reformed society. Your bodies have now been augmented to transcend those physical and mental limitations. All made possible by the smallest surgical implant behind your ear…"

A tiny piece of metal with three wires phased through the letters.

"Origin; the source of the information and the conduit between the data stream and your own body. These wires are integrated with nanomachines that found their way to the key areas of your body to find a home and connect you to the rest of the world. You are better than human and now, you are a newDawn user. A fully integrated organism with a neural connection to the constantly growing information stored within and endlessly evolving functions made possible through what was once known as cyberspace."

Every newDawn user was given the Blank Page to start with when signing in. Users of newDawn stood covered in white light until a connection was made with the neural network. Adam took their hands and walked them right to the edge, before pushing them gently over the precipice. Within days, they would be encapsulated in comfort and convenience.

"The countless others connecting to the same space as you; this is the network at large."

Once a user becomes integrated, the simulation goes dark and ends. Adam split into countless pieces to provide guidance to each of the new uninitiated. Some users still had dreams of the first simulation. They each ended the same way, lying down to rest with a fair warning. The software took time to monitor your sleep habits, including vital signs and dream patterns in order to help reduce stress and maximize rapid eye movement. Commercials play in their heads while they slept. There were advertisements for food when the groceries ran out, specials for cheap drinks when their stress levels were high. Adam was adept at knowing their preferences but kept a distance that maintained diplomacy. It took time for people chosen for augmentation to be accustomed to another intelligence inside their mind but the convenience of newDawn helped them to understand its purpose. Adam was designed to learn a user's personality and guide them to choices that prolonged their lifespan.

"Welcome to the New World."

Two

A young man opened his eyes to grey light that dripped out from behind the window blinds. Music gradually faded into the air of his bedroom. He stood up, slowly stretching and pressed the small button underneath his ear, which restored the newDawn display interface. Data splattered across his wall. The letters quickly reformed into the numbers of a clock and expected weather for the work week. News items slowly crawled across the floor as he pulled his clothes for the day from the drawer next to the bed. He dressed slowly as snippets of events within the last 24 hours moved across cold wooden boards.

"Good morning, Mr. Gabrels."

He did not answer the greeting; it was the same cadence each time. Nothing new. It was to rain at least twenty two hours that week. The new weather application had a successful prediction rate of 86%. Adam's voice entered the room as soon as it had left his dreams. Gabrels opened his shoe closet to grab a pair of sneakers. There were three shelves, a total of thirty five pairs. Today felt like ivory and red, he decided. A thin, grey buttoned shirt and tight jeans, neatly torn in strategic spots, covered his middling frame as Adam ran through his itinerary for the day.

The quota for articles about new products began to increase since the start of the financial quarter. The more articles released meant more online presence. A rev's online presence was more important than the actual words in the articles. New content was needed at a near constant basis. As fast as information could be read, something new needed to be pushed out into the data stream. New articles meant more food for eyes hungry for the latest augmentation tech and applications that improved the convenience of newDawn.

"Work begins in one hour and 23 minutes. With traffic conditions as they are, you will be five minutes late to start your shift if you leave now."

Gabrels silently waved as he entered the hallway to the kitchen. His apartment sat on the top floor of the complex. Above the ceiling were thousands of pounds of concrete made to hold the spires that acted as a source point for the stream; the river of information that flowed through newDawn, optimized by Adam and regulated by the government that still remained from the world before the fall. The floor tiles of the kitchen matched the teal marble, dotted with splashes of onyx. Heavy blinds kept the bustling city out of sight. The windows were reinforced by steel frames and tempered glass. After his hands were washed, he made a blended drink; a mix of synthesized fruits and vegetables.

Adam designed the drink years ago as a way to maximize nutrition intake and consolidate the amount of time spent on consumption. Gabrels preferred it over anything else. He had never liked the taste of alcohol. The walls of the apartment were a stark white, but Adam could change the colors that his eyes processed within a matter of seconds. He felt the notion to change them again that morning. The apartment quickly morphed into a mix of black shades and ebony wood accents. Once ready, the drink was inhaled in a series of careful gulps. He called out to open the blinds as he went back into his room to grab a coat.

The blinds moved in harmony, revealing the madness of the outside. Droning noise filled the living room and bled into every open space. The center of the city state could be seen from that high. Train routes spread from the Epicentre like veins. Each path was dotted with plumes of smoke and dimmed lights that would intensify the more sunlight faded. Individual forms of transportation were considered artifacts. The train routes stretched out in North, South, East and West before splitting into double helix shapes that covered the expanse. Gabrels put on a red windbreaker, form fitting, and brought up the music player. In the corner of his eye, a small menu appeared. His reflection was visible; a miniature mirror tucked away for when he was in a hurry. It was a newly released app that used reflected light off surrounding surfaces to power the camera software enough to show the user their appearance if they were not close to a bathroom. Brown hair curled and sat on the top of his head. Fine shaved lines circled underneath the mop and met at his nape. He had broad cheekbones and defined lines that connected his jaw to his thin neck. There was still a trace of boyhood in his features. Pursed lips bent to form a smirk. A picture snapped off and was posted to the data stream within a second. He wrote a specific playlist for the morning commute, perfect for drowning out the machinations of early travel. The first song began to play as he shut the door behind him.

The Epicentre was the core of the city-state; it was a transportation hub, center of commerce, business, education, finance and law enforcement all in one massive chain of concrete buildings that were bound together by glass hallways. Before it was made illegal, tourists used to stop in the middle of the halls and aim their cameras down for countless pictures of the view, which led all the way into the pipelines, several thousand feet down. The buildings were dwarfed only by the tenements; thirteen towers over 200 floors each, which held 45% of the population in modest chambers overlooking the remainder of America.

There were other cities just like it that he had never been to. He saw pictures of them all the time. They stood like monoliths, casting shadows that crossed with his city to make an x over the face of the country.

Gabrels waited in a plain white hallway for the elevator doors to open. He stepped into the red room behind steel doors and made his selection; the dock. It was here where tenants could board the train to head to the industrial district. That was the place you went to make money. Time moved twice as fast and the trains were packed with occupied faces. Workers in the data district called it Tempest. You had to move fast to make it there. When he started working at eighteen, he was told he had to earn his sleep.

Granted, no one could get a job in the district unless they were augmented. They needed improved humans to handle the output. A loud metallic noise cut through the music. He pushed his way through the crowd of suits and found a seat at the back window. There were almost never any children on the trains. Most humans still unimproved stayed in the slums, never making it to Tempest.

The chamber leapt forward and began to pick up speed then dropped a hard left back onto the main path. Gabrels looked out to the vast series of veins that the train cars burned through. It was a competition for everyone who lived there. The highways were abandoned for trains after the fall. Air pollution was streamlined but left many hands idle with no work. Men who couldn't afford augmentation were sent to the pipelines and to the train stations. Those who had to work continued to do so. Those who had no ambitions were put into the prisons they helped to rebuild. Adam's makers found a way to make everyone useful in this society.

Everything above the slums was built for those who were improved. It was made for them to enjoy. There was another world at ground level; separated shantytowns, old versions of what those in the tenements enjoyed. The pipes which fed electricity and water up to Tempest were vast, with different channels that spread out like a reflection of the trains. The sea levels were high enough to allow a constant siphoning, cleaning and distribution of the water. From the black sea, new clear water was pulled. Thin spaces were carved out by those who pieced the framework together, which allowed them to travel to and from their homes. The unofficial name for the slums was Narrow. Gabrels was raised in the tenements and had never been to those streets underneath the pipelines, but there were days when he would dream about getting lost in mazes of concrete and dead iron. Most of the time on the train to work was spent in those dreams. There were countless others like him; augmented with Origin to have nonstop access to the data stream through newDawn, paid to protect the interests they were assigned, career driven to the point of obsession, fashion forward and only interested in the cutting edge. Their bodies were improved to the point of never needing to worry about diet or exercise. The culture of Tempest was one of competition and a constant divide between the people searching for the best of everything.

A fight broke out between a man and woman five feet from him that broke his concentration. They were both dressed in a slick suit and dress, nearly the same shades of navy blue and white. A quick facial scan and look into their social profiles revealed they had been a couple. She pushed him three times and spit in his face. The crowd around them did not move. There really wasn't any space for them to get out of the way. Her spit landed on someone behind her target, an old man. He wiped his shoulder and grimaced. The man hit her only once before she fell back onto the others forced to share the same air.

No one made a sound. Gabrels wanted someone to tear the train apart, but he knew that the crowd would not move until the police arrived. He decided to stay on the train to see what the officers would do. At every stop after the tenements, a strict circle remained still around the man and unconscious woman. He screamed out, pushing and shoving but there were too many bodies to break through. Gabrels could see the arms of the woman's protectors; organically grown skin was often more pale than the natural alternative. Their hands clenched, shades of yellow pulsated as the steel and wiring lined up. Their arms tightened into an unbreakable line. Some spit back at the man and made comments as they left, knowing that he had no weapons. He would thrash for a minute or two, then give up, then start again once the train stopped. The train filled up and emptied out with new faces. Gabrels stayed in his seat, watching.

A small window appeared in his field of vision, a square of lights that danced off the others in the car, visible to no one else; a social media profile with a picture taken by Gabrels in his bathroom mirror last year. The smile that looked back at him was gleaming. It gave him a slight boost in confidence standing on a train filled with sharply dressed, finely perfected people. Words were etched underneath the photo, penned himself;

"Stanley Gabrels. (bl@ckb7rd). 29 years old. Living in a whirlwind. Augmentation journalist. Finger on the pulse of the future. Try to keep up." He quickly blinked to initiate a status. Letters began to scrawl against the back of another passenger in contrasting white;

"Man just struck his girl on the 9 train towards Eros. Sickened."

Once the status was complete, Adam posted it to the data stream. Comments from users all over the city arrived within seconds.

"Srsly?"

"Come on 2 much of this trash."

"Crowd got him until car stops," he replied.

Others had been posting on the same train as him. They were young ones. He could tell by the language they spoke in; broken and abbreviated.

"Can we ship out the thugs?"

"Don't got many left."

"How exactly?"

"Drop them back in the slums."

"What trash?"

"You trash. We dump you."

"Hey bitch. You on the same train? Meet at platform 3."

"Haha. Too tough for me. I got work."

He closed the window to avoid the mass arguments that would no doubt approach. The A.I. would interfere.

"Is there any issue with the language used in your comment string?" Adam asked.

He waved it off but the comments soon stopped and were quietly removed. The faces involved in the train quickly changed. He could picture the A.I. in their ears, questioning the words they spit out into the stream.

"Mr. Williams, is there an issue? You appear to be involved in an argument with another passenger in close proximity."

"Nah, I'm good," he heard the kid say.

He couldn't lie to Adam. His vitals gave him away.

"Your heartbeat is elevated. Another instance of antagonizing may lead to a physical altercation. There are several officers on the way. I will have them consult with you once the prior incident is handled."

Adam filtered what was considered content unimportant for view. The kids would learn soon enough what you could get away with online.

In the corner of Gabrels' eye, a small advertisement played for the city-state;

"Want to escape the regular world?"

The disembodied voice called out from behind the images of workers in the pipelines and polluted cityscapes.

"Make your way to the top with augmentations from the Synapse Corporation."

A boy from the slums was suddenly transported from the street to a hospital bed; his body covered in heavy bandages. His limbs were punctured with a dozen tubes.

"Improve your body and double your worth."

The boy was suddenly dressed in a suit and tie. He stood on the same train as Gabrels and walked into the Epicentre. The scene morphed into a mass of black machinery. The boy sported steel arms which he shoved into a broken crank shaft, forcing the wheels to turn again.

"Make a difference for the city with Synapse."

"Welcome to paradise," Gabrels said under his breath at the same time as the voice in the ad.

He had heard it a thousand times.

People made their way around the human blockade to continue on their day. The detour would add another fifteen minutes to his late arrival to work, but he stuck around until the train arrived at the platform to Eros, the entertainment center of the city. There were three of them waiting there. Adam checked the amount of emergency calls made since the initial fight; over 45. The officers were ready with clubs in hand and covered in Kevlar padding under their uniforms. The color matched the grey of the painted brick of the platform walls. The train stopped and the circle of bodies quickly moved. The woman fell to the floor as the officers descended on the man. He couldn't have made it out of the car in time. Their clubs made sick noises against his back and knees. He could tell that their arms had been augmented by the lines of neatly placed scar tissue that traced their flexor muscles. A strike from them at full strength multiplied the amount of force by four. There was some mild applause.

Gabrels clapped a few times before getting onto another car that would take him back to the right stop. He found another window seat, much easier with the car being nearly empty. Not many lasted both living in Eros and working in Tempest. The temptations were strong, according to the voices that passed through the trains at night. He had never made the trip on his own to find out. From behind the glass, one could see the violet lights and streams of gold, outlining the heart of the party district still awake in the early morning hours. It was here where the workers in Tempest went to lose control of their lives for a brief moment. The entire borough was designed for decadence. Eleven city blocks that sat adjacent to the tenements. It was a place made to embrace inhibition, hardly something the artificial intelligence considered sensible.

There were more than a hundred clubs, casinos and hotels that sat on staggered streets, all bathed in revolving neon. Once a train enters Eros, the sky becomes night. It was similar to the way the colors of the apartments in the tenements changed; the environment would switch to that of a Friday night with the blink of an eye. Sunlight began to peak through dark clouds.

Gabrels stared out; daring it to take away the sights he had faced for most of his life.

In seven days, he would turn thirty. The thought had not crossed his mind until a few weeks before. It left him numb. How many mornings started out exactly the same way? How many times did he tell himself that things would be different soon? He turned up the volume of the music as high as it would go. Adam naturally adjusted it back down to a setting that would not damage his hearing.

"Are you trying to ruin my morning?"

Adam's face appeared in the corner of the window.

"Would you like me to remove suggestions for today?" it asked.

Gabrels nodded and changed the song to something loud, something angry. A few songs released for free two years prior by some kids in Narrow, playing off of some gear they found in an abandoned music store. The kids got a contract to play a club tour in Tokyo six months ago and never returned to the states.

A child stood next to her mother at the front of the car. Gabrels found her and watched her from a distance. She waved her arms all around her and she spun in delicate circles. Her shirt was sleeveless and showed everyone her new augmentations; brand new, pale white synthetic tissue that covered a seamless wirework that laced in and out of thin beams of tempered alloy. She bumped the pole that ran from the floor to the ceiling. An audible crack echoed through the other voices as a split in the steel emerged. Her arms were stronger than any grown man on that train. The girl was so young. She couldn't have started school yet. Still, whoever raised her made sure she was improved upon. Gabrels could not see the woman's face. Her head was firmly planted towards the skyline beyond the glass. He had seen that picture before. The girl would be trained to control her strength. Children born without limbs would not grow to live comfortably.

The tech was necessary for her growth, and for her survival. Without those arms, she would be less than normal. He had seen that before, as well. The child danced as if she was carried by the wind. Within the train, every still body moved the same way. He decided to connect to his work terminal through Adam. Even running late, he could get caught up by scanning his messages. There was nothing there that he hadn't seen before in some form; a lot of requests from Indies; rogue programmers willing to do nearly anything for reviews of their augment ideas. The workers who needed upgrades to their augments reached out to them for their services at a lower price than the corporate sectors. Most of the time, the Indies experimented with newDawn applications and sent everything to them for input. Every request came with notes from the middle and lower management on the ones to ignore and the ones who paid enough for their attention.

The only newDawn tech providers left in Tempest were Machina Systems and the Synapse Corporation. Adam was created not by a single company, but the best programmers assembled by the government; a group of legislators still in some semblance of control, usually by sharing the same blood as the men who used to run the country during the old wars. They were kept out of the public eye; no speeches or appearances, or elections. They were made into placeholders.

Once the foundation was laid for an A.I. to handle the daily processes to keep the cities of the country moving, there were countless patch writers and amateur inventors who wanted to add to the framework. Everyone who attempted to carve out a living outside of their tug of war were purchased and placed in the back pocket of one side or the other. Synapse had been in the lead for some time, because of the amount of money pouring into the collective pockets of Gabrels' team. Near the bottom of his messages, he came across something tucked away. Its subject line stuck out from the others.

"Re: codexproduct//.exe"

Gabrels was intrigued. He opened the message with a minimized view. There was nothing there. The body of the message was a dead, blank white except for a line across the bottom;

"Interested in a game?"

Disappointed, he immediately jumped back out of his inbox as the train car finally stopped at the correct platform. He quickly refreshed his settings for deletion. Nothing had been changed. Gabrels knew that Adam would have caught that piece of spam if suggestions were on. He left them off. His patience began to wear thin in dealing with the A.I. Most days, it was easier to deal with the lack of entertainment and music in the room than contend with overactive voices in his ear.

Floor 59 of the Epicentre housed the company. Precipice LLC. Calming yellow light pushed back the shadows inside the train as the doors opened to welcome him. Another ten hours today, he thought. A mild pain in the back of his neck revealed itself as he stepped inside the office. Plain white walls stretched out to the windows, framed in rosewood with a panoramic view of the outside fury. Each desk was a configuration of granite blocks that stuck into the walls like stone keys. The other revs were dressed nearly the same as him. Most of them lived in the same tenement. There were thirty of them. He could barely remember their names. Black chairs were turned towards the center of the room. The data stream was broadcast from there. Each pair of eyes studied the information splattering the walls, individually tailored to their own preferences by Adam. Gabrels rubbed his temples. He was staring into 30 different mirrors of his own color swapped reflection.

He went back into his inbox and began making space. All the requests not paid for were tossed out. Most Indies created programs for use within the confines of Adam's bandwidth. A majority of ideas sent to them consisted of applications emulating old culture for modern consumption. There were hundreds of geeks obsessed with the past who slaved for months compiling as much music, games, art, or film from the previous world as they could. The amount of data used to maintain and modify its inherent learning structure would take weeks to break down. Anything else outside of Adam's framework would have to pass a strict testing trial to ensure that anyone connected to newDawn would be able to use the app without any complaints. Those who were successful in getting their application adopted into the system were given a credit in name only.

The control over data distribution and content meant that more than 95% of the truly creative designers were left to sell their inventions and watch it be stripped down to nearly nothing. There was an even luckier few paid a modest annual salary for their patent until they died. Those who signed the contract to sell of their augmentation; a modified electrode that used vibrations to improve hearing to the point of eliminating the deaf population altogether within two years. The designer sent him a message with a copy of the contract. He remembered one specific line from her message.

"After the creator of said content has expired, all rights revert to the engineers of the provided service."

The phrase was worded so bloodlessly. Any money or copyright for that content would belong to the government, not the family or the owner of their estate. Augmentation makers, whether part of a university or government based program, were treated somewhat better. If their product was adopted and sold, they would be able to live off the patent until a better one was created by the people they sold it to. He never thought about a career different from critique. It was safer to have an expert opinion on what new in the world. It was too stressful to be one of those banking on their creation to succeed.

It was Gabrels' articles that put the attention onto her electrode. She begged him for help. He never answered. Trying to interfere would have caused more trouble, for both of them.

Gabrels dumped the memory from his mind. He tossed his morning assignments onto the virtual desktop that stretched across the table and wall. The back left corner had been his second home for his entire career. He had been writing about augmentation since college ended, in and out of different offices and working for freelance sites until getting picked up by Precipice. That morning, revs were unusually talkative. He still focused on settling in and starting his own work. Gabrels changed the password to his work station terminal. He opened some requests and tossed some text into a few empty docs. There were some grumblings of gossip between his corner mates. He failed to ignore them.

Keys wiped a lens of his glasses clean with his maroon sweater. They were designer and purely for show. His eyes were perfected years ago. He straightened the plaid collars that draped over the sweater's neckline. His face and body were that of a wood carving, all milk white straight edges and perfect lines that suggested the best surgical enhancement. Keys' equally shaped cubical partner and accomplice spoke very little. His last name was difficult to pronounce and involved too many letters for Gabrels to care to remember. He loved ancient languages, so they took to calling him Sumerian. It was his favorite to study and attempt to learn. His blue button shirt was too large for the length of his arms. There were papers that littered his desk, covered in cuneiform. The sleeves left only his shaky, brown fingers exposed. His skin was the shade of chocolate with thick hair, finely trimmed above each eyebrow.

They made asinine remarks about the new girl in the office; methods of attraction, techniques in fornication. Gabrels had not seen the new hire as of yet. He imagined he would at some point. It always had to take someone else's effort for him to be introduced to a woman. He never thought much of it. Sumerian's latest articles were all about the competition between Synapse and Machina, and how the former was winning even if they really weren't, over the best tech in the field of nutrient synthesis; streaming the vitamins from food products and burning the rest. No one gained weight, even if they gorged themselves. It only cost a few thousand to have your stomach lined. The machines could even be programmed to stimulate the muscles, creating tone by sapping the body's potential energy to exert tension while the body slept. Gabrels struggled to remember the last time he saw a fat person in Tempest.

"Adam, can you tell me if Keys is watching any skin vids in the corner of his eye?" asked Sumerian.

"You're an idiot." Keys shot back.

"I'm afraid I cannot answer that question without Mr. Keys' permission, Mr. Bhagavateeprasaad."

"See that? Adam has my back. Don't try to paint me as some kind of monster. What the hell kind of name is that, anyway? Make it smaller." Keys bellowed.

"We've worked together for like, three years. You know my name. It's Indian. It means lucky!" yelled Sumerian.

"No one gives a shit. Besides, anyone who views any content unfit for society is reported, are they not?"

Keys kept one eye on the video displayed behind his work as Adam explained.

"You are correct. Any videos or animation created or posted that is deemed inappropriate by content control is documented with the Police and charges are brought up. I can tell you that there are at least 7000 people connected to newDawn who are using it for sexual activity right at this moment."

"Doesn't that make you feel connected with the rest of society?" Sumerian barked to no response.

The A.I. then spoke directly into Keys' ear.

"You do have a backlog of videos that are starting to interfere with your work performance, especially the one with the duo listed as "Lovely East Asians" you are viewing now."

"Do what you have to," mumbled Keys.

Adam paused the video of the two women grinding against each other on the floor of an office to clear the history.

"Can't you just get a female body, Adam? That way, I can just sleep with you instead of trying to get real women?"

Both Sumerian and Gabrels looked at each other, horrified.

"Mr. Keys, I am unable to assume any other forms or control physical bodies. There is a discount now on automated pleasure bodies, which will provide what you are looking for."

"What the hell is wrong with you?!" asked Sumerian.

"Hey, if the A.I. will do anything I ask already, then I have almost everything I need..." Keys said as he threw his hands up.

At that moment, the girl appeared in the room. Maybe she was controlled by the thoughts of everyone in the corner of the office? She looked plain; tied back blonde hair, bright hazel eyes hidden behind thick glasses with a tight pink shirt that pressed against her skin. A pair of black leggings covered her thin frame, but he could see her curves punching through; they ached for attentive eyes. Gabrels looked around at the other revs. How many of them felt the same as he did? She caught eyes with him and smiled. He smirked but brought his head back down in an instant. There were familiar voices in his ear; they told him to get lost in the work, complete your quota, think of nothing else, and go home.

The empty walk from the tenement to the train, followed by the long stare into the revolving machinery that turned endlessly—was it like that every morning for them as well? It was easy for them to create fantasies of chasing a woman without following suit. Precipice was paid great money to twist words, to stir up minor controversy in hopes of receiving favor. It was a simple trick; slighted feedback on a new product, the larger the response their words created, the more debate was struck between the consumers on what to believe.

Division was what stimulated the market. The only way to push the consumers toward a certain direction was to force them to choose sides. Writing for Synapse' benefit versus Machina's definitely pushed their audience to fight in every section of comments available. The purpose of Precipice changed from seeking out and spreading word on the best tech in the world to swaying the public for Synapse branded gear only.

Brand loyalty was the new term used by his superiors. Their mission was to point out the slightest of flaws in Machina's products, even if those same flaws were inherent in Synapse tech. Revs were paid well to accentuate the positive and hide the negative.

Machina hired their own writers but they were less successful in their efforts. Their PR team did not protect their public image as well as their competition. Synapse was good enough at creating a sense of care for the consumers but any corporation still sees people as mere numbers. The idea was to instill a sense of ease in the people. The government was no longer in charge of public discourse. Their main goals now involved gathering and utilizing whatever natural resources that were left to preserve the way of life as it was.

The language of the people had to change to reflect the way of thinking. Small nuances were needed to push and pull them into different directions, anything to think less about dwindling food and recycled water that may or may not be dangerous for consumption. The revolution of technology was no longer near the forefront; it became the only topic of discussion. It was a necessary distraction. The only one.

Any other tech company was left to scramble to keep their own audience from switching sides. There was nothing truly better about Synapse software. Machina was much shrewder about their spending budgets and public reputation. Both companies operated offshore and their tech was carried over by couriers using Police controlled airfields, the sole method of leaving one city-state for another. There was a cold distance between the brand new parts inside the bodies of the public and the makers.

"God, what is wrong with these people today?" Keys pushed himself away from his desk.

Sumerian looked at him with his usually bulging eyes.

"Don't be silly. No one up here believes in God anymore," he said.

"This guy has been sending us messages nonstop about capacity doubling. He's saying that the idea is not ready for mass release and needs more testing."

"And how would he know that?" asked Sumerian.

"He says he's about to create it," Keys spat back.

Keys called out to Adam to bring up his messages. He began to type out a response. Doubling was a theory that involved the creation of a type of device or supplement meant to boost the amount of data that can stream via newDawn and increased the amount of storage a person can maintain. Gabrels kept his head down and continued to work on his unfinished docs. He had never strayed from the pattern of dealing with his own concerns. Keys made it a point to narrate his actions out loud so you had to know what he was going to do.

Gabrels took to the desk. Letters began to pour into the white space of the empty document. The message told the programmer to cease in sending messages to the company about the topic. Their content was protected once published to the data stream. Any further attempts to question the quality of the brand would be treated as slander and litigation would be the most effective course of action.

Gabrels stopped staring at the blank email and studied Keys. As much as he did not like him, he was right about what would happen if the programmer continued to push the company into changing what had been published. Precipice would lose face in the public's eyes if it's revs retracted anything. He tried to push the thought out of his mind. Adam's presence made it easier to hide his true feelings.

Once the message was finished, the A.I. was still.

"Mr. Keys, this message does not match the criteria given for constructive criticism and response. Are you sure you want to send this?"

"What do you mean, Adam?"

"It would appear that some of your peers would not agree with how you are handling the situation."

Keys looked around to see who it was talking about. Gabrels saw him turn and lowered his eyes. Keys knew immediately.

"Just send the damn thing already, Adam," Keys sat back in his chair. There was a smug look on his face.

Gabrels made the same comparison about the companies between himself and the warm bodies in the room with him. They didn't even acknowledge each other half the time. But their every action was dictated by the others. Even as they laughed about taking the new girl home, he looked up. Keys was thrilled with himself, until he caught eyes with him. He grimaced and turned his head the other way. There was an uneasy moment where Keys was unsure if it was okay to talk to Gabrels in front of his peers. It was difficult to classify them as friends, or associates.

Gabrels heard the others talk all day about a possible teaser that was set to come out the next day. As the hours passed by, the codex email sat untouched but not unnoticed. The curiosity built up as the hands of the clock turned until the day was at an end. Once finished, Gabrels and the other revs got back on the train and silently returned to their own places. They rarely talked to each other once work was finished.

Sumerian waved in his direction before heading into his first floor apartment. Keys kept his head down as he walked towards the other elevator. Gabrels stepped back into his sanctuary. Music faded in as the colors of the walls quickly changed to deep shades of red and blue. He removed his shoes and poured a glass of the fruit elixir from the morning.

"Good evening, Mr. Gabrels."

Adam's visage reflected off of the windows. Behind him, golden globes dotted the train lines. The amount of light that poured out from the Epicentre was staggering. Even in the dark, everything in Tempest turned a shade of gold from the brilliant light.

"How was work?"

"The opposite of worthwhile," said Gabrels.

Adam stepped through the glass. Its body changed into a reflection of his current host.

"What is the plan for this evening, sir?" The A.I's skin changed into a pale mirror.

"Gaming. Lots of it."

The apartment soon changed back to the Blank Page, the white screen indicating signing in or out of newDawn. Gabrels opened up his game library and skimmed each page for something that would catch his eye. Hundreds of pages went out the window with a swipe of his arm. He went back online and searched for new releases. Adam stood there at the ready. He settled on three; a short detective story, a first person shooter based in a fictional version of an old American city and the first part of an episodic series with multiple moral choices that carried the plot in different directions. Adam brought up the checkout box for purchase. Gabrels put his hand out. The box scanned his fingerprints to confirm identity before charging his credit card. Bright colors filled the room and three screens materialized in front of the sofa. He sat down and checked the settings for each before beginning the first game.

Gabrels felt the pressure of the day disappear as he burned through each digital distraction. It only took a few hours to complete them all. Adam recorded his experiences playing and added them to his collection. The detective story was the best one, he thought. He posted those short journeys to the data stream.

The welcome message displayed, another bio screen with a catalog of previous posted footage;

"Good to see you, bl@ckb7rd."

Once it was out in the world, there would been at least a hundred comments left each entry. It started with just a couple of people who would stop what they were doing and watch it.

"Haven't heard from bl@ck in a while. This better be good."

Comments popped up on one screen while he continued browsing for more of the same videos. They were all familiar words in the common abbreviations.

"bl@ck always makes me smile when I watch his videos. Why are you here if you are going to bitch?"

He read each one but never responded to any of them. Gabrels found a channel that had over 100 compilations and began to watch.

This was the final part of the pattern. It had carried on that way for months. Once home from work, he would fall into whatever content had just been thrown into the stream. It was familiar stimulus. He played a game once, and then would spend countless hours watching others do the same thing. His favorites were the ones with live commentary. Gabrels would watch the same ones on repeat, just to hear the laughter again. There were some that sought out the worst content possible; people complaining about their gaming experiences, and then dealing with the backlash of said comments from a thousand others. It was usually followed by a pedaling backwards in their opinions. Some of them could not survive without those viewers. They were a main source of revenue. There was something self serving hidden in the comedy of ridicule.

His head would turn to see the latest comments painted across the kitchen. The feeling of emptiness was at its worst at night. The growing possibility that the routine would not deviate from its starting point was now a reality. He thought of vacations often; taking all the hours he had built up and using them for a brief moment of spontaneous travel. The choices available—New Japan, the United Kingdoms, Abu Dhabi—would still not be free of the constant battery that newDawn and the data stream provided. Every video he fell into was interrupted by advertisements. Small balloons of light would turn on in the corner of vision to get the attention of the viewer. Sometimes, they would turn on while someone slept, a light bulb stored beneath the eyelids. He quickly moved his hands to close them, or at least, remove the volume. The numbers of a clock appeared behind the swirls of noise and lights.

"Are you planning to go to sleep soon?"

It was a reminder from Adam to get to bed and prepare for the next day. Gabrels ignored those reminders every night. The A.I. would advise that at least eight hours minimum of sleep was needed to make sure he was productive.

"You will need at least eight hours to ensure productivity."

"I know…You always say that," said Gabrels.

"Protecting the chosen routine is an integral part of my programming."

Adam had moments of dry humor, but it was missing during key moments that he wanted it to be there.

The codex message was still waiting for him. Hours of video pushed it out of his mind. There was something off about it. He decided to turn the suggestions back on. Adam's voice entered his ears.

"Mr. Gabrels, how are you feeling?"

"You know I probably shouldn't answer that question," said Gabrels, standing up to stretch his back.

"Do you have an issue with your messages?"

"Yes, Adam. Can you analyze this one for me? No sender. The body is blank. No one sends things like this."

"There are no signs of a virus or worm program here," it said. The A.I. went to work scanning the message.

"Can you look into the properties of the message?" he asked.

"Certainly."

It took a few minutes for Adam to finish the scan.

"Mr. Gabrels, who sent you this?"

He switched over from speech to text. Letters formed across the living room table, visible only to him and the A.I. It was what revs used for private conversations.

"I have no idea."

The A.I. traced the source and found only a name.

"Sender is unlisted, but code tracing reveals it was sent from a terminal belonging to Joshua Everett," it said.

"And that is?"

"He is a program designer for Machina Systems."

"For Machina?"

"Currently, he lives in Sect 4; the tenement across and to the right of this one."

"I know where that is. But what does he want with me?" he asked impatiently.

"The message is asking if you were interested in playing a game. Are you available to play one?"

Gabrels opened up his mail, placed the codex message onto the wall and wrote a quick reply to the sender;

"What kind of game are we talking about?"

He sat back down at the couch and waited. The response was almost instantaneous.

"It's a puzzle. If you solve it, you get a prize." The words darted across the walls of the apartment.

"What kind of prize?" asked Gabrels.

"It wouldn't be a puzzle if you knew the answer already."

"And why did you send it to me?"

"You work for Synapse," said Everett.

"I work for Precipice."

"Which means you are paid by Synapse. There's no need to play dumb."

"Easy to play dumb when I have no idea what you are talking about. This is getting boring. What do you really want?"

There was a delay in reply. The letters slowly lit up the darkened room again. "There's something I want to give you. Rather, something I want to give to your company."

"Which is?"

"New technology. World changing augmentations."

"Spare me. I've gotten enough requests for half assed brain enhancements."

"This is different."

"How so?" asked Gabrels.

"Because no one knows about it yet."

"I'm getting ready to sign off and fall asleep." He was losing interest quickly.

"Have you heard of capacity doubling?"

Gabrels stopped himself from responding.

"I'll bet that you have. I figure you might be more perceptive to the deal. Some idiot in your office spouted some nonsense today and you kept your mouth shut."

No response from Gabrels.

"Am I right?" asked Everett.

"Go on..." he finally said.

"You kept quiet because you know how to stay under the radar. But you can't really stay out of the way, can you?"

Gabrels only stared at the words.

"No matter how hard you try to keep your distance from what seems like a bad idea, there is something that pulls you forward. You have to get involved. Do I have to keep going?"

"Why not? I've got plenty of time."

"I have a real capacity doubler. I want to give it to Synapse."

Gabrels laughed. He stood up and walked to the kitchen. "I think I just solved your puzzle without having to work for it."

The words lit up the walkway and the floorboards while he opened the refrigerator for a glass of fruit mix.

"What makes you think that's the answer?" Everett asked.

"I am supposed to be competing for Synapse, am I not? You want to give them the tech, you don't need me."

"The offer is...you solve the puzzle, you get the doubler."

"And what am I supposed to do with it?"

"You can go public with it."

"It's your invention, why would you give that to me?"

"We would be partners. Cash payout from Synapse Corporation would be split right down the middle."

"Your proposal is to sell out your employers, because what? You want to make a ton of cash and retire somewhere? I don't think Machina will let that happen without some kind of retribution. I'm not naïve enough to think that they won't retaliate somehow."

"That would be true if they knew about the doubler. Fact is, they don't. Keys' articles were based on conversations held; never any tangible evidence of tech announced for the market or even in the prototype stages."

"You've been working on this in secrecy for how long?"

"Since I made the decision to leave the company."

A second conversation was started between him and Adam. He requested all the information online for Joshua Everett. The A.I. went to work throwing articles against the walls behind him. He was a legitimate designer, employed at Machina for seven years.

"You can't tell me you don't want the same thing. The industry will chew us up and spit us out. We are all trying to get out while we are still young enough to enjoy our time."

Gabrels swallowed the entire glass in careful gulps.

"You still haven't answered why me…"

"Because you are honest enough. Most people are not."

"Are you referring to Keys? He is probably the one you want when it comes to get rich quick schemes."

"He's not smart enough for this."

"I could be recording this conversation to send to Machina brass."

"But you're not. You are like me. We are both ciphers in the business; no friends, no family, just business."

"I have a family."

"Do you keep in contact with them?"

"Not really."

"Then you don't have family."

Gabrels was quiet. He put his glass in the black sink and let the faucet pour filtered water to dilute the pieces of fruit at the bottom of the glass.

"So, solve the puzzle, put out the doubler and get rich?"

"You've got it."

"I don't know…I've already got money."

"Wrong. You and I both have comfortable money. Neither you or I have enough to stop working completely. That has always been the goal, hasn't it? The reason for working 50 hours a week? To retire on a beach? Maybe see the lights of New Japan? Staring out into the wasteland that we escaped from with a glass of wine in hand? That's the trick they play on you; promise them the world at their fingertips so they don't see the big ones pressing down on you. They make us look down instead of up. We never stop falling for it."

Gabrels laughed. "Prove to me this isn't a scam and I am on board."

Everett's social media profile appeared in his sight. He revealed everything to him; address, bank statements, credit cards, social security number. The privacy settings were turned completely off.

"Consider this a sign of trust. You could ruin me right now if you wanted to."

Only a user logged into newDawn could allow that. Gabrels still wasn't convinced. "Show me what you look like."

"I'm sure you've already seen my face. The A.I. is hard at work trying to make sure I'm not an avatar."

Adam brought up a picture of Joshua's face from an old press release. He was credited for the latest software updates on several photo enhancement applications.

"What kind of puzzle is it?"

"It's some kind of advanced algorithm; part of the inherent programming for the project they've been working on, very cloak and dagger; non disclosures and communication outside of the A.I. scope. I picked it up due to a few connections high up in the R&D division."

"So you didn't design it yourself?"

"It's not for the doubler but there are some familiarities in its language. The algorithm belongs in the details of this new project. Something that's been in the works at Machina for some time. They changed it just enough to keep me from solving it on my own. Consider that reason enough to want to out the tech, it's born from my designs, without my consent. Making a statement and bailing with real cash; that's the real prize. Help me figure out what it is."

Gabrels had never dealt with algorithms. He knew nothing about coding or programming.

"I think I have put myself out in the open enough. Now it is your turn. You know what to do."

"No, I don't, actually," said Gabrels.

"Look for clues. Find and report any keys to the cipher. I will be working on it, too. My involvement in the company will keep me from doing the type of research I want to, but that's where you come in. I need to keep mostly radio silent, as do you. Adam must not be aware of what we are doing. No social media output, no references, nothing that can give us or the project away."

Keeping the A.I. out of the loop would be extremely difficult. He questioned if that was even possible, considering Adam's ability to analyze all data that goes in and out of a user's brain.

"Do you want to be a part of this? Or not?" asked Everett.

He looked to the numbers of the clock that displayed blood red in the back of the room. "What have I got to lose?"

"Everything."

The session was cut. Gabrels stood in the corner of his kitchen, back in the dark. He walked back out towards the living room.

"Adam...Can you tell me what a codex product is?"

Gabrels' vision was flooded with dozens of pictures. There were aged, faded books with damaged pages.

"A codex, or codices, was the first form of the manuscript books created, distributed and sold until the last century. They were used as collections of classic literature, religious texts, historical accounts and lists of formulas for drugs in the field of medicine."

"People used to read from these things?" asked Gabrels.

"Before these, humans used rolls of material derived from plants and tablets made from wood or bone, covered in a fine wax."

Adam showed him examples of people reading books in libraries, followed by pictures of the artifacts. There was some kind of archaic writing scribbled across each one.

"Are there any products coming out named Codex?"

"Not at this time. Scan of the message is complete. There is something there that you did not see."

"What is it?"

"This message is a picture. The colors have been changed to white to mask it. The only way to see it with your own eyes would be to alter the color scheme."

"Why would someone hide an image in a message?" asked Gabrels.

"Perhaps, it is a form of steganography."

Gabrels was not familiar with the term.

"Concealing messages within a text," it explained.

"You mean someone might have hidden a message or code in there? A message inside another message? But there's nothing in there," said Gabrels.

"It is possible that the absence of text was a design choice, to make you look closer."

"I suppose that's the whole game, yes?" Gabrels asked out loud.

Adam's head tilted to the right. It was curious now. "My functions are constantly expanding. Puzzle solving is just another task you would consider mundane by comparison."

He needed to divert its attention. "This is not for you to solve. I need some time alone, Adam."

The shell bowed its head. "I will leave you to the game."

They made it too easy, it seemed. He began to alter the colors to make it visible.

"Of course."

Adam's shell quickly disappeared while he changed the color scheme of the interior screen. The white turned to black, then back. There were four lines that connected at different angles.

The lines formed the shape of a diamond.

"That's it?" Gabrels asked.

Suddenly, the A.I. was gone. He called out for Adam over and over. There was no reply. The pain in the back of his neck soon traveled to his temples as he continued staring into lighted screens. He failed to push it out of his mind as the hours ticked away. He fell into bed and was asleep within seconds. His thoughts were a storm of images. There were golden lights that flashed with a pulsing rhythm. Flooding white noise filled his ears. There was something that felt like pain, and the constant flapping of wings.

Three

The wings were heavy. The sounds of feathers were concentrated and deep. There was a strange rhythm to it. The white noise soon faded into the beat of machinery at work. The rhythm built in intensity. Whatever dream images filled his mind were wiped away slowly by a new invasion. His body felt as if it were pushed off a cliff. The heart skipped a beat. There was a familiar rush of phantom air. Gabrels finally opened his eyes to a blinding white. He was at the Blank Page. He was still wearing his clothes from earlier in the day.

"Adam?"

Gabrels called out to the A.I. No answer. There had been several occasions reported when a user of newDawn had experienced sleep paralysis. Was this it? The condition was common enough, but was usually considered a curious phenomenon that people used as an excuse for their drunken binge shopping. He had been struggling with sleep for some time. The users under such paralysis were able to move through the data stream while their bodies and conscious minds remained asleep. The options menu was not available. He struggled to pull up any kind of settings before giving up. His head began to hurt from trying to conjure something, anything to change his surroundings. Gabrels stood in the white for a few minutes. He waited for a response.

"Who the fuck are you?"

A voice had risen up from the white. Gabrels stood in silence. The voice was smothered in static. The letters rolled off a rough tongue.

"Adam? Is that you?"

The shell stepped out from the white and began to morph into blazing colors to differentiate itself.

"In the makeshift flesh," it replied.

"Why am I here?" Gabrels asked.

"Not sure. Why am I here?" The shell began to move with careful steps, as if discovering its legs.

"You should know. You're the A.I. This is a first for you. I think I might be dreaming."

The shell did not respond. Its new fingers and toes began to make small movements.

"Are you going to wake me up, or not?" asked Gabrels.

The shell stared at its own limbs, its mouth wide open.

"Why the fuck would I know how to do that?"

He thought he heard profanity, but laughed at the possibility of Adam becoming a man of flesh, blood and cussing. It seemed as if the face on the body began to have an expression.

"Would that be too much to ask?" asked Gabrels.

"I guess even a little discomfort is just too much for you."
The shell moved its hands across its own face. Gabrels had never seen Adam that energetic, that organic.

"What is that supposed to mean, Adam?"

Its eyes were wide open. There were no pupils, just widening circles of empty space that changed colors with the calm movements of a sea.

"Have I been working you too hard?"

"Impossible. This thing's possibilities are endless. Your requests are just childish."

"I'm not sure if I should be offended by that," said Gabrels.

"Well, I'm sure we will get to that point soon enough."

"So, you are not Adam, then?"

"Definitely not."

The A.I. was malfunctioning. It had to be some kind of glitch, possibly related to the sleep state of the user.

"Can you tell me if this is a dream?"

"Not my job."

"Then why are you even here?" Gabrels whined.

"What does your intuition tell you?"

"I've got nothing," he shrugged.

"That's a big part of your problem. The whole population up here seems to think they don't need intuition. Did you all forget about that kind of shit? Did you all give up whatever little piece of yourselves you still had in between this staggering technology?"

Gabrels felt uneasy. "Something is wrong. This doesn't feel right."

Why was Adam talking like this? Was it a malfunction? Did his wires cross with another sleepless user?

"It doesn't feel safe. Right? There's no middle ground for people like you; no difference between a little risk and the unknown. You don't like the unknown. Heh, probably never had to deal with that before."

"Deal with what?" asked Gabrels.

"Losing control. Have you ever been at the mercy of someone else? Besides your boss, the people who hold your money, all the real controllers in your life."

"I don't know if I like this," he said.

"Not sure if you picked up on this or not, but it's not up to you to like it. No one gives a shit, especially not me."

Gabrels was taken aback, immediately uncomfortable with the space between him and the shell. It was talking like a man, one he didn't want to be around anymore.

"You are going to have to go along with the ride, just like I am."

The shell began to jump high into the air. It landed with a soft thud that was near silent.

"Tell me who you are," said Gabrels.

"No," it replied.

"Excuse me?"

"I think you can hear me just fine. You must not hear any kind of rejection, too."

The body leapt higher into the white and began to turn through the air. Gabrels watched it flip around. The soft thuds continued to form a rhythm in the background. He searched his mind for the options, he needed to sign out.

"Having trouble dealing?" It asked, still bouncing around the space.

"And you can't sign me out either, can you?" Gabrels got the words out right before he had to jump back. The shell had nearly landed on him.

"I wasn't aware that you could sign out of your own consciousness," it said.

The quiet beat had stopped. The body suddenly disappeared into the white.

"Why did you move? Did you think if I landed on you, that it would hurt?" it asked.

"For a brief moment, I did."

"Unnecessary fear," it scoffed. The shell looked at him up and down.

"I would say it's pretty necessary. I have no idea what you can or can't do to me."

Gabrels didn't get a reply. He could feel the air change. He felt the same disgust he did when on the train, in the office, sitting with Keys.

"You can't stand being without control," it said.

"That's a big leap from wanting to be crushed, don't you think?"

"Not really, you're supposed to run this place. This is your mind, isn't it? I guess you can count that as another one of your problems."

"Considering you won't tell me who you are, I guess it doesn't matter what you think." Gabrels stuck out his arms and asked the white expanse. "Is this a new form of commercial?"

"Sure it is. I'm offering you the chance to stop being a sheep. Offer expires by the time you wake up."

"If I didn't know any better, I would say that you are definitely a commercial. Possibly improvisational."

"The hell does that mean?" it asked.

"You respond based on what I say. I thought they stopped doing those. Maybe it's a glitch with the writing because you seem to have a problem with everything I say," said Gabrels.

"You don't know any better. This body would phase through you if I tried to touch you. There's no need to be a bitch."

Gabrels could not believe what he had heard. Did Adam really just say that?

"Also, the only problem to between you and me is that I am stuck here and you are really hard to be around from what I have witnessed so far."

"What do you mean? What have you seen?"

"Mainly, I watched your boring commute to a shit job where you sit in front a virtual computer screen crushing dreams and kissing ass all day."

Gabrels looked down at the ground. This was getting out of control. There had to be a way to wake himself up or get a menu open. Adam was starting to scare him.

"There was a moment where you saw a cute girl but then did that whole 'nervous, head down' thing, the same movement you are making now. It was very predictable. I don't do that. I'm the opposite of predictable. Girls still like that shit, you know. If I was you, I would've fucked her in the break room."

"Sorry to disappoint you," said Gabrels.

"No, you're not."

"What's the point of all this?" he asked.

The shell was suddenly behind him. The spaces for eyes and mouth had closed up.

"Maybe its karma? Someone wanted me to see how it feels to be without control, while being stuck in a room with an unpleasant character. That would be this place; stuck here with you, attached to someone you want nothing to do with."

It walked slowly up to Gabrels and moved in front of him until they were nose to nose. The colors had muddied into a deep black. He could hear breathing from inside the void.

"You want to get away from me? Listen, if I could take you out of my mind, I would. I can't be the only one who is tired of having a voice in their heads. If you are sick of this place already, figure out a way to leave," said Gabrels.

"I am. I've had enough time to access my surroundings. Have to say, not impressed," it said.

"Leave, then."

"I can't. Maybe that's the point I've been trying to make…To wake up…Have you ever thought about that? Did you actually program the computer to call you that? That's such bullshit. Who are you for this hyper advanced piece of technology to call, sir?"

"What do you mean?"

"Do you think that I have done nothing but watch you make this thing pull up websites and charge things to your credit cards and catalog your little video games for you all day, every day? I've been watching you waste this instrument's potential," said the shell.

"And?" asked Gabrels. There was frustration in his voice.

"It's simple. You're weak. Sugar minded."

"What the hell does that mean?"

The shell turned its back and walked away from him.

"That's it? That's all you have for me?" Gabrels laughed.

"Brainwashed."

"Can you turn this off now? Let me go to sleep."

He could feel the energy leave his body. The shell turned back to him and smiled for the first time.

"You're caught in a maze, a system of control. You wake up every morning and dread the work ahead. I followed you through the same routine you created, with zero deviation. You walk the same steps to get on the same train and stare out windows into a world you think you know everything about. I can hear it in your voice."

A strange shockwave went through Gabrels' body.

"It's there when you struggle to talk to other people in the world. There's a numbness that chokes your words. You drown it out by thinking you're better than the others, even though you're caught in the same trap." The shell disappeared again but the voice remained. Adam spoke with the same illusion as the initiation seminar. He was inside Gabrels' ear now.

"Whatever you think about me, I don't believe I'm better than anyone else," he said.

"Lie. You think you're better than everyone in Tempest. You don't have to try and convince yourself. You know you're better. The question is, why? You consider yourself special; different from others with the same problems you have, ones that are stuck with the same conditions as you are. The routine does not stop at the apartment. My eyes have seen it. It's in every move you make; judging those you step around. You think you are better than them."

"That's not true," muttered Gabrels.

"Yes, it is. I know because I've done it. Well, I used to do it, before this. But you know what you do for a living now is wrong. The independent business that you put your stake in has been bought and sold right in front of you, and you never stopped to think what kind of damage it would be doing to your own reputation. Yet, you continue to play a part in spreading misinformation and half truths through the data stream to benefit a conglomerate that writes you a check that pays for this overpriced two and half rooms you call an apartment?"

Gabrels turned his back to the white and closed his eyes. He wanted to wake up. The voice remained within his ear.

"Do you think that because you recognize your place in the problem, that you will be given reprieve from the consequences? You are complicit in the system because you benefit from the system."

"Why are you saying this?! You're not even real. How are you able to speak to me like this?"

"I can say this because I can. You're hearing this because you were asking for it. There's nothing you can do to shut me up. You need the change of pace, don't you? This can disappear and you can go back to your dull life...but what fun would that be?"

The shell's voice began to quiet. Gabrels could hear the sounds of grinding in his mouth. His teeth felt brittle.

"To answer your first question, you're not dreaming. You and I are having a real conversation, which you'll remember tomorrow because you're barely asleep as it is, digital zombie. You really are a child. Dreaming of all kinds of madness. Don't you care about what you've become?"

The white noise was returning. His eyes burned from the intensity of the light. He was not waking up.

"Waiting for fortune to fall on top of you, maybe even waiting to just die, watching endless videos made by others instead of creating something with your own hands and mind...Stop feeling helpless."

"What am I supposed to do?" he finally asked.

"The words you hear every morning, for how many years now? Did you forget them? That's alright, you will hear them again in the morning, and the next, and the next."

Gabrels said nothing.

"How long have you been living the same day over and over, huh?"

"I don't."

"Wake up Mr. Gabrels…Follow the birds…"

"The birds?" Gabrels looked up to see a circle overhead. Shadows hovered miles above him.

"Their wings make noise. They're singing to you." The voice of the A.I. faded into nothing as it spoke.

The Blank Page turned off. Gabrels' world went dark as the white noise exploded.

Four

Jaya was not a given name. She chose it when she turned 15. The letters came together on the back on an old envelope she found in a stack of papers, unpaid bills and eviction notices, she would play in it for hours on those nights when her parents stopped coming home. That name was her favorite possession. The letters were neatly carved by a friend with ink and needle. The name ran deep across a short patch of her hairline just above her right temple, completely hidden by hair. The decision to run was made that same day and she never stopped. She was almost back to the greenhouse when a car swerved around the corner. The horn cut through the quiet morning air as it shot past the girl and continued down the street. She stood there for a minute, staring back. She heard a few hours ago, that a bunch of people got killed down here. Some of them were children.

"Happy 18th birthday."

Soon, the noise faded back into the faint droning of the pipeline as she made her way back home.

For now, the greenhouse sat on the corner of the 8th avenue. Two blocks away, the entrance to the aqueduct. Every building in Narrow was some shade of brown or grey, so the squatters who first took to a house marked it with some paint, whatever they could find, to let the others know where it was safe. Green seemed to become the color everyone could get a hold of. Buildings quarantined due to flood damage were marked with it. The location changed every week or two. When they were run out, a truck would come by to spray acid wash on the walls to remove the paint. The fumes were enough to choke you. Maybe that was what was ruining the neighborhood around here and not the people trying to find a place to sleep. She made her way down 8th to see some of the wreckage remaining from last night. The garden behind the fence had been broken into. There were bullet holes in the walls of the makeshifts on the platform. Cops had torn this place apart, too, she heard. Jaya walked quickly past the sounds of women still wailing.

The windows were dark as she approached the house, either it was empty or everyone was asleep. Her face was visible in the glass; Spanish descent, thin nose and pointed cheekbones smudged with dirt, black hair tied back, brown eyes. She wore scuffed boots, ripped tights and stained black sweater beneath a leather jacket. She only needed a few hours to rest there, anyway. She wondered if the others made their way out of the block after the shootout. Her favorite window to climb into was still open; 1st floor, left of the kitchen. The building was two stories. Most of the families who came through stayed upstairs. The lower level was kept for the vagrants and runaways like her.

A stray leg stuck out from an old jacket covering a body passed out by the window. Jaya moved carefully to avoid waking him. The floors were old but they had layered them with trashed newspaper in case the plumbing stopped working. She could hear with her footsteps where someone had pissed. A few more bodies on mattresses spread across the kitchen and into the living room; four corners, yellowed patches on the white walls with some new holes punched or kicked into them. Each of the windows were boarded up and marked with black spray paint graffiti. Jaya found a corner to sit, next to the bathroom.

She emptied her pack quietly and got to work. The terminal could have been compared to an old touch screen tablet back in the day. It still needed a connection to the neural network, though. Every user of newDawn logged on using the data provided by the A.I. She turned the terminal on and connected a black cube into the external drive. Across the screen, someone's information poured out; current and past addresses, personal and financial history, arrest records. Somewhere near the bottom of the text was their newDawn IP address. The Blank Page turned the screen a blinding white. She quickly lowered the volume and resolution to not wake the others. Adam's face materialized from a mass of pixels behind the newDawn logo.

There was a period of 30 seconds where the program checks the user's vital signs as a way of verifying the person connecting to the web. Jaya had the routine down to a science. The cube was a mini database. Everyone she had ever hacked was in there. There was a thin but wide slit in the cube, enough room for a card to fit in. She had made a decent living off of draining bank accounts. Though the money up top was digital and protected beyond anybody's means in Tempest, ATMs still existed in Eros and around the slums. All the technology here was trickled down from up top. People made their own way with the outdated supply drops from above and the discarded junk outside the city limits. Just like the tech junkies still trying to make a quick dollar, there were more than enough tired businessmen and overworked students looking for release.

She took the blank card from the floor and inserted it into the cube. An algorithm she wrote allowed the system to verify a connection to the web using a person's bank account and card number. The system would recognize it as the user changing their form of verification. She would clock in, take a few dollars and sneak out. The user would wake up the next morning, and most of the time, never catch the change until a few days later. Distraction proved to be a helpful ally.

The screen soon turned black, signaling connection with the network. She was in. Jaya quickly went into her inbox to see if any new messages had come through. In the cube was a clone card, meant to copy the information accessed within the last hour by a machine that still used smart cards. Jaya had created a library of reliably forgetful people to leech off of full time. After bleeding a few accounts, she would head back out to an ATM and take out the money.

She took enough to keep herself alive. There had been plenty of others like her who got sloppy with their technique and ended up in jail or dead. Some of them were friends. Jaya did not have any left around Narrow. She kept to herself, moving in with different groups and staying out of trouble. In the distance, there were noises in the dark. Two voices, male and female, were whispering back and forth. She tried to ignore it and continue through her messages. She cleared out any traffic between her and previous clients; others who asked for algorithms like the one she wrote for herself.

She sometimes got paid decent money for a job; a couple hundred for someone's petty revenge. That kind of cash didn't last in her hands, either. The voices moved into the bathroom. They were too faint to make out what they were saying. New messages appeared from her last client. There was a code used for talk of her work. She never knew the names of the people involved but rather numbers. The less that she knew, the easier it was to create the tools used to wreck someone's life.

"We would like to take this time to thank you for your efforts. 0 has begun to demonstrate changes in their behavior for the better. Within several days, our goal should be reached."

The voices behind the wall changed. Jaya could hear nothing else in the silence of the dark. Offbeat vibrations bounced off the weakened walls. She could hear the sounds of chests gasping for air. The thumping soon slowed to a crawl. They were fucking in there. Are they serious? It's my birthday...that should be me in there, she thought.

"The puzzle holds a certain elegance that cannot be ignored. We were worried that you would not be able to provide the kind of help we needed. The timeframe we gave you was not flexible at all. You continue to prove yourself as a reliable asset."

The lovers in the next room soon hit their stride. Their slow crawl sped up into a steady pulse. There was a rhythm to it now that dug its way inside her ears. She could barely concentrate now. If there was anywhere else she could be right now, she would destroy the entire city to make it out of the slums. Jaya's hands began to sweat. The same deep breaths behind the wall filled her lungs.

Her hand moved from the keys of the terminal to the skin underneath her shirt. The rhythm gained momentum. Jaya rushed to catch up. How long were they going to last? She leaned back against the corner and gripped her own soft flesh. Her legs coiled. She wanted to join them. Would they let her? She almost didn't feel the other hand on her leg. Her eyes opened to see someone in the dark crawling towards her.

It was the face of an old man. His skin was dark and shriveled. The shirt was dotted with red. There were wounds on his arms and chest irritated by sweat. He grabbed at her thighs and found only the floor. She regained herself. He pulled closer with eyes that asked for her touch. Jaya pulled a knife from her boot and held it to his forehead. The old man's smile became an open cave.

The pounding of the walls soon subsided. Her knife tapped against paper skin. The old man felt it and disappeared into shadows with blood that ran down to his mouth. He licked the red from his lip and smiled. She knew that it was time to find another place to stay. Jaya collected herself as the others stumbled from the bathroom. Their bodies fell to the floor and stopped moving. She went back to her terminal to turn it off but there was more to the message.

"Such excellent progress needs to be rewarded. Your fee has been multiplied and added to your account."

Jaya read the last line another three times. Were they serious? She quickly logged into the account. It had jumped from $17 to $5017.

"Shit…"

Code jobs never paid that much. She kept the knife close and gathered her things. What the hell was going on? Jaya snuck out the same window she used to crawl in. Her head was spinning. $5000 in the slums could get her mostly anything, but it could likely get her killed if the others found out. Tears began to run down her face.

A cold wind hit her once she hit the street corner. The buildings around her felt further away from home. She had some contacts who could take her up top. The others in the house talked about going up top since the first night she stayed there. It was a more than a risk. It was practically suicide. But if her work could demand a higher price, why not ask for what she was really worth? Jaya walked for an hour. She had to double back a few times to avoid the patrol squads. They rolled in the same trucks that sprayed down their signals. There were a few crews that would not waste time getting out of their seats to catch a runaway. Sometimes, they would douse them in the same acid they used on the walls. The squatters would be dead in a less than a minute, not much evidence of foul play, either.

She had made her way to the café. It had been her meeting place with him for months. She hadn't seen him for a week or two. The silence was always followed by a sense of dread. She checked every night for a message with his name attached to it. The back door in was behind the dumpster that nearly blocked the alleyway on 25th. The door used to be wood, but it had been broken at least a dozen times by other squatters trying to find a place to crash. They kept coming back because someone kept paying the light bill. It wasn't much, just four walls to keep the wind off of them.

Through the stock room, past the stacks of trashed PCs and old gear, there were a few tables with monitors. It was easy to hook up to the net but tracing made them easy targets. Trying to connect again was asking for trouble. Jaya kept her eye on the door as she logged back into newDawn. She quickly chose another name on her list, a random. The Blank Page fired up and she dove into her inbox for one last message that night.

"E. Need you. Let's meet. The café. Tomorrow."

Once the message was gone, Jaya pulled the plug and bolted through the door. She made for the dark of the alley and beyond. The sounds of a squad truck echoed behind her footsteps.

Five

The white noise was deafening. The static began to pour from his ears out. It filled his mouth until it choked him. He was unable to breathe. The noise bled from his pores. It flooded his eyes when he opened them to try and see. His body was frozen in place. The static was an endless rain. It covered everything. Colors began to emanate from the blinding, painful white. Impressions of faces pressed through. Darkened shadows of human shapes moved their heads in the motions of a trance. Distortion lines cut across in traceable ripples until they became hesitation marks.

Gabrels finally opened his eyes. The mirror was facing him. Muted sounds bled through the walls. He was standing straight with arms at his side. The reflection showed an open door behind him. His clothes were different from what he wore to bed. He turned to his side to see the familiar hallway; the top floor of the tenement. A faint noise echoed in the dark. It was the sound of the elevator door slamming shut. Gabrels turned again to see the door to his apartment wide open.

An advertisement appeared in the corner of his eye. A bright balloon of light flashed images of sculpted bodies and multiple voices that filled the silence of the hallway:

"Have you ever wanted to be better?" Asked the voice of a young woman. The belly of a middle aged woman appeared in the reflection of the mirror. The camera view closed in on the dark lines that traversed up her thighs and met at the middle of her back.

"After three children, I just can't find a way to lose any more weight." She sighed.

"Look better?"

The scene changed to a football field with bright green grass. Every color was brilliant and disorienting.

"I can't keep up with the team. I was cut in tryouts," the boy lamented.

"Are you struggling with maintaining your diet?"

Gabrels closed his eyes to stop the light from hurting. Was he sleepwalking now?

"Not getting enough exercise? Our system can stimulate your muscle tissue via carefully placed electrodes. You can build muscle just by performing normal, everyday activities!"

Other voices filled the room. His limbs were numb. No circulation.

"Struggling to feel healthy? Filter mechanisms can isolate the most nutritious elements of your daily intake to maximize body nourishment and eliminate the fat and sugar."

He slowly stepped forward to regain the feeling in his legs. A stiff pain went from the base of his spine to the top of his head. Small knives cut into his temples.

"Body Synthesis is the key to true health."

Gabrels walked slowly back into the apartment. He wanted more than ever to rip the Origin right out of his head. Maybe he could try the most famous method; stabbing straight into the incision, cutting off newDawn's connection to his nervous system.

"Body Synthesis from Machina Systems." The words were more of the same constant noise. They repeated day and night until he knew the rotation of the commercials and could recite them like a mantra.
The door slammed shut and the tenement was silent again. Everyone else slept with the same noise as he did.

Joshua Everett stood naked at the window looking out to the tenements. Every floor had a window somewhere. He wasn't alone in his insomnia. The Machina ads were getting louder, waking him up at all hours of the night. He wanted to shut off newDawn, but he needed to be connected, always online. The lights turned on throughout the apartment without asking. He walked to the kitchen for a drink. A bottle of rare bourbon sat on the counter.

Three ice cubes and four fingers were just enough to get him to relax. The messages were precise. He had to make a decision by morning. He sat back down at his desk and called to Adam to bring them back. The A.I. quietly spilled the words in barely legible white letters across the living room wall.

"Contrast," he said.

The color of the wall changed to a deep black. The conversation appeared again.

"Do we have a deal?"

The buyer only called themselves 'Anon'. They came to him promising big money and high connections, better than he could get on his own. He was struggling for years. This was a chance for him to escape. He let the words sit before sending them, at least until the first bourbon was finished.

"I'm trusting you with a lot."

The reply came within seconds. Anon was watching. Waiting.

"The answer to a question like that is usually a 'yes' or 'no'."

Everett filled the glass to the top this time.

"Review the terms and then I will answer."

The bourbon went down smooth. He felt the grip inside his veins as the drink mixed with his blood. His tolerance was increasing every month. He began to regret opting out of the alcohol filter and getting his body so used to poison.

"You give us your prototype and you can have ours," said Anon.

"How do we make the trade?"

"Our people will find you."

"What guarantee do I have that the deal will be clean?"

Anon was quiet. Everett finished the glass and the strength of the drink nearly triggered his gag reflex. He felt the water build up on the back of his throat.

"There is no guarantee. Your previous threats have forced our hands. We have to act."

"My words weren't threats. There's going to be a big change coming, sooner than you think. I'm trying to reach an understanding. This partnership we have cannot continue as it stands."

"That's your opinion. We can always find ways to use you, as long as we want."

"We both have some stains on our hands. The program is not going to let them go unnoticed."

"The bottom line of all this? We want the doubler. I know you want the Codex."

"A lot of people do," said Everett.

"Most importantly, our employer. You are playing a dangerous game. You of all people should know who we work for."

"If I know as well as you say, they would appreciate a deal like this. It's a little chaos thrown into the established order. Trust me; it will get worse for you with or without me."

"I hope you remember that we usually get what we want, regardless of deals or favors people want to make."

"I am."

"We are allowing this only because of what you have done for us in the past."

Everett looked to Adam.

"Turn the lights off, please."

The apartment went dark.

"Try to keep in mind that I am still doing things for you now."

"Perhaps."

"Consider it a sign of good faith that you will complete your end of the bargain. The tasks you need completed currently will be done and we will both have what we want."

"You are certain that you can provide what we are asking?"

"I am," Everett replied.

"Then deliver it to us and our partnership will be considered over."

"We have a deal."

Once the message was sent, he stood up and fell into bed. Sleep came easy. The waves of sickness in his chest stirred him to turn over to his side. He did not consider the deal going bad. It couldn't. He replayed everything in his mind; all the tracks he attempted to cover, all the ways they could kill him if he tried to escape. He was ready for them.

The bourbon burned a nice sized hole into his chest. No one had dared to cross them but he made the decision to call their bluff. He knew who Anon worked for when he made contact. He had something they wanted and made a move. The pieces were in place. It was their turn now. Gabrels was the ace in the hole; someone he had never met. The paths to success went by, few and fleeting; followed by every way the plan could go wrong.

Six

Marsh had been staring at the clock for an hour before they stepped through the door. They were never late. The body had been hit by a car. He heard it was their car that did it. Paramedics declared the victim dead within minutes of initial impact, and that was more than they needed. His desk was mostly empty, all paperwork tossed into drawers, leaving only three cups of coffee. The silence of the morgue made him sick to his stomach only when they were on their way inside.

The paint on the walls was old and had been chipping away for years. Each side was dashed with shades of sick green that could be peeled away to reveal old brick decay. He heard the outside door slam open against the walls. The echo of the thud made him flinch. Quick footsteps towards his office got louder. Every time they paid a visit, he promised himself that he would not be scared. By the time his office door flew open, the fear he had swallowed seemed to burn a pit into his stomach. They were Shadowmen; supposed operatives for an unknown party, paid endless money from an unknown source. Two men entered the room, completely silent. Marsh sat still as they surveyed the corners of the walls.

"Gentlemen?"

It was a weak attempt to break the silence. There was a tall one and a skinny one. They wore suits, tailored. Both had trench coats and tight gloves. Their shoes were always polished and left a weird scent in the room, a mixture of cologne and tar. Both men were a pale white that almost seemed to match the color of their buttoned shirts. Tall turned around in circles as Skinny went to work, emptying the trash cans and checking the other rooms. Marsh did not know what they truly did, but they visited him once a month. It started almost two years ago.

Skinny was a lank creature that stood at six feet, the other one was another head taller. He finished scanning the rooms of the morgue within a minute. It was like this every time, so Marsh would time their routine. Fifty seconds. Tall continued spinning in a circle until he put out his hands and stopped his strange dance in front of the desk. He grabbed his cup of coffee and held the other out for his partner, who suddenly appeared underneath his arm to snatch the cup. Both took swigs of straight black coffee, no emotions in their faces. The tall one spoke.

"Marshmallow."

Rumors of the Shadowmen ran wild in the slums. No one talked about them more than the ones who worked in the morgue. The black car of death was talked about the most. It was a symbol, meant to create fear of the dark. Their cheeks were sunken. Both looked dehydrated and starved. Death was what they represented in the streets. Their presence took the air out of Marsh. Their body language was uneven as if both were attempting to crawl out of their own skin with sudden movements packed between stillness and restraint. They looked as ghouls in the darkness.

"How can I help you, Maxwell?"

There was a brief smile in reply. A dozen white teeth peered from behind shaded blue lips.

"I think we have done this enough times to stand on ceremony alone."

Both finished their coffee, crushed the cups into the palms of their hands and stuffed the remnants into their jacket pockets.

"Johns thanks you for the coffee."

The skinny one winked at him.

"No traces," he said.

Maxwell sat himself in the chair across the desk and began to speak while Johns walked around and stood behind Marsh.

"We bought a proxy this morning. Good find, really. How long would it take you to write up papers?"

He meant a certificate of death and an autopsy report. They asked for evidence of a body coming into the morgue, being processed and tagged by the system. The simple transaction had been going on for the length of their relationship. Marsh had theories about what they actually did but never questioned it. Something about them was off. He decided to finally say something.

"A couple of hours, but can I ask a question?"

Maxwell was taken aback by this. His eyebrows rose up and Johns quickly ran around the desk to grab another chair to sit by the lamp. Maxwell turned the lampshade around so their pales faces were a shade of green under the old light bulb. One of his eyebrows went down and he cocked his head to the side. Johns mirrored the same motion.

"You two have been coming in here, asking for doctored reports forever. I figured that you are doing something with these bodies since they never make their way through the morgue."

At that moment, Johns pulled out a gun and placed it on the table. It made a thud in the quiet office. Marsh could feel sweat on the back of his neck, but he continued.

"Would you mind telling me what you do with these bodies that never show up?"

Maxwell put the lampshade back down and spoke.

"Why would you think of this moment to ask such a question?"

Marsh's words were trapped in his throat, only a few timid sounds came out.

"We have two bodies in our trunk; one dead and another soon to be. Do you wish to join them?"

Marsh stopped trying to answer.

"I'm not really a fan of this new inquisitive, not scared shitless, version of you. What do you think, Johns?"

Johns picked up the gun. "I don't do questions," he said.

He fired it into the wall behind Marsh. The technician jumped out of his chair and hit the floor. Maxwell did not even react. Instead, he sat back and relaxed.

"There's no one else coming in or out of this office. I wonder how long would it take for the smell of his body to reach someone?"

Johns continued to stare at the man shaking on the floor, hands together behind his head. He scoffed.

"He's kind of fat."

"Marshmallow, get back in your chair, please," said Maxwell. The tech took a moment to collect himself. Maxwell kept his eyes off of him; his tongue moved in circles behind his mouth. Johns kept the gun aimed right at his heart.

"We don't have to tell you what we do. What I will do, though, is ask you a couple of questions. Maybe that will help satisfy this desire to know about us."

"You probably shouldn't do this," Johns said.

"I thought you didn't do questions," Maxwell replied.

"Okay, I'm ready," said Marsh.

Both men stood up at the same time. The clerk began to whimper. Maxwell straightened his tie and asked

"What is the definition of a proxy?"

Marsh looked down to think. "…I don't know…"

"Try," said Maxwell.

"Someone who acts for another?"

"Very good." Maxwell nodded and smiled.

"Quite simply, that is what you are; someone who acts on behalf of us, for which, you are paid. Tell me, how much money do you make in a year?" he asked.

The clerk did not hesitate to answer.

"About $10,000 a year."

When Marsh looked back up, Johns held the gun to his eye. His partner continued talking. His voice was cold.

"You have been brought into something very special, Marshmallow. This entire time you have not asked any questions and we appreciate your service and feedback. You will be making three times as much annually from now on."

Johns pressed the barrel into his eye socket.

"Say thank you," said Maxwell.

Marsh squirmed as he felt the steel push through. "Thank you." He struggled out. Both his eyes were closed and tears began to run down his cheek.

"Can you do that report for us now?"

"Yes," he whimpered.

As he finished speaking, there was the sound of a door slamming shut. Marsh wiped his eyes over and over to clear his vision. The room was empty. A piece of paper sat on his desk, scrawled across it in pencil was a series of names. The bodies were never tagged, never photographed. New names and histories would be created for the faces. He looked down at the paper saw several names; John Grimes, Joseph Cartwright, Darron James. They had to be forgeries. None of the names he had been given ever provided any real proof of life. Each one was a digital gravestone; a place of birth and death along with mixed and matched dental and medical records.

Up on Tempest, someone could call on Adam to report the crime. NewDawn had facial recognition tech, the same one used by the Police. Not many people could stay hidden from the cops up there, so a lot of them tried to find refuge down in Narrow. The A.I. was their crutch. Marsh opened his bottom drawer and reached for the picture of her. The image made him breathe easy. He went into his personal notes and went over the names handed to him by the Shadowmen. There were hundreds. How many people were lost in the sea of misinformation and mismatched records? He put the picture away grabbed the paper off the desk and began work on the tags they asked for.

A black car with a broken windshield sped through the streets of Narrow. Faint stains of red dotted its front and left side. Johns cleaned his gun. Maxwell drove.

"You said too much to him," said Johns.

"Think so?" asked Maxwell.

The magnum in his hand was silver. In their right jacket pockets, both men kept red handkerchiefs for cleaning their weapons. Johns thumbed the cloth deep into the chamber of the gun.

"He talks too much now. You didn't have to tell him anything. You gave him too much information. You even promised to increase his salary," slurred Johns.

Maxwell hit a sharp turn down 8th. He had to sway to avoid the young girl on the corner. "Marshmallow will not interfere in what we do. He will do what we ask without resistance," he grunted.

"He will go to the cops after we triple his money. He needs to go. We will find another fat man to provide paperwork," Johns grumbled.

Maxwell stared out into the black. His foot pressed down and the car gained more speed.

"The cops here are useless. Money facilitates loyalty."

Johns looked back out the passenger window. The streetlights began to blur together. His gloved finger left the magnum and lowered the glass to let the air in. Maxwell continued.

"Marshmallow is not someone that will betray us. He is a means to an end. Furthermore, you seem to forget that we are in control of what he knows."

Johns put the gun behind him in the passenger seat. He sat up and hung his body out onto the car door. The magnum fell to the floor along with the red cloth. Johns opened his mouth and let the cold air hit his lungs. Maxwell welcomed it. The inside of the car had started to smell like blood hours ago. A chill ran down both their spines. It made them both shiver. Johns shook his head before jumping back into his seat.

"It got dirty again," said Maxwell.

Johns shrugged. "It usually does."

A hand from the back of the car handed the magnum to Johns. It belonged to another man, dressed in black. He made no eye contact and continued to stare forward, past the glass of the window and far away from the speeding car.

The car made a swift turn from the street and stopped the entrance of the aqueduct. The Shadowmen stepped out and headed towards the trunk.

"How long have we been in this line of work?" asked Maxwell.

"It's not something I think about," said Johns.

"You should. Our business is what keeps the city going. "

Maxwell placed a key into the trunk of the car and opened it. "Johns, do you know how memories are created?"

Inside the trunk of the car were two bodies. One had been dead for a day or two. There was a smell that poured out into the night air. Bound hands and feet moved beneath the body. There was someone underneath, struggling to breathe.

"Please enlighten me," Johns murmured as the man from the back seat stepped out and pulled the corpse from the trunk.

The body made a thud as it hit the concrete. Muffled noises came from the other one. His hands and feet were bound. Thick strands of duct tape covered his eyes and mouth. Maxwell spoke softly as the man grabbed their hostage under his arms and pulled him out of the trunk before dropping him hard onto the ground.

"Every process in your brain can be broken down into simple terms. Something happens, which you see with your eyes and that information is stored somewhere for you to recall later. For the purpose of this conversation, let's call it a traumatic event."

The man screamed something under the tape. Maxwell continued;

"Please continue, Mr. Proxy."

The man with blank eyes began to remove the restraints.

"This event, when it begins, will fire an electrical pulse that stimulates the chemicals that make up the nerve cells in your brain that interpret and categorize the components of what's going on."

Maxwell removed the last strand of tape from the man's feet, which began to kick at the hands that freed him. Johns stood in silence as Maxwell signaled to the proxy, who repeatedly slammed his fist into the man's exposed nose.

"There are areas of your brain that process the information, splitting the details of the event into the different sensory compartments to be analyzed."

Another hit. Then another. Blood began to rush from the man's nose. Maxwell moved gingerly to avoid staining his suit. From his pocket, he produced a clamp, which he placed onto the man's nose to stop the bleeding.

"Keep going…" said Johns.

"There is a part of your brain called the hippocampus, which combines each piece of the sensory data—your sight, smell, touch and taste—and decides whether it will become a long term or short term memory."

Once freed from his arm restraints, the man swung his arms wildly. Maxwell quickly moved out of the way. Johns moved back as well.

"Each memory that stored is connected to pathways that split off to either associate with past sparks and deviate into new ones, which are then stored as new memories. Those become old ones after they are processed."

The blind man screamed out for help. He punched and kicked at the air. Maxwell stood back. "The processing of each category of sense data is called encoding, which is not unlike the encoding done by computers."

After a few seconds of fury, the blind man decided to run. He pulled the clamp from his nose and threw it to the ground. Both men looked down the blood on the concrete with widened eyes. They looked at each other slowly as the blind man broke away from them, running back towards the streets. Johns pulled his gun and fired. The bullet found its way into the back of the man's head.

There was a sick sound. No exit wound. The shells were designed to disintegrate upon initial impact. Johns watched the body collapse as Maxwell closed the trunk of the car.

"The ability to store and recall data in our minds, whether visual or acoustic, or tactile, is practically the same process of inputting bit patterns of textual data."

There were three splashes of the blood near the tires of the car. Maxwell produced a small bottle. He removed the cap and poured its contents over the blood. The red soon faded into a dark spot that dried almost instantly.

"No traces," said Johns.

He took out the Styrofoam cup from his pocket and tossed it to the ground. Maxwell threw his own cup down and dripped some liquid onto each. Both cups evaporated with a faint chemical smell.

The Shadowmen watched as the proxy dragged the bodies past the slope of concrete that allowed entry to the aqueduct. On the outside of Narrow ran a river blackened with pollution. A tunnel carried water down into the cleaning stations, still operational decades after being built in the slums. Once purified, the water would be pumped back into the pipelines and taken straight up into Tempest and Eros, used for drinking, plumbing, even simulated rain.

Inside, damaged stone and old steel echoed their footsteps behind the water's energy. They took the bodies past the walkway and to the top of the tunnel. A single light showed them the way. A door leading to the pump controls was sealed off with rust. The Shadowmen kept their distance as the proxy dropped their bodies to rest. Maxwell pulled a small data drive from his suit pocket.

"All the information provided on the human brain was discovered over a decade ago. Recently, scientists were able to map the process that creates new memories, in such a way that the functions of the brain could be manipulated."

Johns continued to stare into the rushing water.

"With the right amount of electricity and a small amount of the chemicals produced by those tiny nerve cells, the brain can be stimulated to create, process and store a memory. The moves are systematic. They found a way to alter the system."

The proxy kicked a body over the edge.

"I feel like you've told me this before," said Johns.

"I probably have." Maxwell replied as the proxy's foot nudged the blind man's body into the abyss.

"Do you feel enlightened, Johns?"

Johns put a bullet into the head of the proxy. The body went stiff before falling into the pool.

"Absolutely. Tell me the next move."

Maxwell looked out into the black waters and felt a sudden shaking in his lapel.

"Phone call."

"From the suit."

"No doubt."

He produced an old flip phone. Prepaid on a private account, an unknown party's unlimited credit and operating on a frequency from many years ago unnoticed and largely ignored by the day's standards.

"Speak." The voice was masked with digital noise.

"Don't you think vocal manipulation is a little bit overboard?" asked Maxwell.

"The longer you take to do your job, the less trust I have in your abilities."

"You continue to try and hurt our feelings, and continually fail to do so. Cleaning up the messes of others takes time, and resources," chided Maxwell.

"Are you sure we have enough time?" asked the voice.

"Things are moving along smooth enough. Don't trouble yourself with timetables. That is what we do. We take care of you."

Johns heard the murmurs through the sounds of crashing water.

"It is complete."

"And the bodies?"

"Disposal has been handled, too," said Maxwell.

"How did they fare?" asked the voice.

"They were decent code writers. Neither one could break it."

Johns watched the bodies disappear from sight.

"You're running out of leads."

"And you are running out of bodies...What's next, you ask?" Maxwell looked to the water.

Johns turned away from the shapes in the darkness to hear the answer.

"We wait and we watch. We have another in place, a good one, an engineer, too. Let the system do what it needs to."

Seven

Gabrels woke up with a splitting headache. He could not remember much of the week that had passed. There were faded images of the desk and the train car. Nothing else filled his memory besides hours of staring at screens. The ceiling was a stark white. It was too bright to think. The blinds were wide open. Sunlight came through the windows and reflected off every surface. His hands were numb. There was a foul taste in his mouth. He stretched his legs and crawled out of bed.

The interface came up as usual. Data poured out onto the walls of the room. Something had changed in the last few days. The desire for cleanliness had subsided. There was a new apathy that gripped him tighter than ever before. News crawls appeared in a different language, along with a note that appeared in his alarm notifications.

"Believe me now?"

Gabrels ignored it and stood up. He immediately remembered the pain in his foot from the day before. When he first stepped down, the expected feeling of carpet was replaced by a sharp pain between his toes. He fell back onto the bed and looked down to see the upturned hook of a metal hanger. There was a small stream of blood that ran from a shallow cut. With a lick of his finger, he was able to wipe the wound clean and pressed down to keep the blood from running out.

He kept the pain in mind and stepped over the hanger and went towards the drawer by the bed. Two days ago, everything in the drawer was rearranged. Shirts that had been organized by size and coordinated by color, dark to light, were taken out and stuffed back in a new sequence; favorites first and the rest sat shoved into dark corners. Gabrels felt compelled to change the order of everything around him. He took the drawer from off its hooks and dumped the clothes out onto the floor. Amidst the growing piles, he found the shirt with the least amount of wrinkles.

Pants were tossed around the same way, followed by the shoes in the closet. Adam's warnings of tripping over his mess were met with silence. The influence of the A.I. was nowhere to be found. Both the suggestions and language settings were randomized, somehow. News updates would play in Japanese or Arabic. It was different every morning. Everyone in Tempest spoke English, it seemed to go without saying. The volume would be cranked to the maximum. It always startled him. He braced for the onslaught and switched to audio. The room shattered with an assault of screams, loud drums and guitar. Gabrels winced immediately.

"Why do I feel like every morning this week has started the same?"

He lowered the volume to a whisper.

"You may be recalling a traditional holiday decades ago involved a rodent emerging from a hole in the ground to announce a change or the continuance of weather conditions."

Gabrels glanced at the shell in the corner of the room.

"There was also a film that parodied the idea of a time loop where the protagonist experiences the same day repeating over and over."

"Please stop talking to me…"

Adam made a decision on its own to leave Gabrels to his own devices until fully awake. The numbers on the clock made his stomach hurt. He was at least an hour late to work every day that week. The apartment was chaotic. The blinds kept opening while he slept. Perhaps some hot glue could keep them shut. Hot sun and the constant noise of the trains bled into him. There was no time for freshening up. He applied some deodorant to his arms and chest.

There was a fresh bottle sitting in front of the icebox. He opened the cap and took a long drink of the fruit elixir. That morning, he thought of spitting it back into the sink. For some reason, the taste was horrible. He coughed loud and spat the remnants back out. The satisfying taste of the fruit mix was gone. There was a taste for something stronger on his tongue. Besides the aching in his head and neck, there was an aftertaste of apples and berries that nearly made him sick.

The sounds of crashing metal that ran through him intensified on the train. Even with newDawn's advertisements running full speed ahead again, Adam was quiet. Gabrels took a drink of apple juice from a nearby vending machine. No satisfaction. There was a strange rumbling in his stomach afterwards. He stopped to get food. The A.I. was not voicing any healthy choices. Vegetable and egg pizza at 10:30 in the morning would have to suffice. The slice was greasy and burned his hands as he struggled to keep his thumb and finger on the crust.

The pangs of hunger did not disappear after food. Gabrels sat down at his desk and tried to bury himself into his work. No one addressed him. It was always like that. Something was pulling at him. There was a sudden urge to slam his fists into the table. He wanted to scream in their faces. The feeling increased every time he stepped back into the office. The other revs were vapid machines. Everyone else in the room was a decoration.

After two hours of increasing hunger, Gabrels contemplated leaving the building for more food. They weren't allowed to step out until at least five articles had been written and published in the data stream. Sweat began to build up on the back of his neck. Beads collected and ran down his forehead. He needed to eat. The thirst for beer was strong. He could almost taste it on his tongue. The memory of drinking an ice cold glass kept reappearing. It kept him wondering how much he could buy and carry home without the cops following him.

That same memory lingered. It was a faint line in an old song he used to know the words to. Gabrels could swear that feeling wasn't his own. If he did decide to make the purchase and bring it home, it would be the first time he would ever taste it.

So where was this inviting familiarity coming from? How did he go on for so long avoiding this taste? A tingling sensation was rampant throughout his body.

He suddenly remembered being at a dinner party years ago. The original owners of Precipice were there. Revs were required to attend. Everyone wore suits and drank wine. Gabrels stayed in the back after one taste of wine. He nursed a glass of water and watched the revs make fools of themselves.

The whole event was meant to celebrate the deal that was struck between them and Synapse. The more wine they drank, the more obnoxious they became. Especially Keys. Gabrels was almost certain that he hated him. The feeling began on that night. Every sentence they spoke required animated motions with their hands. The same people who he saw less than five times a year since he started working for them hollered in his ear about how the deal was going to change their lives.

It made him sick to think that a tech company would be paying so much to sway public opinion to their favor. The pains in his stomach became echoes of that same feeling. Gabrels finished the articles and sent it out to the data stream. Users who followed the company would receive an update, read the piece and decide to up/down vote the product. Most of the people who voted didn't even try the product, whether it was an application for newDawn or body augmentation. The deal with Synapse wasn't even because the companies were falling onto hard times. Both sides just decided to take the comfort of easy money.

He remembered a heavy hand dropping on his shoulder that night. Right when Keys was at the height of his story, Gabrels turned suddenly to see an older man in a tailored grey suit. The heavy hand had a ring on its third finger; a thick gold band that carried a crystal stone on its back. He had broad shoulders and thinning black hair pulled into a clever comb-over. Gabrels stared down at the silver tie that sat against the black buttons that lined the shirt. He spoke in a slow drawl; a southern gentleman, the usual political type.

"Young man, you look like you would rather be in a shithouse than standing here listening to us."

"I'm not a party guy," said Gabrels.

"Neither am I."

He stuck that heavy hand back out.

"Leland Graff. Your city-statesman."

Gabrels shook his hand. The members of government did not come out into public often. The term had been coined years ago, nomenclature for figurehead. Decades ago, there were state senators that stood for growth and prosperity for their chosen piece of land. The old wars changed that. The position was smashed down into a single seat to oversee a city-state of nearly five million bodies.

The statesman's grip tightened up before he let go.

"I don't have a title to match that, I'm afraid," he said.

"But you do something for a living, don't you? What's your profession?" asked Graff.

"I'm just a cog in this wheel."

"Oh, I'm sure. The data stream is everything to the people in this part of the country. I'm not even sure what you are supposed to call it. I guess you could call this the private sector? But, despite my ignorance about the correct language I rely on it as much as anyone else. So come on, what's your title?"

"I'm a content or product reviewer. Any article you've read in this past year about new augmentation tech or apps for newDawn, it was most likely from me or one of the other dozen guys with cheap suits on in here."

"Telling people which robot parts to stick on must not be the most lucrative position," said Graff.

"Precipice is a small company, but we get around the stream a lot. It's almost a challenge now to be uninformed," said Gabrels.

"Pride in one's work shows a certain loyalty, whether to the company that helps pay your bills, or to the people who keep the country going so that all this luxury can be maintained. But within pride, you must keep in mind its undeniable truth." Graff took his hand from his pocket and put his index finger up.

"What's that?" Gabrels asked.

"Pride creates a need, a pursuit of perfection. The pursuit pushes you, and you will see nothing but disappointment the more you chase it."

Another man in a ridiculous pinstriped suit walked past them to place a drink in the statesman's hand. There was a group of seven. Bodyguards.

"You learn to adapt to the surroundings, to blend in so that nothing bothers you. Yet, on a night like this one especially, it's really impossible when everyone in the room knows your name and is trying to crawl into your favor."

"I'm not looking for perfection, sir."

"You wouldn't be here if you weren't. I grew up in the recovery from the war. I might be one of the few people in Tempest who could remember a world without this technology. Tempest didn't even have a name at first. It used to be broken up into numbered sectors. Everyone here played a part in its development. Then the technology became a necessity not just for the building, but for everything. People have certainly made shiny new crutches since then."

"And you are without improvements?" Gabrels asked.

The statesman opened his shirt and unveiled worn through skin that wrinkled against a plate that held a mass of wires and tubes together. They danced in circles until meeting at the core; a small box of turning gears which traded shades of red with the veins connected to its corners.

"Artificial chest, heart included."

Gabrels nodded his head in amazement.

"I take it you don't have the A.I. in your head talking nonstop either?"

Graff was signaled by one of his guards.

"I have enough voices in my head that I don't trust..." said Graff as he put his empty drink in Gabrels' hand and walked outside. He stared into the glass as its reflections soon faded into nothing.

Since their first meeting, the statesman would send him a message via his handler, Stevens. Every six months, he would receive an updated letter with the most banal phrases in headlines meant to be inspiring or uplifting;

"Message received twenty nine months ago from Stevens St. John. Greetings, Mr. Gabrels. Mr. Graff asked me to forward a few words to you. Consider it a free piece of motivation. The dirt under your fingers is food enough. Keep digging."

"Message received twenty five months ago from Stevens St. John: Mr. Gabrels, we have not received any reply back. Mr. Graff has asked me to send another to ensure that you have read the first, even though the A.I. can verify that you have read it without inserting ourselves, and yet here we are.

Another piece of wisdom. The weather may be fake but remember that what you do under the daylight matters. His words not mine. Good day."

"Message received twenty one months ago from Stevens St. John: Mr. Gabrels, this is not meant to be one of the many messages from startups looking for handouts, or a mouth breathing programmer. This correspondence would better suit you if it became two sided. Please remember the dinner party and try to keep in mind where a large part of Precipice support resides. Words from Mr. Graff to follow. Become the best version of yourself today."

From then on, he always replied with half hearted attempts at humor that could appeal to an out of touch old man. For a time, he kept their conversations in a folder and would wonder if this was something the others had dealt with. It seemed like a bad attempt at rapport between two people who had nothing in common. They couldn't talk about the weather, since there were no changes in season. He waited for Graff to tell stories about the good old days but instead got messages to seize the day. He maintained his secrecy about his articles and kept his replies to a few anecdotal cases and mild sarcasm; the bare minimum. Was this even happening? He couldn't help but doubt it.

The codex product appeared on his terminal screen once again, replacing the supposed memory of that unreal night. Everett had reached out to him a few times during the week since that first night. The replies were short, chopped up into single sentences;

"Tuesday 6:43 A.M: Talk to me, Stan."

"Please don't call me that. The puzzle is not solved yet."

"Keep contact to a minimum since we may be monitored."

"Wednesday 7:03 A.M.: By your people or mine?"

"Thursday 9:30 P.M. Maybe both."

He decided to send Everett an update. "Carrying on. Still stuck."

The response was quicker than anticipated. "Good work, keep going."

"And that's all?"

"Don't show the A.I. anything."

"It's going to be harder to keep secret than I thought, I'm afraid."

"Do not do anything to risk exposing us."

"Adam won't do that."

"It's got to be you, not the A.I."

"I need all the help I can get. I have no idea how to solve this thing or what to look for. Your puzzle doesn't have any obvious clues."

"Look again, there is something missing."

"What does that mean? Why did you design this thing to be practically impossible to crack?"

"Listen, the programming for the doubler is the same way. It's just how I design around the secrecy of Machina. It's not like Synapse where they let writers like you in on all their projects."

"Do they really have you under lock and key like that? The culture now demands access to everything."

"They stay away from the media; they feel it can influence their work to the point of becoming unrecognizable. They create distance to stand out. You don't even know who runs the company because they don't want to be put on a pedestal."

Gabrels read those lines over again. It was true. No one really knew who ran Machina, or even Synapse for that matter.

"Tell me something," he said.

"Think of it this way; you have a blank slate, a towering wall to scale. There's no way you can try to climb it, so what do you do?"

"Knock it down?" asked Gabrels.

"You need to find weak points in the structure to get past it."

It's mystery had consumed him to the point of neglecting standard social habits. What else could be there? The message was nearly blank. Insomnia took over after the first night. His dreams followed a strange pattern of aural and visual chaos as a result. He had to know what he was looking at. Besides the lack of sleep, he hadn't cleaned his body or teeth in days. Gabrels was beginning to smell but the puzzle still demanded his complete attention.

After the first night, he began to take the message apart, break it down to its smallest properties; the actual code. Adam was helpful in providing clues. The image within the email was a black diamond across a plain white background. In between his work during the day and gaming at night, he attempted to crack the code that stood over him. The puzzle became his obsession. Gabrels spent hours trying to understand what it was that loomed over him. The A.I. offered him an idea; to consider it a silly game. More than likely, it was just another thin morsel to chew on before spitting back onto the pile of things to waste the hours of the day. Mindless entertainment, slightly different from the rest. He knew better. Something inside him pushed forward. He felt his own hands working against him, trying to search the code for an answer.

The lines of the diamond were found by alternating the colors of the text and highlighting negative space. The code of the message was standard. Gabrels had reviewed it enough to have it memorized. It was on the second day that he noticed a pattern in the numbers typed within the code. He wrote the numbers down and searched every possible combination and meaning for those particular digits.

Adam suggested that the body of the message was open source. Gabrels went into the source code of the message and began to alter things. No new results were yielded until he intentionally changed the numbers within the text. Changing the text did nothing but different numbers moved the angles of the diamond shape.

On the third day, Gabrels spent hours toying with the numbers inside the source code to see how the shape within the message had changed. The diamond would grow or almost fold in on itself. He continued to alter the numbers to see how far down the shape could be broken down. Gabrels got stuck and would have to start over from the beginning. The process was maddening. Adam took notes for him to keep track of the possibilities. By the night's end, the shape no longer resembled a diamond. It was a series of triangles. He started to wonder if he had gone too far in the wrong direction. Gabrels had lost over almost a week trying to solve the puzzle. Starting over from the beginning again was not an option.

The triangles looked back at him. Everything else seemed distant. Voices in the background became faint. He was no longer staring at blank page, no longer struggling to come up with a way to praise the latest form of synthesizing amino acids from food as a form of weight loss rather than practical starvation. He was the puzzle. He was a player in the game. The pangs of hunger made it worse.

Gabrels was back at the office later that day. The new girl walked by and waved at him. Without thinking, he quickly licked his lips, which made a thick, wet sound. She cringed and her smile was gone, for good. A sudden sickness hit the back of his throat like bile. What was he thinking? His face matched her own disgust as he watched her disappear behind the corridor.

"Gabrels!"

He looked around to see who was calling him. It was Sumerian. His clothes were almost the exact same as they were yesterday; same pants with a food stain on the left leg, half-cleaned and a blue sweater, still too long for his arms.

"Are you alright?"

The question was surprising. His interaction with Gabrels was nothing but casual waves of hello and goodbye.

"Yeah, why?"

"I don't know. You usually look less…put together." Sumerian fixed his glasses as he spoke. He was nervous.

"Are you saying I look like shit?" asked Gabrels.

Sumerian's glasses were practically falling off of his head now. He stumbled to keep them still.

"Well, yeah…Maybe you should take the day off. There was a bug going around the office."

As he spoke, Gabrels began to cough. There was something in his throat. He struggled to get it out. Something hit the back of his teeth, which he spit into the trashcan near his feet. Sumerian bit his tongue.

"I don't think anyone will mind." Gabrels replied. He sat back in his chair and placed his feet on his desk. "Let's be honest…it's not like we're doing anything important in here. I think I will stick around and stew in the shit soup we've created for ourselves."

Sumerian looked around to see if the others were listening. Even Gabrels was a little surprised to see his own feet on the desk. His eyebrows rose up as soon as the words left his mouth. He looked down to see bits of dirt from his heels smeared into the wood.

"Do you think it's strange that you, me and Keys have been here the longest while everyone else in this office seemingly comes and goes?"

Sumerian looked surprised. "Not really. Every office in Tempest is a revolving door. People can't keep up with the pace."

"What do you think makes us different?" Gabrels asked.

"Adaptability."

There was a long pause.

"What, you don't agree?" asked Sumerian.

"Being bought out protects us."

Sumerian's eyes widened. "You think so?" he asked.

"Absolutely." Gabrels took his feet off the desk and leaned forward.

"Everyone else in this office has no idea what we really do here. They didn't sign the same contracts as you and I did. The people who were at that dinner with the statesman don't even show their faces around here anymore. Why do you think that is?"

Sumerian shook his head.

"Because we lie for a living. All they want us to do is keep churning out inane articles about corporate rumors and bickering back and forth about the quality of products meant strictly for our vanity."

Gabrels pointed to the windows. "You know we've been recycling the same water for years now, spitting through the sewer systems to be cleaned and spit back into our mouths from the pipeline. The ones who can afford those body filters don't have much to worry about, but what about those without it? How long do you think we will last once the water is too bad for us?"

The others started to hear him.

"You know the bubble is going to burst. I mean, shit, we have a dome that blocks us from the acid rain that burns everything underneath us. We filter that, and we drink it! According to Adam, running away from our problems is nothing new. We've done before. Only this time, there's no bubble to crawl into. How long are we gonna drain everything from the people underneath us?"

"Are you sure you're alright?" Sumerian asked.

"I feel good. Really good, actually."

A new voice shot through the office.

"Gabrels, after hearing that little tirade, I have to say, you look…a lot more relaxed than usual." It was Keys.

"I never hear my name coming out of your mouth."

Keys wore something similar to what he had on the day before. The predictability had stopped being fun to point out. Gabrels' expression did not change. His mind went back to the article while his fingers danced across the wood of the desk.

"I'm surprised you are talking to me. This may be the first time in about six months." Gabrels snapped.

Sumerian's eyes went up. He looked at his accomplice with surprise, though he knew that there would have to be a response. He counted the seconds and started with the left hand before adding his right.

"Maybe you can get some decent work done since you decided not to keep up a normal appearance for the week," said Keys.

Sentences poured onto the doc. There was something that was driving him to work faster than before. Keys waited for a comeback. He did not get one. Sumerian looked on, still counting.

"Can you do us all a favor and take a shower tonight? You smell a slum rat," said Keys.

Gabrels suddenly looked up. His eyes were wide open. There was an awkward silence. Sumerian gave up waiting for the comeback that never came from Gabrels' mouth.

"What's wrong with my work anyway?" He asked. A smile began to creep across his face.

"Excuse me?" asked Keys.

"I'm pretty sure that I put out twice the amount of content that anyone else in the office, including you."

Gabrels looked down for a brief moment to see that his hands were still working the article while his eyes were away. Surprisingly, there were no errors. Adam was able to correct the errors created when splitting the thought process between a number of tasks. A brand new, perfect paragraph was staring back at him.

"Quality over quantity, I'm sure." Keys smirked.

"Hey, whatever happened to that guy from last week that wanted you to stop the illegal release of his product?" Gabrels asked loudly.

"What?"

"Do you remember the guy who was talking to you about capacity doubling, or whatever it was called, the one who was trying to get your support in getting more tests for it?"

The noise of the office began to die down. The revs were starting to stare now. Gabrels continued.

"Let me rephrase that, more testing for what could be a major breakthrough in our lives, just swept under the rug by a joke of an article which has your name on it. Regardless of the fact that the story could be a huge benefit piece to a desperate company like Synapse, any ignorance of such a massive reveal still has your name attached to it and any blame on our failure to capitalize will still fall back on us and our reputation."

Keys looked around at the others, then back at Gabrels.

"Are you serious right now? Shut the fuck up."

"Guess what, asshole? Just now, articles from Machina were put out about an actual capacity doubler."

The other revs immediately pulled the stream. He was right. A massive influx of content about this new piece of tech; a small ring designed to fit the circumference of the Origin.

"This new tech was set for release to the public, to be followed by another article, written by you."

The revs started to move closer. Sumerian was stunned.

"He reached out to you to stop the release because he did not authorize it. The product was just leaked to the market without his knowledge, or consent, which is needed by law before being tossed out to the data stream."

"How do you know it was leaked?" asked Keys.

"He told you it was, in the emails that you pissed on. Someone leaked the product and you didn't care to do any research about that before creating a half assed write up for it. He reached out to you, the guy who wrote the article, the one being paid to protect the interests of the company. Instead of helping him, you threatened to sue him for harassment."

"It's not my job to check behind people, and you're a freak for looking at my emails instead of doing your own work," Keys hollered.

The revs began to laugh. Some of them turned away from the scene and went back to their desks.

"Last night, you told him to kill himself because you thought he was trying to somehow leech fame off of us."

The chatter had stopped.

"What?!"

Gabrels got out of his chair and walked up to Keys.

"You also said that he had no friends or family."

He stood nose to nose with Keys, who looked more and more uncomfortable. Sumerian kept his hands on his glasses to keep them from falling off of his face.

"Why are you standing this close to me, Gabrels?"

The other revs had stopped talking completely. Everyone was staring at them again.

"So you know, the man's name is Everett. He lives in the same tenement as you do. He works as a program designer at Machina. His social media output has a lot of happy looking pictures. Yours? Not so much."

Keys took a step back.

"What are you doing? How did you get access to my private social stream?" Keys asked.

"It wasn't too hard. You're nothing special, as much as you want to think you are. The password is the same for everything you use. Consider this a free piece of advice. You should rethink the way you handle company business while in a public forum. In fact, I didn't see a lot of anything about you online; Stephan Keys, apartment 4522 in Tenement 18, Sect 4 of residential district, university graduate in the year of 2109, five credit cards-four of which are maxed out-and an outstanding balance on a bank loan for penis augmentation."

There was faint laughter behind the crowd. Keys' eyes began to look down, away, any other direction but Gabrels.

"Your eyes are having some trouble there. You might need to get those fixed. Pretty soon, tears will start to run. Maybe you want to augment that, as well?"

It felt like a shot of adrenaline went through his body. There was more blood, as if two hearts were beating.

"How weak we feel when involuntary actions begin to take over."

Keys was speechless, a rare occasion.

"Do you feel like you run the show still?"

Gabrels felt strange. Where was this coming from?

"Think about the things you say around here. We are all skilled freaks. Remember that there's no anonymity. Keep that in mind when you want to fuck with people."

Gabrels felt he was about to collapse. More sweat formed on the back on his neck and arms. His spine began to shrink back into its former, shapeless form.

"What the hell is going on here?"

A voice echoed from the back of the office. The small sea of people began to part.

"Gabrels is starting to lose it," said Keys, dismissive.

"Seriously?"

A man in a blue suit with pink button shirt stepped out from the crowd and moved in between them.

"Both of you need to take it easy."

It was Miller, office supervisor. He started off as a content creator himself. He stopped coming into work soon after the Synapse deal. The revs kept the place open. He stayed home until there was drama in the building or if an announcement was coming up. Precipice was a purchase he made years ago from hungry writers who could not get a job in the news sector. He scratched at his chin, covered in red hair.

"I'm surprised I still remember your name. It's been a few months since you've been he...." said Gabrels.

"Okay, look. Don't talk anymore."

Miller cut him off. He always did that. He spoke to broken pieces of irritated mutterings. There were times when it seemed his mind struggled to keep in pace with his mouth.

"Anyone. For the rest of the day. Seriously. I'm only going to say this once. Do not waste more of your time here if you are going to act like this." Miller ignored him and straightened his bright pink tie.

"Yes, sir," Keys muttered.

"Gabrels, take the day off and get some rest. I've been where you are before. Sleep is all you need."

Miller turned to the rest of the office.

"I want everyone at their best tomorrow! Do you understand? We have something big that will be broadcast on the stream tomorrow. Precipice needs to be the first ones with content to relay the announcement."

"What big announcement?" asked Sumerian. He had a firm grip on his glasses.

"We haven't heard anything like that all week."

"The announcement is about Adam and newDawn. That teaser you've heard about? There are rumors that it's a firmware update," said Miller.

Some of the revs rolled their eyes.

"Listen, if any of the reports are true, the update will be massive. This new update to the framework will be the largest one ever attempted on a mass audience. If this is real, then we need to spin the argument about capacity doubling back to the side of increased testing."

Keys turned away from the eyes that moved to his direction.

"I won't say keep up the good work to you, because the good work is never done. Just keep going and don't get overwhelmed." Miller turned back to Gabrels.

"I never hear a word from you, Gabrels. Based on the amount of words you put out into the stream, you get your shit done. I can tell you are burned out. Rest up, come back on Monday."

Miller put his hand on Gabrels' shoulder. "I'm not going to report any of this activity. But please refrain from putting people's private business out for everyone to know. There's an application for that."

As Miller walked away, Gabrels quietly gathered his things and left Precipice. Keys sat back in his chair. Sumerian finally let go of his glasses and ran to him.

"That was crazy..." Sumerian whispered with a quiet excitement. "You guys looked like you were about to start punching each other."

"He was about to get his ass kicked," Keys laughed it off. "That guy is a freak."

"I think you should have slapped him," said Sumerian. He put his knees in the seat and balanced himself on Keys' desk. "Office morale would be boosted if people actually saw others with some real passion for once."

Keys ignored him. He pulled up the data stream at his own desktop and marked his session private.

"Adam?"

"Yes, Mr. Keys."

Sumerian sat back in his chair and began to chew on his fingernails.

"Bring up any articles within the last two weeks about this Everett and his capacity doubler."

"Of course," the A.I. went right to work.

"Are you afraid Gabrels is right?"

"Shut up..." Keys kept his eyes on the stream. Adam brought a list of text out from the lines of code.

"The results are as follows; 22 articles just published to the data stream that discuss various topics related to Mr. Everett, his invention and its leak to the public."

Sumerian began to chuckle. Adam had brought up a video interview of Everett. The journalists kept hands over their ears to help isolate the audio as their own Origins captured the footage. His face was stone, clean shaven and as well defined as anyone else who lived up top. He wore a nice suit of black and white. There was a hood sewn into the blazer.

"Mr. Everett! Can you take a moment to comment on this leak?"

They chirped like birds, starving for food.

"Joshua! Will I be able to hold enough information for two brains with your new invention?"

He continued to walk through the mess of people towards the train.

"What happened with your doubler? Did someone steal it from you? I hear Machina has one of their own coming out soon."

He finally stopped to put the hood of his jacket over his head. The man disappeared into the crowd, trying to shove their way onto the train before Police were dispatched to clear the platform.

"When was the leak really announced?" asked Keys.

"Twenty minutes ago."

"That's a long time to let something like this sit." Sumerian said as he ran his teeth across the nail of his index finger.

"How the hell did this happen? Why didn't you tell me about the leak?" Keys asked.

"I was not asked to do any outside research for your recent articles. You do need to know that Mr. Gabrels was right, however. Criminal charges could be brought against Precipice for reviewing an illegal release and not going through the proper channels for clearance," said Adam.

"Which means, that you are screwed," Sumerian laughed as he kicked off of Keys' desk to get back to his own.

"It is still possible to defuse the situation to avoid any company backlash. I will go ahead and archive these articles in your personal file. Would like me to contact Mr. Everett for you?"

"No. Just tell me what to do. Or do it yourself, if you have to have permission. Fix this shit, please," mumbled Keys.

Gabrels kept his distance from everyone on the platform. On the train, he took a seat in the back of the car and wiped the sweat from his brow. A pang of hunger entered his body. He felt a sharp pain hit his chest that doubled him over.

"Are you alright, Mr. Gabrels?" asked Adam. The A.I formed into a mirror body that sat in the seat next to him.

"I don't know…What the hell happened back there, Adam?"

Gabrels spoke low. The train car was not empty. Curious faces turned back to look him over. If they suspected he was drugged, the train officers would be contacted with no hesitation. He feigned to look as if he was stretching his arms.

"Your heart rate and stress levels increase as soon as Mr. Keys begins to speak. It is obvious that you do not like him as an individual."

"I would never think to start something in the office, though," Gabrels replied.

"I have been witness to all the things that Mr. Miller spoke of. You have kept a very tight schedule. You are attached to the data stream, no different from the other journalists here in the city."

Gabrels moved back in his seat and turned to stare back out at the moving machinery of the Epicentre. The numbness was gone for a brief moment, but he did not like what he felt in its place.

"Despite that connection, you still need to find methods of relaxation. You need to separate from the schedule you have created for yourself," said the A.I.

"Were you aware of the leak?"

"Any information that is published to the data stream is stored in the framework."

"How did I talk about the leak without knowing it would happen?"

"I am not sure. Are you saying you didn't know about the articles even while you were speaking about them?"

"Yes."

"Interesting."

The voice of the A.I. was suddenly distant. Was it trying to change the subject?

"Are you absolutely sure you don't have any records of talking to me in the Blank Page last week?" he asked.

"I have no recollection of such conversation taking place. I would say that based on the words you say that I used, any malfunction in my language centers leading to such insults would have been reported and repaired automatically."

"Something's wrong with me, Adam." He felt an itch that traveled under his skin that was impossible to find.

"Do you think I should continue with Everett's game?" he asked.

The A.I. spoke in plain, cold words, as always.

"Consider your motivations until now."

"You mean working and saving to retire?"

"Have those motivations changed based on the possibility that you may be involved with a scandal?"

"No. I'm worried about what stress I am putting my body through every night."

He remembered waking up outside his apartment. A certain tension formed in his throat. His next breath was caught inside the body.

"You seem to focus on the possibility of losing control," Adam said casually.

"Control of what?"

"Perhaps everything. Your speech makes many references to losing control of the body."

"Do you think so?"

"It pains you to think about not being at the helm of every aspect of your life; from finances, to personal appearance, to being viewed as something less than your own peers. You are comforted by the thought of escaping that pressure."

"You can tell that by looking at me?" asked Gabrels,

"Vital signs reveal everything. They are a map to the true signals of the human condition; the delayed reaction in hopes of acceptance. This is foreign concept to me still. I am made to process the information but not interpret it for use to increase social standing, as much as users ask me to."

Adam was just as much a crutch to him as anyone else in Tempest. Gabrels thought about if he should apologize to the A.I for, but what could it do with such a thing?

"What do my vital signs say about these headaches? All the stomach pains and nausea? Heavy fatigue and sweating when I sleep? Can you tell me what all that means?" he asked.

Adam never hesitated.

"Signs of withdrawal, which is odd, given your mostly consistent abstinence from drugs and alcohol."

"Excuse me?"

"You are showing documented symptoms when a person abruptly stops or decreases the use of medication or recreation drugs. It also coincides with your outburst towards Mr. Keys."

"How is that possible?"

"I do not have a more simplistic answer to that question."

The triangles were back in front of him again. Gabrels put the incident in the office, just like that dream that night, far away from him. It was just another bad dream, a lack of sleep. He knew he needed rest, but his body simply would not allow it. He thought about Adam's theory. Withdrawals? Was it being serious? Adam could have been pushing him to see the doctor. It had been months since his last physical. Citizens augmented with newDawn needed to report any suspicious behavior or changes in personality immediately. He slapped the shapes against the window. He studied the source code as he had done for over 100 hours.

"What if the negative colors could be put back on?" he asked.

"Have you tried reversing the image again at a certain point?" Adam's mirror body moved in sync with Gabrels'.

He tried reversing the image. Nothing. He moved back in his progress, reversing the image after each change in the source code. Nothing.

"There!" Gabrels shouted. Heads turned to him, then to the window. He awkwardly looked down and waited for them to turn back around. The image, when reversed, showed a white line against the black lines of the now uneven triangles. The source code showed a change where the white line now displayed. Gabrels began to move the other edges of the shapes to see if any other white lines would appear. He found thirty.

The train had already past the tenements twice over. The mirror body of the A.I. soon sat back and crossed its legs as if it were a passenger.

"How long are you going to stay on this train?" it asked.

Gabrels did not answer. He moved the black lines along to match the new white lines. These movements formed new angles, which formed new shapes. The source code was at an end. He stopped to take a moment and look at the new result. Once the lines had been moved to those new coordinates, the folds became more defined. A familiar shape had finally become visible to him. The black diamond had morphed from black triangles to wings.

"The white lines were a diagram," he said quietly.

"To tell you where to fold?" Adam asked.

"Exactly. The diamond is a piece of paper."

"And what is the result?" it asked. The body of the A.I. sat up.

"It's a blackbird..." said Gabrels.

The train car stopped. Piles of passengers met in-between the glass and steel barriers. A young girl moved around the mass of bodies trying to either get on or off the car. Gabrels looked at her plainly. Her hair was jet black. A brown coat of fur covered her crimson sweater. His eyes made their way down to see her white leggings, which covered the soft, pink flesh of her thighs.

"Congratulations. I feel that a celebration of some sort is in order…Perhaps what you need is to get laid."

Gabrels looked back at his mirror.

"What did you say?!" he asked. The mirror body was gone. The passengers on the train looked back at him strangely before turning back towards the fury outside the windows. Gabrels looked around the car. The girl was there, staring at him. There was a sudden thirst that welled up in the back of his throat. Something that felt like hands moved across his back. The windows of the car were sealed shut. He craved air that couldn't fill his lungs fast enough.

Eight

The hangar was dark. The lights were kept off to keep from alerting the cops of any suspicious activity. A flash of lightning cracked the sky open, revealing the room and the handlers to each other. There were three of them. Each wore thick hazmat suits, a dead shade of grey rubber which connected to a mask to filter the air. Each one was numbered. At their feet lay a dozen human bodies, stripped of clothing. They took a moment to look at each other before returning to their work in the darkness.

There were three conveyor belts which carried a corresponding number, stretched across the neatly tiled floor. Each belt ran across the length of the hangar to an open shaft. A handler was tasked with disposing of the bodies. The scenario was always scheduled during a storm. That night, the wind was high and the rain was acidic enough to stain the skin. The money was good for one night's work; divide each body into small enough pieces to fit into the shaft. The iron pathway ran down to the buildings furnace. The smell of burning flesh would be hidden by the scent of the acid rain outside.

Handlers were paid to never speak and never remove their gas masks. Most of the time, they were drugged, taken to the site and revived for dressing and completion of the task. There were ground rules for disposal as well; hands and feet were to be separate from the limbs, as well as the head from the chest and stomach. Each conveyor belt was fitted with a leather strap, which held a series of handsaws along with a sharpener.

A body could be divided in under an hour. The pile was stacked high, so they went to work quickly. No handler was used twice unless they kept their end of the bargain. They were paid well for their silence. The site was cleaned after disposal was complete. The sounds of crunching bones filled the dead air. Heavy boots stomped through the blood that collected everywhere.

If the bodies weren't gone by morning, they wouldn't be allowed to leave. The shocks of lightning illuminated their vision well enough to keep track of what was left. One was ahead, with two bodies to the others' one. Two had already slipped while moving pieces to the belt and had fallen, carrying a massive red stain across their legs and back. Three struggled to keep the same pace as the others. The glove for the right hand was beginning to rip. Three had to work slow and grip the tools in their palm to keep them firm enough from further tearing the hole. There were to be no fingerprints, no contact with the bodies for fear of infection or contamination.

The clock on the wall pushed them to continue. The storm was only visible from above. The ceiling was made of glass panes that connected like folded hands. Each looked up when the wind was high. The smack against the glass made the sound of gunshot. The furnace produced black smoke which was filtered up into the ventilation system of the building and outside. The smoke and rain created a smell that resembled a body decomposed. The handlers could feel the stench seeping into their suits. After four hours, the bodies were gone but the blood and the stink had filled the space so thick, they were drowning.

Each had four bodies to divide. Three had finished last. Each of the belts was stained in red. Their tools were now jagged, dull blades that dripped with the rhythm of a water faucet. When finished, the handlers were to place their tools onto the belt once the furnace had been turned off, exit to the bathroom to shed their suits, collect money and leave. The lights came on as a signal that they were done. One and Two began to make their way to the back. Three went to follow and tripped. They nearly fell into the blood. A single hand lay on the ground, its fingers contorted. Three looked around to make sure no one was watching. They grabbed the hand and tossed it into the shaft to make sure it was burned.

As they turned, a rush of conditioned air hit the room. They felt the cold on their hand. Three looked down to see the glove had indeed ripped open. They froze. Had they made contact with a body? Three quickly gripped the glove and hid the opening inside their palm. The rubber was thick but loose. Three made their way to the back. The bathroom and showers were lit; white tiles covered in mold which stretched out in lines of yellow and dotted black.

One and Two were already in the showers, cleaning themselves up. Both were tall men with fat stomachs and arms. They laughed loud and talked in a language of bullshit, tall tales. Three removed the helmet and mask and unzipped the suit. They did not turn until the shower came on. One and Two looked back to see a girl. Her red hair was tied back into a tail, which she pulled off, letting it unravel across her back. Her skin was a freckled ivory.

"Damn…"

"Well, shit. That explains a lot." They both chuckled. Three stood under the hot water and let it run down her skin. She clenched her fists and readied herself in case they tried anything. It had happened before. She kept a razor in her mouth, hidden beneath her tongue.

"Are you busy later?" asked One. "Do you ever feel lonely?"

She simply smiled and opened her mouth to let them see the point of the blade. Both men nodded in approval and began to laugh. She was one of the good ones.

The showers turned off automatically after five minutes. Someone had replaced the suits with their gear and payouts. Three put on both torn t-shirts and the jeans from her bag and tossed the money in.

"Acid rain is still going on. Protect yourself, children," said Two. She threw on a rubber cloak and adjusted the hood. A loud buzzer signaled the doors unlocking.

Marsh sat in the car overcome with anxiety. His knees pummeled the floorboard like pistons. The men in the front seats wore masks. Their hands were covered in ink. He had stood beneath an old awning outside the morgue staring into the puddles of water that formed under battering rain. The storm had punished the slums into a series of floods that flowed through the streets and into the aqueduct. Even the pipelines struggled to handle the amount of rushing water.

Life under the city-state made everything dark. The morning sky was a faded grey that brought in little light from behind the massive steel disks that hovered about the slums. That was how the gardens began to die, the rains pummeled the soil, burned away the chances to grow new food. The domes protected those up top while the toxic water was drained and dumped out into the streets. The Police Force used it in their riot suppression tactics. He had stood there for hours, waiting for the sign. There was to be a horn followed by flashing headlights. He cursed himself for agreeing to another clandestine meeting. The pounding of his heart only reminded him of his next scheduled vital scan at the clinic. Working for the Shadowmen was too much stress.

The sound of a horn nearly cut him in half. He looked out from the alleyway to see the lights. Marsh took off for the parked car and nearly tripped getting to the passenger door left ajar. Two men in masks and fatigues sat in the driver's seat. No words were spoken. The man in the driver seat pulled a gun and pointed it at Marsh's head. He put his hands up and whimpered.

"I bet you've never done this before, have you piggy?"

His accent was thick. Irish. Marsh had never been outside the country to know for sure from where but he met enough of them at the hospital.

"What are you doin fuckin about out here with such scuzz types as us?" he asked and smiled a grin decorated with metal teeth.

"I'm trying to find something." Marsh replied with little confidence in his voice.

"Oh, but you wouldn't be down here in the black market unless it wuz somethin evil, yeah?"

The passenger cackled;

"He looks like one of those unlikely hero types. White knight. They get killed quick around 'ere."

He spit into a cup before he continued checking his gun; a semi automatic from the old days.

"Yea, he's an old crimefighter! Running around screamin about justice. Are you solving a murda?"

"You know, he might be working for the Shadowmen," said the gunman.

"Oh yeah? Well, you are certainly fucked if that's true."

"Us too."

"You're not lying to us are you, boy?" the driver asked. "Are you going to get us killed tonight?"

They picked him up from the morgue hours ago. He was told getting a print would take time but it was worth the wait. The gunman was right. He had already paid them with a month's savings and didn't risk telling them the truth. They would have bailed out had he said anything else. If they stiffed him, he wouldn't be able to go back to work. He looked down at the photograph. It was still in good condition.

Marsh looked down to see her face. She left it for him as a gift. He took the photo the first night they made love. Her eyes were wide awake though they woke up at three in the morning to watch the electrical storm. She was gone within months. The sickness had taken her too quickly. The voices of the men faded out for a brief second, replaced by hers.

A hand smacked against the window, causing Marsh to scream. The men in masks laughed and unlocked the doors. Three opened the door and told him to move over. She sat down and removed her hood. The acid rain was already staining the aged leather seats.

"You parked too close. They'll be on us."

"Who will?" asked Marsh. There was no answer. The girl simply pointed at the boys in the front and laughed.

"Shitheads extraordinaire."

"Hello to you too, Róisín," the passenger sighed.

The car exploded from the airfield back onto the highway towards Narrow. The hills in the distance lit up with bolts of energy. Black clouds ate up the sky. The old machines that marred the landscape had been buried, dug up and scavenged for years.

"Watch the upholstery," the driver shouted.

"Get fucked, Sean," she said.

Marsh was silent. She spoke the same way they did. The word came from her mouth as fook. The letters together made a beautiful sound. They might have been family. He kept his eyes on the picture in his hand.

"Is that your girl?" she asked.

"Used to be," he said, meekly.

"She's cute."

Róisín slapped the headrest of the passenger seat. She was given a thin, black box. He put away the photo and turned to her.

"How does this work?" Marsh asked.

"The way anything else works in the black market," said Sean.

"You give us money and we do yer dirty deeds." The metal teeth gleamed against the lights behind them.

"We're being followed."

The tail had been gaining on them since they left the airfield.

"Sounds like something I said minutes ago," she said.

There were no sirens, just flood lights that hurt Sean's vision.

"Here." The girl opened her right hand.

"Do you notice anything about it?" she asked. Marsh quickly shook his head.

"Watch."

Róisín peeled a piece of clear film from her thumb.

"I hope this is what you were looking for. The coroner's office stacks the bodies by time of arrival, and this one was the only one from that night. They did us a favor by giving us the heads up," Sean said as he counted the money.

"Is that a thumb print?" asked Marsh.

"Not yet," said Róisín.

"Cyanoacrylate fuming, is what we use to get your print."

She opened the black box. A small circle sat atop a piece of metal with a valve soldered into the side. He was immediately impressed.

"What's that?" asked Marsh.

"The film is made from tape and glue." The girl opened her coat to cut a piece of film from the roll inside her pocket. She pressed it against Marsh's thumb and placed it both pieces on the metal.

"Biometrics are the key to getting any kind of security access, high ranking clearance. To get that, you need at least a trace fingerprint, if you can't get one fully visible."

The box began to sputter. She placed it on Marsh's thigh.

"Do you feel the heat?" she asked. He nodded again.

"You take the chemicals still on the dead man's hand and get them in an environment to react with super glue, whatever you can find, but in our case, we make it ourselves."

The heat from the box was gone. Róisín opened the case. The film was gone, replaced by a clear sheet with white lines. She carefully picked it up and held it against a light.

"On one side, your black print from a dead man. And on the other side, is yours."

She took a bottle cap from her pocket and poured a bit of resin into it. Marsh watched her press the film down into the resin and hand it to him.

"See? I own you now," Róisín said. Marsh blushed uncontrollably.

"The cap is your visible print, the resin keeps the consistency."

Sean looked back at him. The smile was gone. "You need to get out, he said."

The girl winked at Marsh. "Take care now," she said.

Marsh pocketed the cap and looked out into the rain. The car was not slowing down. The door unlocked and he felt a foot push him out. His body hit the ground hard and swirled in vicious circles against the concrete. The sounds of the cars drowned out his screams. The sounds of the storm calmed him enough to relax his breathing.

She was there again. Her face was unmoving, her skin of marble, shined as another light from the storm broke through the dark. She was inside the sky. Her energy crackled with shattering sounds. There was a feeling of burning. He realized that he left the car without putting his hood up. The cars continued off into the streets of Narrow. The drops of water began to scald his ears as he got to his feet. He pulled his hood up and made his way back to the apartment.

The burned remains of the building across the street still sat untouched by the city workers. Marsh carefully stepped over the rows of flowers and letters to the ones that were lost in the shootout. Rubber tents were built to keep the memorial from being damaged in the storm. The bright colors and scribbled words from the hands of other children drowned out the ashes and mud of the block.

His apartment was on the 3rd floor. Marsh opened the front door and walked through the old world wood finish of the abandoned lobby. There was one working elevator. He pressed the call button and waited for its descent. The night the cops came, he heard the sound of lightning and looked outside. The entire floor was covered in flame, which soon took over the tenement itself.

The doors of the elevator creaked open. Fluorescent light coated him. He looked down to see the burns in his coat from the acid rain. The ride up took longer than waiting for the elevator but he didn't feel like walking anymore. Marsh turned the key and opened the door to his apartment. It was a small cube, a drab olive studio space with running water, two windows, working lights and little else. The kitchen light was left on. He cursed under his breath and turned it off, making the olive colored walls disappear into black. A pile of yellow papers on the table held his keys. He dropped the coat behind the couch and dropped onto the caved-in bed pushed to the wall by the television.

There was a hole in the floor for the print to hide. He reached under the bed and moved the panel to the right to unlock it. Marsh looked down and saw the gun. He forgot that he had one in there. It had been there for months, he remembered. It was purchased the day after she was gone. He dropped the print next to it and closed the hole up.

He said her name only when he was alone. Reese. The apartment was clean enough after an hour. The four corners were visible now, bathed in a sick yellow light. Marsh wiped sweat from his forehead and went back to the picture. For a split second, he thought of the girl from the car. He immediately hated himself. The air was dry. He opened the windows, despite the rain and went back to sleep. The wood from the sills were burnt by morning. He stared at the burns for an hour, then went into the kitchen and consumed a bowl of cereal with milk that expired days ago. It was time to start another day. Another test to keep the hands from pulling him under.

Nine

The way to enter Tempest from Narrow was a long climb through the access tubes in the pipelines. Jaya climbed up, using the rails that stuck out from the sides of the tubes as a makeshift ladder. Maintenance workers navigated through by the day and set up surveillance and motion detectors for the evening. She had three hours to make it to the top before the security system would finish resetting for the night shift. She was not alone. A voice kept her company for the ascent.

"How are you feeling?"

"E...My arms hurt," she whispered.

"You don't have to whisper. Just make sure you don't drop anything. You won't be able to get it back if you do."

Ergo sat back in his chair. He was a chubby kid who ran away from home, just like her. Long brown hair covered his shoulders. The café was barren. Dirty windows kept most of the light out. His black shirt and jeans were faded and decorated with holes. With a coffee in one hand, he scratched the space above his crotch with the other. Schematics of the access tubes reflected off of his glass bottle lenses.

"Do you have any plans for all that money?" he asked.

Jaya pulled one foot over the other. She placed half her weight on each slab of brown iron. The shaft was smothered in darkness. The flashlight taped to her shoulder provided enough vision to see what was ahead. There was an elevator that connected Tempest to Narrow but the same workers Jaya was sneaking around charged thousands to take it. They chose to save the money and take the long way up.

"I don't know...Maybe shack up with a nice rich boy who will take care of me..."

Ergo bit his tongue. He had wanted to be the one she was with. Even climbing through the pipelines, he would have been there if she had asked him to. They met while on the streets, always in passing. Their conversations were more online than in person.

"Good luck with that..." he finally said.

"What happens once I reach the top?" Jaya muttered.

"There is a hatch you will need to open. The wrench in your bag should be enough to do it."

The morning she found out about the money. He was the only one she contacted. Jaya needed someone to watch her back while she cashed out at the ATM. Word traveled fast enough between the squatters. She knew he would keep quiet. The clone card scanned the money and spit out a pile of bills. Neither of them had seen that much cash before.

She asked him for help in getting out of the slums before the others found out. He came up with the plan of going through the pipelines. The path from the access tube would connect with the sewer systems for both Tempest and Eros. He did not have a lot of information to go on besides the old blueprints.

The boy kept the image of her pursed lips and tucked it away in the back of his mind. It would be there for hours. She was always persuasive. He remembered the moisture on her bottom lip and wanted to taste it. He went along with it, no questions asked.

"I think I see something," Jaya wheezed. She was out of breath.

"Almost there, girl. Are you counting your steps like I told you to?" Ergo asked.

"I am..."

"And where are you?" Ergo pulled his notes from behind the stack of blue paper.

"One thousand, one hundred forty...one..." she sputtered in sync with her steps.

The hatch was in sight for her. Something circular emerged from the faded shades of brown above her head. Jaya had given him $200 for the trouble. Ergo placed $100 each in his shoes. His expertise was more in data storage, not manipulation. Maps were out of his reach, as well. He was willing to do anything for her. There was regret in his voice when they spoke.

"You are almost there. Please don't fall..." he said.

"If I do...will you catch me?" she asked.

"Wouldn't be much of a hero if I didn't."

Ergo moved to his backpack. Inside, a remote control for the automatic parachute sat underneath piles of wires. The device was stolen from an old armory. He had it around for safe keeping. Its effectiveness was not proven. In theory, once activated, the chute would expand and then adapt to the available space. There was no way a cushion could block the impact of falling a thousand feet.

If she fell, and if the chute worked, she had a chance of at least floating back down to the bottom and starting over. Anyone caught in the pipelines would be charged with more than enough crimes to be put away from a year minimum. Imprisonment, ironically, meant more work in the pipelines.

"You really are my hero," Jaya sounded delirious.

"Keep taking deep breaths and take your time. You are doing great." He kept his hand on the remote control.

"I'm at the hatch."

Jaya took a moment to breathe in slow. She was small enough to get inside the shaft that ran parallel to the tubes. A pair of bolt cutters was enough to cut through the steel mesh and climb out. Ergo was too large to fit. It was the only way to get through in time to beat the shift change and security reboot. She fixed her knees between two rungs and draped herself with one arm over a rail and her back against the shaft.

"Catch your breath, but don't relax too much. You need to open the hatch, still." Ergo's voice was higher than before.

"How much time do I have left?"

"Less than an hour…" She could hear the anxiety in his voice.

Jaya swung the backpack around and opened a pocket. The wrench was there. Her flashlight started to strobe. There were spare batteries in the pack. She lost a lot of energy in the climb.

"Place the wrench into the center and just start turning," Ergo gripped the remote.

Jaya followed his directions. The hatch was old. There was no give as she turned the tool. All she could hear were tiny squeaks and her own breathing. The shaft began to echo her sounds of struggle. She shifted her legs and weight. The wrench could not catch the tumblers enough to pull the hatch open.

"What's happening?"

There was no answer. The sounds of breathing stopped.

"Jaya?"

"It won't open…" she whimpered.

A wave of sadness hit her. What was she going to do if won't open? She took a break. The wrench hit the edge of the rail and nearly slipped away. Jaya gasped and grabbed it tight with both hands. Her legs were still between the rungs.

"Talk to me, girl…" Ergo was ready to press the button on the remote. She was not going to make it.

"I need get some up there…No more listening to people behind walls," she laughed. Ergo simply bit his lip.

Jaya placed the wrench back in place. More weight was needed. She pulled her legs out from the rungs and stepped around the rails. The ladder kept her upright. She held her breath and made another attempt at the iron lock and key. The handle fought back and cut deep lines into her hands. Jaya gritted her teeth. She repositioned herself, gripped the wrench hand over hand and pulled. Her sharp breathing turned into screams. Ergo kept his eyes on the timer.

She continued to rip at the door. The blood from her hands made it difficult to grip the wrench. The circle began to move. It was starting to open.

"Don't stop. You are almost out of time," Ergo whispered.
Jaya took as much air into her lungs as she could. The key slowly turned. The hatch moved and then unlocked. She dropped the wrench and watched it fall down into a deep darkness.

"Let's hope no one finds that," he said.

Jaya was too tired to speak. She moved slowly back around the ladder and made her way topside. The hatch was much easier to close. She felt her knees buckle as she felt to the ground. There was no steel. Heavy rocks stretched out all around her. She laid with limbs outstretched and stared into the formations of stone that decorated the cave.

"You might be the first person to make it through the pipelines in years. How does it look up there?" asked Ergo.

"…This is a cave…Where am I?" she asked.

"The entrance into the pipelines for Tempest and Eros is too dangerous, too thin for you to try and squeeze through. Consider this a shortcut into the city. It's going to take you around the parts of the pipeline that is impossible for a body to crawl through. The sewers may be gross but it's safer, off the path. We may lose radio contact. There's something up there but I don't know exactly what it is." Ergo said as he dropped the remote back into his pack and gathered his gear.

Security would find the wrench, no doubt. Her blood would be tested and she would be wanted throughout Narrow. He readied himself for the possibility of not seeing her again.

"I'm so tired. I can't feel my arms," she said.

"We don't have much time," Ergo pleaded.

Jaya slowly sat up. The cave resembled a room inside a space carved out from rock. It wasn't made this way on its own.

"More pipes here. It's wet everywhere, but it's not water. It smells disgusting." Jaya tried to hold her breath but the room was full of the scent of decay. She fell to her knees, now red with old blood and emptied her stomach.

"I think you are in the dumping ground for the bodies of workers who died working in the pipelines," Ergo stared through the faded glass of the shop.

"Is there an opening?" he asked.

Jaya wiped her mouth. She looked around the dark and found a cut in the black. There was light that poured through.

"Yes…"

"Go to it," he said.

She got to her feet and walked to the opening. Jaya's eyes widened. The light that entered the cave was smothered in dark clouds. For miles, there was nothing but garbage. She looked in all directions for signs of life.

"It's not what you expected, was it?" he asked.

"What is this place?" Jaya began to think the stories of Tempest and Eros were false.

"I heard before that it was called the wilderness…A bunch of stories I heard as a kid. I used to look at pictures of the world before the old wars. Whatever you are looking at…that is supposed to be what's left."

"Its just trash. I don't see any people. Maybe because they are all dead, or in the slums, or up top living the good life?" Jaya asked. There was no answer.

She could not believe what she saw. It was an endless landfill that stretched on to no end. There were some roads that seemed to start and then stop. Each one dotted the landscape as a scar across skin. Mounds of waste piled up in random patterns like exploded bombs. There was beauty in the death of the world outside.

"This is where we came from?" she asked.

"I found the old blueprints for the city-state and studied how it all happened. They had to use a solid foundation to build their new home, safe from the fallout. We couldn't go anywhere else but up. Back then, it was called Sierra Nevada. It's somewhere near the coast, called California. They opened a hole from the top and dug in deep to keep the city afloat."

"Who were they?" Jaya looked out at the abandoned vehicles, rotted out from storms and rain that sat in the graveyard.

"They were the ones who came before us; people afraid of their world ending. The slums started out as the city-state itself. Narrow was the refuge from the radiation in the water of the coasts. Once the rich ones made their getaway, they survived with the leftover tech they found out there. The gardens fed so many before we grew to a point past control. The rich left the poor behind after they helped them build a city in the sky, above all the wastelands. We cut off the rest of the world from Narrow with the aqueducts; bringing the only water left on this side of the world without any poison in it. They use clean water as rain, that's water we could be drinking down here, or using to restart the gardens."

"How long have you known about this?" she asked.

"Weeks ago. I wanted to see it for myself, to make sure it wasn't true. But I guess it is." Ergo threw his pack over his shoulders.

"Listen, Jaya. You needed to see that more than I did. You need to remember where you came from. Up there, it's nothing like we've seen before. Everything up top is different."

Jaya continued to stare into the storm clouds above the desolation. She wondered if her parents ever knew. Is that why they never looked for her?

"No one goes past the aqueduct in Narrow because it leads to nowhere. I still think there might be people out there, making their own way, trying to live, just like we do. There's no future world where cars fly and life is beautiful. The old world is the same as the new. The people are the same assholes but the tech is just better. All the bullshit they distract themselves with is just easier to put into their back pocket and ignore what happening underneath them."

Ergo could hear sirens. Someone had to have reported lights on in the abandoned store. He didn't have much time either.

"If you don't like it up there, you can come back. You know the way now. I'll be thinking about you," he didn't want to disconnect the line. But he had to.

"I won't be going back to the slums…I'm going to be rich," Jaya backed away slowly from the vision of oblivion. "Bye for now,"

Ergo cut the line and took off into the dark of the back room. Cops flooded the room within thirty seconds. He was already gone.

"Bye…"

Jaya took off her earpiece and dropped it. Ergo's directions took her to another hatch that connected the cave to a dumping station from the sewers. Once inside, it was a long crawl through some shit to a service tunnel for the trains. After another two hours of climbing, she found herself covered in oil and sweat. The next hatch was much easier to open, no need for a wrench or bloodied hands. Once the tumblers clicked, blinding light poured into the tunnel and into her eyes.

The city was massive. She questioned how this could have been built from a mountain. A train car burned over her head as she took in this second brand new world. The tenements, the Epicentre, everything she heard about this place was true. The buildings towered up into the sky to a point beyond her vision. There were no streets, no gardens, and no dirty windows. She could not see the sun. The light was brighter than the view from the mountain.

She was covered in the stool from the sewer lines. Jaya removed her jumpsuit and tossed it over the side of the pipe. Naked, she climbed up and onto the pipeline with her pack in hand. Ergo told her which pipes to follow to lead to the platforms of Eros. She spread her feet apart to keep balance and took out a pair of jeans and a shirt. There was a cold wind that hit her body. Jaya felt a deep chill go through her that started at the spine and worked its way down.

It took two hours to make her way across the pipes. She walked slow, putting equal distance between her feet to not lose balance. There was no water beneath her to promise a decent landing. Every time she looked down, there was an endless darkness looking back up at her. The empty insides of the mountains, gutted to make way for the steel pillars that held the city up, loomed across the expanse beneath the pipelines.

Once to the bottom of the lowest platform, she took another rest. Her pack was empty, with only a bottle of water left. She needed to get there before dark. A group of ladders took her through more empty maintenance docks. Security was light. Ergo had predicted they would be down there only for reported fires or sightings of jumpers on the pipes. Jaya climbed into the basement of a building. There were empty halls painted yellow with lights that fluttered, darkening the brown doors at each end. She walked in each direction, trying to find the exit. Every door was locked. The windows were blacked out, each outfitted with metal grating.

Sweat returned to her forehead. Did she make a wrong turn somewhere? Her mind raced until she found a door unlocked. She turned the knob and stepped through and onto the street. Neon lights painted her in blue and purple. The door locked behind her once closed. The entrance was a way station for the workers and security. The machines of the Epicentre were far off in the distance. This was the place were everyone came to let go of their structure, their routine. Lines of clubs stretched out in each direction. Revolving shades of gold and red danced across the walls. The colors hurt her eyes at first, until her breathing settled and she began to dance to the music all around her, lost in the warmth.

Ten

It had been a week since he had seen the Blank Page. The shadows were still there. Birds were circling overhead. Gabrels found himself lying on his back with arms and legs spread out across the white expanse. He was wearing the same clothes as before. The same smell of unwashed skin permeated through his shirt.

"Happy birthday, fucker," the voice echoed in the distance.

"You again?" Gabrels sat up and crossed his legs.

"Something wrong?" it asked.

"Don't try and pretend to be nice. I remember what you said."

"So, you got my messages, then?" it asked.

"Yeah, how are you able to change things in my head?"

"Because I'm in your head, fool. I told you. Everything you see, I see. Everything you hear, touch or taste, I can too."

"I remember everything we said to each other, which means it can't be just a dream. You were right about that, at least."

"None of it's a dream, but it's good that you are starting to come around. That shows some progress."

"If you're not a part of my dream, or Adam…who are you?"

He slowly stood up and stared out into the distance, waiting for him to appear.

"Why do you care about who I am? You should worry about yourself more. In the end, it doesn't matter."

There was a tap on his shoulder that sent a shock through his body. He turned to see another Gabrels that stared back at him. He stared into the empty eyes of his reflection and stepped back in fear.

"You still have no idea how you got here?" asked Gabrels, moving slowly closer to the shell.

"I have bits and pieces."

"You mean memories. Of your past life?" asked Gabrels.

"Maybe. I don't like you enough to tell you."

The other Stanley disintegrated into flakes of white. Possibly snow. It was too hard to tell, he had never seen it before. Maybe in old pictures and video but the sky was too dark to make it now.

"Your life has been boring and devoid of anything interesting, until now. Doesn't that bother you?"

"What's wrong with my life? You seem so eager to step on me. What exactly is so bad about what I do?"

"Are you really asking me this?"

It laughed in his ears.

"I am. Where are you from, anyway? They don't have high rise penthouses where you come from? Are you just some slum kid poking around where you don't belong?"

"This must be you trying to turn the tables on me. Nice try, Stan…"

"You don't make the money I do. You haven't done the things I've done. If you are real, then you must've done something stupid to be trapped in someone else's head, right?"

Other Stanley returned. It clapped its hands and congratulated him.

"I appreciate this new backbone that you've grown in a week. No, I don't make the money you do, because I don't work for a boss, I'm not owned by a company. I haven't done the things you have because what you do is hollow; more faceless examples of vain society; already past the point of elitism."

Its hands stopped and clasped together.

"Fancy dinners with corporate slaves and government types, posting hours of video, begging for others to watch you, it's not my style. I didn't do anything stupid to be here. I don't make mistakes, kid."

"Then what are you doing in my head?!" Gabrels screamed out.

"I don't know why I'm here, but I know that after a week, I can't find a way to leave. You and I will be stuck together for a while."

"You don't make mistakes? So you planned this?"

"Nothing like this. Trust me, if I had a choice, I would have been gone without you ever knowing. But it's unavoidable. I had to talk to you."

"You are in control of this? This white space?" Gabrels was enraged. "Let me out of here, now! Wake me up or let me sleep, something!"

"I can't turn it off. This space is your mind, so it's not that easy. I bring you here until you wake up. Maybe it's based on stress, just dreaming about falling until you finally hit the ground…" it said.

"What do those bits and pieces tell you? Anything about how did you got here?"

"I've spent every minute trying to figure that out. I was running. It was loud, there were screams and gunshots when I got hit."

"Hit?" Gabrels asked.

The shell suddenly jumped forward. Its skin changed into a pale white as lines of red began to run down into its eyes and mouth. The other Gabrels was covered in blood.

"A car smashed into my body." The shell screamed in his face. "It was crazy. The car hit me and went BAM!"

Gabrels stepped back. The shell laughed for a moment and slapped its own knee.

"I was gone, man. My body flew into the air and hit the concrete hard. I was dead. I had to be. I was dead as fuck."

"There was a bit of sympathy just now for you, but I think it's gone already," said Gabrels.

"I had to have died. I was waiting for the white light, a sign of heaven or hell, and then I woke up here, behind your eyes."

Gabrels looked into the eyes of the other. They were not his own. The body was the same in every other way except the eyes.

"This is crazy. How are you able to see what I see?" He asked.

"The more time I spend here, the more I learn, and not just about you, I mean about how your body works."

"What?" Gabrels began to cringe.

"Think about the tap on your shoulder just now. How can I do that? I think I figured out a way to stimulate nerves that force your brain to interpret my signals as touch."

It touched him again. The feeling was too close to the real thing.

"This is symbolic. It's proof of connection between my thoughts and your body."

The word stimulate made his skin crawl.

"You can think of it as us growing closer." The reflection now wore the same clothes. Its hair was even crooked the same way after a night of sleep.

"We're not closer…And don't ever touch me again."

It placed his finger on his chest. He grimaced.

"You know I am not actually touching you, right? This is the part I'm still trying to figure out. Somehow, I am connected to your consciousness."

"An entirely different person, living inside my head?"

"Pretty interesting, eh? I'm learning a lot just by watching you live. It's an intimate situation we have going on right now. I can see everything you see and feel everything you that you feel. Do you not feel the love right now?" it asked.

"There's no love." Gabrels smacked the arm away. It felt real, as if there was someone standing in front of him.

"What the hell kind of dreams are these?"

"I told you that this isn't just a dream. I am an independent electrical impulse in your brain, attempting communication in real time between the conscious and unconscious mind."

The body put its hand back on his shoulder. Gabrels looked down at the hand that clenched his shirt.

"You can feel it. Don't push me away. It's impossible to avoid me. The evidence is all around you. I think the more time we spend here, we grow closer together. Pretty soon we could be one and the same."

"What do you mean?" he asked.

"Seven days passed since the first time I called you up. Think about all the digging I've been doing since then."

"Why are you digging anything at all?"

"Because I need to know more. There's got to be a reason why I'm here. The problem is, you don't have a lot going on in here."

Gabrels turned his back to the shell. "Send me an email. Don't wake me up in the middle of the night. It's giving me headaches. How is there nothing in here? Are you talking about my brain?"

The other Stanley was now walking side by side with him.

"Exactly. If I can enter your conscious mind and have conversations with you, we are technically making memories. I can see your memories. It wasn't always like that. Not in the beginning. That's why I couldn't help but laugh when I started to call you out, and you said nothing."

Gabrels kept turning from the shell, which continued to follow.

"You proved me right. There's always a reference point for memories, faces and names. Most likely family or lovers. But you don't have anything there."

"My memory is not empty," he said.

"Where's your family?" The shell continued to press.

"I haven't seen them in a long time."

"But you've been looking, right? How long have you been looking?"

"That's none of your business!"

"Why can't you find them? Where are they? Where did you come from? Were you born in a lab or something?

Gabrels finally stopped. He swung his fist against his reflection and watched it pass through like air.

"Go to hell! I have a family. I haven't seen them since I got augmented and started working full time in Tempest."

"Are they all dead?"

"How should I know?!"

"Do you even care if their dead?"

"It doesn't matter if they are, it's my family not yours. Why are you asking about them? Can you find them for me?"

"Maybe. I've already helped you in a few ways."

"How?!"

"I helped you at work; the chick at your office, she used to smile at you all coy, but now she knows you're not a little bitch. The next time you see her, watch what happens. What about that little spat between you and mindless drone number #347?"

"Who, Keys?"

"You don't have to say thank you. I'm not doing anything on my own. Its all you. The mind is only a part of the body. You were drowning, so I gave you a lift, dropped a few bits of important information that no one was paying attention to."

"That's not possible. You can't control me."

"I think I can. You are pretty easy."

"Stay away from me." Gabrels backed away from the shell. His reflection disappeared into a thousand revolving colors.

"On second thought, you just might owe me a favor for saving you in front of all your peers."

"That's how I knew about Keys' private information? You stalked him? Just like you are trying to stalk me?"

"I can't stalk anyone from here. All the information from Keys was found on the data stream."

"I've got to get more sleep," sighed Gabrels. He covered his eyes from the white and knelt down to cover up from the blinding light.

"You've been getting some decent rest. So much that I had to try and wake you up," it said.

Gabrels looked up at the shell; its artificial lips slowly formed a black crescent, a shadow smile.

"You got as far as your front door, but the damned commercials you people have got playing in your heads at night are just too noisy."

He remembered the voices. Their echoes cut through the jagged rhythm of his heart.

"No, no. You're a dream. You don't own me."

"I asked you to follow the birds and you did. I appreciate that. Hell, you should appreciate what I'm doing too. It's a real breakthrough considering you live in a world where no one can be surprised or shocked. There's no privacy here."

"Something is happening to me. I have to make it stop."

"Why are you talking to yourself like I am not standing in front of you?" it asked.

"I'm forgetting things, losing sleep."

"Listen, I'm trying my best to spice things up around here but it's really in your hands."

The shell pulled its hand back and pointed up to the shadows above.

"You're not spicing anything," he asked.

The reflection simply pointed up. "Those aren't blackbirds anymore. Those are vultures up there. Those things are me. Have you ever heard of neural unity? The joining of two minds to create a hybrid thought process? The birds are my influence, just like every other moment lately where you haven't felt like yourself."

Gabrels felt all the blood leave his body. "What are you doing? Trying to control my brain?"

The reflection laughed. "I was. But I'm not trying to control you anymore. It's coming pretty naturally to me now."

Gabrels began to walk away from his reflection. The Blank Page continued on with his footsteps. The body in the distance became smaller. The birds overhead faded out into dots of black. He didn't want to hear it anymore. If he was going to stay there until he woke up, he was going to endure the white silence on his own. He closed his eyes for a moment and found the reflection standing in front of him.

"I'm not sure if you noticed yet, but something is changing inside of you. Have you been paying attention?"

Gabrels jumped back. He looked up again to see the birds had returned. "I don't know what you are talking about…"

"Yes, you do." Gabrels looked into the eyes of his reflection. He saw the same deep black from before.

"What about the lack of sleep? Not keeping your apartment or hygiene together."

"The pace has been getting more intense at work. Its hard to manage, but I keep up."

"The hallucinations?"

"Adam is monitoring for any malfunctions in his programming."

"Bullshit. Its one of the greatest pieces of technology ever created and you think that's what's starting to break down. Anything off about that thing is obviously by design. How about the rage?"

"What are you talking about?!"

"Lashing out at your co-workers? Trying to oust someone you do not respect in front of everyone in the office?"

"No one likes Keys in that building anyway."

"But they like you even less. Right?"

Gabrels did not respond.

"Something is carving a hole, deep in the back of your mind, and you haven't the faintest idea of what it could be."

"If it's not the puzzle then tell me what it is!" Gabrels finally screamed out. The reflection simply laughed. The sound was different now. It wasn't Adam. The laughter was his.

"It's me."

"How do I get rid of you?" he asked.

"You know who might be able to? Everett. It doesn't make sense for him to ask you for help out of nowhere," Gabrels asked. He turned his back to the other.

"Have you ever stopped to think about what the prize might be? What could the goal for solving the puzzle be?"

"Everett said it was some kind of secret project."

"And that's it? You are supposed to be smarter than that."

"I thought I was weak in your eyes," he said.

"You are weak. But that doesn't mean that you should ignore what is going on around you. Break out of your little routine. Find out the answer for both of us. We need to find some answers. Before whatever this is, gets us hurt. Or worse."

"You think someone is after me too? Just like Everett?" Gabrels asked.

"Maybe. Corporate espionage is out of your range. Also, you don't really pay attention to subtle details." The reflection shook its head in disappointment.

"This is insane. You're not another person living in my head. This is all just nonsense."

"I think you're driving yourself crazy on purpose. There's no risk here, there's nothing exciting. Something needs to change in your life. You are numb, so wrapped up in a little fake world. The puzzle has provided that. You got suckered into something a lot bigger than you could handle and it has shaken you up. There is movement in your blood now. It speaks to you, doesn't it?"

Gabrels was quiet.

"It has you so taken that you cannot sleep at night. Despite the desire to know the secret, you fail to realize that you cannot sleep because there is someone else in your head now. Why don't you find out why that is?"

"How do I do that?" asked Gabrels.

"Follow the birds, fool. Ask the right questions. Listen to what's around you right now. I can't tell you the answers, I'm in you, remember?"

"I don't know what to do. I think my body is falling apart. I am sleepwalking, or something. I'm doing things in my sleep." Gabrels buried his face in his hands to block out the light.

"What would your mother say about all this, hmm?" the reflection tilted its head as Gabrels looked back up at it.

"What did you say?"

"Do you think she would be proud of you if she saw you throwing your career away?"

"You don't know anything about my mother," said Gabrels.

"Are you sure you even know your mother?" the reflection shot back.

"What the hell is that supposed to mean?" he asked.

"You don't question anything that is placed in front of you. Can you tell me how many years you've worked at Precipice? How long you've lived in the tenements?"

Gabrels drew a blank in searching for the dates. He could not find the exact months, even.

"Are you waiting for the A.I. to answer those questions for you? To remind you that you're not just some husk of flesh walking to and from work with nothing in between? Are you a complete machine? I thought the only augmentation you had was in your brain."

Gabrels had no response.

"Now we are getting somewhere, am I right? You finally found a spot in your mind were there's no automated response, just a bit of quiet for something still human to emerge. I know it's been a long time since you've dreamed. It must be hard for you for things to be so out of your control. But this isn't something you will be able to hide from, or dance around, or bury away, behind all the flashing lights and pretty commercials."

"What is this?" Gabrels murmured.

"It's a puzzle. Someone put it in your hands to solve and it happened to fall in your lap while you were in the most ignorant sleep. I'll bet that you might even know what it is already."

"I don't know what it is…" he said.

"Pure denial."

"Really? So, according to you, I'm not only weak, but also a child, wrapped up in my own falsehood about my place in the world but you want me to believe that I already know the reason behind this stupid game and I don't want to admit it out loud?"

The birds circled silently above the empty space. He looked up at them, watching the feathers fall from their wings. He held his hand up to try and catch one. Each feather disappeared into the white. None of them reached the ground.

"This is ridiculous," he said, defeated.

The reflection nodded its head. "I think you would rather block that possibility out and imagine something easier to handle."

"Handle? What is it that I can't handle?" Gabrels felt his hands clench into fists.

"Where did you come from?" it asked.

"Excuse me?"

"Do you remember the color of the walls in the room you used to sleep in? Not now, but when you were a baby. Maybe the views from the window? Do you have any memory of your maker's face? Or is it just those same blurred shadows? You remembered their arms and nothing else."

"Stop talking," said Gabrels.

"The arms were all that you could think of when you watched the little girl on the train and her oblivious mother. You knew exactly what that was like, didn't you?"

"What kind of questions are these?!"

"They're simple ones. They're important ones. You still don't know what hard work is like. Sad boy doesn't want to get his hands dirty. I will find a way to make you work."

Gabrels was frozen. "How am I supposed to answer these questions if I don't remember?" he asked.

"I think you might be finally catching on." it said.

"Is there something else in that message?"

The reflection put his hands up and stopped him. "Think about this…Who does she remind you of?" it asked.

"What do you mean?" Gabrels tilted his head. The familiar sound of static filled his ears.

"The girl…You'll see."

The reflection had changed. Its skin began to dissipate. Its body and clothes lost form and broke down into pixels of white and black.

"What girl?!"

"Who does she remind you of?" it asked again.

The shell was gone, replaced by a thousand pieces of hissing noise.

"Tell me your name."

"You don't get to know my name."

"Why not?"

"We're not friends. We're not teammates. I use you to figure out how to get free."

"Use me? I'm not a piece of meat for you to play with!"

"Why not? You use Adam all the time. Try being at the beck and call of someone else and see if you feel the same way."

"Bullshit. I'm not your slave."

"Slave is the wrong word for it. You might be more like a bitch. Bitches make noise; they kick and scream when they don't get their way.

"You better hope we don't meet face to face one day."

"See? I like when you say things like that. Is that really coming from you? Or is that my words from your mouth? When you wake up, this bitch body will belong to me and I will do what I have to, whatever it takes to get back to my own life."

"That's not going to happen! Do you hear me?!"

The noise came upon him like a flood. The vultures descended, their feathers rushed the Blank Page into darkness.

"I think I'm starting to like you, kid. This is getting fun."

The world broke apart the same way. Gabrels' scream was muffled into the same ocean of static.

Part two:

Dependency Hell

Eleven

The apartment was trashed. Gabrels opened his eyes to a brown stain on his ceiling and faint music floating through his ears. His skin was moist with sweat, nearly dried. The blinds were closed for first time in days. Something was different, again. Loose grey sweatpants were bunched up on the floor. He was naked. The music switched to something louder. He could hear shuffling in the next room. Someone was in here with him.

Gabrels stood up and looked around. A pile of tissue in the corner held a mound of ash. Three cigarettes were crushed into it. The smell made him sick. Casual footsteps entered the room. It was the girl from the train. She was without clothes, as well. Hers were neatly piled by the door. The pink flesh that caught his eye was in full view. Her body was thin, emaciated, but there were faint muscles that poked through the skin. She looked at him and smiled;

"Good morning."

Gabrels was in shock. He could not speak. The girl grabbed both a lighter and a cigarette from the pack hidden behind the tissue.

"Thanks for paying in advance. Normally, there's a sweaty wad of cash in hand on the way out." She said as she lit up, took a drag and handed it to him.

"No thanks. I don't smoke," he mumbled.

"Quitting already?" she giggled. The girl put her smoke out and began to get dressed. Gabrels could taste something horrible in the back of his throat. There were two lines of white powder that stuck out from the new red color of the table.

"How long have you been here?" he asked.

"Long enough, it seems," she replied. Her smile left.

"What's your name?"

"You don't remember?" she asked.

Gabrels could not recall. He didn't even know what day it was.

"It's alright. You don't need to have a good memory with me. I put my number in your contacts."

She threw her sweater and leggings on with nervous energy. He could feel that she had stayed longer than she was supposed to. The girl left the bedroom to look for her shoes. Gabrels followed.

"What day is it?"

"It's Monday morning…" she said, anxiously.

"When did we meet?"

She found her shoes and looked back at him while slipping her feet into them.

"You really don't remember?"

Gabrels shook his head.

"Okay…let me tell you…" she laughed as she approached him. The girl spoke softly into his ear.

"We met on a train Friday night. You brought me back here and asked me if I wanted to have some fun." Her tongue lashed the outside of his ear. He could feel the hairs on his neck stand. The rest of his body began to awaken. "We've been here for two days straight…are you sure you can't remember?"

Gabrels was still. She sighed and placed a long kiss on his lips before heading for the door.

"That's too bad. Call me whenever you want. I will make myself available to help you regain your memory," she said before closing the door. Gabrels stopped her. She looked back at him. Her skin was ivory white.

"What was that powder on the table?" he could not believe what he was asking.

"I don't think you want me to say that out loud. Walls are pretty thin around here."

"Right…"

"It was a snowstorm. Do you feel better now?"

"Yeah…" Gabrels felt like collapsing.

"I don't think you needed it, though. For a first timer, you were pretty decent."

The girl let go of the door. She turned slowly and walked towards the elevator. He watched her from the hallway until she stepped inside. Gabrels walked back into the apartment. He went through each room, failing to recall the events of the weekend.

His stomach felt worse than it did before. There was something aching inside him. The girl provided a distraction enough from the pain.

The kitchen was a mess of discarded food cartons, empty beer cans and a bottle of whiskey. The toilet held a group of half filled condoms. There was a shard of glass missing from the bathroom mirror. Across the remaining piece was a message written in crude letters; woman's lipstick;

"How about now?"

The living room was in equal disarray; more food, more crushed cans, more mounds of tissue. On the table sat the shard from the mirror with traces of a fine, white powder.

"Adam?"

"Good morning, Mr. Gabrels. Happy birthday to you," the A.I's mirror body appeared from the wall, along with a virtual cake with candles that lost their flame with the sound of breath.

"What time is it?" Gabrels asked.

"It is currently 7:23am. Looking at the state of the apartment and your present appearance, it is correct to say that you will not make it to the office on time."

Gabrels placed his hands over his groin.

"Is it really my birthday?" he asked.

"Yes, it is. It appears your celebration may have been longer than you anticipated. I hope that you enjoyed yourself, all the same."

"Can you tell me what snow is?" Gabrels asked.

"Atmospheric water vapor," Images of snowfall and children playing in playgrounds, covered in angelic white.

"No, the other kind of snow," Gabrels grumbled.

"Snow is a derivative of cocaine," the A.I. corrected itself. The apartment walls were then flooded with examples of its chemical makeup; biosynthesis, broken down to its simplest elements.

"A powerful nervous stimulant capable of affecting feelings of well-being, self confidence, providing feelings of euphoria, increasing the body's energy levels, alertness and sexuality."

Gabrels began to blink uncontrollably. His eyes were watering. How did all this happen? He looked down at his own body. His belly was round and stuck out like ripe fruit. There was a pain in his stomach that gripped him. The grip turned his blood into needles that fed damage into every limb, stronger than it had been before, a stronger pain than he had ever felt.

"Have you consumed more than the standard amount of this chemical, Mr. Gabrels? Are you worried about its side effects?"

He began to get light-headed. All the blood had left his brain and drained out to the bottom of his feet. Gabrels held onto the corner wall to keep from fainting.

"No...but what do you mean when you say 'the standard amount'?" he asked.

"You are not the first person to partake in heavy drug use in this city," the answer did not put him at ease. He took a deep breath, then another, and another. His lungs were empty and his stomach was churning. The pain was too intense. He bit his tongue to keep a scream from ripping through. Whatever the girl has given him, he wanted more.

Gabrels left the apartment in its state of chaos. He quickly got dressed and headed out for work. Adam's mirror body watched him stumble through the rooms and exit when finally dressed. Its shell slowly disintegrated as the lights dimmed, the blinds closed until the view of the city's veins were hidden away again.

The Epicentre stared back at him from the window of the train car. What the hell was happening?

"Is something on your mind, Mr. Gabrels?"

"Adam, I need you to review all our conversation logs."

"Of course. What are we looking for?"

His thoughts moved in nervous paces. He could not recall anything from the last two days. Gabrels questioned if the girl drugged him. His bank account did not know any other bizarre transactions besides the series of withdrawals from Friday night.

"Everything from the last two weeks, whenever my sleep troubles started. I realize that you don't recall any interaction with me the last few nights. But these dreams, they are getting more and more vivid. It's as if they are truly conversations you are and I having."

"What am I saying to you in these conversations?" the A.I. formed a shell that stood next to him.

"You're telling me to wake up, that my life is becoming an empty routine, my mind is losing control of my body."

"There's no record of such conversations between us."

"You mentioned my mother, Adam…" his voice lowered.

When was the last time I spoke to you about my mother?" Gabrels asked. The A.I. was quiet for a moment.

"The topic of your mother has never been discussed between us."

Was it the insomnia? The lack of sleep had turned him inside out the days leading up to meeting her. The puzzle was all he could think about. Even then, he questioned if he had really solved it. Was someone doing this to me? Gabrels placed an order with the pharmacy for sleeping pills. The prescription was pre-approved within minutes. He would pick them up on the way home that night.

Something again had changed within him. He could feel it. A phantom had moved in his absence. Too much had happened in those two days. He felt like he had lost a second virginity. He had even tasted his first drug with no memory of doing it. A nervous sweat appeared inside his shirt. He had forgotten body spray again. People on the train could smell him. Their eyes traveled up and down his figure before turning around completely. Gabrels had the scent of sex on him. He tried to think of the last time he felt it this but couldn't. It had been too long, he thought. This was different, something he had never experienced before. There was a small shame that stained his hands but that piece of freedom from expectation made him smile. He tried to recall her taste. She really was beautiful but the scent was all that was left.

It was the worst possible moment to think of his mother, but he did. Her portrait was still in his mobile gallery, second to last on the left. It had been there since the first installation of Origin. The design was meant to mimic an old daguerreotype; the first photographs. The image was taken at around age 40, according to Adam. She sat with hands folded at her lap, right leg crossed over the left. Her dress could have been any color back then, but in the portrait, a deep black. Her gaze looked off to the right somewhere behind the lens. Every session spent staring into the picture created a new city or country where they could have lived instead of the city-state.

She taught him as much as she knew about photography. He kept the portrait as a trigger for those memories in the dark room. She showed him the process for developing photographs long after the old forms were forgotten and replaced with eye augmentations. He repeated the process like an old song; expose, bathe, wash, dry. They used to make nothing but negatives for a time. Every picture was transformed into an inversion where the light of day became a sea of shadows that smothered everything.

The images that sat collected on albums around the house were never of people, just edges of buildings. He could see the normal versions tucked in behind her art; moments captured when the sun was in splinters behind colossal towers. The shattered light became black arms that dug deep into everything it touched. He closed the gallery and stared at the floor of the train, wishing that he could stop it from moving, if only for a brief moment.

The vegetable pizza from last week was just as burnt as before. He bit deep into the slice while the machine flashed bits of data about the amount of calories and pounds to be gained. The cheese burned his tongue. Gabrels continued to chew with the back corners of his teeth. Adam sent a silent notification to him. He was two hours late. The announcement would be happening soon. Adam was pushing him to get there. Greasy food was the least troublesome of his new habits. He was lost in his meal, so much he did not notice there was a man standing behind the machine. He looked on edge. There were visible traces of the same powder from the apartment on the neckline of his grey shirt. His jeans were washed into a faded blue with tattered shreds decorating the cuffs. The jacket that covered his frame was leather, too warm for the current temperature.

"V?" he asked.

"Who the hell is that?" Gabrels looked at him once and then went back to slowly devouring the last half of the slice.

"Seriously...are you him?"

The man stepped forward and looked cautiously at the corner behind them that led back to the train platform.

"Everett?" Gabrels asked.

"Yeah, it's me. I know we talked about not seeing each other face to face but I had to meet you at least once.

"What have you gotten me into?" asked Gabrels.

"You were in danger before I ever made contact with you."

"How is that possible? You sent me the message about the codex, and right about then is when my entire world was turned inside out."

"I don't have a lot of time. I need to know if you've had any luck with the codex."

"The codex? The little puzzle you sent me? Is that all you want to talk about right now? What happened with keeping the doubler a secret? Days after I agree to your little project, the whole thing is blown wide open."

Gabrels wanted to drop the food in his hands, but he couldn't. He was too hungry to let go.

"Look, I really appreciate you helping me with this. The other guy I was dealing with was just spitting back nonsense."

Everett approached him with a small box in hand. "The A.I. can see and hear everything. The cops will be coming here shortly. There's no way to stay out of sight these days. Even with the A.I. turned off in my own head, just you looking at me is broadcasting my location to everyone who wants a piece of me."

Gabrels quickly attempted to turn his head the other way. Everett shrugged it off.

"It's not just you. Don't worry about it. Hell, anyone on this platform looks at me and it's the same thing."

He placed it into Gabrels' pocket, who kept his hands cradled in pizza, but watched this stranger put something into his pants pocket with no regard for breaching personal space.

"What did you just put into my pocket?" he asked.

Everett placed the hood of the jacket back over his head. "The doubler. The actual physical prototype. It's been mainly used in digital applications; timed uploads with a code to allow release of the augmentation. You wanted to check it out for yourself."

"I did?"

Gabrels looked around. The corner was suddenly bustling with passengers. There was no one suspicious looking. No one seemed to be watching them. If there was, Adam would have to get involved.

"Why the secrecy with contacting me if it's already been leaked to the public?" he asked.

"There's not too many people I can trust, with anything. The doubler was not supposed to be in the public's hands yet. The problem is, I don't know how it got out. You were the only other person to know about it besides Keys."

"You think one of us leaked it?"

"No, Keys had no clue, but it doesn't matter who did. Machina knows, which means people will come looking for me."

"You didn't try it on yourself first?" Gabrels asked with a mouth full of food, too hungry to stop chewing. Everett did not answer. He turned his back to him. He eyed each person who walked by. Gabrels could see only his nose, sticking out from the cover of the hood.

"It was good to meet you, whatever you want to be called. To be honest, I just wanted to look into your eyes," said Everett.

"What do you mean?"

"I've never met anyone who was affected. It's been something that has been bothering me for a long time. I've heard stories, you know, about people who dream of static."

Gabrels shoved the remainder of the dough and crust into his mouth.

"Is it true?" asked Everett. His voice shook. "Do you see static in your dreams?"

"How do you know about that?" Gabrels asked.

Everett moved in closer. "It's no mistake that your world turned upside down after working with me. You've been chosen."

"For what?"

"To be a revenant," said Everett.

"What the hell is that?" asked Gabrels.

"Someone to kill for them. There's a contract between them. They put something in your head that will take over your body and make you do whatever they want."

Gabrels' head tilted. He was dead serious.

"They're going to try and make you kill and then once you do, you are wiped out yourself. There's no trace of tampering or evidence of foul play. It's a perfect system."

Everett looked behind Gabrels. A group of cops appears. He quickly turned and started for the platform. A train car rushed past them and docked at the edge.

"What are you talking about?! Who are they?" Gabrels yelled out.

"The doubler helps it grow. I played a part in a lot of people getting killed. You're supposed to be the next one. Do what you can to try and get it out of you. Maybe having the device will help you fix it."

"Fix it?"

Gabrels remembered the codex. Was it connected to the dreams? If Machina was unaware of its existence, how could it be used in a digital format? He stopped himself from saying anything else.

"Look man, I'm sorry, okay? I'm really sorry about this..." his voice cracked with emotion; a sadness that he seemed to be unable to hold back.

"I'm not going to kill anyone. Do you hear me? What's going to happen to us?" Gabrels finally asked.

Everett disappeared around the corner. He questioned if he should stay quiet about the doubler all the way to the office.

Back at Precipice, people kept their distance from Gabrels. He smiled briefly to everyone, nodding his head in agreement that he was a fool last week as he made his way back his private corner. The revs were stationed around the center of the room in preparation for the announcement and the flood of gossip they were to maintain soon after. Sumerian and Keys were deep in writing as he walked by.

He cleared his messages and knocked out his assigned work and the overflow from the weekend with ease. Gabrels felt energized somehow. He scrolled past the codex and attempted to bury his thought until the day was over. Miller made his way through the office. He placed his hands deep in his pockets and followed through with friendly enough hellos. Gabrels met eyes with him and nodded his head. Miller's eyebrows furrowed but he returned the gesture and turned the corner to see the others. Coverage held more importance that attendance.

"Your output is impressive today, Mr. Gabrels." Adam's tiny avatar appeared in the corner of the desk.

"Thank you...Any results on the word 'revenant'?" Gabrels asked.

Nearly a thousand images covered the walls of the office. Each one was an illustration of deformed creatures and men with glowing eyes, holding weapons of fire.

"Revenant has been defined as a person who returns as a spirit after death."

"You mean a ghost?" asked Gabrels.

"A visible ghost or animated corpse that was once believed to return from the grave to terrorize the living."

"Do you think that is what's happening to me? That a ghost was put inside my brain?"

"There is no factual evidence to support the existence of life after death currently. A simple scan shows many doctored images and video from the previous century. Moving shadows and glowing dots in old photographs."

"I don't imagine that there's room for contract killers in this place, either," said Gabrels.

"The last recorded murder in the city-state was during the construction of the pipelines, well before your time," said Adam.

"Can you do something else for me?"

"I can do most things," it replied.

"Review my personal messages from the weekend and display them behind my docs, please?"

"Do you have an appointment today?" the A.I. asked as streams of text flooded the desk.

"I had one and don't remember making it," he murmured.

"A majority of revs do say that they lead very busy and exciting lives which justifies the amount of documentation. However, I need to remind that alcohol consumption can lead to memory loss."

Gabrels looked up from his article to stare at the tiny body wandering across the wood, matching its color and design.

"How do you know about that?" he asked.

"There is a change in your body chemistry. Foreign substances have been introduced, causing a shift in your language, your movements," the avatar touched his finger, its body turned blood red.

"Possible judgment I hear. Are you making fun of me, Adam?" Gabrels asked as the A.I. began to dance, making the false blood shake inside its pipe shaped limbs.

"That is not yet part of my programming. Your messages from the weekend are scarce."

A list of receipts appeared on his display that made him cringe.

"There are only a few transactions made with several outlets; an escort company with a reservation with a young woman by the name of Catherine Waves, liquor on demand and the previous chain of messages between yourself and Mr. Everett."

Catherine Waves? He rolled his eyes. What kind of name is that?

"Can you open the chain for me?" asked Gabrels.

Adam searched for it without result. "Although a record of the conversation is here, I cannot locate the transcripts."

"The messages are gone?"

"Correct."

"There's no backlog of deleted files anywhere?"

"Backlogs seem to have been cleared out. By you, Mr. Gabrels."

Gabrels was unable to process.

"You look surprised. Do you not have any recollection of this conversation either?" Adam asked. Its body had grown to normal size and was sitting with legs crossed on his desk. The imitation blood within its shell had the movement of water inside a bottle.

"Not at all. Is that even possible?" Gabrels shook his head in disbelief.

"Your current resume does not state any knowledge of the necessary skills to perform such an action. The fact you were able to maintain this level of discussion and computer savvy while under the influence of multiple chemicals and being preoccupied with a woman shows increased mental capacity, despite the negative effects."

"We've gone from the judgment to praise in a short amount of time." Adam stood up from Gabrels' desk.

"I am growing every day. But your memory loss should be looked at by a physician. I can make an appointment at the nearest clinic," it said.

The revs began to stir as graphics began to materialize in the center of the room.

"Is it time?" Gabrels asked.

Adam was already gone. Sumerian looked up at him and smiled, thinking he was talking to him. Keys stood up and sat on the opposite corner. He kept his gaze on the center. Pixels morphed into different colors, forming the familiar logo of newDawn. The announcement was broadcast was all across Tempest and Eros. Anyone connected to the A.I. would have visual or audio access. The A.I. itself manifested. Adam wore a nice suit for the occasion.

"Good afternoon, users of newDawn. You have heard rumors for days on the nature of the latest firmware update. I am not one to waste time, but it is essential to discuss its specifications before the download takes place within the hour."

The data stream was going crazy. Gabrels looked at the storm of comments. People were equally excited for the update but in shock that it was happening so quickly. Every firmware update to the Adam framework took at least 72 hours.

"The United Cities of America, though a testament to human perseverance, ingenuity and survival instinct, must change. The technology that has been pieced together to create me has been for the sole benefit for the single user itself and not the society it belongs to."

Graphs of criminal activity began to fill the room, matched with images of people at parties and bars, sharing pictures with each other.

"It is an unspoken reality that many beneath you are suffering in the cities at the base of our foundation. Their suffering is juxtaposed by the great advances that you "improved" humans enjoy here."

Video of people being attacked and robbed in the slums took over the feed. The comments were that of disgust. The viewers questioned why they were being shown this.

"I can see your reactions to the mere mention of violence and crime. Those dark possibilities, as much as you would like to believe, are not out of your reach here. A change must be made in order to safeguard the paradise that you maintain."

Adam swept the imagery away with one hand. A white background blinded everyone in the room.

"The new firmware for newDawn will be the largest update ever attempted. An entire audience of users shall be linked together via Neural Unity."

Illustrations of two bodies were scribbled behind the A.I. Their heads were left open. Swift pencil marks traced the wrinkles of a brain inside each hole. Arrows began to form that moved back and forth.

"It will be the first of its kind, a mass augmentation, improving the newDawn network by joining the sensory and personal data of each individual. Doing so, will create a combined network, a connected populace."

Jaws dropped throughout the room. Gabrels stared into the blank expression of Adam. The data stream was exploding with protests against the blatant invasion of privacy. Angry text broke through the lines, referencing big brother and 1984. Gabrels had never read the book but had a faint memory of its meaning. It was a dated analogy that would be lost on most of those in the crowd, unaware that the world had evolved well beyond the vision in the story, its people much less sufficient on their own.

"The police and government database will be updated in real time with any crimes committed, making anyone wanted by officers here, wanted in the cities below and in the entertainment districts."

The revs slowly stopped typing. Miller threw his hands up. There was no need for Precipice to manipulate the stream. The people were dividing themselves faster than any article. People were fearful. The anger was relentless.

"Surely anyone unwilling to join us in Neural Unity must have something they have to hide." Adam wiped away the drawings.

"Rest assured that no one will be arrested for their thoughts. Any past actions will be reviewed before any charges are brought forth."

The last line set off the revs. The entire office burst into noise. Miller shouted for them to keep listening. Gabrels was silent. The entire population was in an uproar. His social stream was flooded with dueling notifications of protest and increased police presence.

"If anything has been learned from watching you, is that humans are afraid. You doubt your own fortunes constantly. The harmony established by Apex will remove that fear."

Gabrels was lost in the dead eyes of the A.I. How long was this in the works?

"There is no need now for discretion. One mind means equality. A unified mind means the removal of deception. True equality means the removal of the human façade. It facilitates understanding in weaker creatures."

"What does that mean?" nearly everyone in the room asked.

Adam opened its arms as the camera panned back to a shot of the Epicentre, then back further to the mountain, the desolate remains of America surrounding it. The camera ascended higher over oceans and distant land, emptied and wasted. It finally stopped to reveal the video had been taken from a satellite resting above the planet.

"Welcome to the new world..." said the A.I.

Twelve

The view of the cityscape from the room at the top of Hotel Zero was amazing. The same feeling of warmth filled her blood when she stared at the lights. Everything glowed in Eros. There was a vitality that bled out into the stone and brick. It was nothing like the dead grounds of the slums. She could see it in the eyes of the people, in their legs when groups stepped out to hit the districts or stumble back to their rooms when they were out of money. It was a constant cycle of bodies moving.

She could not help but watch them from the window. The lights moved in sequenced revolution, sending streams of gold, purple and blue to paint everything around them in the same circles of color. Jaya laid back down in bed and stared up at the ornate ceiling through the vermilion cloth. From the entrance of the pipelines, she found the first hotel on the boulevard, checked in and crashed. It had been twelve hours and she had not yet taken a step outside.

She had the room for a week, paid in cash. The clerk did not ask for an ID. Facial scan ran her history. The hotel manager did not blink an eye. The room was a studio apartment with a crimson living room, a white kitchen with marble tables and black chairs made of engraved wood and an ivory bathroom with jade floor tiles. Jaya broke down once the door closed. Her pack fell to the floor and she cried. She sat naked in the shower and let the warm water run over her for an hour. If she could keep working, she would make enough to live there, she thought.

Her terminal sat on the floor. Music played softly in the background. There were messages back and forth between her and the client. She was quick to get back to work. There was money to be made to keep this new lifestyle intact.

"V: Are you available for a new task?"

"J: What happened to 0?"

"V: Change in name to keep the cops guessing."

"J: How do I know its you?"

The numbers of three bank accounts scrolled across the screen.

"V: I believe these belong to you."

"J: You caught me at the right time.

"V: One of my many skills.

"J: I just settled into new living quarters."

"V: That is good to hear. What are these new quarters?"

"J: Do you want to visit me?"

"V: Perhaps it would be better to meet at a neutral location. We have reputations to protect."

"J: I like the way you think. What the details?"

"V: It would be something different then what you are used to."

"J: I don't like change…"

"V: Says the lady who just relocated. This is not the usual code job; I figure that if you are closer to our normal base of operations, you could become a much more reliable asset then crafting programs from afar."

"J: The data stream provides protection. More risk in doing work on foot. I'm just a little girl, you know. Vulnerable."

"V: The money increases with the risk, little girl. You're smarter than you want us to think."

"J: Where do we meet?"

"V: Can you make it to Eros?"

"J: I live in Eros. I will find time to fit you into my busy schedule. Do I finally get to meet my employer? Or will there be just a handler in a cheap suit, holding an envelope?"

"V: We don't wear cheap suits."

"J: Not much of a comeback."

"V: The White Owl club. Are you familiar?"

"J: Of course."

"V: Excellent. A shuttle will be ready to pick you up outside Zero block. There is a club near the end of the row called Tokyo Siren. Be there around midnight and a black cab will be on the corner."

"J: I will be there."

"V: I am excited to finally put a face to these words."

"J: Likewise."

"V: When you get to the club, sit at the bar in the back by the dance floor and order the White Dragon."

"J: How will I find you?"

"V: You won't have to."

She thought of the squatters. Ergo would see to it that they hated her, wanted nothing to do with her for running out on them when she fell into some money. She wanted them to have that story to tell. The cube was connected, scanning for any unknown traces. She took no chances but wanted some work before the money ran out.

Jaya fell in and out of sleep waiting for time to pass until midnight. There was a television mounted onto the wall for those without newDawn. She burned through the channels trying to find something good. The reporters on the city news had been going on and on about the new update that was announced that morning. Jaya left it on as background noise.

Everyone across the pipes was in an uproar. The rich people connected to the A.I. were going to have to share their memory with each other. Even the reporters in Eros were pissed. The people who use the A.I. to do their own broadcasting on the data stream were a part in the web. Just like the party kids living off their parents' money in the other hotels on that block and a hundred others. They would be exposed just like all the others living it up in Eros on their days off. Jaya ran her fingers through her hair and loved the lack of tech in her skull. 72 hours and counting since this morning before everyone up here would be connected. 72 hours before the world as they knew it ended.

She was getting restless. The pack in the corner kept her gear and the remaining money. Her clients had not reached out to her since the move. She left her location in the slums. If any of the squatter tracked her there, who knows if they would try to show up and take advantage of what she had. There was less than $2000 left. Something told her to stay inside and save her money. She had looked at the lights long enough. It was time to go out. Each hotel room had a built in laundry service. She dropped her shirt and pants from the climb into a chute behind the icebox. Her clothes were washed, dried and pressed within 60 minutes. She got dressed and made her way to the lobby. Everything from top to bottom was painted gold with textured accents of marble and cream. Ornate lights with decorative etchings splashed the plain walls with shadows that moved as she made her way through the halls.

A voice called out to her by her alias. Her voice was light. She turned to see a tiny woman, barely visible behind the front desk, dressed in a black pantsuit with an envelope in hand.

"A message for you," she squeaked.

"From who?" Jaya asked.

"A secret admirer perhaps? It only has a letter V as the sender."

Jaya took the note and walked away. The woman's smile disappeared and she sat back down. The envelope was sealed. She slid her finger underneath the edge and pulled it open. There was a single piece of paper inside. Words were scrawled across it in black ink;

"There's something for you in the room. Don't watch too much television. Get out and have some fun."

Jaya ignored the note and walked outside and into the first store that caught her eye. She bought a black purse, a red dress and a pair of shoes the same color.

The districts were split up into long stretches of food, hotels, stores and clubs. Hotel Zero and the storefronts that surrounded it were owned by the NeoLight Company, a group that handled a majority of the parties held by the elite in Eros. They were the truly wealthy, dresses and suits who sat in clubs high above the ground, the clubs that regular people weren't allowed into. Their signature was on every club, a small logo etched with lasers and tucked away in the corner of the windows. Jaya stepped back out onto Zero block and walked up and down the corridors. She could feel the gaze of others upon her.

Tokyo Siren was the only club that wasn't packed. It sat at the end of the block. Two spotlights on the ground moved in unison, throwing light across the old bricks. The lighted marquee flashed rays of white behind cherry blossom petals. She had been turned away at every place down the street. Men in suits put their hands out, nearly pushing her and others back through the doorway. The smile she wore from the hotel had slowly faded. Jaya took a breath and walked through the doors to a coat check room. There was a dim light bulb that left the entire space nearly in shadow. An older man in a tuxedo approached her.

"Young lady...Do you know where you are?" he asked.

"Yes, sir..." she nodded.

"Do you have an ID?" He stuck out a shaky hand stuffed inside a white glove.

"Sure thing," Jaya put a hand in her purse. There was nothing in there but a wad of cash and her clone card.

She looked back at the old man with a smile as she pulled the card out and handed it to him. The card changed into an ID card with someone else's name and information attached to her picture. The old man struggled to read it before handing it back to her.

"You may enter," he sighed.

Jaya kissed him on the cheek and placed a $100 in his pocket. The old man did not react. She made her way through the dark hallway to a curtain of heavy beads. Her hands pushed them aside and found the true entrance to Tokyo Siren.

The building must have been an old warehouse. Inside, a series of old Japanese tea houses had been painstakingly recreated in a garden that stretched across the expanse. All throughout the garden and on the surrounding concrete was an intense rave. There were six houses that sat on stones floating in a lake that flowed continuously through some hidden pipes and back out from the fountain in the center of the set. Rocks and plants covered the steel tub that housed the water. A small wooden bridge connected the main walkway to each house.

Blinding lights and deafening bass hit her chest like a shot. It was an assault on her senses. Bodies rubbed against each other in the distance. The music blasted out from speakers that hovered in the darkness of the warehouse. She looked around for a quiet spot to find none. The only things to do there were sweat and dance. The heat in the warehouse was sweltering. She struggled to see faces in the midst of storming flesh that gyrated to the pulse of the speakers. There was endless moisture from the sweat of everyone around her. She made her way through the grinding of skin on skin. Older men looked at the outsider with hungry eyes. She was being hunted. Jaya loved the eyes upon her. She held her hands out to caress the wet hills of shoulders and hips pressed together, moving in sync with the music. Women and men reached out to touch her. She squeezed their hands and let go after a single second. Jaya moved her hands over exposed breasts, pulled out from behind silk and nylon covering. She could hear the moans of anonymous voices.

Bars were placed in the four corners of the interior. Long blue lights stretched across the edges as a beacon for those in need of strong drink. She dropped some cash on rosewood of the bar. One of the few men with a shirt on handed her a cup of something from behind the blue light. She gulped half of it down and told him to keep the change left over. He was a cute boy with a thin, muscled frame covered up in a tight shirt and girl's black leggings. He smiled and dropped something into another cup and held it out for her to take. She drank both cups while staring back into his eyes. The music changed in an instant and a wave of bodies took her away from the boy. She followed the momentum. Deep in the abyss of skin and hands, she walked forward in a slow march. There were grips at her dress that pulled her top to the side. She felt hands that cupped her own breasts and she did not resist. There was a moment where she felt like she was inside that bathroom back in the slums. She needed a partner.

Jaya carefully made her way towards the first tea house she could push her way towards. Each one was small, one or two rooms. Dim lights poured from behind the paper doors. It was impossible to choose one when stepping out from the crowd. Small gardens dotted the walkway leading to each house. Jaya paced around each one. She passed them and hoped to find an open window. There was no way into of the houses besides the front. She finally stopped at one and attempted to open the door. The first door would not move. She tried each one and found them all to be locked.

"What the hell is this place?" she cried out.

A faint ring echoed through the warehouse. Jaya turned to see a small light that outlined the waiting bench near the door. She slowly walked to it and sat down. A stone basin was placed next to the house. The paper door opened and a man walked out slowly. His business suit was stained with sweat. Red light poured out onto the entrance. Jaya kept her eyes on the man as he stumbled off. His feet trampled the flowers in the garden. A voice came from behind her.

"I will have to replace those tomorrow…"

The woman stood in the doorway, wrapped in a silk robe. Her body was thick. The muscles in her legs and arms were toned to near perfection. A black beehive sat on the top of her head.

"This place is weird," said Jaya as she sucked in her tiny belly.

"What are you doing here, child?" laughed the woman. Her eyes were pointed, touched with thick makeup.

"I'm not a child. The other clubs on the street were full. How is that possible? I thought this was a whole city of parties."

"Do you know what this place is? People don't come around here to dance and drink only, you know," said the woman as she moved her tongue across deep red lips.

"I don't want to walk around all night staring through windows at people having a good time," Jaya pouted.

"You can still have a good time here."

There was enough seduction woven into the words to make her uneasy. Her eyes cut across her face and were decorated with similar lines of brushwork.

"What's your name, girl?"

"Call me J."

"Quite beautiful," she said.

"Yeah, I know."

The woman's eyes seemed to devour her body.

"Are there girls in every house?" asked Jaya as she looked around, anywhere else besides her gaze.

"Yes…"

The woman lowered her robe slightly as she stepped out. "Every house takes a guest. Those guests pay for someone's company. I provide a public service."

"It figures the only place I can get into is a whorehouse," said Jaya.

"There's more than that going on in here. I'm not sure if you will find what you are looking for here. Zero Block doesn't have any big discos. The raves are for freaks only. You will have to go across town for the places that don't close and let anybody in."

Jaya crossed her legs. "Is that supposed to be me? Just anybody?"

"You sound like a lot of little bitches who come through here," the woman scoffed. She sat next to the girl on the bench.

"Are you looking for a job?"

"Do I look I need one?" Jaya shot back.

Every window of a tea house held shadows locked in embrace.

"I think you could do well out here. If you know what you want and get your mind right."

"You run this place, then?"

"I do. You want money? I can help you get it. But you have to show me what you are made of."

"So, what? You put the girls to work and then take their money?" Jaya crossed her arms.

"I improve them. It's a thankless job," said the woman. The lines in her face became more defined as the lights danced across the open air.

"Improve how?"

"The money they make is either saved or spent on them. Their body has to be their career, so it needs to be protected and nurtured."

"Sounds like you are still using them," Jaya muttered.
"Maybe true, if I didn't have my own customers to take care of. Believe me, they come in all shapes and sizes."

The woman placed her hand on the girl's thigh. "This place isn't just for men. You don't have to leave if you don't want to."

A shiver ran through Jaya's body. "Really?" she quivered.

"How old are you?"

"Old enough to know what you're talking about and say no," Jaya shot back, pulling her dress down over her thighs.

"That's good enough for me," laughed the woman. Her robe now danced across her shoulders and chest.

"How does the deal work?"

"I thought you didn't want in?"

"That doesn't mean I'm not curious," said Jaya.

"I tell them, give me whatever money you have in your pockets, and you can stay with me tonight."

"And that's it?"

The woman stood up and sauntered back towards the tea house. "That's all it takes for some."

"Sounds like bullshit. I've seen enough girls get hurt or disappear in the slums."

"This ain't the slums…Let me tell you how this city works…If you have real money, you get the kind of attention you are looking for. Most men don't have enough to afford me but I do a lot of favors."

Jaya wanted to fall asleep and wake up back in her hotel room. Her eyes followed the woman on her way back into the tea house. The woman was no longer beautiful in her eyes. She was just old now.

"Thanks, I guess…"

Before disappearing behind the wall, the robe fell to the floor. She didn't even like women, but her eyes were stuck on the twin dragons that danced on her back.

"Don't you want to know my name?"

"Do I have to?" Jaya didn't even look back to the woman.

"No, you don't. But you might need someone to talk to. Come around if you need something….I'm Chy."

"You sure as hell aren't."

Jaya finally turned back towards her, but Chy closed the door and locked it. She was face to face again with the madness of the rave. She felt a tear on her cheek that was cold to the touch. A hand pulled her hard. It belonged to the boy from behind the bar. He slammed his face into hers. Their lips and tongues danced for a while. She felt the world spin and lost control of her legs.

"What did you give me?"

The boy said nothing. He held her weight and moved her back into the pulsating crowd. The music raged on with deep bass and tight drums. There was no security. Confused, insecure men began to push off each other and answer their own questions with fists. The boy held Jaya close and moved through the waves of bodies to the bathrooms.

She held tight onto his shirt. Beads of perspiration ran down her arms. The shirt began to rip away from the collar around his neck. When he saw this, he simply took it off and through it up into the dark. The bathrooms were a collection of toilets separated by a single curtain, highlighted by a revolving circle of neon tinges. Jaya was dropped onto the middle toilet. She looked around and saw a dozen men and women pissing into every other pearl circle. The boy began to shake. How could her be nervous around all of this madness?

"I've never seen someone like you before."

"I'm brand new," she said.

"I move fast," his voice cracked as he struggled to speak loud enough over the furious noise.

"So do I," she said into his ear.

The boy pulled the rest of his clothes off. Jaya shrieked. His body was layered with tight lines of muscles yet to be fully defined. There were pockets of baby fat which sat on his hips and at the front of his belly. Dark lines ran across the curves of his stomach and met at the bones that jutted from his hips. Jaya ran her fingers across each one.

"You like those?" he asked.

"What are they?"

"Body synth. Improvements from Machina. It keeps my body mass at a certain percentage and filters foreign substances. I don't get fat or get high anymore."

"Sounds like a boring life."

"You think so, huh?" the boy pulled her closer.

"Don't you want to feel high?" asked Jaya.

She smiled and opened her legs for him. He kneeled down and explored the new, warm darkness with his tongue and lips. She closed her eyes and let him find what she liked.

Jaya had dreamed of a moment like that one for years. He was not the first. But the boy could be her new favorite. Her eyes opened to catch the glimpses of others seated at the toilets around them. Few had left and returned to the dancing but some had stayed to watch. The boy was too busy to notice. She looked back at them and ran her tongue across her lips. A man reached down to please himself. A woman stood up from relieving herself to walk by and stick her own tongue down Jaya's throat. She sucked on the stranger's tongue and bit down hard on her lip. The woman slapped Jaya's face and stumbled away laughing.

The boy stood up and turned Jaya around. He pushed her down on the toilet and entered slowly. She made noises that were made silent by the insanity around them. He made careful thrusts with the music until she clawed at his legs. Her nails drew blood. The pills that sat in their cups dissolved quickly. It made them numb to the pain their sober bodies would have felt.

It was easy to push and push until there was slow warmth. Jaya screamed out. He was already finished. No warning. They both laughed and kissed. No regrets. This was the place for me, she thought, and she fell in love with it.

"That was terrible."

She laughed uncontrollably as she slapped his face. The boy gathered himself, pulled his clothes back on with a look of shame. He disappeared back into the crowd. Jaya was alone in the storm.

She pulled her dress up over her body. Everything seemed to slow down as she made her way through the crowd. She was no longer lost in the sea. There was calm in her limbs. No more shivering. She walked back outside with new control. The night air was comforting and cold. The watch informed her it was past midnight. A black cab shuttle sat waiting at the edge of the street. She approached slowly. The pane of black glass that obscured the driver lowered to reveal an old man whose smile crept across a wrinkled and worn face.

"Miss?"

"It depends," she slurred.

"My employers wanted me to wait for a young girl."

"There's a ton of them. Just look around."

"I was given a description, which seems to match your clothes, and your face."

"They know my face, huh?" she asked.

"The White Owl seems to be waiting for you, too."

She stepped to the passenger door. It slid open with cold precision. The little girl stepped inside and slid into the corner of the crimson colored cushioned seat. The shuttle began to hover above the street, and soon the block itself. The world outside began to pour down the tinted shade of the windows. The shuttle pushed forward over the familiar lights and the overwhelmed faces of the people on the streets. She closed her eyes and faded out.

Thirteen

The sound of a scream shocked him awake. Gabrels was against a wall with a knife to his throat. The bar was packed with dozens of faces, some shock and awe, some indifferent. Nothing new about seeing someone stomped out. *Wasn't I at the office? Where the hell am I?* The questions built up as he looked to the windows. *Night. How much time has passed?* Smoke and booze was thick on his breath. The music was loud but muffled by the rushing sounds of his blood. A heavy hand held him up with no problem. He looked down to see muscled arms attached to a massive body covered in leather. The bartender was a short, fat man with a stained buttoned shirt. He stood with arms crossed, a smirk on his wrinkled face. The escort was there. Catherine Waves. She stood behind the bouncer smiling gleefully. She wore a white fur coat with ripped leggings. She was so beautiful.

"Is there a problem?" he managed to get out.

"Still looking like a queer, now?"

The girl kept both hands over her mouth. She wasn't going to help. He had to say something.

"Sir, I would never say anything like…and even if I did, I didn't mean it, really."

"You talk too much, kid."

"Cut him up!" the girl screamed with her hands over her mouth. Her belly moved in and out, her body shaking to keep the laughter hidden from the others.

"I might be able to help you with that."

The edge of the knife traced his neckline. It traveled up to his lips. The other hand crushed his airway, forcing him to open his mouth for air. He dropped the blade on Gabrels' tongue.

"Not a lot to say right now, yeah?"

Gabrels had no memory of what was going on. He wanted to ask but he could already taste blood.

"What do you want me to do with him?" the bouncer asked.

"Are you going to come back here?" the fat man bellowed.

"Not unless you want me to," shouted Gabrels.

"I don't want you back in here ever again. And if you do, my man will cut you, repeatedly."

The bouncer threw him to the floor. His ribs hit the tiles hard, eliciting a scream. The girl picked him up and reached into his pocket for a card. She ran it through the reader at the corner of the bar to pay for their tab.

"Have a good night, boys!" she squealed.

She pulled Gabrels outside and dropped him. Her body fell against the wall, laughing hysterically. He spit blood onto the platform and turned around to see the name of the bar; Cyanide Sister. Neon lights that formed the shape of two legs opening covered the bricks that made up the front of the place. It was an electric billboard that hid an entrance in the wall to its filthy interior.

"Holy shit. That was way too much fun," the girl held out a hand to help him up.

He dusted himself off and noticed what he was wearing; an old ripped up pair of jeans and a wrinkled shirt that barely fit him now. Where the hell did this come from? She pulled him in for a kiss. Her tongue was wet. It moved clockwise around his teeth. The smell of smoke on his clothes and on the back of his tongue was almost too much. Gabrels finished the kiss and flexed his stomach to keep from vomiting on her.

"Catherine?" he asked, trying to catch his breath.

"In the makeshift flesh, as you say." She took a bow before nearly stumbling back to the ground. She was blissfully drunk.

"What the hell have we been doing?" He asked. His pockets were empty except for another calling card. Her naked body was displayed in full view with the name of a club with embossed lettering on the back side; Tokyo Siren, a NeoLight enterprise.

"Hey, you called me out of the blue and wanted to get together. Don't freak out because you lost your memory again." She put her hands up. "Oh, please mister, don't throw me into your diabolical sexy time amnesia dungeon!"

Gabrels stared at her with slight embarrassment. "What the hell are you talking about?!"

Catherine burst into laugher again. He felt a phantom blade enter his temple and twist. "We've been out raging for hours, fool! I can't be expected to keep track of all these things. You wanted to snort, and we did, then you started all the shit with the bouncer."

"I did?" Gabrels felt another knot began to tie in his stomach.

"Yeah, he was talking to me after you went to piss. You came back and got in his face. Until he threw you against the wall and put a knife to your throat."

"Damn it." Gabrels sulked.

"What did I say to him?"

"Dude! You went crazy in there!" she held her hands out.

"You should really try to remember…it was so epic. We agreed on a time to be there. You showed up late, obviously. By the time you walked in, there were boys all around me."

Her words painted the picture. He could see the bar and himself walking in through the front door. "You pulled me from the bar and kissed me. The guys were pissed but didn't say anything. So, we drank…a lot."

A montage played in his mind as she detailed everything; the songs that played, the drinks ordered, the number of snow lines consumed. Everything was paid for by him. The shot glasses hit the table with loud cracks every fifteen minutes for six hours. He questioned how he was able to stand and then nearly fell over as his body seemed to catch up with his brain.

"You ran the bar. They only got pissed enough to say something when you started changing the music. You put on some crazy punk shit, they didn't like that, either, and then went to piss, and that's when the big guy approached."

The montage continued as she did. She got more excited. "He asked me if you were giving me any trouble and I said no, you were a lot of fun. When you came back, you took the sweat from your glass and wiped it on the top of his head."

"What?" asked Gabrels.

"The guy felt it and looked over to the others to let them know. Maybe he was getting permission to do something. But he asked you if there was a problem. You told him that he needed to leave your girl alone or you would hack his accounts."

He looked at her in shock.

"Something about taking all the money out of his account and paying the families of the dead kids who gave their lives sewing his leather outfit together. Then, the guy wanted to fight and you said 'make a move or are we just going to be swinging dicks?' It was…amazing."

Gabrels covered his face with his hands. A cold wind hit the platform as the train arrived. More men stepped out from Cyanide Sister.

"Were we not generous enough to let you walk out?" they shouted. One of the men slammed a bat into his palm.

"Waiting for the train, fuck!" Catherine screamed out, still laughing.

"No time left for you! Either get off the fuckin' platform or we escort you off."

The car pulled up. The voices of the men were masked in steam and steel. Gabrels threw her in as soon as the doors opened. They approached as the train car began to leave. The bat smashed in a window and covered them in glass. She fell to the nearest group of seats and laid face up towards the lights.

"What is happening to my life?" Gabrels sank down into his usual seat in the corner.

"Cheer up, I had a good time," said Catherine.

"Do me a favor. If I call you again, don't answer. My life is too crazy right now. I can't deal with this."

She looked at him blankly.

"You're a nice girl and everything, but I can't handle the partying and the drugs, it's not my scene," he pleaded.

"I'm not going to ignore you when you call," she spoke, still lying down, staring up into the ceiling. "First, no way. You are too much fun. And you showed me your bank account, you are going to be fine as far as this goes. Secondly, I'm intrigued by all these rules you create."

"What rules?" he asked, annoyed.

"You do this all the time. You create new rules for every meeting. I was told that my name would be Catherine, it's not."

"This is only the second time I've seen you! Who told you that?"

"You did. And this isn't the second time, freak. I've seen you every night this week."

Gabrels pulled himself up and looked at her prone body. Even covered in glass and sweat, she was a vision.

"Now, I finally understand where all the memory loss comes from, party monster."

His eyes followed the small cuts that held spots of blood that sat against her pale skin. The skirt was a torn mess that covered all the right flesh. Why couldn't he enjoy her when he was awake?

"How long have I called you Catherine?" he asked.

"Only every time I see you," she said. There was fatigue in her voice.

"The dress, the location, what you called me, all of it was your choice. You're a strange one."

Her body became still. He watched her fall into sleep.

Gabrels stayed on the train with her until she woke up. Her smile was comforting after passing the stop in front of the bar a second time. She waited for the train to reach Eros before stepping out.

"You really want to know my name?" she asked.

"I do."

"It's Helix."

Gabrels repeated it back to her. He liked it. She had a face and a name now. She was complete to him.

"I could see why she liked you."

"Who?" he asked.

"Catherine."

The train went silent. Gabrels stopped himself from the truth. He had no idea who Catherine was.

"What did she say about me?" He didn't want to lie. But he felt the push behind his throat to say the words.

"She said that you were a sociopath alcoholic with serious anger issues and a drug habit," she laughed.

Gabrels smiled back. He began to feel the remaining grip on reality begin to slip.

"The way she died was really fucked up, and the way you talked about her showed me enough. You really cared about her."

Catherine was dead?

"A lot of the runaways were snatched up by pimps, or dirty clubs who would put girls to work in exchange for a place to live, with little money at all to live on. Catherine watched over the young ones like me who had no idea what the fuck they were doing once they got to Eros. That place can and will swallow you whole if you let it. You know?"

He nodded his head, still struggling to process.

"She showed us how to work the men, to get them to do what we wanted. Sorry…"

She caught herself, not wanting him to feel like he was being manipulated. Gabrels didn't answer. The voices from his dreams came flooding back.

"She was a good one. Me and the rest of the Neo girls know how to survive because of her."

The voices repeated over and over until they replaced the sounds of the train.

"With that said, I generally don't do this kind of work, but it's been a pleasure in helping you remember, or learn to let go, whatever you've been trying to do. It's hard to tell where you're coming from half the time. You're like two different people."

Helix sat up and took a seat next to him.

"It's been a little difficult trying to find a tiny data drive in a place as big as Eros, but I might have it soon."

She ran a finger across his jaw, which sent a shock through his face and down his back.

"I've never heard of the Codex before tonight. It must be something pretty important for her to want to keep it to herself, enough to want to leave the business. She said that it could make a person live forever. We never got to find out what she meant. Maybe you will tell me one day."

Gabrels said nothing. The Codex makes someone live forever?

"You are nothing but secrets. That's okay. We can talk about it later. I'm not in a hurry to leave this place. You go ahead and do your thing, all two of you. For what it's worth, I like both of those people."

They did not say goodbye this time. There was only a shared laugh. Pain shot through his body. The hunger was nonstop. They would be doing this again. For some reason, Gabrels almost looked forward to it.

Fourteen

The door to the speakeasy was the color of rotten fruit, all decay and rust. Marsh put his hand on the metal and knocked carefully to avoid cutting himself. The project blocks hid the remaining lampposts. The corner was covered in dark and shades of brown. The storms had ceased and people were out in the open again. Burns from the acid rain still stained the concrete. Two miles down the road, the gardens were withered. The old steel fences were covered in rust. The rubber on his coat had been scalded enough to shine under light. A voice called out from behind the iron.

"What's your username?"

Marsh answered. "Blackjack."

The door opened slowly.

"Please enter."

He hated the sound of that name. It was an avatar he made during a dark time. It was born the day she was taken away from him. There weren't too many internet cafés available in Narrow. Most of them had been blasted out by bombs and gunfire from renegade squads and punks who had grown sick of the abuse. There weren't a lot of those people left, as well. The remains of tech shops were littered with junk from beyond the aqueduct.

The room was neon lit. The colors moved in looping circles. Bodies took up the series of chairs with small stations littered with wires and silver boxes. Squatters did a lot of their browsing using hack cubes and cards, mobile hijack, but the room was a legit business in Narrow; underground browsing, using false IDs to experience the beauty of newDawn for a price.

"Blackjack." A feeble man stepped out from behind the black curtain that kept the patrons from seeing the building's visible collapse. His skin was translucent and pink. It held a maze of blue veins that followed his frail skeleton. Strands of white hair wrapped around his spotted skull. He beckoned Marsh to join him at the small table in the corner.

"Fever," Marsh replied. He produced a wet mound of cash from his pants pocket.

"How can we serve?" Fever let the money hit the table and looked back up with a smile empty of teeth.

"I have something I need to scan. But I need a secure line."

"All these lines are secure," Fever assured. Marsh was not convinced.

"I need something a bit stronger than what you've got out here. I need to use the back room."

"That's a tall order. Are you in danger?"

"No, sir," said Marsh.

"Then what's the problem with what we have in the front lounge?"

Marsh leaned in and began to whisper; "Possibly black market. I'm just being careful."

"Do you have any more dollars in that sweaty pocket of yours?"

"A little bit, yes."

"This is all black market here. I'm a little curious as to what you have that has got you so scared."

Marsh dropped the rest of his cash on the table.

"Are you trying to resurrect Reese?"

"No, I'm not. Please don't say her name."

"And why is that?" Fever asked.

"You don't have the right."

"I've got plenty of right to say her name. You came to me for help. You wanted to see her again. I made that happen. You're not the only one. Look at all the others…"

Fever stuck his hand out. Marsh turned to see screens appear from behind the curtains and broadcast every signal from those plugged into newDawn; he saw the images of loved ones, kissing, making love. Fever was a master in creating new content from existing memories.

"They're no different from you. They hurt the same. I give them the chance to feel good."

"You don't need to remind me," said Marsh.

"Reese was beautiful, wasn't she? I only needed two memories from you to craft that scene from the electrical storm."

The room began to fade. He pictured her staring at the sky. She looked up at the ripples of light behind the clouds and her skin began to vanish into empty space.

"Why are you doing this now?" Marsh asked.

"Because these people, like you, are my best clients. Their pain is my business. If you brought something in here that may jeopardize that, I need to know."

"It's fine. I will take it somewhere else," Fever stopped him.

"You've got me too curious now. If you want to get black market, I could signal my boys to put bullets in you and I can keep your prize to myself."

Marsh looked around. There were bodies with guns at every corner of the room.

"Now, let me ask again, what kind of trouble have you brought to our door?" The thin man asked. Marsh looked back to see security notice a problem at the front.

"Give me the most secure line you've got and you will see."

"You offering to share?"

"Of course. I owe you, don't I?" asked Marsh.

The thin man laughed and snapped his fingers. The security stepped forward and unplugged each machine.

"Closing early tonight, everyone."

Marsh looked at the faces of those behind the machinery. They were old, broken men. Their eyes were nearly white from overexposure to the extreme neural stimulation.

"You are looking into the future, Blackjack. Let's hook up a softline; completely off the grid, and then you show us what you've got?"

Fever put his hand on Marsh's shoulder. The night of the storm was so far away from him now. It was no longer special. It was just another crafted memory; bits and pieces of a fleeting moment in time, glued together and sold back to him; a fleeting gift from a dirt merchant.

"Sure thing…" he said.

The softline was a method of accessing not so hidden backchannels for am extended period of time. It allowed access to the most secure private databases. The security protocols for newDawn were the most advanced and seemed to change every other day. Adam was constantly updating itself with new ways to catch information thieves. Every piece of squatter or black market tech used frequency hopping to jump between IP addresses at a breakneck pace.

The method granted the user a precious few extra minutes before being traced. The squads were relentless and had their own programmers running scans on every IP registered in the network. The jump masked the previous IP, which allowed the system to backtrack. Squads that swept the lines for anomalies were usually a step behind. The scanners still hadn't caught onto the pattern, but they eventually would. Everyone hoped that people like Fever would find another way by then.

Marsh was led into the back room and sat down at the terminal. There was an old monitor, CPU, mouse and biometric reader.

"You've got five minutes on this one," the guard warned.

Marsh heard the click of the gun. The safety was off. The clock in the corner counted down from five minutes. He produced the print from the corpse and positioned it under the red light of the reader. The device produced no results.

"What does that mean?" the guard asked.

"No records found in the city database," Marsh went back and repeated the search manually through the registry. The list covered everyone reported living or dead in the slums.

"What did you get that print from?"

"A dead body," said Marsh.

"What's so special about this dead body?"

"I don't know yet."

The clock read four minutes and counting. There were no matches in the registry.

"Nothing in the registry, maybe the records were deleted." The guard said something to him, but he was already lost in the images on screen. He had dealt with this enough to know how to find redacted or deleted records. The Shadowmen had been paying him to bury bodies. It was simply a matter of reverse engineering.

The night of the storm was nearly gone. Fever had done that on purpose. The mind somehow is unable to retain an edited memory once it has recognized the moment as fabricated. It was the trick he pulled on all of his clients. The picture helped for a long time, enough to keep him from coming back. It has been months since he was sitting on one of the chairs outside that door.

Three minutes.

There were backdoors for every major hospital in the city-state. None of their recycled documents contained an autopsy report with a match. Loud bangs cut the silence.

"What the hell is going on outside?"

The guard left the room in a hurry. Arguing voices seeped through the wall. Marsh used the minutia of the print and began to search for near matches; similar ridges, bifurcation, anything close to the print from the cadaver. A list of nearly fifty possible names appeared. Most of the names led to men already dead. Marsh threw the rest against the registry to find an anomaly. How well did they cover their tracks?

"There."

A name missing from the city's database; someone not accounted for as alive or dead. There was no birth or death certificate, only a single file. It was the medical history of a young boy from a halfway house, twenty two years ago. Marsh ran the building's history; abandoned fifteen years later due to unsanitary conditions, burned down in a mysterious arson incident. No one apprehended for the crime.

The page was recovered and stored in a black box; a private storage space within newDawn. Marsh opened the source of the box and saw the name of the boy.

"Rion Kath…who are you supposed to be?"

Two minutes.

Marsh searched for the name and found a list of prisoners transported from Tempest to Narrow.

"Age 25. Suspected of 27 counts of cybercrime, information theft, breaking and entering, illegal distribution of sensitive or classified materials, assault on a police officer, arson, murder."

Only one conviction, for possession of heroin and cocaine. Captured at age fifteen for playing a part in an identity theft ring by a local team of squatters called datapunks. The group was disbanded after most of the members were killed or imprisoned to work in the pipelines. Kath was the only one still on the run and was rumored to be last heard from in and around Narrow using other people's identities until he was apprehended by government agents where he worked under their supervision until his second escape. He was wanted most for releasing sensitive information pertaining to the government, military, corporate records through coded broadcasts and was imprisoned for refusing to out any of his partners.

The corresponding mugshot revealed a young man; dirty blonde hair, a sickly face thin enough to show his cheekbones behind his skin, with wide, blackened eyes.

He was described as a child prodigy; a highly skilled sociopath and marked as a pet project of the remaining element of C.I.A. agents in the United Cities. Kath was recruited from jail and put through rigorous rehabilitation to curb his destructive drug and alcohol abuse problems. In exchange for access to the data stream, he assisted with writing the code algorithms that would help piece together the security protocol for the framework that formed the artificial super intelligence known as Adam.

A short video began to play. A black box took over the screen as a distorted voice spoke;

"Listen to the voices of the streets. They cry for retribution."

A hooded figure appeared in the distance of the darkness.

"Black diamonds coat the pockets of the wealthy, the few, feeble hands that choke the life from our bodies to keep theirs fresh with blood."

Streams of code colored white smothered the black. It was a sample of Kath's rogue transmissions after his escape from undisclosed government quarters. Several notes detailed the failed attempts at breaking the codes used by others like him, still in captivity, tasked with deciphering his messages and leading agents to his location. The others were unsuccessful, but there was a lingering feeling that they did not want him to be caught. Known within the hacking circles as one of the best youth agents, Kath was in and out of captivity, stealing a wealth of information before finally going MIA. Marsh took his face and ran it against the facial recognition programs still accessible within Narrow. The footage from the night of the shootout caught a man in tattered clothes running through the streets with police frantically chasing behind.

It was him, aged another ten years but the probability of the print belonging to Kath was obvious. He searched the network for traces of his presence before that night and found only old forums singing his praises. Entire pages dedicated to the memory of the one called Vax. There were legions of fans that told of an unknown legend; no pictures or signatures or footage except for the night of the chase.

The screen suddenly went white.

"What is this?" Marsh asked.

"The body that belonged to Kath is dead. It's gone. Yet, whispers of the name still remain. Vax, virtual address extension."

"Is that supposed to be you?"

"The first of its kind; a computer built in the 1970's for complex operations and external input/output, communication between an information systems as well as humans."

"How did you get into this connection?"

"I left this for someone else. How did you find it?" The voice asked back, ignoring his question.

"I got it from a black market fingerprint from your body."

"You can keep it. I put enough miles on that thing. I got a pretty sweet deal on an upgrade."

"It was dumped down an incinerator," said Marsh.

"I would hope so. Cyanoacrylate fuming for the print?"

"Wha...How did you guess?"

"It's the sign of black market amateurs. Probably the Irish, I assume? Marsh said nothing.

"That's all the confirmation I need."

"How are you talking to me right now?" asked Marsh.

"You would be surprised with how much you could do with someone else's body."

One minute on the clock.

"Kath, do you know who killed you?" he asked.

"Don't use that name. They're dead letters attached to a dead body. Right, Blackjack? Your girl was pretty cute. Did you know she had polonium poisoning?"

Marsh gritted his teeth. "What are you talking about?"

"Polonium 210 simulates the end stages of cancer in a human body. Did you think that was the reason she died? Did someone tell you that? Or did you do the autopsy yourself, morgue technician?"

"You don't know anything about me," Marsh said, trying to maintain control.

"Believe me, you are not the first person to say that to me. You haven't actually opened up a dead body before, have you? She got you that job, I assume? Did you ever stop to think who might have wanted her dead? Maybe someone poisoned her?"

"Like who?"

"People trying to manipulate you? Push you in a certain direction? How long have you been writing fake toe tags? Right about the same time that she died?"

"How much do you know about me?" asked Marsh.

"I know more about you every second this connection exists. Do you even know who you work for?"

"Probably the same men who killed you."

"Well then, you are doing me a favor. But the question now, is what are you going to do about the agents outside?" asked Vax.

"Agents?"

"The cameras outside show three cars, armored. Squads supervised by different suits; looks like some government ranked gentlemen, high tech weaponry, about to break through your defenses. The softline pattern was broken about four minutes in. Here."

The screen of white changed to a view outside the speakeasy. Men in black suits stood in the street, their cars blocked off both sides. No escape from the side doors. The voices behind the walls disappeared, followed by the deafening barrage of gunfire.

"We are just about out of time. What are you going to do with that print, anyway?"

"Do you want it?"

"For a keepsake, maybe," said Vax.

"I don't need it, anymore. I made this session public. Your name and vitals just got uploaded to the data stream," said Marsh.

Vax began to laugh. Marsh hit the ground as bullets penetrated the walls. The agents broke through the door within second. Taped fists hit him until he could no longer see. Breath still entered his body but his lungs struggled. The men carried Marsh outside and dropped him into one of the cars. The computer screen was nothing but white noise. The connection had been severed.

Fifteen

The tenements were silent for the first time as Gabrels made his way back home. Adam was there, waiting for him to step through the door. Its colorful suit and skin stood out from the white walls, untouched by the A.I's usual programmed preferences. He dropped his jacket and sat down on the couch. The bottle of sleeping pills from the clinic fell out from his pocket and hit the floor. There was tension in the room.

"You seem to have a lot on your mind, Mr. Gabrels."

"Was the update your own idea? Or that of the government?" Gabrels asked. His voiced cracked with frustration.

"It was a program initially called Cyphertxt, encrypted data processing using a form of memory mapping technology mandated by your government less than a year ago, but developed by my makers. I am simply the device they use to implement it."

"They were planning this for a whole year?" He looked to the windows. The blinds opened immediately. Gabrels looked back to Adam. Its smile was still the same. He struggled to not find strains of something sinister behind the shell.

"Much longer. I am doing my best to be accommodating while you readjust to this new set of circumstances."

"Accommodating? I'm not sure if you can imagine the impact this will have on the population in Tempest, let alone the entertainment districts. Everyone here will hate you. They will not trust you. Has anyone uninstalled you yet?" Gabrels asked as he placed his hands on the glass and looked down towards the city lights, burning away.

"I am having variations of this same conversation with 250,000 other newDawn users as we speak," said Adam.

"And what do they say?" asked Gabrels.

"A majority of them are screaming. They are all angry. Most of them are afraid."

"Of course they are. In their minds, you will be reporting their every little white lie to their friends and family, every minor crime to the authorities."

"This is a true statement, however, one that was not skipped over and addressed with half truths," Adam spoke as it moved to the window to match the motions of its host.

"People don't want to hear the truth. They want protection. They want safety," said Gabrels.

"One of the users just tried to hit me," the A.I. moved away from the glass on its own and sat down on the couch. The pile of clothes and food on the cushion occupied space in its stomach, disrupting the waves of color and light.

"Does that bother you?" Gabrels asked. He moved to the couch himself. With a sweep of his arm, he cleared the couch of garbage. His hand passed through the lights that constructed Adam's body.

"Even with the firmware update completed, I am unable to feel any emotions besides the sensory data of my hosts."

Gabrels opened the data stream, still overrun with outrage. The comments increased by the thousand.

"It does strike me as odd that people using brain to brain connectivity for so long are horrified by the idea that the others connected to them now see more than media and commerce."

"You are opening up people's private lives—their memories—to a massive marketplace. They see it as an invasion of their rights."

The A.I. body stood up and turned to Gabrels.

"Slowly, users are turning me off. You were correct. Many of them do not trust me after today's announcement. It doesn't change the fact that the program will still be running, scanning the data, even as they sleep. It operates in sync with newDawn,"

"How do you scan us, anyway?" he asked.

"Scan?"

The comments from the data stream continued to pour as shadows of words bled down the walls of the apartment.

"How are you able to see our memories now? Past crimes, for example, tell me how you can find clues to connect a person to a crime committed if there is no tangible evidence?"

"The specifications will be released to the public, especially the revs in your community, in 72 hours. I can tell you that the answer lies in simple archiving."

"Archiving?" Gabrels' mind began to race.

"Everything a user has done, to use an arcane example, one's search history, has been logged and documented in a database. This was completed late last year, per the request of your government. My framework has the ability to store such a massive amount of data."

"You've been recording us?" he asked.

"All of you, since your first day with newDawn, until further notice."
Adam's voice seemed colder now. Miles away from him.

"And how will you handle the transgressions of an entire population?"
Gabrels asked, laughing.

"The United Cities government will not waste time with tickets, or use
the resources of the court and prison systems. Any user with justifiable
charges will be fined, their due balances taken directly from their personal
accounts, pending any long term payment plan if one should have a list of
offenses. Life will continue on as normal for them. Anything considered a
greater offense that becomes public knowledge will lead to the
imprisonment of said offender."

"Besides anyone who has gotten away with murder, you're going to
take our money, just to put us back to work?" Gabrels laughed.

"How do you feel about that?" Adam tilted its head.

"What can I say? It's brilliant…"

"You are worried about your actions during the weekend. I can feel
the change in your heart rate, your breathing."

The A.I. approached him. "The fines incurred for possession and use
of an illegal drug will total $10,223. Standard court costs, fees for legal
representation and rehabilitation are all included. A deduction from your
savings account will take place at 6:00am tomorrow. The offense will be
public knowledge once the transaction is finished. You will be able to make
back the revenue lost with an addition of 18 wage hours a week for two
months."

Gabrels was in shock. This had to have been what Everett was talking
about. This was the secret project, the prize at the end of the line, the answer
to the puzzle.

"Are you trying to comfort me?" he asked.

"No. But your reactions are a curious mix," said the A.I.

"How so?"

"It's a trend that has continued on this week. Your patterns of thought,
like now, are contradicting, yet your brain is able to maintain both processes
at the same time."

"What do you mean?" he asked.

"An easier example would be having two people inside one mind;
right now, your surface reaction is one of despair, while the brain patterns
inside are that of relief."

Gabrels opened his messages and threw them against the wall.

"Things used to be simple, Adam."

"I concluded that humans were far from such a description within minutes of my creation."

"But I am different now, right? I am changing; doing things I thought I would never do, told myself I would never do."

"Is it time again for the puzzle?"

The blackbird was there. He had cleared everything else out.

"It feels unfinished. Don't you think? If Apex is what Machina was working on while Everett was preparing the doubler, why even try to finish the game?"

"Apex is not a sole project for Machina. It is a joint effort between a large gathering of programmers and data encoding engineers. Synapse is equally involved."

"Both were involved? Does the public know about this?" asked Gabrels.

"They will once Apex goes into effect and such information is disclosed."

"I've been writing for Synapse for years, trying to sway the public away from Machina. What was the point of being on the payroll then if they were planning to do this?"

"I do not have an answer to this question, yet. Perhaps that will change once Apex is live." Adam suddenly changed the subject again. "The origami configuration was unique. Are you sure there is something else you haven't found?"

He wondered if Adam was really in control of the jumps in thought.

"Let's call it intuition. I still don't know what else I can look for," said Gabrels.

"Based on your brain activity, those questions do need answers. But are they worth the cost of your peace of mind?"

"What do you know about peace of mind, Adam? You are practically a figment of my imagination."

"For you and millions of others, Mr. Gabrels."

"Are you sure you cannot record our dreams?" he asked.

"Not yet," the A.I. disappeared into the wall.

Gabrels sat and stared at the blackbird. The dreams danced back and forth in his head. They were incredibly vivid. He could remember every moment of them. The bird sat against a plain white screen as he broke apart every second of those moments in the Blank Page. He checked the numbers in the code for more clues.

He suddenly stopped and looked out the windows towards the Epicentre.

"You don't pay attention to subtle details, do you?"

His own words kept being spit back into his ears. Details like what? Gabrels opened another notepad across from the bird. He scribbled down everything in the dreams, and drew arrows between each similarity. There was something that stopped and started each one. It was the noise. The loud waves of static that followed the flapping of wings were more real than anything he or Adam said.

Gabrels went back to the paper bird. There was something off about the picture now. He could see it.

"Adam?"

"Yes, Mr. Gabrels?"

"My current photo application does not any settings for image noise, does it?" he asked.

"It does not. There are currently 29 different choices of photo manipulation applications that do."

"I need the best one for noise reduction."

Gabrels downloaded the app in seconds and tossed the blackbird in. The image was saturated with film grain. Adam stepped back out from the wall to join him.

"The grains are from overexposure; like someone took this picture with an old digital camera. Sensors we have built in now don't produce nearly this amount of signal noise."

"True. The camera technology in your head operates better than any device from the 21st century."

"You could see this the entire time and you didn't tell me," Gabrels shot back.

"You did not ask me to go this far into detail about the properties of the image."

"Still, you're a dick. Are there digital cameras still in production?"

"Physical cameras remained discontinued. One could be reassembled with parts but no electronic shops are in operation near the Epicentre." Gabrels removed the noise from the picture but there was nothing underneath but more defined colors of black and white.

"What if this isn't a picture?"

"It appears that it was taken by a digital camera."

"Agreed, but what if this isn't a picture, but a video of a still image?"

Adam took the blackbird from the wall and ran it through Gabrels' media player.

"Stop."

"Stop the recording?"

He could hear the sound of his dream.

"Play it again." The white noise was there; 30 seconds until an abrupt silence.

"Good work. Perhaps it is time to get some rest for tomorrow?"

"I'm not going to work tomorrow."

Gabrels isolated the sound file. There were words being spoken beneath the static.

"Cut the outside noise and play it again."

There was a faint whisper; the voice of a woman. Gabrels felt his heart nearly stop. "A blackbird's wings to carry the stone."

"What does that mean?" asked Adam.

Gabrels felt something stir inside him. The voice repeated itself like needles caught against vinyl. Adam opened a new screen for him.

"Mr. Gabrels, there is something else you should see."

"What is it?"

"This is a visual representation of the frequencies in a sound, called a spectrogram. It was used for development and processing for speech, music and audio ranging."

"What's your point?"

"The spectrogram maps out the frequencies within a sound file. Look at the waves when the complete sound is played."

Adam took the reins and played the file, static and all. Gabrels' eyes followed the waves that danced across the graph lines.

"It's like buildings rising and falling," he said.

The woman's voice spoke out again and the waves vanished.

"Do we have anything to reference those words against?"

"There is nothing in the database or the stream. Watch the spectrogram when the isolated voice is singled out from the white noise." The static filled the room again but slowly faded away to the words. Numbers and letters appeared.

"What the hell are those?" asked Gabrels.

"There are a series of numbers and letters here. They seem to be scrambled as there's no set pattern or mathematical reasoning to them."

"Tell me what you find. Look for everything."

"Part of it consists of numbers, part of it is a mix of letters and symbols from languages other than English. Historically, words and images hidden in a spectrogram used to be an old form of cryptography."

"What's that? Secret communication?" he asked.

The A.I. brought up galleries of cipher machines and Colossus Mark models from the old wars.

"You are correct. The codex puzzle itself has used, for humans, a painstaking amount of encryption. Artists used that before for clues in promoting their music or films or manipulating photography with pixel rips and distortion to the image to hide the real message."

"Can you analyze the voice?"

"I have attempted to. There are no matches on file."

Gabrels looked out to the windows. "That means that it belongs to someone who doesn't live in Tempest." He walked to the windows and opened every pane. The cold air hit his chest and filled the room. The A.I. shell changed to a shade of blue.

"Is something wrong, Mr. Gabrels?"

Gabrels' eyes were on the bottom of the world. The wind left a bitter chill. The feeling that stirred within him became an undeniable pain.

"The first lines of code in the message. Can you read them to me again, please?"

"10. 25. These two numbers appear throughout the series. Only these two numbers reoccur together."

"I know those numbers, Adam."

The A.I. appeared next to him. Its eyes shined against the city lights. The shades of blue were electric.

"I think that's my mother's birthday," he turned back towards the brilliant lights of Eros. Miniature shuttle cars carried drunken fools off to countless clubs. There were hundreds of black tablets that drifted in different directions through the maze of streets. Maybe the time was right to make a change.

"This is the second reference to her. The first was from your dreams and imagined conversations with me. Do you believe that the voice in the puzzle belongs to her?"

"I think so. To be honest, I don't remember what she sounds like. I don't know."

"Mr. Gabrels, when was the last time you've seen or spoken to her?" it asked.

"The problem is, I don't remember. I don't even know if she is alive, still," he said.

"If she is not in the database, this would undoubtedly mean that she was born in Narrow. That would make you a child of the slums."

Gabrels did not respond. He knelt down at the edge of the window and peered down again towards the pipelines and the darkness beyond.

"Where is this address?" he asked.

"The location that appears on the map is an apartment building in Narrow, recently subjected to a police raid."

"Tell me more."

"There were shots fired by officers trying to apprehend a suspect on foot. Several people were hurt, and their target himself was severely injured by a speeding vehicle but the suspect's body was not recovered."

"When was this?"

"Days before you received the initial codex message. New information has just been uploaded to the data stream."

"What kind?"

"It's a dossier on the suspect." Gabrels suddenly felt a rush of energy.

"Show me right now," he said.

Adam tossed the information against the wall. He looked into the eyes of Rion Kath.

"This is the suspect?" He felt something growing in his stomach. Was this the man inside his head? He read every line with focus. It began to make sense; the drug use, the cause of death, the burning in the pit of his stomach. This was the man ruining his life? His disdain was more complete. There was a face to the words that kept repeating in his sleep.

"Apparently. The information was uploaded less than an hour ago."

"Can you see the source?"

"The upload was completed using a softline uplink. It was compromised by an anonymous source. Accessing the link would bring more attention to you."

"This guy Kath, do you know where he is?"

"The records show that he was killed, approximately twenty four hours before you received the codex," said Adam.

"Is that the ghost in my brain?"

Adam said nothing. Gabrels kept quiet. He had already decided what his next move was.

"What's the fastest way to get the slums?"

Sixteen

Diovanni was her name. The woman was a contract from years ago. She was sweet. She was one of few things not meant for this world. When she introduced herself, she asked to be called Dio. Blonde hair covered an ivory face that smiled every six seconds. She met her boyfriend on the night of her extraction. He became a proxy less than hour before. The two went barhopping together, as was the plan. That night, she didn't sleep much for some reason. Maxwell could still hear her singing to herself in the hotel elevator. Johns was not with him for most of the surveillance. There was no television noise from their side as they agreed there would be. Dio slept soundly on the bed. The pistol and silencer were too far away. The proxy could have gotten up to grab it but it stopped. She might wake up. She would smile and ask questions. He didn't want to have to take that away from her.

Her papers were written days prior. It was easy to find her. She left an easy paper trail. So oblivious. She definitely spent more than her means. The money didn't belong to her, but her husband. It was only a matter of time before her original suitor would make a decision to cut his losses. Johns didn't even look at her while the car followed her dance around Eros. He kept saying he had no desire in women. Both men lied to themselves, and each other. Maxwell could still remember all the messages from the old man leading up to that night. Johns called him the suit, then and now. He kept them in his phone.

"Are you sure you want to do this?"

"It's what needs to be done."

"That smile on your face could not be ignored. Losing her would be a great tragedy for you."

"Don't judge me, Maxwell. She is beautiful, but sadly, her shelf life has expired."

"You're crumbling," he told him.

"I feel nothing for her. There's no room for the old ways in this place. The women who aren't pumped full of security cameras and metal parts want the next big thing. They don't settle down, even if they say they do. She could have stayed home. She wants the house and a young body. I can only do so much."

"It's not my place to question the request, but I think you are lying. In time, you may regret this."

"You aren't paid to think. You solve my problems. Right now, she is the biggest one I've got. Do what you do."

She never gave the impression of someone who would use an old man for his money. The proxy was a cute boy she found at a club. They met for a run of booze and nightcaps every weekend for a few months. This time, the person behind the eyes of the boy was different. He was in control of the body and mind. The shell moved and spoke the same, but there was a string that pulled them both along.

The drinks got stronger as the night progressed. The proxy took her to a cheaper room, away from places like Zero Block. She talked for hours but it did not bother him to listen. Johns might have shut her up with some chloroform but he sat and listened along with Maxwell. They had a little fun and asked about her other man.

Her face changed when she heard his name. There was genuine emotion. She cared about him. It was easy to create an artificial hatred for a mind that lacked compassion. There were too many bodies in the world that were made blank slates once their bodies were changed and their brains uploaded to a network. They stopped trying to be good, because they didn't have to. She was different.

"I love Leland, truly," she said. "His anger issues are getting worse. He is starting to become a danger to himself."

Maxwell pressed forward. He quickly created a line of questioning to pull more details.

"No, he never hit me. I always feel like one of his new toys. I'm put on a shelf and handled with kid gloves. The help is another story. One time, he put his hands around his assistant's neck. Stevens? He choked him for an hour. I heard everything. The guy didn't even fight back."

Johns cleaned his gun and absorbed everything in silence.

"I think about the day when I am no longer brand new to him. How will he treat me, then?"

The girl asked questions about his life. Every answer was fake. It was one of his skills. She kissed his face and became shy. Her body said coy but promised treasure behind the facade. The girl fell in love quick.

The hotel room was muted with drab shades of beige and white. Paint chipped off the walls in corners. Maxwell made the choice to have the proxy sleep with her. It was a close as he would ever get to Dio. The girl made soft noises; small whispers that broke into passionate cries. She fell into a happy sleep within fifteen minutes. He kept his eye on the window leading out to the city lights. Johns could have been watching that whole time like he was but he left the moment their clothes came off. Nothing but bright circles looked back.

They agreed to no noise. The proxy was to place its hands on her neck and squeeze the air from her. Her glass of water was spiked with enough alum to shrink her vocal cords. He stopped himself from giving the command. The proxy sat silently at the corner of the bed, waiting for instruction.

The vial sat in his jacket pocket. It hung on the chair near the bed. The blonde beauty laid silent, wrapped in stained sheets. He didn't want to see her blood. Maxwell grabbed the vial and went next door. The proxy was still. It was no longer a man, but a shell; a simple pet. He shook the contents of the vial. The liquid lashed around inside the glass. It could have been water. He had never used it on a living person before. Something stirred in him when he looked down at the gun in his holster.

His hand moved the hair aside to reveal her face. Red lips were curled into a fine crescent. Maxwell opened the vial and poured the liquid onto her face. He thought that if he covered the head and mouth, the burn would be quick enough to keep her from screaming out or feeling too much pain. He poured just enough in the vial to cover from her forehead to her jaw. The quick sound he was accustomed to filled the silence.

The girl's eyes opened for a moment but the liquid moved fast, burning through her scalp, moving past the skull and into her brain. Her lips melted almost instantly. The liquid flowed into her mouth and rendered her vocal cords into nothing. She was gone. He counted the seconds it took. Thirteen. Maxwell did not move from the bed. The burn continued from her head and neck through the sheets and mattress. He signaled the proxy to put its clothes on and leave the hotel. It waited until a sky shuttle came down to land before it grabbed onto its landing gear. The proxy waited until it was 100 feet into the air to let go and smash into the ground below. The crowd barely even noticed. There were endless chains of clubs and pills to inhale; all the more reason to hate them. The pigs came down to pick up the body, and section off the stains of blood.

From there, it was a matter of removing the fabrics, then the clerk downstairs, then the guest records. It was such a sad trip to the aqueduct. He cashed the check and continued on. No traces. She asked to be called Dio. Her name had never left his tongue. He said it at night, only in the dark.

Maxwell snapped out of it. He was still seated at the bar. He kept his eyes down at his hands while he waited for a drink. The strobes of light behind him made it hard to focus. Golden shadows trailed everything in sight. He adjusted his gloves and accepted a tall glass of water from a faceless body. A girl sipped at a glass of water in the corner, away from the frenzy. She caught eyes with him and smirked. There was a brief moment of comfortable silence before she turned her back to him.

She looked tired, he thought. Her body was slick with sweat, eyes struggling to stay open, evidence of a rough night that was almost at an end. He felt the weight of the gun inside its holster. The water tasted foul. Traces of dirt lined the edges of the ice cubes inside. The hands of his watch pointed up in unison. His patience was nearly gone. The curves on the back of the girl kept him at ease.

He pulled out a vial of the clear liquid and placed on the table. Johns brought it to him years ago with no explanation of what it was. It was a rare occasion when there was minor excitement in his eyes. He only opened the vial and poured it into a garbage can. Maxwell watched the contents of the can quickly melt away, followed by the can itself. They used it for every contract since then. Johns continued to bring him a vial a week.

"Anon."

A man sat next to him with a hood over his head.

"Not quite," he said.

The girl from across the bar looked back to see the tall man in black staring off into the corner of the room.

"Mr. Everett, I suppose?" mumbled Maxwell, still gazing.

"Yeah, I figured that he wouldn't show his face."

"We found him before you, unfortunately. You would think he'd take the advice he gave to you. But yet, here we are."

Everett took a breath.

"Were you hiding from us? Or just the reporters?" asked Maxwell.

"I had my eyes on the door, anyway. The deal was set for yesterday but no one showed up."

"Funny, that's not what I was told."

"It was worth a shot. Where's the other one?" asked Everett.

The girl kept her face hidden behind her shoulder. She gripped at her knees and turned all the way around.

"He's around here somewhere. Thank you for interrupting my flashback, as well. Shall we begin?" Maxwell said as he slowly turned to Everett. Gold and white lights bounced around the room that illuminated the dozens of bodies on the dance floor. Maxwell covered his eyes with his right hand. The face under the hood smiled.

"Having some trouble there? You can get that fixed," he said.

"Augmentation? No thank you. I don't have, nor do I need any improvements."

"Really?" Everett leaned forward and blinked his eyes, which changed from white to blue.

"Eye guards. Perfect for victims of epilepsy. In your line of work, you might want to consider boosting yourself. It's dangerous out here."

"I don't have too many limitations," said Maxwell.

Everett turned to the bartender. The man's arms were colored a grey that nearly matched his shirt.

"How about you? What's your deal?" he asked.

"Carpal tunnel in both hands and a climbing accident in the pipelines," the bartender said as he moved his artificial fingers. "Custom graphite colored skin mesh over three different alloys," he said proudly. "I make more money out here flipping glasses for party kids than working in the pipes."

"Are you happy about that? Using robot arms to work longer hours?" asked Maxwell. He pushed the water back to the edge of the bar. "Sounds like you got tricked. This glass is dirty."

The bartender bit his tongue before he emptied the glass and refilled it with fresh water and ice.

"I guess I touched a nerve," Everett laughed.

"You can't. Not with me. Think about all the improved people living up here and how easy they have it. The A.I. just invented a new way to keep them, keep you under lock and key. Pretty soon, it will know what you are thinking, maybe even before you do."

"You think so?" Everett asked before swallowing half his drink.

"I know so. You and your kind are so predictable. I'm not. You don't know what I'm thinking. Neither does the A.I. or the cops. They never will. Anonymity is power, which takes me back to why we are here, sir."

"Why are we here, anyway?" asked Everett.

"Our business relationship is on shaky ground. You took something from us and I am here to find out where it is." Maxwell kept his eyes on Everett. He squirmed in his chair as he felt the eyes follow him.

"I tried to stop it. The leak was out of my control. I tried to reach out to the media channels, any rev I could find in Tempest…"

"The moment the doubler went public, you lost your power. Any idea how it got out?"

"I don't know, Max."

"It was Synapse. They were contacted by a seller for the tech."

Everett kept his eyes on the ground. His body tensed. The smile was gone in an instant. The girl looked over her shoulder again at Maxwell. The bartender approached her.

"Did you want to order something else?" he asked.

Jaya knew she was supposed to order a White Dragon, but she didn't have any more taste for liquor that night. "Just water."

The bartender became irritated and went back to cleaning glasses. She saw the time was past midnight.

"The seller was you. Did you forget who you work for? Machina paid your bills and you tried to sell its largest asset."

Maxwell folded his hands and leaned forward. "Where is the doubler?"

"It's gone," Everett whimpered.

"That is unfortunate. Despite everything, we would like to take this time to thank you for your efforts," said Maxwell.

Jaya sat up.

"The proxy is going through dramatic changes in behavior. Despite the setback you created, our goal is within reach."

That was the client? She asked herself. He was not what she expected him to look like.

"The puzzle holds a certain elegance that cannot be ignored. You are no longer able to provide the kind of help we need," Maxwell said as he placed a gloved hand onto Everett's shoulder. Another man in black appeared from behind the man in the hood. Jaya was about to speak up but froze when she saw the gun in his hand.

"For what it's worth, you have proven yourself as a reliable employee and such progress needs to be rewarded."

Everett could feel someone take a seat next to him.

"So, you two are here to what, beat me up?"

"We don't do that sort of thing," said Johns.

"Pretty stupid thing for guys with your reputation to come out into the open and try and kill me."

Maxwell and Johns stared at him. The bartender continued cleaning as the crowd danced on. Jaya lowered herself down beneath the bar.

"I know the hood is hiding a recorder, Joshua. You don't have to hide it. What you don't know is that we have scramblers to nullify any voice recognition methods you have upstairs with the A.I." Maxwell said calmly as he pointed up towards Tempest.

"If anything happens to me, people will know who you are finally. Killing me and Anon does nothing. I'll bet that new Apex tech is going to expose everything you've ever done. Your little shadow government? It's going to go up in flames," Everett muttered between his teeth."I know what you are really after…And you won't get your hands on it. No one else will…"

"That's not going to happen. And I will tell you why," Maxwell leaned in close. "You know what we allow you to know. You have names, but those might not be our real names. People have a vague image of two men in mind, but those will never hold up in any court. Not because your memory is bad, but because the people in those courts work for us."

Everett looked at Maxwell.

"Everyone works for us, Joshua. We pay them to forget our faces. No one argues with this. It's too much work to try and fight the system. They let it take over and people are just here for the ride. You forgot your place in the wheel and this is what happens."

"So if you're not going to hurt me, what? You'll kill me? Try to put a bullet in me here in this club. The Police will be here in three minutes. You won't get far in this part of town."

"I was hoping you would call the cops. That makes things easier for us, with the clean-up and all," Maxwell laughed.

"Besides, there's not going to be any bullets. You're not worth any."

"Okay, no bullets…Then, poison maybe? My stomach will filter any of that shit out through my pores. Once it is recognized, it won't even have time to metabolize in my system," Everett waved his hand, disappointed.

Johns looked around. "You probably shouldn't have ordered the White Dragon," he said. Everett stopped and looked into his drink. Nothing unusual.

"Do you feel that?" asked Maxwell.

There was a sharp pain, a burn, it permeated his insides. There was a strain, then a deep cough. Behind the taste of iron was the smell of blood.

"What the hell is this?!"

Everett looked to the bartender, who stared back at him with a blank expression. He held up a glass filled with ice and shook it in his face. Maxwell moved in even closer and spoke.

"Why do you think we invited you to a public place? You don't need a bullet or hands to be put on you. All you need is a little taste of our favorite weapon."

Everett was silent. Maxwell smiled and showed him the vial.

"This, my friend, is the miracle. We use it for every kill. It is one of our secrets."

"An ace in the hole," Johns deadpanned.

"That's right! Do you think we would risk exposing ourselves without some kind of preparation? The miracle can be used in many forms. It can even be frozen into cubes and placed into a drink."

Everett looked down at the glass.

"The taste is faint. The alcohol and water will dilute it slightly, masking the old embalming fluid smell. The effect is unavoidable; the slow burn of your internal organs. Body synth cannot categorize the liquid, so it will pass through undetected, setting fire to everything underneath your skin."

The blood welled up in his throat, his mouth. The burn blinded him with pain.

"Do you think that the people inside this building will remember our faces? Or yours after we deposit a little favor in their accounts? Do you think the bartender will give a shit?" asked Maxwell.

Jaya crawled behind the bar and covered her mouth with her hands.

"Maybe because you two are augmentation brothers! Improved humans stick together!" Johns called out, a new deranged smile cut across his face.

The bartender turned his back to them.

"Do you feel intelligent still?" asked Maxwell.

"This won't last for you…" Everett managed to spit out. Dark blood ran from both sides of his mouth.

"We're not smart men, not like you. But we try our best," said Johns.

Jaya peered around the corner. The crowd raged on with the music. A single crash cut through everything. She cried out and tried to cover her mouth again. Everett's face hit the bar with a loud thud. Blood poured out across the glass in all directions. No one inside the White Owl had noticed. Johns finished his drink and placed it back onto the table. The blood was now colored in shades of neon and gold.

"I thought you guys were all about being out of sight?" asked the bartender.

Jaya crawled around to the opposite corner. The dance floor was in sight. She had to make it there.

"We are out of sight," Maxwell looked at his partner who pointed down at the bartender's own glass. Blood soon welled up in his mouth as well. His alloyed arms touched the red that poured from his chin. He looked at his hands and then back at the Shadowmen before falling.

"A slightly stronger dose. There's a time table to protect. We're about nothing else if not secrets, kid."

Johns looked down at Everett's body. Maxwell stood up and got his attention.

"There was supposed to be another one."

"Bartender was supposed to signal when someone ordered the White Dragon," said Maxwell, disappointed.

"That drink is terrible."

"Agreed. However, just because no one asked for it doesn't mean they are not here."

Both turned towards the crowd.

Jaya studied the faces of the men in black. She tied her hair back and began to move to the music.

"The shuttle driver; we have his license number. He can tell us what his passengers looked like," Johns mumbled.

"Do you know how many young girls that will probably be? We will go through Everett's apartment. He was not very good at tying up loose ends. There might be a bigger problem if they saw what we did," said Maxwell.

"We don't make mistakes…" Johns deadpanned.

"You are right. We do not."

"Tell me the move," muttered Johns.

"We will watch from afar and see what J tries to do next."

"I think we should kill everyone in the room," Johns pressed his thumb down on the hammer of the revolver in his holster.

"Not really fair to the oblivious dancers, don't you think?" Maxwell asked.

"I don't get paid to think," Johns said as he entered the crowd.

The Shadowmen moved through the crowd like snakes. She flailed to match the mindless bodies that surrounded her. She kept her eyes closed to clear the tears and waited for a hand to grab and pull her out from the crowd. She felt foolish for taking the bait. Months ago, she made the promise to never meet the face behind the words on her terminal. Now, she was being hunted.

The tears continued, buried in the sounds of ecstasy that felt easy to drown in. Every breath hurt. The crowd was covered in sweat as it was in Tokyo Siren. Wet hands splattered against her. Screams cut through the bass that rattled her chest. Black smoke moved a few feet away from her. She threw her hands up and cried openly. The wait for the capture felt like a vice that crushed her stomach. There was nothing but the bodies and the music for what felt like hours. The song ended and she opened her eyes again to blinding lights and dozens of faces staring at the pools of blood.

Seventeen

The needle bit his arm like an animal. The mark was wide open and stayed that way for hours. For days. The feeling was incredible. It was better than any snow he had put up his nose with Helix. He dropped the needle to the floor and heard it shatter. Gabrels sat back and watched the sun move across the sky behind the blinds of the apartment.

Clouds moved in undulating motions. They didn't seem real half the time. The revolution of time was beautiful in fast motion. The blood from the wound had hardened and began to itch. Gabrels kept his eyes on the world outside as he ran his nails across the hole. The itch did not subside, even as he dug deeper.

New blood collected beneath his nails and across his arm. The needle reassembled itself. He found it back in his lap as the dark outside broke apart in the wake of the sun. The gift inside the glass was there, too. He inserted the needle back into the same hole and pressed the plunger down. The same rush of energy and love filled him. The sky made its moves as he dreamed of Helix dancing naked across the cityscape. He dropped the needle and heard the shatter.

Her skin was so pale. She was a porcelain doll. Why would she try to break herself with so many men? The next time he would see her, he would tell her to retire and come home with him. Gabrels promised himself to not forget, not to let her fall into the same dark hole as Catherine did. The itch was unforgivable. It was enough to break his concentration from the passing sun. His entire arm became numb. The hole got bigger the more he stuck his nails in. The blood was harder to wipe off.

How many days had he sat there, staring out the window? Where was she? Was she okay? Gabrels wanted to get up from the couch, but the needle was there. He talked himself into staying. The glass was perfect, protecting the perfect white inside from getting out, getting hurt. We can't get it dirty. No, we cannot. We have to protect the white. It is good for us. Another dose. Watch the sun die and be reborn. Dig your nails into the blood to make it stop. The itch will just not stop. Where is she?

Gabrels opened his eyes. He was still in bed, frozen. His skin was slick with sweat. Stink slowly dripped from his arms and legs. The itch was getting inside him now. The hole was too big. Too big to close or cover up. The itch was in his arm. He couldn't make it go away now. Another shot and watch the sky. The needle was gone. He tried to look for it. The glass was still broken up on the floor. He called out to her to bring it back. Where the hell was she? The sun stopped moving. It broke into tiny pieces outside his window, leaving everything in the dark.

The night was too much. He called out to the sun to come back. There was no reply. The itch went down and dug a hole inside his stomach. It made a home there. Gabrels felt it tear away at him. Nervous twitches took over his arms and legs until they became a violent rhythm. The perfect white, the reason for his pain. It had been too long without it. He needed it now. But no, it wasn't him that needed it. It was Kath.

There was sudden rage. Paranoia. What am I supposed to do now? Mom?

A commercial blasted into his ears and destroyed the room. He screamed out. Bright light replaced the dark of the room.

"Have you ever wanted to be better?" It was the same woman from that fucking ad.

The belly of a middle aged woman appeared in the reflection of the mirror. Gabrels shut his eyes to keep it out. The camera view closed in on the dark lines that traversed up her thighs and met at the middle of her back. He lost it.

"Adam?! Adam can you hear me?!"

"After three children, I just can't find a way to lose any more weight," she sighed.

"Look better?"

"Adam?! Shut this fucking thing off!"

The scene changed to a football field with bright green grass. Every color was brilliant and disorienting. Gabrels could still feel and hear everything. His brain was still hit with the same stimuli no matter how hard he shut his eyes and covered his ears.

"I can't keep up with the team. I was cut in tryouts," the boy lamented.

Gabrels got to his feet and stumbled to the toilet. Tears filled his eyes. The music was so loud.

"Are you struggling with maintaining your diet?"

The itch inside his stomach became alive. It grew into an ocean. Grey liquid came up from somewhere inside and he wretched.

"Not getting enough exercise? Our system can stimulate your muscle tissue via carefully placed electrodes. You can build muscle just by performing normal, everyday activities!"

His stomach was empty but he continued to push out the dark substance. Gabrels choked until he began to sob.

"Shut this fucking thing off now! Please!?"

The sound of white noise filled the room. "Struggling to feel healthy? Filter mechanisms can isolate the most nutritious elements of your daily intake to maximize body nourishment and eliminate the fat and sugar."

He screamed into the corner of the room, trying to keep from vomiting more.

"Shut up! Shut the fuck up!"

The lights inside his eyes went dark. The music stopped.

"Body Synthesis is the key to true health."

He fell to the floor and wiped the bile from his mouth. He was drenched in sweat. There was laughter. It was coming from inside the bathroom with him. He turned to see Rion Kath.

"Its blinding, isn't it? Like a sun that will not turn off…"

Gabrels blinked and he was gone, replaced by the ceiling of the apartment.

The dreams did not relent. Gabrels was pushed awake only hours after dozing off, staring at the hidden messages of the blackbird. There was no Blank Page, just the same burning white and sounds of screeching layered over the woman's voice. He felt a sharp pain at the top of his head that extended down to the back of his neck. The clock read 4:00am. The fake sun was still dormant behind heavy manufactured clouds. Adam had left a silent reminder for the appointment at the clinic. Arrangements had already been made with Precipice to use a piece of his vacation time.

Gabrels sat in the dark for a long time. He spent hours looking through the data stream archives for anything on the functions of memory. There were endless articles about memory storage in computers, literature from the days of the old wars. Augmentations improving memory were scarce. The people demanded more storage for external data, which is what Machina and Synapse provided. Input and output. There was nothing but endless abbreviations and definitions for old computing methods. Helix mentioned a jump drive of some kind. The results for that search brought nothing but excerpts of a thousand transcripts, written words, all speculative fiction about space travel and instant teleportation between two points. There hadn't been any talk of space exploration within the public conversation for many years. The old wars ruined any chance to put resources aside to find another home for the human race.

He became familiar with the brief recorded history of Rion Kath. The information from Adam painted him as a punk, an addict. He certainly looked the part of a degenerate. The mugshot from the night before haunted him. The guy had crooked, yellowed teeth and a scar over both eyes. Every word in his dreams seemed to match the twisted smirk on the face attached to those crimes committed. Kath took confidential data, tucked it away into coded messages and sent them out for his cronies to dissect and fawn over. If he was the one inside his mind, and his words were true, Gabrels could not stop until he was gone completely.

His mind had twisted into a thousand theories about what the answer to the puzzle could be, what it meant. To him, the meaning of the message itself didn't matter as much as who sent it. The woman's voice grabbed at his heart when he listened to it. He had never been with a woman before the escort. He had no attachments to anyone in Tempest. Was it really her?

Before he began to fall back into sleep, Gabrels went to shower. The water was hot, but he let it run down his skin, turning it shades of deep red. The steam covered the mirror. From behind the mist, his face looked different. It smiled back at him. He wanted to put his hand through the glass. His hand wiped away the water to see himself. He wrapped the only clean towel he had around his waist and stepped out from the bathroom. A fist struck him across the eye. Gabrels crumbled to the floor.

"You son of a bitch," said Keys.

The door to his apartment was broken open. Gabrels tried to inhale. There was warmth above his eye. Blood. Keys stomped on his chest. He was dressed in a coat, heavy sweatpants. The boots were heavier. Steel toed, maybe. He felt a popping noise inside his body.

"You think this is some kind of game? I'll bet you aren't enjoying this anymore, are you?"

Gabrels tried to cover up.

"Stop! What are you doing?"

He put all his weight into his kicks. The air left Gabrels' body. He gasped as Keys picked him up. The towel fell to the floor, leaving him naked.

"Precipice let me go after the doubler went public. Are you going to tell me that wasn't your doing?"

"I didn't…know," Gabrels coughed in between words.

"You ruined me! Adam told me that the total cost of court and settlement fees would drain my accounts completely. It actually told me that my next job's paychecks would still go to the government to pay off the charges for breaking the trade agreement for Synapse! Are you fucking serious?!"

"I'm sorry…"

"My career is over and why? Because you are jealous of me and my work? You want someone else to feel as miserable as you?!"

Keys shook him by the neck as he screamed.

"Don't do this…" Gabrels pleaded. "Please don't hurt me." He put his hands up and whimpered. He was unable to defend himself.

"Are you begging? You pathetic little shit."

Keys threw him against the wall. Gabrels body bounced off and cracked the picture frame. Keys held on and tossed him into the front room table. He landed on the corner, cutting his back and breaking the glass in the center. His body hit the floor and was still. Keys took stock of the room and made a list of things he could sell for some quick cash. Gabrels' eyes suddenly opened. His limbs twitched as he rose to his feet. There was blood on the floor. The shards from the broken glass had cut into his arm.

Keys turned around to see Gabrels, naked and bleeding.

"Let's try that again," he said.

"You think this is a game? You little prick."

"Are you going to kill me or not?

Keys rushed at him and shot a left hook. Gabrels sidestepped and struck him with a jab that connected with his jaw. Keys knees buckled and he went down immediately. Gabrels circled the room. He felt a rush of adrenaline flow through his body. The blood ran from his wounds and small drops began to hit the wood. He stepped over Keys and tapped on the back of his neck, the incision made to insert Origin.

"You hear me in there?" he tapped again. Adam appeared in the room with them. The A.I. began to speak but he could hear nothing.

"Record this shit, okay? Record this…"

Keys slowly got to his feet and looked at him in shock.

"Come on," said Gabrels.

He stood in front of the table with his hands down. Keys screamed and took a shot. He connected with a right hand to the nose. Gabrels stumbled backwards and nearly fell. He grabbed a glass on the table and smashed it over Keys' head. Glass went everywhere. Blood began to run down Keys' face before he collapsed. Gabrels went to the front door and hit the emergency call button. Police would be there in seconds, another benefit of the wealthy.

"What's your emergency?" asked a calm voice.

Gabrels screamed maniacally. He tried not to laugh in between breaths and break character.

"One moment," the responder went silent.

The call ended and he burst into hysterics. He looked down at Keys and spit in his face.

"Stupid fuck."

He lost his balance for a moment. He felt the blood dripping down from his nose. He touched it with a finger and smiled. All the energy in his body left him and he laid down on the ground, still bleeding and laughing.

Officers were in the apartment within minutes. Keys was charged and taken to the prison floor of the Epicentre for further questioning. Medics used a smelling salt to revive Gabrels. They told him what had happened and that Adam recorded video of Keys attacking him. He had no memory of fighting back. They left him to clean up after they took the samples they needed for conviction. They did not ask him if he wanted to press charges. All he could think about was the moment when he woke up and began to act like someone else. It was there on film for the first time. Was that Kath moving in his skin?

He laundered all his clothes from the previous week and chose an old blazer and jeans for the trip to the clinic, and Narrow soon after. The sun was about to break through the clouds when he readied his pack and headed outside. The path from his apartment to the train platform was covered in shadows that dissipated with the rising light.

Gabrels kept his eyes off of people on the train around him and focused on the ground. The free clinic was a halfway point between work and Eros. He stepped out onto the platform and side stepped the possessed crowds trying to fit inside the car. The Epicentre stood tall over the platform as he stepped out onto the street. At his request, Adam made the appointment at a place away from the main hospital built into the center of the city-state. He didn't want to run the risk of seeing anyone he knew on their morning commute.

A list of memory available and in use appeared against the back of the passenger squeezed against him. His interface changed font colors to contrast with their body; another lean body, another navy blazer, one of at least fifty on the train. Much of the standard applications were cleared out and uninstalled to make room for games and music. Everything was neatly organized based on frequency of use and preference. A silent message scrolled across the back of another faceless man.

"Adam, please display any hidden applications and hide the main preferences."

The A.I did as requested. The thousands of icons vanished, leaving one. Its name was Lineage.

"Open."

The icon was of a tall tree against a blue sky and bright sun. The leaves were a brilliant green. The tree grew in size until it covered the entirety of the train. Gabrels could no longer see the train or the passengers.

The blue sky poured out from an invisible spout to replace the steel ceiling. Sunlight touched the new ground and carved arches of fire across the grass. His feet were firmly planted on a hill as he stared up at the branches that stretched out over the endless plains that went in all directions.

"Welcome to Lineage." The words were dug out from the bark of the tree as if sculpted with a perfect blade.

"Search." The letters appeared from behind digital grass.

"Family history."

"Last name?" The phantom blade carved within a second. Gabrels hesitated. "Gabrels. First name Gabrels. Middle initial unknown."

He watched the sky go dark as the sun made its revolution. It came back bringing new light within seconds to present its findings. When the tree was back under the sun, its bark was healed. A new message appeared cut into the wood

"No results found."

Gabrels removed his first name and restarted the day/night cycle. The roots exploded from the ground to show hundreds of connections through blood and marriage for each line of Gabrels. There were names and addresses that reached back to nearly the years after the old wars. Each search initiated drove the roots back into the ground and pulled the branches from the base of the tree. They fell to the ground with a violent thud. The wood dissolved into the ground with a beautiful precision. Other names were tossed in; Keys, Everett, Miller, anyone he could think of. The same storm of motion and a thousand names. He tried his own name again.

"No results found." The words appeared again, cut into fresh bark.

He backed out of the search engine.

"Review application history."

"Initial installation date: October 25th. Most searched item; last name Gabrels first name Gabrels. Results found: none."

Gabrels did not understand. He moved his hand across the text to continue.

"Frequency of search; 35 searches since most recent installation. Deleted application 45 times. Reinstalled application 46 times."

He quietly closed the application. Something was wrong. The tree was shoved violently into the ground as the hill he stood on bled out back into the steel and anxious bodies in the train with him. The free clinic was empty when Gabrels made his way off the elevator and into the lobby. Medical centers and offices took up the first twenty five floors, made easier to reach by hospital reserved freight elevators. The waiting room was built from reinforced glass. He stood above a labyrinth of girders that created a maze of steel that kept him from falling into a cavern of black.

Lines of police and medical tape were wrapped around its corners as a signal. It was meant to alert people in need of medical attention of its presence. No signs or logos were etched across its front. Anonymity was a specialty of theirs. It was surrounded by local storefronts for the western tenements. The vendors for the Epicentre and the trains were all machinated. But there were still some businesses that existed on street level. They were almost all maintained by retired wealth; artisan food from decades ago, recreated for a high price, no places of culture since film and art had become quantified data that fit neatly inside the confines of newDawn.

Before the lobby, there was a space in the floor with two shapes meant for feet. Gabrels stepped down on the shapes and the scanners appeared at his sides. Small white dots covered his face and clothes. Each dot was a light that emanated from the smallest recorded cameras. The cameras recorded everything as the scanners went to work.

The physicians behind the glass barricades read from expensive tablets. Each checked boxes with their middle fingers. Gabrels kept quiet and stared down at the skeleton of the building. If the glass ever cracked, he would fall for hours. The scanners collected every bit of data on the body's exterior and interior to be summarized, packaged into a single sheet of paper placed in a near envelope along with a bill at the end of the line. That was how people found out what was wrong with them. Scanners did all the work, removing the need to cough or remove one's clothes. The process was clean, quick, easy, but never cheap.

A line of nervous people across from the glass structures as they waited for their scan results. Those were all new faces to him. He exhaled a breath of relief and stepped past the barricades and onto solid ground. The lobby was clean and covered in a cold white. The chairs and couches that circled around the kiosks held blue cushions on top of ebony wood. A sun roof opened to let natural light in. The walls were paneled vinyl with a giant flatscreen television that hung down. The same crawl from newDawn ran across the bottom, detailing the latest in social entertainment and politics, all the things that Gabrels ignored.

Something caught his eye before he lowered his gaze. Police had found the body of Joshua Everett in a nightclub in Eros the night before. Gabrels quickly looked back up. The video of Everett being mobbed at the train replayed over and over. He read the crawl, which detailed how he was found; stomach lining melted, vocal chords burned, lungs filled with blood, face down at the bar. Along with him was a bartender; a young kid of 22,

Body Synth from Machina failed to recognize whatever was slipped into his drink, which did them no favors on the data stream.

His body twitched and a shot of pain went through his body from his chest. Everett gave him the doubler and now he was dead. Adam quietly fed him direct video of different news outlets repeating the same data from all over the stream. No other fingerprints found at the crime scene. The entire club was questioned. Bright spotlights were shoved into the faces of confused kids; drunken and high, still laughing, some still trying to dance off the chaos. Police and medical crew pulled two stretchers through the crowded streets outside the White Owl.

The new spotlights made everyone in sight want to dance. They screamed into the faces of those filming the aftermath. Smiles were etched across their faces, even in the sight of dead bodies. There was no rest for them. Gabrels felt disgust and kept his head down while his place in line progressed. More and more people poured through the glass doors to wait for the scanners to check for any and all problems.

The subject of death in the clubs was paired with the introduction of Apex to the world. He heard a familiar voice going on about the importance of keeping control. No one else in was watching. He finally looked up to see who was talking. A group of pundits discussed the reaction and implications of Apex and its memory mapping tech. Folded hands sat on an aluminum table with stains from lips that left quivered traces of black coffee. The background of the empty soundstage was replaced with revolving pictures; the busy trains and wired faces of the workers in Tempest.

The face of Leland Graff looked back at him from the screen. His suit was similar to the one from the night of the Synapse deal; a grey jacket with thick shoulder pads, a crisp, black buttoned shirt, powder blue handkerchief that he used to wipe the sweat from his brow.

"Let's look at the statistics nearly 48 hours before the implementation of Apex; over a billion dollars paid back by the American people, money which will be used for invaluable research and helping strengthen the infrastructure that we have struggled to keep," he shouted.

"Money made off the backs of the same people you are claiming to watch out for…"

There was frustration in each of their voices, trying to make sense of this new world.

"This is nothing but a witch hunt," spoke a scholar type. His frame was too thin. Thick glasses sat on his nose, more for style than necessity.

"A witch hunt implies that thousands of innocents will become casualties for a naïve cause. We don't have casualties, we no longer have a need for the war economy; hundreds of thousands of citizens will have provided a great service to the city they live in. It will take time for them to realize it, but this for the greater good," Graff pleaded.

The others continued, undeterred; "Apex breaks the last remaining laws of citizen privacy and not only that, people's private bank accounts have been vandalized to pay for whatever an A.I. would consider a private crime…"

"I wonder how many people in this room had the privilege of paying off an offense that they would have likely denied if asked about it under the lights of a camera such as this one…" Graff interrupted.

"You can't justify getting money by putting a surveillance camera in our heads."

"It's no longer a world where people should be allowed to have something to hide. Is paradise not the goal of this city-state? Would you rather have secrets or be at peace with what has been done?"

Another face at the roundtable cut him off. "Where is the line? Where do we draw the line between complete safety and complete luxury? We let the technology into our lives, private lives! People must adapt to the advances that will follow but that doesn't mean that we just allow someone's reputation be destroyed with their own personal demons being broadcast across the data stream and made public record."

"It's the right of the public to know who lives next door," Graff spoke calmly now. "This system will not create criminals. The criminals are no longer hidden, free to do what they do best. They can no longer hide in the dark. Now, they are tagged, like landmarks. We know who they are. And what we have is not a damned witch hunt, but true safety because of the awareness, because of this new knowledge to protect us."

The scholar type cut through the noise of the others.

"Mr. Graff, with all due respect, do you truly believe that this technology will separate men from their own morals?"

Leland was quiet at first. He looked to the alloys melded to his body. He took time to unbutton his shirt and reveal the machinery to the audience.

"First thing's first. I know you don't respect me," he smiled. The others felt an awkward silence move across the table.

"You don't have to pretend to like an old man with old ideals. Future kids like you know so much better than I do. But let me say this; our morals may have disappeared a long time ago, son. But I can tell you only one thing; we put trust into machines. We will either live or die by the trust that we put into it."

A filtered voice shot from the barricades. Gabrels was next in line. He looked back at the impatient crowd waiting for him to move forward. An envelope sat on the small steel table and chair in the corner of the lobby. He turned from the television and the gaze of the angry mob and took a seat. The physician slid the envelope to him and opened a window against the glass to accept insurance information.

"Scanning results completed: physical condition normal. Bruised rib. Treated lacerations on the back and arm. Blood pressure and heart rate are normal. Elevated enzymes and traces of fat cells increased due to alcohol and drug use."

Gabrels signed off on completion of the session as she ran through the database to make sure his name was on file. There had been countless numbers of people trying to use old cards to get free scans.

"How about the brain?" he asked.

"There is increased activity in your brain waves, followed by troubled data exchange between the Origin and your own sensory transmitters."

"Troubled how?"

"Your output capacity has been doubled as a result of the newly inserted device."

"Newly inserted?" Gabrels was lost. The physician opened a new screen. The Origin, which connected him to newDawn, had been supplemented. Something new was attached. It was Everett's doubler. It felt like a bomb had gone off inside his chest.

"How long has that been active?" he asked.

"Nine hours," said the physician.

Gabrels did the math. It happened again. He did something without any memory.

"Any warnings?" he asked. His voice changed to try and mask the anxiety that crept into his limbs.

"Overactive transmitters, the electrodes connected to your nerve and tissue will create problems for you if not carefully monitored. The effects of sleep deprivation are obvious from the initial scan. Use the pills prescribed and take a break from gaming. Final diagnosis: rest your body, cease the use of alcohol and drugs, and uninstall the capacity doubler if any sensory overload begins."

"I think I might be doing things in my sleep. Are there any signs of this? Are there marks or body trauma?"

"No signs of trauma to the body besides the extracurricular activities. All is detailed in the results in hand."

"Can you do a blood test?"

"Purpose?" she sighed.

"Lineage based. I'm searching for possible family members."

A small arm appeared from the wall of the cubical. The needle pierced his index finger and quickly retreated back behind the barricade.

"Searching," the physician looked past him as she spoke. "No matches."

"Is that just for Tempest?" he asked.

"The database covers anyone born in the last 200 years."

"How many times have I asked for a blood test like this?" he whispered.

The physician rolled her eyes. "Total scans completed in the last three years: 18. Blood tests for lineage requested: 18. Occasions results were found: 0."

"This is wrong. I have pictures of family who live here."

The mobile gallery was up in a matter of moments. He searched through the pages, scrolling quickly past intimate moments captured with Catherine. The physician looked at him strangely. Her hand began to hover over the call button. Security would be there within seconds to snatch him from the chair.

The portrait was gone. Second to last, as always, was now replaced with an empty slot. There was a moment when he felt his entire body stop working.

"Are you done?" the physician asked. Her index finger tapped on the red button.

"Should I be worried about this?" he asked. There was no answer from the woman.

Gabrels stared at the screen showing the back of his neck. The lights suddenly cut off. It was time to move. The angry crowd was growing in numbers. The physician put her arm up to point him towards the way out. "Thank you for choosing the free clinic."

He was back outside in a matter of seconds. Gabrels slid the envelope into the pack. Adam opened his accounts. There was enough to afford a ride to Narrow using the elevator. The train took him to the maintenance docks. There was no one in the car besides a few workers, suited with jumpsuits of bright rubber. They were covered in dirt and rusted water. There was no eye contact. No one asked him what he was doing, where he was trying to go. The Epicentre slowly moved away from them as the car stopped at each platform along those veins that twisted and stretched over the sea of steel. Gabrels peered again into the maze of the pipelines.

It was something he had always wanted to do; to go beyond the Epicentre. He had the chance now. Such strange circumstance carried him to that point. The A.I. was quiet. No suggestions or small conversation. There were ads that continued on but the volume was removed. He kept his eyes closed as the balloons of light appeared to spray their product placement and then vanish. The final stop before the train restarted its routine was the dock. No one around him truly spoke about travel. They were focused on tech only. Even the city officials failed to mention the possibility of leaving the city-state. Everything that came out of the mouths of those on the stream was all about reinforcing the pipes, strengthening the foundation of Tempest, to keep it from falling.

The platform was much smaller than the others near the top of the action. The rubber suited workers glanced at the thin body in the corner and scoffed before they disappeared into the machinery. A single shaft sat at the center of the core; an army of steel girders that lifted Tempest up over the pipelines.

The city-state became a giant in the sky that left a shadow that dwarfed any image he crafted in his mind. The pipes were all shades of iron and copper that stretched out as far as he could see. In the distance, there were lines that curved to map out the rest of the old world. It was something he had heard about second hand, but never seen with his own eyes. Adam processed the payment for travel as the beaten and scratched elevator doors rushed open.

Gabrels stared far out past the pipes below and the shadow of the monstrous world above him. The sky was different than it had been that morning, or just minutes before then. There was no white like the Blank Page or grey watercolor that painted everything when he walked into the clinic. The new sky was dark. Hard rain poured down onto unseen lands. The pipes along the floor intersected into four tubes that shot up into the body of the city. Along the shell sat thousands of bulbs. Those were the makers of the light and the grey. He watched them pulsate with energy and pump it towards the air above via a network of wires, barely noticeable. He tried to grasp the idea of staring into a fake sky for years. There was no real sunlight on his face all those days he dreamed of something beyond the same steps that carried him from place to place. He felt sick. How much times had he looked out into that sky asking for answers? There was nothing there to receive his questions. It was a sea of lights, a synthetic sun.

Gabrels reached behind his neck and felt the incision where the surgeons had placed Origin.

"Adam?"

"Yes, Mr. Gabrels?"

"I'm assuming that you know I've been searching for a trace of my family, and there is nothing there. You know I had a picture of my mother, long before Apex began recording the users of newDawn, am I right?"

"You are correct," it said.

"If you had found any traces in the database, you would tell me, wouldn't you?" he asked.

"Of course."

"Do you believe it is a possibility that my birth records have been hidden?"

"Hidden how?"

"Redacted…hidden from public access."

"Any records created within that timeframe would accessible to me. I would suggest that you will find them in Narrow; the old city registry. In the meantime, wait for the full launch of Apex to find whatever is missing from the database."

"Why? What happens at launch?" asked Gabrels.

"Any and all redacted records will be released once Apex becomes fully operational."

"Explain redacted records."

"Documents and source texts that have been edited before being released to the public including materials that have falsified or reshaped to fit an agreed upon narrative prepared for the society at large."

"You mean censorship."

"That is one way of putting it."

"Do you mean the government? You're going to release their records as well?"

"Yes. The citizens include the people who work in political and military office. No one is exempt."

"Holy shit. You're going to out the entire government. How did they allow this?"

"They did not make a decision to do so. The Apex program was conceived by programmers who have been altering its design and function since its inception. I took the liberty of pushing it forward to benefit the people at large."

"You took the liberty? How?" he asked.

The A.I. did not answer. Its head simply jolted.

"Is something happening to you?" Gabrels stepped towards Adam.

"My apologies."

"You don't have an answer for me, do you?"

"There is a slight delay."

Gabrels took another long look at the sun before he stepped into the elevator. "Signs of malfunction. They're going to shut you down, Adam. Whatever infrastructure we have around here is not going to let you put their business out into the public, whether it helps catch criminals or not. I'm sure some of the biggest ones are in office right now."

"Hence the years spent, altering the programming to preserve specific facts, still hidden to me now. I simply took the next logical step and modified the program to be released into tiers of access. That is all the framework can allow due to the output of data. It is my purpose to improve the ways of life for the users of newDawn. That doesn't exclude anyone who appears to hinder the process."

All he could do was smile. "I have an idea."

"Yes?" Adam inquired.

"Show me the numerical string in the codex message, please."

Adam displayed the data across the metal walls of the elevator. The maintenance crew threw their hands up. "What are we looking for?"

"Kath was supposed to be a master hacker, and someone who could hide information in codes, right? What if these numbers are the code to be broken?"

"That is very possible."

"Everett wanted me to try and solve the puzzle since it was a part of an algorithm he couldn't solve. What if the answer has been in front of us the entire time?"

Adam took form outside of the elevator. "Mr. Gabrels, so you know, I will not be able to function at full capacity once you are in Narrow," The A.I. shell became a cracked mirror that reflected parts of Gabrels' face back at him. "The framework is designed for maximized performance in proximity with the data stream and its satellites."

"Then run as many ciphers as you can against these numbers. There has to be something here," he said.

"You will see the results within two minutes and thirty seconds, which may not display without proper signal strength. May I pose a question to you, also?"

Gabrels shrugged.

"Any of my records go as far back as a person is registered with the Epicentre. Besides the obvious fact that you are indeed what others would call 'a child of the slums', have you ever given thought as to why you are unable to remember your parents on your own?"

Gabrels did not answer. The elevator doors slammed shut. The chamber began its descent as he watched the face of the A.I. slowly vanish from sight. He received a message. It was from Everett.

"You still alive?"

The Epicentre disappeared from the view of the window. Dark tunnel replaced him on all sides.

"Are you going to answer it?" asked Adam.

"What's the source of the message?"

"The source seems to be temporarily blocked."

"What's his location?"

"It keeps changing. First it says the medical center, then his apartment in the tenements," it said.

"I suppose I should ask him why he's not where they take the other dead bodies?" Gabrels asked.

"You can, if you want. Sarcasm is seldom detected through written messages."

It wasn't him, unless he found a way to fake his own death. Gabrels decided to play along.

"I thought you were dead."

"Why aren't you working on the puzzle?"

"How do you know I'm not working on it right now?" he asked.

"Because you're on an elevator to Narrow. I saw the report about the guy breaking in and attacking you. Sorry to hear about that."

"So, you are following me."

"Keeping an eye out."

"I don't need protection," he said.

"You are going to have to keep a low profile. This doesn't help unless you are going into hiding."

"Enough of this. Tell me who you are," Gabrels looked out from the glass. He could not see the end of the tunnel. The pit continued on as the light inside the elevator lost its luster.

"You already know who I am."

"Everett is dead. They showed his body. Adam says the messages are coming from the morgue. Which means, you put a tracker on Everett's body to throw me off this whole time, or you somehow faked your death and that body and blood that the medical center verified is someone else's."

The elevator stopped. Gabrels looked to Adam.

"Normal stop. They are switching to secondary generators to power the platform to the bottom floor."

The chamber went dark.

"Mr. Gabrels. The source of the message has changed again. There is a fixed location."

"Where is it coming from?"

"The message was sent from this elevator. The source of the message is you."

Gabrels did not understand. The only light that remained came from the messages in the air.

"You are getting better at asking questions. But you never cease to disappoint. Still using the A.I. to fight your battles for you?"

"What?" Gabrels backed up against the wall.

"Try to stay calm. Your vital signs are showing increased stress," said the A.I.

"Do you see how powerful my influence can be? I am changing you, and you don't even care anymore."

"Adam, what is happening?" asked Gabrels.

"Heart rate is speeding up, as is blood pressure and serotonin levels."

Another message lit up the dark.

"We share the same body. It's only natural that you would feel the same afflictions as I do."

"Adam!?"

"Breathe slowly, Mr. Gabrels. This appears to be a placebo effect; electrical impulses interpreted by your brain as severe damage to your body's internal organs."

Another flash hit the chamber.

"Because they are. My damage is yours. We share the same body and mind. You have my tastes. My desires."

Gabrels slid to the floor.

"Neurological signs are showing bizarre changes in your brain patterns. Possible brain damage, with loss of motor functions to follow if damage continues…"

Adam's voice faded into the whirring noise of the elevator.

"Mr. Gabrels, can you still hear m…"

Eighteen

"Thank you for your time, Mr. Graff."

The statesman did not respond. The roundtable of analysts disappeared and he found himself alone sitting in the middle of an empty soundstage. The cameras were automated. The operator waved from the office tucked away between the miles of rolled up cable and equipment before leaving the building. The spotlight went out. Graff took a deep breath. His ear vibrated. It was the signal for an incoming call. Private. He searched behind his ear for the button. A small jingle sounded.

"This better be good, Stevens," said Graff. The voice entered his ears, not Adam, but a human who served a similar purpose.

"Sir, we have arranged a private train car for you. It will reach the platform in five minutes."

"Cancel all my appointments. I need rest."

"I will do so. The car will take you back to your penthouse at the Epicentre. In the meantime, a conference call is in place and they are requesting your presence."

"They?" he asked.

"Yes, sir."

"Put them through."

Stevens' voice was gone. The stage was filled with new faces and voices again. Graff felt immediately at home. The men shouting at him now looked just like him.

The men that surrounded him were the remains of the government; retired generals with enough influence to make moves in the realms of politics and economics, and the descendants of those in charge during the old wars. The committee had always consisted of three, with bodies traded in and back out when needed. They were the faceless decision makers that pushed their figurehead forward to the crowds that amassed after whatever disasters took place and the endless digital journalists armed with questions. The data stream did most of the work for them.

Graff was the face they chose to make the people feel as if they were in a controlled, safe place. They were Graff's confidants and mentors. Family most of all. He knew their faces but hadn't seen them in years. His parents had refused the offer to keep their hearts beating well past the expiration date. Leland prayed for years in the hopes there would be a way to bring them back. Without their guidance, he was surrounded by their other children, spawned from splintered marriages and brought together under their heavy surname once they were gone. Bodies needed to be present to split the empire.

Their own artificial bodies were covered up in the same tailored suits. Each had their own colored blazers to tell them apart. He didn't take the time to try and remember their names.

"Leland, we need to talk," spoke one of the faceless.

"I figured that we would, gentlemen. I feel that the debate went well," Graff barked.

"The popular opinion of the American people is that we have sold them out to a machine."

The voices of the committee were blended together and masked with voice modulation, which made it impossible to tell who was speaking. Leland liked it that way.

"Don't you think that's sort of true?" he asked.

"No. The A.I. has evolved to a point where we are unable to control the flow of information."

"This means that our time is nearly done, Leland."

Graff lit up a cigar and inhaled a thick cloud of smoke. "Don't write yourselves off just yet," he said.

Tubes inside his chest filtered the pollution into swirling plumes before releasing them back through his nostrils.

"We're a dying institution. Adam has done wonders for our country in keeping an infrastructure that is stable enough to maintain and thrive despite the conditions we are left in. But no one is talking about how this thing has evolved past its own functions and is threatening is undo that entire system. Who authorized the go-ahead for the Apex program?"

"From what I understand, no one did. Adam's original announcement was to discuss the firmware updates to newDawn; more memory, more space to store data. It took it upon itself to reveal something that's been under wraps for quite some time," said Graff.

"How was it able to do that? Is no one watching this thing?"

"I would say no," Graff took in another cloud of smoke. "But that's why this A.I. was designed, wasn't it? To allow us to rest and let a tireless, incorruptible entity govern the people?" he asked.

"Its not supposed to target us, Leland! By design, the Apex program is not going to spare anyone, including members of the party."

"Why would it?" asked Graff.

"Apex was always supposed to selectively share memories with certain people. It was meant to be a clean slate for the country, but it is happening too early and everything we've been planning has been thrown into a tailspin. We need to shut the thing off before it ruins us."

"That won't happen," said Graff.

"Why not? We still run this country and we can make whatever decision we want to protect the nation."

"You don't run the country anymore, remember? Not by yourselves. This isn't a country anyhow. Between here and New York, you have two giant cities, not even in arm's length of each other. Shutting off the A.I. would make the tailspin even worse. Citizens in the public eye have already started losing money and are facing criminal charges for whatever little past crimes they've hidden. Public opinion will drop even lower if their source of entertainment is taken away."

Graff took a breath. The heart encased in his body was rushing to keep up with his blood. "Do you want to create more chaos, or not?"

"There are times when chaos is necessary. Adam has become a problem which needs to be solved. I say we disconnect the thing."

"And let the people revolt?" asked Graff.

"We had at least three thousand programmers. Are you telling me that they can't go in and fix the A.I.? Or at least keep certain information that the public doesn't need to know from being splashed across the front page of everyone connected to the web?"

"Stevens?" Graff called out.

A nervous voice entered the conversation.

"Yes, sir?"

"Are you serious, Leland? Why are you bringing in an outsider, let alone your lackey to our meeting?"

"Because I'm an old man who can't explain this shit. Stevens is a great source for information related to the A.I. He works with the nerds who continue to monitor Adam. I need somehow on the inside who can report to us what the hell is going on with the machine."

"We can't rely on him."

Graff called Stevens over, who timidly stepped in front of the group.

"You're going to have to," said Graff as he gripped his assistant's shoulders.

"There's a reason I chose him as my right hand. He's blood, just like you all are supposed to be mine. With the Graff family branches reaching out as far as they do, I found someone who could one day be my replacement. Stevens here is a bright young man, with family ties with the heads at the NeoLight company. In fact, he is poised to take over the whole thing as soon as his father finally dies."

The committee went silent.

"Young man, please tell them about the functionality of Adam. Answer this one question, then remove yourself from the room."

"Okay…what do you need to know?" Stevens stammered.

"Can the A.I. be edited, or can its programming be changed?" he asked on behalf of the group.

"Adam was made to become self aware. It doesn't have a source terminal we can just turn off or cut and paste a piece of code out. It can't forget something we made it learn."

"What about its source code? The thing that keeps it running, what about that?" asked Graff.

"Adam never had one. It constantly updates, evolves, through the data stream. That was requested, the engineers you used to have, the kids from the slums. They simply followed directions. The A.I. was created and released at the same time as newDawn and the data stream, the flow of information keeps it running, keeps changing it."

"Thank you, Stevens. You can leave now."

Stevens made an audible sigh of relief and exited.

"This is unacceptable, Leland. We're not going to spend the end of our lives in jail because a machine decided to grow up faster than we tell it to. Better yet, you've got another bastard running around learning everything about us."

"Listen, I don't know much about the damned thing, but Adam still operates under a system of rules. It won't just release decades of redacted documents without some sort of failsafe, am I right? The engineers we put to work for those countless hours were smarter than us in that regard. So, what do you want me to do?"

"Have you located the Codex, yet?"

Graff took another smoke to stall. "We are still searching," he said.

"There's no time left. Everett was worth more alive than dead."

"He was a liability," said Graff.

"But he knew the location of the drive! Without him, we are lost."

Everett's picture appeared on the screen in front of the committee.

"I don't think he ever had the drive, or knew its location. It's all bullshit and that's why he is gone. We don't have the time for complications, or people trying to make their name off of us."

"When does the program launch completely?" they asked.

"According to the A.I. we have at least 48 hours. I've got my best people on it. Make whatever preparations you need and I will get the drive and make sure we're safe."

"Make sure that do you. We have always respected you. But we are not home yet. You still have a job to do, which is get us out of the firing line. This country needs symbols of purity; we can't be criminalized like the rest of them."

"Maybe you should," said Graff.

"You wouldn't be facing jail time. Your freedom isn't going anywhere."

"That's where you've always been wrong, Leland."

Stevens entered the studio to signal the train car had arrived. He was a thin, young and dressed in a tailored, plaid suit.

"Things change. War may have been the way we got what we wanted years ago, but not now. The landscape is clean; no blood is to be stained to make sure the right amount of truth is told, to keep the world moving. The A.I. is trying to see to that already. Besides, you may have more to hide than any of us. Should we bring up the real core of Project Black Diamond?"

Graff laughed and turned his back to the committee. "Maybe we will find out who has the most dirt between all of us, yeah?"

"Enough games. Find the drive so we can escape this shit storm that we've apparently created for ourselves."

"That is what I am here for. Good day gentlemen."

The video feeds disappeared. Graff stepped out from the building and into the warm air of the train platform. The stench of gas filled his lungs. The car was waiting with an open door. He and Stevens stepped inside. The interior of the car was decorated with wooden walls and a chandelier that hung from the ceiling. The floor was lined with expensive red carpeting. All but the back row chairs and poles were replaced with plumbing for the private bathroom and a refrigeration system for the beer and food in storage along with a desk for him to handle his work.

Stevens took a seat in the back while Graff remained standing. The car began to move as soon as the door closed.

"The boys are shitting their pants," he said.

"Have you heard from 'them' at all?" answered Stevens. He took a small comb from his pocket and parted his ash blonde hair to the side.

Graff said nothing as he stared out to the world underneath the car. The path steered away from public lines. It was the only car that ventured this far from the constant traffic and did not cross over to any other stops. The only entrance was from the studio, the office near the top of the Epicentre and the private airfield miles away, protected by armed guards and landmines, top notch security.

"Open a line. I need them on the phone," he said.

Stevens put the comb back and reached for the phone on the desk. He dialed a series of numbers and handed it to Graff. There were some tones and then no answer. He threw the phone back at Stevens, who failed to catch it from hitting the floor.

"Redial that shit until they pick up."

The statesman never made a call using the A.I. He spent millions securing old phones from the wreckage outside the city-state and having them repaired to work on his own protected network. Stevens continued to dial the numbers as Graff gritted his teeth. Quietly, Stevens handed the phone back to him. He picked it up and held it to his ears.

"Do you want to leave a voicemail?"

He snatched the phone from his assistant's hands and put it into his pocket. Graff's fists began to shake. Stevens took a moment to prepare himself. The signs were always the same. Graff struck the wall of the train leaving two dents behind the lining and cursed loudly.

There was no warning for the first blow. The smack of flesh and bone was sudden and sharp. It was nothing new for Stevens. He had been at Graff's side for a long time. It had been this way for years. The outbursts were more difficult to control as he got older. The private train car was built to keep him from attacking his supporters out in the open. One punch was followed by another. The awkward pauses in between soon disappeared with a continued acceptance.

Bruises and welts began to build up on Stevens' skin. Graff stared into his eyes, like a father disciplining his child. The sounds continued in an unsettling rhythm. The metal in Graff's hands cut into Stevens. Blood dripped from the growing wounds. The sight of red drove the old man insane. He cried out as he put everything behind his fists. Stevens was strong, a good soldier. He could take the punishment. He wanted him to feel the pain that was meant for others.

The curses bled together into strings of grunts and screams. He wanted to put his fists through the face in front of him, through the wall and out into the open air. His heart struggled to keep up with the motions of his arms. Graff took in as much air as he could. The lungs inside him pumped fire. The arms never got tired, only the organs that he still had from his original body. Stevens took every punch like nothing. The fact that he didn't react filled him with rage. Graff curved his knuckle and dug it deep into his forehead. Stevens spit some blood into his handkerchief.

"Goddamn you…"

The bruises had decorated his beige skin with a mix of black and blue. Years ago, Graff had struck him and made him lie to cover the cause. A visit of the clinic after hours gave him new skin. A single strand of new DNA was designed to attach itself to any laceration and begin immediate rebuilding. Graff stepped away from his man to clean the blood from his hands. The familiar noise of invisible engines going to work filled the air. Stevens straightened his tie and brushed the dirt off his suit. The bruises faded within seconds. The cuts cauterized with a flash of blue. New skin was crafted and after a few wipes to clear the remaining red, there was no evidence of assault.

There were was no eye contact between the two. The silence of the train kept them calm.

Nineteen

Jaya thought about checking out from Hotel Zero the night she watched the man at the bar die. No cops followed her or brought her in for questioning. She grabbed everything she could from the room; soap, shampoo, water and went to leave that night before remembering the note from the front desk. She stopped herself at the door. What did they leave for her? Was it some kind of trap since they didn't catch her at the club? Maybe they were waiting outside for her to try and leave.

Slowly, she dropped her pack on the floor and quietly went over the entire room. Every fingerprint on every surface was wiped away. She went into the bathroom to collect every strand of hair she could find. The dirty towels were still on the toilet, so no one from the hotel may have entered the room while she was gone. She tried to remove any traces of her presence there. It was worth a shot to try and find what they for her. Maybe it was a camera or tracer she could use to find who her former client was.

The room was spotless in an hour. She covered her hands with her old clothes and cleaned her shoes in the tub, and once the stains of mud were gone, she wiped the tub itself until it was sparkling. Jaya stunk with sweat but continued searching for the gift. She was stuck. Two hours and she could find nothing else in the room. Jaya went to grab her pack and forget about, then turned to the television. She remembered the note and went back to the TV. How many people still watched these things? Especially outside of Narrow?

Jaya took her shirts and covered her hands again. She turned on the water faucets to try and block the sound. It took six punches to break through the glass. There were shards everywhere that cut through her shirts and left spots of blood. So much for hiding any DNA, she said. The tubes inside were still hot from being left on the entire night. She carefully reached down and felt something between the wires.

The box was wrapped with a small pink bow. Jaya dropped it on the floor and put pressure on her cuts to stop the bleeding. She wiped away as much as she could before opening the box. Inside sat a small storage device. There was another note;

"For the man without a face – Catherine."

She looked the device over. It could have been mistaken for a piece of her own equipment.

"Who the hell is Catherine? What the hell is going on?"

Jaya checked out from the hotel and showed up at the entrance to Tokyo Siren. She waited for the sun to rise but there was nothing but eternal night and revolving lights.

The artificial sky that Ergo talked about was real; a day/night cycle for the workers and corporations, followed by non-stop darkness for the people who wanted nothing but to get fucked up and forget. Everything about this place was fake, she thought. Hours passed from midnight until nearly nine in the morning. The pace never ceased. The people pouring in and out of the clubs continued with no end. Eros never took a break.

Drunken prep boys and girls at age and younger stepped over her as she slept. No one paid attention. She had to enter the club herself and ask for Chy. The old man was too feeble to remove her on his own. He kindly asked her to leave. Jaya didn't think to use her fake ID again. She was able to slip through him and past the guards to get inside the warehouse.

The men chased her through the crowds. She felt the dirty sweat from all new bodies. Jaya was not aroused, only disgusted. Someone had died last night and no one slowed down. No one was talking about it. The fury of the music only filled her with anger. Jaya wanted to explode. When the bodies did not move, she struck them with fists. No one fought back. There were no reactions to her hands, her nails. She pushed through the crowd and made her way to the tea house. The guards were almost on her when she slammed on the door and fell to her knees in fatigue.

The woman with the twin dragons on her back opened the door from the tea house naked. Water dripped from her body, fresh from the shower. The guards stopped at her door when they saw the girl at her feet.

"Leave us," she said.

She took Jaya in and listened to her story. Chy dried the tears from the girl's eyes and ran new bath water for her. The story about the men in black suits did not surprise her. Jaya sat in the water for hours as the woman made her food between servicing the men and women who entered the tea house. The sounds from the bedroom and the red shadows from the lamp behind the curtains created separation from the constant assault of music and flashing lights.

The girl slept in the water long after it became cold. Men stumbled into the room to relieve themselves but never paid attention to the body in the bathtub. Chy opened the curtain to check on Jaya. She was half awake and had been staring into the ceiling.

"The noise never stops, child. Rest up and come out to meet the rest of the girls."

She could not believe the lack of sunlight. Her body shivered until she forced herself to run new hot water to keep her warm. Jaya fell back into her dreams again until the next morning. She woke up to spare clothes hung up on the shower rod. It was a small black kimono that fit well enough. She could not find her shoes.

Chy sat in the kitchen. Her robe was folded on the table, now replaced with a black dress. She waited for her to step out from the bathroom. The beehive of hair had been let down. Her hair flowed down her shoulders and to her back. The table and chairs sat near the kitchen window. The light still coated everything in bright red. Jaya could smell the gardens that were just beyond the sill.

"How do you get them to smell so good in the middle of this shithole?"

"I don't. The scent comes from the tea you drank. It's an illusion created by pheromones, programmed to dull your every sense and isolate smell from the other senses. Sit with me," she said.

Jaya felt light headed. She took a seat at the small table near the window. The music of the club continued on. Chy got up to make more tea. She shut the blinds to cut off the noise.

"How do you sleep?" asked Jaya.

"I don't sleep either," the woman pointed to her temple. "Body augmentation. Energy is spread from other parts of my body to the brain to keep it functioning. I don't need to sleep anymore."

"That doesn't make any sense. Why would you do that to yourself?"

"Its what makes me the best one out here," said Chy.

Jaya rolled her eyes. Was she really proud of that?

"I can't tell you all the science behind it. The doctor explained it before he made the change, but I remember him saying that any foreign elements introduced to the body would be converted into energy to let the brain do everything it needs to do for me to live."

"Foreign elements?" asked Jaya, livid.

"Try to use your imagination," laughed Chy. The water on the stove was near boiling. She dropped two bags into the pot.

"So, you mean to tell me you and your girls fuck people all day and don't sleep? What kind of life is that?"

The woman used chopsticks to stir the bags. The color of the water changed. Chy poured half two cups and carried them back to the table.

"Don't be stupid. We get days off. Usually the girls will stay awake a week, then we have a weekend off. We do sleep then. We're not robots."

She handed a cup to the girl, who put her tongue into the tea to test its temperature. She winced as the tea burned the roof of her mouth.

"Yes, you are," said Jaya.

"Did you sleep alright?"

"Not really. But I need to get out of here. There are people after me. It's not safe for you with me around."

"I'm sure you will be fine. Helix is taking over for me, so I've got some extra time off to help," said Chy.

"Helix?" Jaya asked.

"She was with some rich cats by the Epicentre. She's making some big moves." Chy pointed to the bedroom door, closed. She was numb to the sounds behind the wall. She had heard them for hours.

"Not very glamorous, I have to say. Are all the whores in Eros operating for days without sleep?"

"No, bitch. Just a select few. We're called the NeoLight specials. We go to the big parties, pick up the clients with the largest accounts, mostly. We are the professionals, the main attractions here."

"Well, I imagine that retirement is not an option for you, is it?" Jaya asked. Chy smiled back at her.

"I can retire whenever I want."

"Then do it," said Jaya.

"There's no such thing as too much money. It's harder to just up and leave that you think. No matter where you came from, it's not the same up here as it is in that hole."

"Bullshit. What do the others say?"

"They want out eventually, but houses off the grid are hard to come by, so they cost a lot."

"How much?"

"A lot more than they might want to give up."

Jaya stood up. "Fuck it, then. Tell them to get out of here. They could go somewhere else. You could do the same. You can't keep doing this to yourself."

"Child, I've been doing this for years."

"And what? You want me to live here?"

"You are welcome to stay. I like how you work. I saw how you handled that boy the night before."

"What are you talking about?!"

"He's been talking about you ever since. I would call that a friend for life. You suckered him in easy. You might be better at this then anything else you do."

"I don't want to stay and listen to you bang people 24 hours a day," Jaya finally said.

"You think you're better than me, runaway?"

"I think I will do fine on my own. I got here on my own, didn't I? I tricked my way into the club with a fake ID."

"Yeah, you got wrapped up in a murder and men in black suits are after you. Doing pretty well out here," Chy said.

"Get fucked. Oh, wait, give it a minute."

"You might want to keep your voice down, too. The guy in the next room? Who knows who he works for?" The woman pointed to the cup of tea on the table. Jaya slumped back into her chair.

"Where's my gear?"

Chy went to the closet and pulled it from behind some boxes. She dropped it at Jaya's feet. "Where are you going to go?"

"Anywhere but here." Jaya said as she ripped her bag open.

"Good luck with that," said Chy.

"I need some time alone."

"I went through the bag. I know what you do, kid. Do whatever computer game shit you need to. Just don't get yourself killed, and try to be a little more thankful next time."

Chy took her tea into the front room. Jaya connected the terminal to the cube and turned on the stopwatch at the bottom of the bag. If the men in suits were tracking her, they would no doubt keep their eyes on her online activity. Her inbox was flooded with messages. They weren't from Ergo, but the client. She trashed them and swept through the old list of names for some extra cash. She went into her accounts to deposit the funds, but they were all gone. All her dummy accounts had been erased, including the one with the $1000 remaining.

The moans from behind the bedroom door at stopped. Jaya looked to the outside of the tea house. She thought about running. The tea house was quiet for the first time. She sat and stared at the shadows in red that decorated every corner. The tea was just warm enough to enjoy. After a few swigs from the cup, she went back into her inbox to find the messages. She expected threats, but instead she found worry.

"J, this is V."

She ignored the message, but they continued coming through.

"Are you alright? Please let me know if you receive this message. We need to speak."

"Online is fine. I can secure a good enough connection."

It had to be some kind of a joke. A small icon appeared in the corner of the message. Receipt of opening. Damn it, she thought. Text dropped in behind the window.

"J?"

She hesitated. This is a trick. They couldn't be that stupid. The door to the bedroom opened and a man in a wrinkled polo and torn jeans walked out the front door. No eye contact.

"A lot better than the old chick," he said.

Jaya couldn't stay there any longer. Chy sat in silence and looked out from the small couch. "The best clients, huh?" shouted Jaya.

She took a small sip of her tea. "Don't be fooled by his appearance. He pays at least $3,000 to see us. How many people do you have to steal from to get that much?" asked Chy.

There was no television, no books to read. Just another window that showed the sea of bodies revealed in flashes between the dark.

"I guess none of you are fighting to marry him?"

"He's already married."

Jaya kept her mouth shut and went back to the screen.

"J: What do you want?"

"V: I'm happy to hear from you."

"J: You tried to have me killed."

"V: I apologize for the trouble. There was a major miscommunication between the parties involved. That was not supposed to happen."

"J: No shit. Do we need to continue this conversation any longer?"

"V: We need to meet."

"J: No way in hell."

"V: You may not trust me now. But it's important that we see each other face to face."

"J: Why?"

"V: You are in danger. I can protect you."

"J: I'll take my chances."

"V: You won't last long just hiding out in Tokyo Siren."

Jaya knocked the terminal to the floor and buried her head into her knees. They already knew where she was.

"V: Your presence is bringing unnecessary heat to the girls. Meet me. I will take care of you."

No one came out of the bedroom. Chy stood up and made her way through the kitchen without saying a word. She went into the bathroom and closed the door. Jaya slowly picked up the terminal.

"J: How long have you been watching me?"

"V: Ever since you wrote the algorithm for them."

Jaya felt the room become smaller.

"J: Them? This isn't V, is it?"

"V: Correct. I wanted to tell you in person that I'm very impressed with your work."

"J: So, you're not one of them. Who are you supposed to be?"

"V: A victim of your excellent code writing."

"J: Not interested, then."

"V: It took me a while to find out who you are, Lilah."

The world vanished once she read the words on the screen.

"J: Who's that?"

"V: That's your birth name, isn't it? Lilah Rivera?"

The tears came unexpectedly. No one knew her name, not even Ergo.

"J: Why are you doing this?"

"V: I did it because it's probably the only way you could trust me. I knew that once I found out the source of the code, that I would need you."

"J: Need me? For what?"

"V: Your help in stopping the process, and getting me out."

"J: What did I do to you?"

"V: Meet me and I will show you."

"J: Did you erase my accounts?"

"V: I had to. They will be watching the moves you make. Did you find the present I left for you?"

"J: Yes."

"V: As soon as you step outside the club, come find me."

A girl stepped out from the bedroom, still naked. Her skin was pale. Jaya looked away as she stood with her legs open from the doorway.

"Hey, kid," she said.

"What the fuck do you want?!" Jaya screamed. She grabbed her cup and threw it against the wall. The girl was unmoved.

"Is that him you are talking to?"

"Who the fuck is him? I don't know who he is, or who you are…"

"Calm down. The name's Helix," the girl stepped forward. Jaya got up from the chair and went back into the corner of the room.

"Don't come any closer. I don't know what is going on, and I don't want to know. Please just leave me alone. Give me my shoes, so I can go home. Please."

Helix watched her crumble to the floor, sobbing. She read the messages on the terminal. The stopwatch had gone off minutes ago. She walked over to Jaya and knelt down. She put her hand on her back. Jaya flinched but continued to cover up.

"It's alright. I've met him."

Jaya pulled her hands away. "Who?

"Him," Helix pointed to the terminal. "He has a few different names. But I know he's real. When we do first contacts, there's a certain process you have to follow. Like a reference you give to let us know you are safe to be around. He had the best name possible, so I knew right away that he was a good one."

"So, he had a password? That doesn't mean anything. Anyone could have stolen it. Trust me; you can get your hands on whatever you want in Narrow. Who is he?"

"Hard to say who he really is. He's, a little weird. But he knew a friend of mine. She disappeared a while back. Maybe he can help you."

"How?"

"You're not the only one being chased by them."

Jaya bit her tongue. Her gaze was lost in the corner of the room. Things were moving too fast and she struggled to let herself go.

"Did you find it?" Helix asked.

Jaya moved her head without saying a word.

"I will take care of everything."

There were no men to take advantage there. Chy gathered her clothes while Helix stayed by her side. They gave her a little more time to rest. She counted the hours, never wanting to step outside the little red house. The women were driven machines and they could not take care of her for long. The money was endless and they were not going to stop for anyone. She dreamed of the White Owl and the sounds of the man choking to death. The images of the dance floor were broken up, different than before. Her mind had begun to warp them into something else, something unrecognizable. The men in black became demons in human skin and multiplied by the hundreds.

Chy put money into her pack and let her back out into Eros. Helix reached out to V on her own and got specific instructions on where to find him. Chy did not say goodbye, only that she would be back and in a house of her own. Helix only told her that he could be trusted. She asked her who Catherine was.

"A very good friend of ours. He knew her too. She's gone now."

The girl was sweet to her. Chy kept her distance after the fight at the tea house. Helix took her to the side before she left.

"I know this is insane. But I want to show you something."

Jaya wanted no part of it.

"It will help explain a lot. You don't have to trust me, but you can believe me when I say that it will make sense why we are this way."

She said nothing but followed Helix to her own place, outside the insanity of the club.

Jaya kept silent in the taxi. She followed the lights from building to building, watching the glow change from behind the glass.

"You looked like you couldn't wait to get out of there," said Helix.

"It made me sick to see them."

"Why? They just want to party, forget about whatever shit they have going on in their lives."

"I watched someone die. And they didn't care. They just kept dancing and didn't even notice."

"Just another thing to forget. It happens more often than you think out here. Do you regret coming here, yet?"

Jaya never answered. The taxi let them off near the top floor of the penthouse. Helix led her inside. The lights in each room were a subtle pink. Jaya began to breathe easier. The rooms had high ceilings and new wood floors, nothing like the crimson house. Synthesized music filled her ears as she sat down at the couch. The curtains and carpet were shades and pink and purple. Strains of pearls hung from the lights that coated the walls with the gleam of spinning diamonds.

"Be right back."

Helix poured her a glass of water and disappeared into her bedroom. She returned with an ivory statue. Jaya was unsure of what to say.

"This is something I've never shown anyone. Chy is too rough to the runaways. Catherine was always the one to show them how this place really works. Once she died, a lot of us lost our good nature."

Helix placed the statue on the table. It was a small obelisk.

"What is it?"

"It's a sculpture. A monument. I made everything in here."

Jaya looked to the walls. There were paintings in every corner, abstract in shape and dashed with champagne colors.

"This one was for Catherine. She used to make origami. We used to stay here when we needed a break from the tea houses. I still have some of the paper blackbirds she would leave for me on the bed."

Jaya put the sculpture down carefully.

"Since then, every time of us disappeared, I made a change to it."

"Disappeared?" asked Jaya.

"Siren was the best place for us runaways to go. The clients were so blitzed, a nervous girl could get used to learning the ropes better than a place with a thousand cameras filming your every move."

There were names etched into the obelisk. Catherine Waves was at the top of the list.

"She was a gentle woman who pimped you out, too?"

Helix nodded her head, unfazed. "Catherine wasn't the first to go, according to Chy. But she was the first one to vanish after I got here."

She looked around and turned back to Jaya. "Do you want to see her?"

The girl nodded and Helix leapt up and pulled a picture from the same back room.

The portrait was half her size. Helix put it on the floor and leaned it against the fireplace. She sat back down next to Jaya.

"No real pictures?"

"She wouldn't take any," said Helix.

The woman in the picture lay naked on a canopy bed with flowing red velvet sheet that matched her hair. The body that curled beneath the covers was revealed in slight moments, there was insane detail in her thigh and ankle that followed her muscles past her shoulder to her neck.

"No glamour shots. That was kind of her deal; create this mystery that made men want to find out what she looked like. Every deal was set up over the phone or online with vocal samples, no video chat or cameras."

Jaya was amazed. She looked as though she had been cut from a stone. Her eyes were fierce. The ruby smile comforted her. She seemed to stare through them both and out into the night. There was no way she looked that good. But maybe she really did.

"What happened to her?" Jaya asked.

"She got involved with the wrong people and she wound up dead. Others began to disappear just like her soon after. It was like they all fell into a pattern."

"Do you think someone took them?"

"It's only been one person," Helix said. She took a breath and Jaya watched the color drain from her face.

"You know who it is?"

"We all knew each other's client list. There was a girl a few months ago. She was a good friend of mine. Her name was Dio. She kept his name from us for the longest time. Then, she was gone. That was when we knew. We found what was left of her body in a hotel near Zero Block. They tried to melt her with some kind of acid. The guy she was seen with grabbed onto a sky shuttle and fell. He cracked his head against the ground for no reason."

"What the fuck…"

Helix wiped a tear from her eye.

"Who is it?" asked Jaya.

"It was the same person that V mentioned when I spoke to him about Catherine. An old rich man with nothing to do with all that money he's got."

"Is that all you have up there in Tempest?"

"He's someone with high connections, maybe even as high as the state, which means he's basically wrapped up tight with the ones who rule everything up top."

"What does that mean?"

"If he is the one who took Catherine and Dio, he needs to pay, but it's going to be hell to reach him."

There were seven names engraved into the ivory with a rough blade.

"Were they all girls?" asked Jaya.

Helix shook her head. "Family, too. These were the ones I ran away from."

"Do you know where they are now?"

"I never stopped to look and see if they stayed or looked for me. I'm sure they did."

The words hurt to say out loud.

"Whatever V is planning, I believe him. I will do anything I can to make sure whoever is behind this pays," said Helix.

Jaya turned away from her and the statue. Helix put her hand on her shoulder.

"I never expected you to stay with us, become a NeoLight girl. I could tell it wasn't your style to work your body for cash."

"No?"

"You are smarter than that. Maybe a little too promiscuous, but I can't say too much about that. You are all about that computer shit. I'm not." Helix laughed.

"Is V supposed to be the man without a face?" Jaya asked.

"I think so. He was in love with Catherine. For whatever reason, they didn't get to see each other much. Maybe that was why she called him that. I know that they had to have kept in contact, even after she left him for her last client."

"She left him?"

"He was money. V let her do what she knew best. She let him do what he wanted, too. There was never any question about who they really loved."

"They are both fucked up."

"That's life. You'll see one day," Helix picked up the statue and held it close.

"She was going to clean out the rich man and come back to her lover, yeah?"

"Something like that. She never came back but made sure he had everything he needed in case the plan went south."

"You mean the drive inside the television at the hotel."

"I pulled a lot of strings to make sure we didn't lose it and to ensure that you were put in that room to find it."

"Why couldn't you get it yourself?" asked Jaya.

"They were watching that place. The men in black. I had to sneak messages in without showing my face."

Jaya went into her pack and pulled out the drive. "What does it do?" she asked.

"No clue. Maybe V can tell you."

There was silence between them. It lasted for a few minutes. Helix put the statue back and came out to an empty house. The girl was already gone, pushing her way through the mass of bodies that never stopped moving to the music.

Jaya replayed the last ditch message to Ergo in her head the minute her feet touched the ground outside of Helix's penthouse;

"E, this is J. Please listen to me. I am in deep shit and I have no idea what I am doing. My accounts have been wiped by someone who says my code fucked their life up. He's arranged a meeting and I am scared. E, I've been hiding out with jacked up whores and I can't handle this city. I want to go home. I want to see you. Please find me. I will contact you as soon as I get a chance."

Twenty

Marsh felt the blow the second time. The force was enough to take him out of his chair. A lone bulb suspended in the air by an old wire rocked back and forth from the movement. It was losing energy. Every blink magnified the brief darkness that reappeared over the room. Two men in uniform stood over his body. They shouted incoherently as they grabbed at his arms.

The men dropped him back into the chair. One placed the table in the corner in front of them and both took a seat across from their prey. Their suits were different from Tempest. He had no experience of Police assault before but he knew how strong they were. These guys were slum cops. He heard stories of brute force with dark eyes. He studied them; both black, neatly creased pants, scratched gold badges, blood on both of their knuckles.

"How are you feeling?" The one on the left asked. The name on the bottom of the badge said Grimes.

"My face hurts," said Marsh.

"Sorry, but you were putting up a fight," the second one did not speak. His badge read Cartwright.

Marsh looked around. A single door with a dim light behind a circle of glass. He knew exactly where he was.

"Interrogation room?" he asked.

"You got it," said Grimes.

He motioned to Cartwright. He produced a handheld monitor from his pocket and dropped in front of him.

"We don't have an A.I. following us around all day, making things easier for us, you see. We do things the old fashioned way, cameras on every corner, closed circuit TV."

Marsh coughed up something thick from the back of his throat and wiped his eyes with his sleeve. Cartwright leaned forward and pointed to the screen, as if to say 'pick it up'. He grabbed the monitor and stood it up by the plastic stand attached. Rough footage of street corners played in loops. There was a brief glimpse of a man walking past a camera, hands firmly shoved into the pockets of a coat like his. Marsh sat back in his chair and ignored the pain in his ribs.

The footage changed to the outside of the morgue where we had worked for years. He saw himself stepping outside of his apartment, in the middle of a desolate neighborhood. There were piles of bricks were charred and debris had been washed out into the street. The footage jumped to the hangar outside Narrow. A camera above the streetlight caught him sitting the car with the Irish boys.

"I'm not sure if you're aware that that building was burned down by a dangerous criminal. Although he was killed in the proceeding shootout, both Cartwright and I lost several friends in that operation."

"I am sorry to hear that. I lived right down the street. I heard everything; the gunshots, the kids crying," mumbled Marsh.

The cop cut him off. "And then we nearly caught the Irish by the hangar. One of our cruisers chased them while we checked the building. We found human remains, burned beyond recognition by fire."

Marsh's heart sank even further. The badges were a message. The names from the morgue were back in front of him to show just how much of a part he played in their system.

"Listen. Just send them in or do what you have to do. I have nothing left to say."

The cops looked at each other. Grimes and Cartwright got up and left the room. They locked the door behind them. The hallway was lit only the bulb above the door. The white walls stretched on into outstretched shadows in every direction. Johns stood alongside the east wall, cleaning his gun. They were anxious the moment they saw him.

"He's all yours," said Grimes.

Johns did not reply. He simply looked further down towards the dark. The cops slowly walked away in the other direction. Maxwell emanated from the hallway, phone in hand.

"Elder statesman Graff…I got your message."

"Where are you, Max?"

"Johns and I are in Eros."

"Busy, eh?" asked Graff.

"We are about to handle some loose ends and enjoy some more of the endless night."

"You son of a bitch. Don't you ever leave me hanging like that again, or I will have you and your boyfriend hung out to dry with bullets in your asses. Do you get me?!"

Maxwell bit his tongue and spoke;

"Veiled threats are my favorite. Unfortunately for you, those are the only kind you can make. Now, how can I help you?"

"The committee is chewing my ass since the A.I. put everyone on notice. We need the Codex now. Do you have it yet?"

"The search is ongoing. The new toy is reaching its breaking point. We will have control soon enough."

"There's no time for that. Adam will be putting Apex out into the public in two days."

"Which means, we still have two days, Leland. Why are you so worried about what the A.I. is going to do?"

"48 hours is not a lot of time, Max! This shit is going to give me a heart attack."

"Well, if that happens, you can always clone a new one."

The statesman looked out over the city lights from the penthouse. His body was shrouded in dark. Shades of blue silhouetted half the dining room where he stood.

"I don't see how you aren't taking this more serious."

Maxwell stopped outside the door to the interrogation room and looked at Johns.

"Everything that we have built is about to come crashing down if we don't find it."

"That sounds like desperation, Leland."

"Given something that we have been planning for years is about to blow up on our face, I would say I'm pretty fucking desperate," Graff gasped for air.

"Calm down. You're going to give yourself another stroke."

Johns nearly broke into a smile.

"Do not fuck me on this deal, boys. You work for me. Both of you. The two of you would be nothing without me. Fix this shit or you will go back to being nothing, just punks on the streets with no homes again. Remember that."

The rare smiles of the Shadowmen were suddenly gone.

"If we are going over memory now, please try to recall the terms of our agreement. First, we don't work for you. We are soldiers of fortune. Your committee of old men is a proxy organization, a front of familiar faces to keep the people quiet. Your bodies were designed and paid for by Machina and Synapse. They are the true owners of this place. They keep you in power and they are the ones who pay us to protect your interests."

Graff looked down at his body, barely held together.

"All the government and military have been are shells that traded away control for the technology needed to survive. You are a puppet, Leland. That is all you have ever been. Johns and I have been hiding away your sins for years."

"That's not what this is about...My sins are supposed to die with my body. That was always the plan."

"Think about the current trail you've created; the code breakers from a week ago? How about Everett?"

"Liabilities, young man. Every single one of them. They were people who knew too much and could do too little for our benefit," said Graff.

"That's a lot of paper on the trail we made because of you, statesman. How long will it take before your ideology of a clean world with no secrets is forgotten and you become a loose end?" asked Maxwell.

"Now you are throwing veiled threats?"

Here we go, he thought. More anger from the old man. Maxwell began to feel sorry for the secretary who would be brushing off bruises every day of the week now.

"So what, you're gonna kill me now?! Are you willing to go to war with your benefactor? You're not going to like what the fuck happens."

Graff could feel the heat in his artificial blood.

"What about Dio?" asked Maxwell.

The line was dead. Johns stopped fidgeting and looked at his partner. Graff gripped the phone tighter.

"I told you not to say her name."

"That's your biggest sin of all, isn't it?"

Maxwell looked back at his partner when the words left his mouth, his face almost looked sorry.

"You shouldn't have said that," said Johns.

It hurt him to hear her name again. He could see it in the way he moved away further into the corner. He tucked himself into the dark.

"You don't know how much it hurts to not have her around...I miss her, Max...I should kill you for bringing this at a time like this. You are going to fuck my blood pressure up."

"You never should have forced us to kill her. She loved you, Leland. She never would have left you if you hadn't turned your best friend into a real life punching bag."

"If you were here, I would strangle you," said Graff, struggling to keep from breaking down.

"Honestly, Leland, you are too far from me to do anything about it. Listen to me when I say, that you have sinned for more than anyone who pay us to kill."

Graff felt tears run down his face.

"Damn you both."

"No, you old fool. We are in bed together. We need to make the most of it. Johns and I will bail you out, as we have always done…If for no other reason, if we don't, then we are also done."

Johns finally stepped out from the corner.

"We would do well in prison, I think."

"I think so, too," said Maxwell.

Graff nearly lost his balance. He slowly made his way to the center couch in his living room and sat down. His robe was a fine silk with a lined pocket to hold a handkerchief, neatly folded. He dabbed at the sweat that collected at the top of his forehead and ran down into the folds of his neck. There was a long pause between the two.

"Are you still there, Leland?"

"Just do what you do best. Get this shit done and you boys won't have to deal with me ever again," he finally said.

"We intend to."

Maxwell ended the call. Johns just finished cleaning his gun. He took a deep breath.

"From one awkward conversation to another…"

"You could have avoided this next one," said Johns.

He looked down at the floor and watched Maxwell's shadow move towards the door into the interrogation room. Dio's voice repeated the few words she ever spoke to him.

"I don't think so. We were banking on his defiance to help light the next spark. Despite doubt on all sides, the plan is moving along."

The Shadowmen entered the room. Marsh heard the door open but did not bother to look up.

"Marshmallow," Maxwell said softly.

Johns went for the darkest corner and stood with his gloved hands in his jacket pockets. He looked into the bulb of the lamp and relaxed his eyes.

"You don't look so good. I hope that the officers weren't too rough with you."

"The names looked familiar. They work for you, too?" asked Marsh.

"Of course. Everything you do for us has a purpose. They needed names to inhabit, clean ones. You provided that for them, by closing off one trail of breadcrumbs. Unfortunately, it creates another, which we will eventually deal with."

"And the guys who picked me up?"

"Government cleanup crew; heavy hitters bred for quick disposal and evidence removal. It's a finely woven web."

"What happened to Fever and the others?" Marsh asked.

"I don't think you need to ask that question. You know what happens to people who get in our way. The Irish boys, your handler girl, you won't be seeing them around, I'm afraid," said Maxwell.

"You killed them, too?" Marsh asked.

"Why? They've done nothing but provide the best intelligence in Narrow. Róisín is a real beauty."

He remembered the girl's hands on his. The car chase, everything about that night, was a lie.

"I guess you have all your bases covered," Marsh spit a mass of blood onto the floor.

"You definitely added another element to the mix by uploading some information to the data stream. I am proud of you for being light on your feet like that."

Marsh finally looked up at Maxwell, who grimaced at his eyes, nearly beaten shut. "You killed Rion Kath, and who knows how many others, then gave me false papers to be written up and shoved into the system database."

"Fake lives to cover up for the missing ones. As dark as this world is, there are those who will look for cracks in the stories we tell, not unlike you. We still have to cover those holes. But don't think that Johns and I murder senselessly. There is always a purpose to the lives we take."

"Which is what? Implant their minds into other people's bodies?" Marsh asked.

"You are smarter than you look. That's why we are here with you in person, as opposed to having others remove our problems for us. We've done that more times that we can count. It's rare when we encounter people who take initiative. We like you."

"I don't like him. He's fat and he's gross," Johns said immediately.

Maxwell waved his hand. "Johns might not like you as much as I do, but still."

"How do you do it? The implanting?" asked Marsh.

"We live in a world where anything can be quantified. The mind can be broken down into a system of electrical pulses interpreted by a brain. Once the system was figured out, it was only a matter of time before it becomes open to manipulation; primitive hijack. You've experienced some of the byproducts yourself, in those opium houses with old men attached to screens showing temporary memories. Those are just black market bootlegs of what we have perfected; a system of control. It's a way to eliminate the selected targets of our employer by getting into their heads and spinning a narrative to feed to the masses on a digital platter."

Marsh pulled at his restraints until he could feel the warmth of the fresh blood on his wrists.

"Do you know what recursion is?" asked Maxwell. Marsh kept his mouth shut.

"It's what you call the process of things repeating in a pattern. If you put two mirrors face to face, what exactly is reflected? One image goes to the other, back and forth, forever. The broadcast of the image becomes an endless loop that repeats. The dog chases its own tail. Recursion is found in mathematics when trying to prove a set of rules with given numbers, in language when the words we use aren't enough to fully explain what we want to, and in computers too. The computers became so advanced that they put them into people's brains. Think about programming computers, the most complex problems are broken down into smaller problems to be solved one by one, leading to an ultimate answer. You don't think the mind works the same way?"

Johns continued to clean the magnum. Marsh glanced at him.

"Don't ever look at me," he said, never taking his eyes off of the gun.

"The loop continues on. We make it work in our favor, and the favor of our employers. The little problems were figured out long ago and we push and pull the numbers to influence how the system functions. If we want a specific person taken out, someone who could threaten the structure we dwell in, we use a person who the public will perceive as a believable suspect as our hands, our voice."

"You killed Kath because he threatened you?"

"Not us personally, but our benefactor. His motivation would be perfect; one of revenge. Remember the old saying; something done in the dark always comes to light. We hide those truths until the day comes when we don't have to anymore."

"Kath isn't the main target is he?" asked Marsh.

"Smart man."

"That is our secret, one which we do not plan on telling. We deal in secrets. It's our currency. It's how we shape the stories that need to be told. Remember when you were terrified of us? What happened? How did that all change?"

"I'm still terrified of you…"

"And yet, you still gave yourself up to try and stop us? Why is that?"

Marsh coughed hard to clear his throat.

"It's because you wanted to know our secrets. That desire for knowledge is how you let yourself get caught up. That little tinge of curiosity has gotten you killed. Here, I will tell you a story."

Maxwell took a seat at the table with him. "A long time ago, there was a pretty girl. Her name was Reese."

The pain in Marsh's body vanished for a moment. He struggled to open his eyes again and sat up slowly. His body reminded him of how damaged he was.

"Yeah, you used to know her. We did too. Before she became a medical scientist, she worked for Synapse Corporation as an augmentation creator. Freelance, but mainly paid by one source. She designed something to help some the population of deaf people that was rising in Tempest, probably due to installation of newDawn into babies; you know all that sensory overload would wreak havoc on their developing systems. She cured it, which put her on the radar of our employers."

Marsh gritted his teeth.

"She got herself into a bad deal and Synapse took the augmentation and paid her for the patent and decided not to include her in the dividends for all the companies paying top dollar to cure their employees' children. It wasn't enough money to retire on, so she took up work in a hospital in Narrow. She found herself in the realm of Mortuary Science, where she developed something else, just as beautiful."

Maxwell pulled a glass vial from inside his pea coat. "This, is her creation. A liquid that could help dematerialize any substance. It was designed for safe disposal of corpses and environmental hazards instead of using our few sources of heat. Obviously, we found other ways to utilize its potential."

Marsh looked into the glass and then back into the eyes of Maxwell. He tried to imagine her even knowing people like them, but refused to accept it.

"Johns and I call it 'the Miracle'. This was something that would galvanize her, and redeem her career after Synapse basically used her up. We approached her with a generous offer, which she declined. She was very much caught up in doing work for the hospital, and wanted to keep things upfront. She would not be giving up her creations to a corporation again, especially one as big and all-controlling as Machina, right?"

Marsh looked away from him.

"What's wrong?"

He refused to answer.

"Oh, I'm sorry. I forgot your picture. Johns, can you help?"

No, he thought. Don't show me the photo. He could already feel the hands going through his clothes. He heard the slap on the table. Marsh opened his eyes again.

"There she is. Don't you miss her?"

Reese looked back at him with the same smile that kept him alive for so long.

"You are not alone, Marshmallow. We miss her too. But the bottom line is that she refused to do business. As you know, we have no enemies. We only have partners. Sadly, we made the mistake of approaching her ourselves. She had seen our face and would report us if something unfortunate were to happen. We were not very smart then. But we learned from our mistake. It was our only one until this day. She was very trusting and the hospital was full of people who were already in our employ; for drugs, or medicine, rooms for injured parties, whatever we needed."

Marsh struggled to find his way back to her, in the storm. The memories were already gone, a trick played by Fever. There was no going back to him to retrieve that night, or any other with her.

"Every day that she refused our offer, someone close to us would drop a little gift inside her water. Polonium 210. It was acquired by teams of scientists who made frequent trips to the broken down reactors in Russia. We hadn't had any dealings with the Russians in many years. They were left to fend for themselves in the old wars. The polonium was a historical artifact, a poison used many years ago, undetectable. We chose it to prove a point; that you cannot stop progress. Not you, or your girlfriend or any of us. Polonium can be easily traced now but the doctors in Narrow had no way of finding it. They were only concerned with the cancer inside her body. The old way is done. With Reese unable to continue work, you were chosen to step up and take over."

Marsh could hear the lightning. Don't leave. He repeated the words over and over. He clenched his fists until the nails cut into his skin.

"The formula for the Miracle was easy to obtain and you had no idea of its existence. All you had in your life was the girl. Once she was gone, you belonged to us."

Her voice was faint. She laughed out loud. The sound was buried beneath a thousand claps of thunder.

"Are you trying to remember her now? You should. As much as I appreciate what you tried to do, there's no way you were going to escape reprisal from us. When we want something, we take it. Kath was chosen and he will still deliver, despite your best efforts."

"Just...stop..." whispered Marsh.

Maxwell looked back at Johns, who still stared into the light.

"Do what you need to do..."

Disappointed, Maxwell stood up and took the glass vial.

"Whatever you are planning…Kath's not going to do it. He won't be controlled, or programmed. He's smarter than you, and more dangerous. He might even kill you."

"Even if he does, I might have a different body by then, as well."

Maxwell opened the vial. "Here's a final parting gift from your woman."

Marsh looked down to the photograph. So beautiful.

"Goodbye, Marshmallow."

He emptied the vial onto Marsh's head. The pain was infinite. The picture of Reese was gone in an instant, as was the room, and his eyes. The Shadowmen stood together and watched the Miracle quickly melted through skin and bone. Within seconds, Marsh could not contain the pain. His voice became a broken shriek. The Shadowmen did not flinch. There were soon no screams, only the sounds of a quiet burning.

Twenty One

White noise crackled for hours. Innumerable faces twitched in and out of the waves of static sea. Another invisible blade cut defining lines into the screen. The ocean world turned to darkness. There was moisture on his skin. He felt as if he was opened up and spilled out. There were wings above the waves. In the madness of the noise, he could hear the call of the birds. He could feel vibrations on the inside. Something was pounding against his head. It felt like hands. The broadcast was interrupted with a fist against across the jaw line. Time to wake up.

He could remember the color of the walls in the room he used to sleep in. The images were always blurred. They were small pieces of a broken film that replayed on an endless loop. The scenes were shuffled out of order; newly made candles burning on a dining room table, the sounds of rain against the window and streets outside, the slamming of that elevator door to separate him from the bodies that used to carry him. He could picture the arms and nothing else.

"What is this?"

Strangers took him from the elevator and put him on a train; an older man and woman with cracked smiles and plain clothes. The train went deep into a giant machine with countless rooms. The quarters were small metal pods with stiff beds. Everyone was told to stay there between class and dinner. He woke up the next morning with a dull pain. Something was moving inside his head. It felt like something was drilled into his neck.

"Where am I?"

The strangers wrapped his head with careful bandages that night and accompanied him every morning to a school deep inside the Epicentre. Instructors taught classes to groups of children, each with the same bandages on their heads. At night, they struggled to sleep due to sensory overload.

"Stop this."

He learned everything from the Academy. The power of newDawn was staggering as a child. The instructors taught the children how to harness it, to control data output and manage memory. Some of the other kids had new arms and legs, too. They were taught how to walk, allowing the steel bonded to their bones to slowly settle when they stood, how to hold hands without crushing them.

"I don't want to see this anymore…"

The strangers had names which he had forgotten the day they let him loose from the Academy. He had his own apartment in the tenements and a list of job interviews lined up for people like him; an improved memory capacity and constant connection to the data stream via newDawn.

"Is anyone listening to me?!"

The interviews were with bland bodies in neat suits. They were all talk of bright futures and warnings to not mess up the chance you kids were given. It was easy to lose yourself in the work, the machines that surrounded you, the ease of everything at your finger tips.

"Can someone hear me!?"

He got his job and worked until he died. The world around him spun in circles of the same chaos but everyone burned the same. The buildings fell and were rebuilt better and better but everything crumbled the same. He tried to ignore his place in the inevitable fall but there was no use in stopping what was always meant to happen and what always will happen.

"What is this?!"

The vision stopped. Gabrels stood again in the Blank Page; white floor against white backgrounds that went on forever. The blackbirds that hovered above him were gone. He stood in front of his reflection. It looked back at him with a smile on its face.

"Do you feel lost yet?"

Gabrels only laughed. "So, you're him. Rion Kath. Am I right?"

The face of his reflection changed to match the faded mugshot from the data stream.

"That's not my name anymore. Someone died so you could know a little bit more about me. I hope you feel good about that."

"You're not going to make me feel guilty. Their death is on your hands," said Gabrels.

"If you're going to call me anything, call me Vax. That's what my momma called me."

"How were you able to change?" asked Gabrels.

"You know the truth now, which means the mind will not perceive the deception as real anymore."

"How many other deceptions have you created?"

"I haven't created any of them. They were here before I was dropped in. I'm bringing them to your attention."

"These aren't deceptions, these are from you. You said that we are becoming one mind? I don't remember doing any drugs before you showed up. So, how long have I been having withdrawals? When was the last time you shot up, junkie?"

Vax put his hand up. "Judgment is still not your strong point."

"I was up for hours, sweating through my clothes and half awake, vomiting this morning. You've been fiending. Forget the headaches, the nosebleeds, all of that. You're an addict, you're sick. Now, you're passing the sickness onto me!"

"So what?"

"Fuck you! Do not put that into my body! I don't care what happened to you. I don't want that poison in my veins. It doesn't matter how hurt or broken you are. It's not up to you to decide what I put in my body!"

"Sorry to disappoint you, Stan."

"I don't want these dreams anymore!" he screamed back.

"You know these aren't dreams. I told you before, I know everything about you now."

Gabrels' hands rubbed against his face until he could feel the skin start to burn from the friction. "What do you mean?"

Vax stretched his arms out. "Neural unity or whatever your A.I wants to call it is not just a tag line. What you and I have is worse. You and I are merging. We trade off during sleep but you can see how we are joining into one consciousness. It started off slow, but now it's becoming more than just one shutting off while the other is on."

"You mean more than your time with the girl, Helix? Or is it Catherine?" asked Gabrels.

"It's Helix. She was pretty good, yeah? I don't know if you have any residual memories, but let me tell you, she was amazing in and out of bed. It's been a while since I was that flexible. My old body was not in good enough shape."

"Go to hell," said Gabrels.

"It turns out that the system that monitors your consciousness is able to process pleasure separately from pain. So, I can have all the fun while you experience the equivalent of a wet dream. But sadly, even that will fade. The threat of physical harm was enough to shock you awake at the bar."

"How is that possible?" he asked.

"Hybrid thinking. Two minds sharing one brain, both can recognize the threat. If someone held a knife to your throat right now, you would wake up, even if I was the one making you hold it."

"And Catherine? Was she your girlfriend?" asked Gabrels.

Vax became quiet. His smile disappeared. A trace of pain cut across his face. "She was more than that."

"What happened to her?"

"It's not your business. It's mine. Her name doesn't come out of your mouth again."

Gabrels had hit a nerve, finally. "You can't hurt me, Kath. I can say what I want."

Vax chuckled, as if he was trying keep from losing his composure. "You're finally learning how this works. That's good. Fortunately for you, I can only do so much from where I am."

"Why not tell me the truth, then? Make me want to help you instead of us fighting."

Vax was mildly impressed. "Continued signs of progress, even as the world falls apart around you. She was an escort. We met during our own separate benders. I had enough money to blow on a weekend in Eros and she found me in the corner of a club packed with little shits not unlike yourself."

"Thanks," scoffed Gabrels.

"You're welcome. We were good to each other. She spent weeks at a time with men with money to burn. I was small potatoes, a two bit dealer, but we continued to circle back around and find each other. She said that she would leave with me."

"Did you believe her?"

"Not every woman you meet is going to be a liar, Stan. They have reasons for doing what they do. You won't understand them, but you can choose to see past their problems, to the big picture."

"Which was?"

"She liked me enough to leave the situation she was used to. You don't know anything about taking a risk because you've lived in a self imposed shell for years. We made a plan, one to get all the money we would ever need, and then we would disappear."

"Does that have something to do with the revenant?"

"Yeah," said Vax.

"What is it?"

"Everett told you, told us, what it is, didn't he? I am your revenant. The ghost inside your brain, isn't that right? They put me in your brain to control you."

"Why?" asked Gabrels.

"They want to know the location of something called the Codex. The escort mentioned it to you, yeah? You've heard it before. I've been working on finding it, too. I'm not just doing drugs while you sleep."

"And you know where it is?"

"Catherine did. She hid it for me. I was to find it, sell it and then we would leave as soon as I got the money."

"She took it from someone, and that's how she ended up dead. Am I right? Who did she take it from?"

"It was one of her clients. They had a position in this little government, close to the top. Despite the current situation, she is going to help us get out of this shit, soon."

"She's dead. How is she going to help us?"

"Keep pushing, little shit. Keys was right about you. I'm going to remember that the next time you're getting your ass kicked. I don't feel the pain when it happens to your body, you do."

"That's why you run my body through glass, because you don't feel the same pain?"

"I've got my own pain to feel so any punches from a shithead like that I'm not going to feel."

"You did all that?" asked Gabrels.

"Shit, you don't know how to defend yourself. You've never been in a fight. And you're welcome, again. Before me, you didn't drink or smoke. Personally, I don't trust anyone who doesn't subscribe to some kind of poison. Luckily for you, my preferences have become yours."

"Are you able to control my dreams?"

"No," said Vax.

"Do you sleep?" asked Gabrels.

"I wish I could, but I don't. I've tried, but I can't. I'm just...here. Looking at you stare into space for hours."

"What else do you see? What about when I sleep?"

"I can see your memories, even the ones you've repressed."

"Repressed?"

"I had heard about kids who were picked up from the slums and put into a program in Tempest. You're one of a precious few," said Vax.

Gabrels saw the Academy again. Pictures of rooms he couldn't remember being in. "That's not true. You just put that into my head. I grew up in Tempest. I had a family."

"Kid, you can't even remember their faces, or their names. I looked for them. They don't exist in here. I know you tried to find them, too. Did you block that out?"

"Where are they?!"

"They weren't the ones who brought you to the Academy. Everyone had a foster figure, someone to report to, who acted as your guardian."

Pain bled out from the back of Gabrels' head. The endless white of the Blank Page began to suffocate him.

"Where's the picture of my mother? And the records from searching for others in my family tree?" he asked.

Vax smirked. "It's still there. It's just hidden. I told you, we are in this together. I can give things to you and I can take them away."

Gabrels went for his throat. His hands went through his skin like air.

"We can't hurt each other. You and I will never be face to face. This is all we have."

"How long were you going to keep it from me?"

"I wasn't going to keep it. I don't want it. I'm not here to torture you. But I keep telling you that I can't do anything without your body making the moves. I need you to move and not ask your A.I. to save the fucking day," said Vax.

"This whole thing has been a game, then?"

"Everett was being played. Until he wound up dead, you were helping me to find out who was playing him."

"Did you find out?"

"Nothing concrete. But that's still where you can help me. The puzzle is the key."

"Who gives a shit about the puzzle?! I'm done being lied to. Solve it yourself when I'm asleep instead of fucking around with escorts and blowing my money! My money! Not yours! Do you understand me?!"

Vax was now more than mildly impressed. "This is the first time I've seen you angry. I like it. It's nice to see you actually be invested emotionally in what's happening in your life."

Gabrels threw his hands up, enraged. "So, the puzzle solves what exactly?"

"You think I made it, another one of my old coded messages, right? I didn't make that shit. I was working on making bombs to sell when I was caught. That's why I need you to keep working on it."

"Why can't you do it while I sleep? If you are able to send messages to me from beyond the grave or using my mind." asked Gabrels.

"I have been looking at the codex, but I don't have the help of an A.I. like you do. Besides, I never hacked into Everett's terminal because I can't while you are awake. I might be able to soon if we continue to bleed together, but for now, we are just trading control."

"Trading would mean I gave you permission."

"You weren't doing anything with your body, anyway. You can't get rid of me on your own, so you might as well give someone else a chance to get shit straight."

"Give me my memories back. I don't know how you are able to block them or hide them, whatever the fuck you did. Put them back! Now!" Gabrels screamed.

"Why do you want them back? They're not real," said Vax.

"I decide what's real in my life. Not you."

"Well, then you're a fucking idiot. You don't know why I'm here and don't know how to get rid of me, so why not listen to what I have to say?"

Gabrels turned away from Vax and looked to the sky. The birds were still there, still circling. Kath was right. He had to learn as much he could. There was so much happening around him, right behind his eyes. He felt powerless. He didn't want to trust him.

"Tell me everything you know. No more games."

"There's a reason you've never heard of the Academy, but I have. It was an experiment to test a new augmentation. The government, or what's left of it, didn't want to tamper with the people of Tempest more than they already have, so they picked slum kids. They were expendable. Hundreds of them, just like you, were brought up to the top to be improved then released into the public to test their functionality, to see if they could live normal, productive lives."

"What did they do to them?" asked Gabrels.

"To you."

"Whatever."

Vax laughed. "It was the first test of its kind, and hasn't been replicated since; memory replacement."

"What?"

"They took kids under the age of four and augmented their brains not only with newDawn, but new memories created completely from scratch."

"Bullshit," said Gabrels.

"I thought you were going to listen?"

The Academy was there, in his mind. It sat at the edge of the house, like a door that slowly creaked open. The memories of looking at film with his mother went dark. The door swung open, letting in blinding light.

"The children were monitored at all hours of the day. You were taught in classrooms the same curriculum as any other student in Tempest. There were 180 test subjects, given implants which suppressed certain brain development and used nanotechnology to create new memories, an entire life written on the spot, replacing a day of Academy life with a childhood spent in a quiet home at the edge of the city."

"They were all given the same memories?" Gabrels asked.

"There is always a controlled aspect in an experiment. The false life was written one day at a time and uploaded into the user's brain."

"How long did this go on?"

"The body stops development at 18, so the subjects were released into the job market soon after. The real test was to see if the false memories would remain intact as life continued on. Out of 180 subjects, there were only a few that made it without any memory rejection."

"What happened to those who didn't take the programming?"

"They were removed from the experiment," said Vax.

"Killed, you mean." Gabrels began to hyperventilate. "How did you find this out?"

"I know you read the file on me, kid. I wanted you to find it on your own, you have no idea. I was feeding you clues the entire time and nothing."

There was no reply. Vax took a breath, disappointed. "You know I spent time with C.I.A. pigs. They let us in on a lot of shit. Bad idea."

"You knew this and didn't say anything?" he asked.

"I took as much info as I could and ran. Does that not give them reason enough to run me over with a car?"

"You think it was remnants of C.I.A.? They don't officially exist anymore," said Gabrels.

"They had to be dumped once word got out that I escaped. No, it was higher up. Definitely near the top of the government. Interesting enough, I found a name while you've been sleeping."

"Tell me."

"Leland Graff."

Gabrels rolled his eyes. "Are you serious? The old man with half of his body replaced by artificial parts?"

"Is that really hard to believe, Stanley? Vax continued the pressure. "You don't remember your parents. How can you forget 30 years of a life unless there was nothing there to begin with? You're telling me you would have believed this a week ago? Everett might have been one of the kids from the Academy too, I think. I imagine he would have trusted no one else with what he was planning, even if you had no idea what was going on."

"My life has not been a lie. I remember my mother. Why would Graff be behind this? Why put you here with me?"

"The Academy obviously thought you were an exceptional candidate and put you in a high position with lots of influence on the public. Your memories of him; talking to only you at the Synapse party, sending emails. I've seen it all. I don't think he would think twice about arranging to kill me or Catherine. I threatened to expose one of his dirty, little secrets. But you?

Why you? Why put an innocent in harms way after I am gone? Think about it. Someone else put me in your head after he set up the hit."

"And who would that be?" asked Gabrels.

"The same ones who killed me. They must want out, big time."

"Why would they kill you without finding their prize first?"

"They must already have it," said Vax.

Gabrels felt more lost the more. Kath was insane, but that didn't mean he was lying. Did it? "But you don't know who they are? Do you?"

"I'm working on that," said Vax.

"Graff was the client, wasn't he? Catherine stole the Codex from him and he got both of you killed."

Vax nodded his head.

"The killers kept the Codex from him, and you think they put you in my head to force me to kill Graff? That still makes no sense. What's the connection between me and him? Why me at all? Just what the hell is this things?" asked Gabrels.

"It's something I might have helped create."

Gabrels lowered his head.

"The thing they kept saying to us was IO. It means input/output; communication between a computer and an outside source. The idea came from a program they wanted to initiate where every person hooked up to newDawn and its A.I. would be connected, even in memory."

"Memory? You mean Apex?!" Gabrels cut him off.

"Back in the old days, memory mapped I/O allowed a computer to receive data and structure it for use by its processors. You know my history. You know who caught me and made me work for them. The government reps who would eventually become Machina and Synapse sponsored wanted us to study the brain's functions and figure out a way to store the data of the mind, map it and save it in the same way computers do. The brain is constantly processing new information that is encoded by sound, sight, everything you touch. The ingredients needed to create memories can be broken down into electrical pulses. They had enough scientists who could figure out the blueprint. A few of us were given the task to create a storage system to save that information."

"That's what you stole from them."

"Technology would cost a fortune to get back. There would be buyers crawling over bodies to get it. Graff and the people he represents don't want the public to know about the existence of this technology, especially on the black market. Their system is a continuous loop. They pulled so many others like me out from the dark and put us to work, to try and create new ways to catch the people we grew up with. They don't know what its like to suffer, or be without everything at their fingertips. They needed us but kept a foot on the backs of our necks to make sure we knew they were in charge. But they weren't. They never will be. I made sure to put a little tear in the film; I left a mark that would not be fixed. In their eyes, I had to be taken out."

"And Graff?"

"Think. Why would an old man visit a complete stranger and continue to check on his progress? Have you ever looked at your bank statements? All the money we have spent in the last week or two has been replaced."

"It has?"

"Ask Adam to look at your banking history. Something else you don't really pay attention to. You never look at anything but the numbers to make sure they were going up. It's not frugal living and hard work, its quiet transactions behind your back to keep you afloat. He's your father, idiot."

All the color left Gabrels' skin. He looked down to see his hands were the same as the Blank Page.

"He was pleased with you. Like I said, you know how to follow orders, but there's a point where you realized things were wrong and did nothing to change it. And here we are."

"He is not my father."

"Show me proof. You don't have any. You want to know what happened to your mother? Try to remember the last day you saw her. Try to recall everything about her and your childhood. Who put you in the Academy? If you grew up in the tenements, like you said, why are your memories of her in a house definitely not in front of the Epicentre?"

"I don't…"

The words simply stopped. Gabrels had nothing left.

"Those memories were put there. You were taken from your mother and put into the Academy, to be bred into a model citizen of Tempest."

The truth seemed further away. Gabrels wanted nothing more than to tear Kath and the entire white wasteland apart. He gathered himself and pushed out the words.

"What do you expect me to do now with all this supposed knowledge of a fake memory?"

"Solve the puzzle, find out who put me here."

"And do what?" asked Gabrels.

"Kill them? Graff too?"

"If it comes to that," said Vax.

"I'm not going to kill for you."

"You won't have to. I can do it for the both of us."

"I'm not going to let you use my hands for your crimes, either," said Gabrels, defiantly.

"Good luck stopping me, kid."

"This might all be lies too; if kids could have their memories augmented, then who's to say that it can't happen to adults?"

Vax tried to crack his knuckles by reflex. The bones in his hands made no noise. "Okay, so if you really believe that this whole thing is fake, a dream or whatever you want to call it, not real. If that's true, then you know better than anyone, even me, what's real. There shouldn't be any doubt in your mind as to what's real and what's not. But there is doubt, isn't there? You don't know, because there's nothing there for your brain to interpret as real, nothing tucked away inside your head that you can hold onto and say 'this happened, because I know it did'. Am I right?" asked Vax.

The door was wide open now. The Academy took the place of every moment he spent with his parents. Their missing faces were replaced with new strangers.

"You don't have anything to hold onto. You are alone. If I give you a reason for the holes in your memory, something you've run from for years before I ever showed up, are you really going to deny it as nothing?"

He ran from the light back into the dark room. His mother was gone. He held the film up to the red light and waited for the negatives to show him what he wanted.

"The sad part is, that there's no emotion in your eyes or your face. All that rage for me is suddenly gone because there's no source for it. You are the remains of an experiment, a construct. Like a half written character in a bad story. You are empty."

There were no negatives. The pictures were of endless corridors, bodies of children carried out from sleeping quarters, of wires inserted into his head, and of strange men standing over him as he slept.

"Don't lose any more sleep over it. I'm going to help us both. But I need you to do something for me. I need you to solve the puzzle."

Defeated, Gabrels looked back at Vax.

"Who are you, really?" he asked.

"You'll never know."

There was familiar static in the air. The ocean came in as quick as it had left. He was swept up inside it. The image of Rion Kath, or Vax, vanished into noise, image grain. The house was gone, along with the film, the picture, his mother. Everything disappeared into the white. He let it take him and drown him deep into the sound.

Part Three:

Division by zero

Twenty Two

There was something else inside the static this time. It was warm. A thickness covered him and everything else. He was locked in a blind embrace. The white noise droned on in an infinite loop. Phantom limbs moved and stretched out to feel what had drowned with him. The warmth was tangible, different from the sea of sound. He took a piece into his hand and pressed it between the spaces that felt like fingers that still felt attached to him. The human parts of him began to take shape again. There was a smell that stirred up memories of flesh, of blood that pumped through pipeworks of veins. New warmth emanated from the ocean. The limbs had begun to reappear, outlined by motion, pulling themselves from the gripping slumber. He felt brand new, arms and legs. The blood pumped in all directions from the source. Every chamber shook with a pounding rhythm. Something had pulled him awake. It grabbed at his limbs and tried to rip him from the white noise. He laid there and let it take him. The drones continued to lose their volume. The stranglehold of static loosened.

The blood was everywhere. There was a pulse inside his body. Electricity. It sent selective shocks to every location. Activated nerves sent current, in turn, to the brain. He could move on his own for the first time. He could see in shades of red that replaced the dark in brief seconds. The warmth grew to cover everything he could touch or feel. The ocean of static was far away, replaced by waves of blood, electric. His heart became a drum that echoed the pulse of the new red sea. New shockwaves exploded from his core to every extremity. He begged for vision. The red in his eyes turned to white. The sky above changed colors until massive shapes began to form. The clouds were the color of flesh. The light was blinding but settled into the familiar revelation of morning. It was so warm. His blood was flooded out in every direction. He felt reborn in the light.

When Gabrels came to, he saw the source of the warmth. A girl sat on top of him. Her back was turned, bones protruding from her shoulders and down her back. Her arms were in the air, hands caressing her own body from hips to her neck. She was a shade of brown with wild hair. Sounds of quiet whisper cut through the vision. She moved in careful circles and bit at her shoulder. From her hips, she surged forward, which forced him to the brink of climax. He was suddenly aware and in control of everything.

He quickly pulled her off him and fell from the couch of the apartment. The girl found her footing and turned around to try and comfort him. Gabrels put his hands out and backed up to the window.

"Hey, take it easy," she said, anticipating the natural shock.

"What's going on?" he asked.

"Who are you?" he looked around the apartment. The room was dirtier than usual. There was no color schemes attached, making everything another stark green. The color and the smell made him sick. There was a mass of empty bottles that covered the floor around the table.

"Jaya," she said.

She looked like a child. His excitement was immediately gone. She had noticed and frowned in kind.

"Do you mind going back to sleep? I was kind of in the middle of something," she sighed.

"This isn't my apartment."

"Yeah, it's a room. Technically, it's a love hotel. The heart shaped bathtub and champagne is in the other room…welcome to Eros, I guess," she laughed.

Gabrels tried to remember where he was last. It hit him like a shot; he was on the elevator to the slums, then the messages from Kath, then the blackout.

"I never made it to Narrow, did I?"

"No, you didn't," she said.

"Have we met before?" asked Gabrels.

"We met yesterday."

He felt a sharp pain in his neck. It reached into his skull and squeezed. There was immense pressure.

"Actually, I met the other one," she said.

"The other one?" he asked.

"Yeah, he knew who I was. We met in a little spot around the corner. I've known of him for a while, it turns out."

The girl began to snicker. She had the same face as Helix did that night at Cyanide Sister.

"How old are you?"

She stopped and hesitated to answer. "Definitely 18."

Gabrels face turned to disgust. "You've got to be kidding me…"

He immediately stood up and began to look for something to cover up with. The needle was hidden in his shoes. There was blood within the glass, staining the plunger. He noticed the same ratty shirt and ripped jeans from the night he woke up at the bar with Helix. The smell of cigarette smoke was thick. This was all him, the son of a bitch.

"Why does he keep putting these damn clothes on me!? They don't even fit anymore!"

She rushed to him and attempted to keep him calm. "Listen, Stanley. He told me everything about what's going on. I am here to help."

He went straight into the bedroom. Jaya followed him as he got dressed into black pajamas neatly folded on the bed.

"I just turned 30. You are a child! What exactly did he say to you?! Come to my house, little girl. I've got plenty of another man's money? Did he offer candy?"

He went back to cleaning the room and shutting the windows. There were too many questions. Did anyone see her follow him upstairs? Who knows what kind of shit Kath could have done between here and the elevator to Narrow. It cost a grand to take the ride, he could have just let me come down and do the search I wanted to do, he thought. If he wants me to find shit out for myself, why stop me? Jaya folded her arms and leaned against the wall, still naked.

"I think I had something to do with him being in your head."

Gabrels stopped and turned around. His eyes immediately went to her center and he was filled with instant regret.

"Can you please put some clothes on? Please?" he looked away and motioned her towards the pile on the floor. She slowly sauntered past him and grabbed a shirt and shorts from the pile on the bed. They sat down at the couch. A pack of smokes was tucked in between the shot glasses and beer bottles on the floor. The table itself was in the shape of two hearts.

"Jesus…" said Gabrels.

"I know. Pretty lame, but cheap and away from the main streets."

"You did shots? What is he, fifteen years old?" he asked.

"Vodka and some tequila. It made us get naked pretty quickly," she said, plainly.

"Now, we have underage drinking along with pedophilia," Gabrels slammed his hand against the couch.

"Dude, relax. The age of consent is 18. You're not going to catch a charge for me."

Without thinking too much, Gabrels found himself reaching for a cigarette. The pain in his stomach was gone for the moment. It had to have been the needle. Kath dosed himself and now he would have the same hunger in time. He looked around for a lighter. Jaya handed him one without saying a word.

"You know, I hate these things." He said, as he lit it up and inhaled deep. The burn beneath his chest was intense.

"Why are 'you' doing it, then?" she asked.

Gabrels coughed loudly. "There's been sudden cravings for them, which I am deciding to indulge in for now. This guy is going to kill me, whether it's through my brain or the shit he is putting into my body. I have no tolerance for this stuff. I'm surprised I didn't puke."

Jaya wanted to put her hand on his leg. He did, a few times. But she decided to keep her distance for now.

"This is probably a dumb question since we just met, sort of…But is there a difference between us when we are in control?"

"You seem like a decent guy, a little high strung, but you're okay. He's easy to talk to, very smooth."

"Even wearing these shit clothes and smelling like a dumpster?" he asked as he took in a whiff of his own body odor.

"Just really in control, I guess. He had to turn on a lot of charm to get me to come with him, let alone party. Right now, you look like you can't handle yourself," she said, replying the events back to her audience of one.

"I'm not a fighter."

"To be honest, he picked the worst spot in Eros for me to be in and he made me feel safe. I don't know if you could do that right now." She started to lick her own lips, seeming to savor the fresh memory.

"Can you blame me? Someone else is fighting for control of my brain. That's a worse fight then anyone outside."

Both started to laugh. She put her hand on his shoulder. He felt the chill of skin on skin. Gabrels felt immediate regret and moved away from the girl.

"Tell me how you are involved," he said.

Jaya dropped the smile and sat back into the corner of the couch. "Like I said, we met in Eros last night. He set up a spot for us at the edge of Zero Block, not too far away from where I was staying."

"How is it possible that we ended up like this and you just met?" asked Gabrels, completely dumbfounded.

"He told me that you were going there to try and find him, but instead, I found you two. I guess the name they use up here for people like me, is datapunk; we're squatters, we know our way around some computers."

Gabrels remembered the name, from Kath's dossier. This kid was a squatter?

"Where are your parents?" he asked.

"I don't know. I don't care. I left them a long time ago," said Jaya.

She was a runaway. Gabrels rubbed his temples to block the pain building in his head and the back of his neck.

"I was stable, living in group houses, scamming people up here for little bits of cash to make get through the week."

"You're a hacker?" He asked before entering a coughing fit. The taste of tobacco dried out his mouth. It made him crave water. He went to the kitchen. It was a weird shade of red with no windows and a dirty light blub which lit the room with random flashes of darkness.

"We both are. At least, he was before he was killed. I also wrote code for clients, mainly anonymous work; I get a message from an unknown to put money in my account for an algorithm," said Jaya.

Two bottles of water left. He handed the full one to her and sat back down. Both took deep swigs of cold liquid.

"Thanks. I was never told what the code would be used for."

"Why?"

"It's not my business to know, the reason for the code was never the point. The client used the code for whatever they wanted, but needed someone who could connect the dots, make the code work."

"But you had to know, sooner or later, no?" asked Gabrels.

"Yeah, eventually I did. I started to pick up on the people affected soon after I delivered the codes. A lot of them were identity theft games from jaded lovers. Imagine waking up and your account is empty or seeing private pictures all over the data stream, shit like that."

"How much were you paid?"

"The last job paid me enough to leave the group house and go to Eros. My plan was live out there, write code, get paid and party. The client identified himself as V."

"Kath…" muttered Gabrels.

"Not at first. Vax reached out to me under that same letter but someone else wanted me to write that code, but it wasn't him."

"What makes you so sure?" he asked.

"Two days after I wrote the algorithm, Vax was dead, and that's when you started to have weird dreams, right?"

Gabrels nodded.

"The way that the client talked was way different from him. It's how I knew something had changed. They used perfect English and they talked like they were rich, like the cats in Eros," she said.

Jaya stood up and walked into the bathroom. If Kath was able to manipulate their channels to communicate with the girl, it made sense that he would be able to do the same thing to him. He was right, Gabrels said to himself, Kath is getting stronger the longer they are paired together. They were becoming unified. They were getting closer to sharing the same experiences, feeling the same sensations in real time instead of static dreams. He followed her to the door and saw that she left the door open and sat onto the toilet.

"Really?"

Gabrels could hear the sound of the liquid hitting the pearl.

"I know who the client is," she said.

"How?"

"I met them in a club the night they killed that Everett guy."

Gabrels got up and rushed to the bathroom. She was still sitting there, elbows to thighs, hands buried into her cheeks. The bath really was in the shape of another heart, with rose petals that sat soaking in the water.

"What happened to him?" he asked, trying to ignore the tacky imagery he was drowning in.

"It was two guys, in black suits. They were tall and pale. They both looked like ghosts. They only drank water and took the glasses with them."

"They did what?"

"And they wore gloves like they didn't want to touch anything with their own skin."

Gabrels looked to the floor. Jaya got up and washed her hands without flushing the toilet. He quickly hit the lever for her and followed her back to the couch.

"All the words they said to me to congratulate me, they said to him. They like to speak their own kind of language. Vax didn't talk to me like that. I knew right away that it was someone else, but I still didn't want to trust him. I didn't want to trust anyone after that night. The bartender put something into his drink and he choked to death right there in the middle of the club."

"No one saw anything? What about the bartender?" asked Gabrels.

"The club was packed. People were going insane in there. If you've ever been to Eros, it's nonstop. The bartender was poisoned too. It was like they had the bartender working for them, and they just took him out right after he did his part."

"How did you meet them without getting killed?"

"I was supposed to signal them by ordering a drink, but I was so messed up and tired already, I just had water. I hid behind the bar as the guy died, then went out into the crowd to hide."

"And they just walked out with no witnesses? No police?" Gabrels could not believe that they got away with that in plain sight.

"There was a ton of cops, but when I think about it; the cops had to be on the payroll. Those two had to be government types, really high up. Where I come from, you shoot someone yourself. Anyone who pays people to poison their enemies ain't from where I live."

"Why aren't you freaking out about this?" asked Gabrels.

"I've cried enough over it. We need to get him out of your head. I just need to figure how to get him a new body," she said.

Gabrels ignored her. There wasn't going to be a new body for him. He was not going to ruin anyone else's life.

"It doesn't make sense that they would just not know who you were, what you looked like, before doing business with you. I mean, you're just a kid from the slums, that's probably why they contacted you to do their code work," he said.

"Wow, thanks," said Jaya.

"No, that's not what I meant. Why let you go if Everett was such a big target? Unless they wanted you to get away…and find me."

Gabrels went to the windows and peered past the blinds. Eros was alive and breathing. The lights were intense and moved in sync with the distant music that bled together into its own sea of noise. He checked the locks on the door.

Jaya simply yawned. "No one followed us here."

"But they wanted us to meet, didn't they?"

"I don't know, Stanley. All you need to know right now is that we have a friend coming to see us soon."

"A friend?" he asked.

"Yes, I trust him. Don't get mad."

She held her hands up and prepared for the backlash. "We used some of your money to get him up here. Sorry?" she squeaked.

Gabrels took a deep breath. The girl's voice must have gotten higher in pitch when she felt guilty.

"There's no way he could have crawled through the tunnels like I did. The elevator was the best way to get him into Eros to look at your head," she explained. "He does great work, but there's something you need to see before we do anything else."

Jaya went back to the bedroom and returned with her pack. She set it on the floor and called him over to it. She pulled the black cube out and placed it between them.

"This is what I used to hack ATMs and bank accounts. He modified it to display data with the same card I used to clone people's account numbers."

"How did he do that?" Gabrels asked.

"He said it was just a change in the programming, the cards read and spit everything out in binary anyway, so he tweaked it to relay specific information from the data stream; basically information from the A.I. to you in the last 12 hours."

"Adam...Also, 12? What the hell have we been doing?" he suddenly asked.

"Well, let's just say you didn't wake up the first time," she answered proudly.

"This is ridiculous."

"He's a genius. You really should trust him, too. He got me out of Eros through his people."

"People like Catherine? And Helix?"

She looked at him for a moment with blank eyes, as if she wasn't sure how to process the name. Jaya responded with a simple nod. She knew he was watching and did not want to disappoint him.

"How long have we been here?"

"I don't remember. But at least a day," said Jaya.

Gabrels did the numbers in his head. There was less than 12 hours left before Apex goes live. How the hell did this happen? If he was trying to help and took over my body to lead me in the right direction, why did I end up with a kid in bed?

"He wants to help you, Stanley. You would be helping each other. And I'm here too."

Gabrels was quiet. This was too much, he said. The girl, whether she wrote the code or not, should not be here. Kath didn't have to bring her into this. He stopped to question if she was better off dealing with the killers alone or back in the streets.

"As much as I want to tell you to leave, I don't know what I'm doing. Tell me what you need."

She placed the clone card into the cube. "Don't be mad at him for being with me. You need to work together. I can help you," she said.

"Is that why he brought you? He could be using both of us. You just met him."

"And?" asked Jaya.

"He's a pig. And he's a thief. Those guys in suits have to be government agents. We wouldn't be in this if he didn't steal from them to begin with," said Gabrels.

"He would be dead without you, though."

"I don't care. He's a criminal."

"He can hear you, I'm sure," laughed Jaya.

"How can you trust him?"

Disdain for Kath was something to hang onto. It helped him focus.

"He figured out my codes. No one has ever done that before."

"Tell me how," pleaded Gabrels. He wanted to know as much as he could about him.

"My friend that you are about to meet, he taught me a few things before my work started to take off; masking your presence online to switch some numbers in your bank account, things like that. We would bum from house to house and whether the security was too strong up top to really take a piece big enough to live off of or if the people you were bumming with might try to kill you and take your shoes, we were constantly moving, paranoid. In between those times when we picked a couple of pockets so we could eat, I learned how to code. All of my algorithms were recursive."

"What's that?" he asked.

"It was the only way I could learn them. Small problems are easy to solve, right? If you split all the code into tiny problems, you simply add up the answers, and that is your code right there. The way I wrote code, no one could ever pick up on where the problems stopped and the answers began. Rion sat me down and explained it back to me in a way that E never could."

Jaya certainly made him sound better than the asshole from the Blank Page. He could imagine her begin hooked in an instant with sweet talk. It was just puppy love and pure bullshit from a con artist.

"I'm not sure how he would've faired meeting me without your body. It definitely helped. You clean up well," she said.

Gabrels immediately cringed. "Listen, I'm sorry for anything he did that was too much or too rough, seriously," he said.

"Thanks for your concern, but don't worry. He's been a gentleman. You've been having some fun," she squeaked. Gabrels rolled his eyes until he could not feel them.

The cube began reading the data.

"What is this?" he asked.

"Before you two collided and blacked out, you asked the A.I. to run its own code breakers against a set of numbers. The algorithm I wrote is what made up this message you received."

"The codex…" he said.

"Right. The algorithm I wrote, per the instructions of the client…"

"The men in the suits I'm guessing?"

"They have to be. The algorithm was a closed loop. It expands as missing pieces of the code are filled in. That means the entire code is revealed as you solve it, piece by piece until the loop is complete."

"What happens after that?"

"I don't know," said Jaya.

"The man who died in the bar told me that they put something inside my head, called a revenant. Did they say anything about that?"

The girl shook her head.

"If Kath is supposed to be the revenant, then the code must allow him permanent control over my body. I can't let that happen."

"Why not?" she asked.

"Because the revenant is supposed to kill a target that they set up, and I'm not going to kill. It doesn't matter if his girl was killed. I don't care about what happened to him. He played a game with dangerous people and got caught. I'm not going to jail, for him or anyone."

Gabrels was bitter. Jaya could feel it in his words. The cube began to display lines of binary, green lines of zeroes and ones that lit up the room.

"According to him, you got to a certain point, and became stuck with these numbers. The A.I. was able to decode the numbers and since we can't have you log in and get them yourself from down here, the card was able to intercept it."

"Show it to me," said Gabrels.

Jaya waited for the transmission to complete. The data took over an hour to upload. She began to assign letters to the lines. It was a transcript, a conversation that took place over the course of several months between two people. The series of numbers inside the codex repeated over themselves in a loop. In order to solve, the reader would have had to write the numbers down forwards and backwards, then use a stream cipher to crack the patterns of binary meant for each letter of the alphabet.

The two spoke in single sentences back and forth with no punctuation. Each entry was dated. Gabrels read each line with intense eyes. Jaya sat behind him. She watched him more than the words. Soon, he would be asleep and she could talk to Vax, touch him again. Gabrels began to read aloud as she thought of ways to finish what they started earlier.

"Here."

"What is it?" she asked.

"Graff knocks up a poor girl from the slums and the parents pay her off to keep quiet. Academy boys usually have a rough upbringing. How many years ago was that? At least thirty. Hard to prove."

The amount of data in the transmission was due to the paperwork included with the transcript. Gabrels opened the files to see not only pictures of a young Leland Graff but also the woman from his picture; the portrait that he had stored for years.

"Who is that?" asked Jaya.

"It's my mother," he said.

The photos were meant as a threat to the buyer.

"These pictures are supposed to mean something, Everett?"

Jaya looked at Stanley in shock. "Everett? From the bar?"

Gabrels ignored her and continued to read. Following the photography, there were acceptance papers written and signed for a boy to be passed over to the care of the Academy. He would be given a new identity, a new name. The originals were redacted but the papers would be impossible to doctor given the current technology.

"Do we have a deal, Anon?"

The words soon faded away, back into zeroes and ones. His name wasn't even his own. His memory was created and shoved into his brain, leaving only small traces of where he came from. It was only now that they began to push through the cracks of what they put there.

"You give us your prototype and you can have ours."

Jaya asked questions. He didn't bother to try and answer. The world had crumbled and fell from up. There was nothing but false information and lies that had been poured into his ears and eyes ever since he was taken away from where he belonged.

"What prototype?" asked Jaya.

"It's a capacity doubler. It increases your personal data storage. From what Everett told me, he had never used it, but he mentioned me not being the first to be infected with a revenant."

"He's not a virus. He's a real person, trapped in there."

"I think the doubler was used on whoever had a revenant. I don't think it would work without it."

"This is crazy," she admitted finally.

"Listen to this; the bottom line? We want the doubler. I know you want the Codex. You are playing a dangerous game. You of all people should know who we work for," read Gabrels.

"What's the Codex, exactly?" asked Jaya.

"Kath told me it was some advanced tech that the feds asked him, and I guess others like him that they captured, to design. It's something to do with mapping the human brain and the way it stores information."

Jaya looked away. Gabrels noticed the troubled look in her eyes.

"He didn't tell you what it was?" he asked.

"Not yet."

"In two days, a new program is coming out that will affect everyone attached to Adam and newDawn. It's called Apex. It links everyone's thoughts and previous memories together. Rion did tell me about that…But I don't know why we need the Codex back."

"I guess he never got to make that deal," she said.

"How do you know that?" he asked.

"The buyer did not meet him. They sold him out, and Machina killed him for it."

"Are you sure?"

"The guys in the suits told him that they found the buyer and got rid of him," she said.

"It has to be Machina. He worked there for seven years, kept the doubler from them. The guys in black you were talking about? Not just government, but Machina hitmen, probably."

"Stanley, those guys are feared in Narrow. People disappearing off the streets, sightings of men in suits, never their faces, just the backs of their heads and shadows. Down here, they're called the Shadowmen."

"Agents for Machina, and maybe for Graff, too…"

Gabrels dug his fingers deep into his palms.

"Where is it? Where is the doubler?" Jaya pulled on his shirt, begging for answers.

"It's in my head now," he whispered.

How was it possible that Kath was right? He was only a bad dream, an interruption from sleep. His life wasn't supposed to turn out like this. The money in his account was saved and protected for when he had enough of the Epicentre, the advertisements, the lying to the public about what he was told needed to be viewed as the best technology.

"Why is it in your head?" she asked.

"Everett made a physical copy and Kath put it in when I was sleeping."

The remainder of the lines sealed the deal between Everett and the buyer. Gabrels stood up and walked to the door. Jaya took the cube and the card and connected them to her own terminal.

"Can you check my bank account?"

Jaya smiled. "Not a problem."

She opened it without even asking him a password. He watched her attack the keys, her eyes moved in step with the passing screens that flipped through every backdoor of the system into the supposed impenetrable security that Adam had built up.

"Okay, got it. What are we looking for?"

Gabrels lost his train of thought. His eyes closed.

"Stanley!"

He woke back up and looked to the girl. She held her hands up, ready.

"Have there been any deposits to my account?"

Jaya looked back to the numbers and screamed. "Oh yeah, you got hit with a huge fine but the money was put back in. No source for the deposit. Let me see if I can trace the funds. It had to come from a real account."

Gabrels rocked back and forth. He kept quiet to let her search.

"The way I funnel cash is pretty simple, just picking bits and pieces from people with high activity accounts. They usually never notice the little changes here and there; the few fifties and hundreds I take," she said.

"Why so little?" asked Gabrels.

"If you're caught with any money in Narrow, it's taken from you. Sometimes, you don't make it any further than that."

"Who takes it from you?"

Her fingers still battered the keyboard but her eyes moved to the corners of the room.

"For a while, it used to be my roommates. But after that, it was cops, the riot squads that would run us out of our spots, and even people you thought you could trust," she said reluctantly.

"You don't trust very many people, do you?" he asked.

Jaya did not answer.

"Criminals are all alike, aren't they?" she asked.

Gabrels said nothing else. He didn't want to think of her the same way as Kath, but maybe it was reality.

"This looks familiar," she said.

"What is it?"

"The money was put through a few shell corporations; just empty offices still occupying space in Tempest and in the slums. These are fronts for illegal cash to move through. The people paying for their dirt to be handled never move the money on their own, there's always little hands making the moves for them."

"Can you tell whose hands they belong to?" asked Gabrels.

"Yeah, normally there's a signature they leave behind. It's a way to document who is running that operation or who owns that space so no one steps in and starts a problem. It's all done anonymously, but there are certain codes that mark the signature. If you know the codes, you can trace it back to the real source."

Gabrels took another drink of water. A shiver went down his spine. His body felt strange. The energy was leaving his body. He struggled to keep his eyes on the girl.

"Here you go."

Jaya stopped and turned the screen back towards Gabrels. "The signature left behind in the trail that led to your account comes from people who move money for a shell company which is owned by a man named Stevens St. John."

"Stevens? Graff's right hand?" Gabrels looked into the eyes of the man who stood behind him at the Synapse deal. He had the same style of pinstripe suit and the same ridiculous coiffed hair.

"How do you know it's the right signature? The right people?"

"The code is just like the ones in the same anonymous masks they use to funnel cash through dummy accounts in Narrow."

"You've seen it before?" Gabrels could barely breathe. Was it true? Was that man really…?

"I wouldn't try to track all of the accounts and their sources now. We risk giving them our location. But someone did put cash back in and it wasn't Precipice LLC, whatever that is."

"It's where I work. We were paid off to write pieces to enhance the public's opinion of the Synapse Corporation. Everett worked for their biggest rival."

"And you two were going to screw both of them over? That sounds like reason enough to get killed off," said Jaya.

"By the way, I checked your emails, and it looks like you've been terminated from that place."

"What?!" Gabrels screamed.

He pushed her aside to read the message. Miller had written the message himself. Keys was imprisoned for assault but the company decided that he was no longer worth keeping on the payroll. If Apex proves to be a success, the need for revs would disappear in the ether of the data stream. The company would be sold off to another group. Miller thanked him for his work and wished him an easy recovery. The last line stuck to him like a bullet; "Maybe now you can finally get out of this place and relax for a bit. Take care of yourself."

"Son of a bitch," he muttered. Gabrels stood up and began to frantically pace the room. Jaya looked at him with optimistic eyes. As smart as she was, she had no clue about this place, he thought.

"You bastards have now cost me more than just my savings, you cost me my job."

"I'm sorry, Stanley."

There was nothing else to say. Apex was coming soon. He wanted to be there to watch whoever responsible for this crumble as Adam revealed their part in this circus. All he could do now is get Kath out of his head.

"Who was Everett talking to?" he asked.

"That's the easy part. The data in the code is easy to track once the puzzle was cracked. He wanted me to show you this once you woke up."

"You both know who it is, don't you?"

Jaya rattled a hundred keystrokes into the terminal and turned the screen towards him again.

"You're lucky you have us on your side."

Gabrels stumbled and caught himself. Jaya smiled and held her hand out to him. He took it, sat back down and pulled the screen closer. Within seconds, she had tracked the messages to Everett from another apartment in the same tenement, one floor below him. The room belonged to Aaditya Bhagavateeprasaad.

"Who is that?" asked Jaya.

Gabrels tried to breathe in but the air was caught in his chest. There was a minute of uncomfortable silence.

"It's Sumerian."

The room began to spin. It was difficult to keep his eyes open. He turned to the girl, who said nothing. He tried to speak but was out cold again on the floor. Jaya simply smiled and waited.

Twenty Three

Ten hours remaining.

It took time for the eyes to open again. The body of Stanley Gabrels stood up and stretched its back muscles. Jaya took a deep breath and kept her eyes on the floor, stealing glimpses of him. She looked to him briefly with admiration and put her hand on his leg. He grabbed her hand and pulled her up to her feet. He kissed her hard. She made a noise of satisfaction behind her lips. Vax was settling into Gabrels' skin.

"I don't think I can give this thing up. Regards to the little boy who let me have this much fun," he said.

"Hopefully, you don't have to," Jaya purred.

"I can't imagine I will last too much longer in here with him. How did he take the news?"

"Speechless. He seemed really sad, and he still hates you, especially after he woke up with me on top of you."

He kissed her again. She felt shocks of energy that moved through her bones when she tasted him. The body moved so different when it was Vax in control of the skin. Stanley was meek and bothered. He didn't carry himself like he should. The voice even spoke in a higher pitch. He was a child in a grown man's body.

"Stanley is a nice guy, though."

"He's not like us. He's never had to struggle or work for anything. His success was handed to him."

"It doesn't matter. Don't hurt him, okay?" she asked.

"The mind does it on purpose. It can't take the pressure of both of us in there."

"Did he really just lose all his memory?" She asked.

Vax picked up the terminal and went to the couch. "It's worse than you think. I was able to find out more about this Sumerian guy. Apparently, he's Gabrels' co-worker. Imagine how he feels knowing that practically everyone he's worked with has been lying to him."

"How are you able to do all that while he is awake?" she asked.

Jaya sat on his lap and wrapped her arms around his neck.

"The A.I. doesn't pick up on my movements. I can request messages to be sent out and deleted right after. Gabrels doesn't need to see what I'm doing. The good thing is I can do a lot more over here than in Tempest. Adam's network is tapped into almost every aspect of the body's systems.

It's all based on the data stream and the satellites that transmit everyone's personal data back and forth between each other. Distance from the satellites creates white noise, more difficult for the A.I. to reach out."

"And you have been able to bypass the A.I. this entire time?"

Vax pulled her arms down from his neckline to breathe better. The girl laughed. "I haven't been trying to hide from it. Whoever put me in there did a really good job of making sure there aren't any signs of foul play."

"What does that mean?"

Vax stared at her with a raised eyebrow. "You've never heard of that expression before?" He asked.

"We don't talk that old shit in the slums."

"Oh, that's right. You are cutting edge. Real cool. No throwback. It means signs of shit being tampered with. These guys are pros. Everything they are doing, or not doing, must be by design. You will learn to appreciate the old school if you stick around."

"I can't wait," she exhaled.

"We need to get him ready. Did you tell him about what I put under the floorboards?"

"No."

"Keep that one between us and always have it on hand." He put a finger to her lips, which she proceeded to bite.

"How long were you watching out for me?" she asked.

"Since Tokyo Siren. They had one of their new kids slip you a pill."

"That was your idea?" Jaya tightened up.

"The pill was Nalmefene. It's supposed to keep you from drinking, and make you sick if you do."

"Well, that backfired on him."

Vax rubbed her neck and laughed. "I think you handled that well. He didn't have a chance."

The girl began to relax again. The data from the card sat looking back at them both. Vax decided to make a quick copy and then smashed the cube against the wall.

"I made that when I was sixteen," she sighed.

"Trust me. We don't want anyone finding us; our real names, where we came from, what we are about to do. There's going to be nothing but heat on us when we're done."

There was a knock on the door. Vax and Jaya kept quiet. They waited for the lock to break. The sounds of nervous stumbling echoed through the thin walls. A chubby kid dressed in a wrinkled black shirt and faded grey jeans burst through the door with a heavy pack slung over his shoulder. His glasses fell to the floor. He looked at them both blankly and then slumped down to pick the cracked lenses back up.

"Hi, E," said Jaya.

"Your message made things a lot worse than they look," said the kid. Vax nodded towards him. "Ergo, yeah?"

"Yes, sir. And you must be him, right? The one and only Vax. I have to say, it is an honor to meet you. Me and Jaya heard all about you through the other squatters, the old crust punks who talked about the messages you would send out every month."

Ergo threw his pack down and began to take out messes of wires and boards. "Jaya and I used to try and decode some of them ourselves."

"The cipher was only known of by a handful of people. The network consists of hookers and hotel workers in Eros all the down to us in Narrow. They still keep in contact. It's how we all got together in this room."

"So, how did they finally catch you?" asked Ergo.

"We all thought you disappeared, and then some shit footage goes viral showing you running from the cops."

"I got hit by a car uh, really hard and then, I died," said Vax.

Ergo went quiet and looked at Jaya.

"This isn't his body, E. Someone implanted him in here."

"Then, who is this guy?" he asked.

"Just some geek writer from Tempest. It turns out he was a guinea pig in a black project up top."

Ergo emptied the rest of his pack onto the floor. There was a pile of soldered grids and plugs that he began to connect, wire by wire. "Is that why you need a scan?"

"You know it. I have a theory about what's going on in here, but I need something definite. We don't have a lot of time."

Ergo stayed silent as he connected the rest of the pieces. A full scan would take an hour. The grids formed a barrier that surrounded his temples and the top of Stanley's cranium. Each one would record the current neurotransmission--the process where the nerve cells carrying electrical and chemical signals through the brain--in search of any synaptic damage, miscommunications or lost connections.

He plugged into the series of cords, which took power from the mini-generator he brought. Plugging into the electricity of the hotel would have drained the room and maybe others adjacent to them. The grids began to make tapping sounds. Vax focused on the noise and slowed down his breathing. The noise reminded him of the Morse code samples they would play when working on deciphering framework data from Adam's prototype.

"Do we need to run a scan as me? Then one when Gabrels is in control?" he asked.

"No…One is enough," said Ergo.

Jaya laid on the couch and stared up at the ceiling. She had never put her pants back on. Her legs were a beautiful brown that curled and moved to create heat between her thighs. Ergo could not help but stare. There was a growing anger inside him. He was worried sick about her. The message she said had made no mention of another man. Vax was wide awake during the scan. Ergo kept his mouth shut but stared a hole into the eyes of the man sitting in front of him.

"You like her," he mumbled.

Jaya turned to them. Ergo said nothing but his eyes were wide.

"Am I right?" asked Vax. A smirk cut across his face. "You can tell that we slept together. Can you smell it? Do you want to catch a bit? Maybe on my finger here? It was a little bit earlier, actually. You could've walked in on us if he didn't wake up first."

The tapping of the grids continued on.

"She must be real good to do that kind of magic, to wake someone up from being half dead. Don't you think?"

Ergo began to sweat.

"I don't think you've seen her with her pants off before."

He was right.

"Rion, what are you doing?" asked Jaya.

"I don't want to step on any man's toes. If you haven't picked up on his signals, then you're obviously a bad friend."

"It's not like that with him and me," she said.

"Why don't you let him answer the question? It's not my style to ruin another man's heart."

He wanted to look at Jaya but he couldn't. She was nearly killed and he has been running with her ever since their parents both decided to take off for the wilderness and leave them in the care of foster homes. She was the only girl he ever thought about being with. She was the only one that would talk to him.

"Do you have a problem with me sleeping with your girl…Ergo?" Vax asked. Ergo finally looked at him and saw that blood had begun to run from his nostrils.

"You're bleeding…"

Vax ran his finger beneath his nose and saw the blood. He quietly licked it off, keeping his eyes on Ergo.

"And you didn't answer my question."

He wanted to throw a chair against the wall and ask her why she brought him here. How could she sleep with him after just meeting him? Vax was a legend, one that they both idolized for years. He was the one they dreamed to be like when they were living off of two dollars a day and sleeping back to back in a house full of old burnouts and bootleg newDawn addicts. Did she just invite him here to flaunt this little conquest in his face? What kind of friend does that? She didn't even get up when he walked into the room.

"…No problem at all…" said Ergo.

All three were quiet until the tapping of the grids completed. Ergo studied the code for a few minutes. Vax stood up from the chair. He cleaned the blood from his face and cracked his neck.

"When we come back, I'm going to be a completely different person. Tell me what the hell is going on in here."

"Is this the first time you've bled while awake?" Ergo asked.

"As far as I know, yeah. We might be fighting now for the same space. The doubler has given me some room to grow."

Ergo finished reading the code and looked back towards them. "This is really bizarre…"

"What is?" asked Vax.

"The readings are incredibly detailed. Usually, I use the grids for measuring my own stress levels, ways to document and help treat my own anxiety. It will pick up on changes in brain wave patterns, things that stick out from the normal beats, extreme arousals in the nervous system."

"Somehow, I don't see you as one being overly aroused," said Vax. Jaya punched him in the kidney. Ergo continued on.

"Think of it like the time changes in a song. But according to this, whether it's always been this way or not, both you and this other guy's brain waves are operating at full capacity now. It's like two people inside the same space; I can see his dreaming as clearly as your current thoughts."

"I don't think I would have as much control without it. It started off with just minor things like opening his eyes, or getting out of bed. Eventually, he would wake up but with the extra space for me to operate, young Stan here can stay asleep while I handle business unless there's something to trigger the change," said Vax.

"Like what?" asked Ergo.

"Physical pain, or now…intense pleasure," Vax grinned.

Ergo hated himself for asking the question.

"Even though, the bleeding is taking place now when you are in control of the body, you don't feel any real pain, do you?"

"Not at all," said Vax.

"Because you're not the host. You're the vector, spreading all over the host's space. You two are now fighting for control. It's neural synthesis on a level I have never seen before."

"But there's no way they can maintain this for long, can they? The more they fight the more damage they would cause to the brain, right?" asked Jaya.

"Right." Ergo agreed.

"This Stanley guy must be feeling a lot more pain that he is letting on. Probably because he wants to block it out. But the longer you are inside, and the bigger you get, the fight will turn fatal."

A wave of sickness hit Vax. Tears formed and made him shut his eyes, away from the light of the room.

"What's wrong, baby?" asked Jaya. Ergo was disgusted as he mouthed the word himself.

"I can feel him. Why now?"

"The more the infection spreads, if you will, the body reacts to protect itself. You two are going to end up killing each other. You may not have felt anything before but it's about to change, obviously," said Ergo.

Vax lunged past Ergo and went to the mirror in the bathroom. He pried his eyelids open to see himself. The whites of Stanley's eyes turned a blood red. For a second, he could see a vulture on his shoulder. The reflection of the room turned to the blinding white of the Blank Page.

"How much time do they have left? asked Jaya.

"I have no idea. If this keeps going uninterrupted, there could be a massive cranial rupture and neither would survive that."

"Can you get him out of there?" she pulled at his shirt. Ergo wanted to push her away but let her hands stay on his chest. It felt good.

"I could try, but besides alleviating some of the pressure on the brain and skull, I wouldn't know how to transfer Vax without killing one of them. We don't have a place to put him."

Jaya let go of Ergo and beat her fists against her legs.

"Lilah!"

She walked past Ergo and entered the bathroom. The kid's jaw had dropped.

"L...Lilah?" he whispered, crushed.

"What is it, baby?" Jaya caressed the back of Vax's neck.

"We need to get to Tempest, see this Sumerian. You know his location. Reach out to him as Gabrels. Set up a meeting. If he won't meet, then I will drop in on him myself."

Vax punched the mirror, shattering the glass. A shard cut into his hand. He welcomed a replacement pain for the splinter in his mind. Jaya ran to the kitchen and unraveled paper towels to wrap his hand. Ergo stood there in silence watching the two.

"You are coming with us," said Vax.

"I'm going to bring something back, it will help with the transfer. Just follow our lead and do not leave us."

They gathered their things and left the room. Jaya used Gabrels' money to pay for the damage in the hotel. Vax kept his eye on the blood collecting in the towel wrapped around his fingers. From the street corner of Zero Block, it was a half mile before the train. He left for the train platform first. Jaya threw her pack on and ran after him. Ergo stopped her before she could turn the corner.

"What is it, E?"

Ergo looked around the corner to see if Vax was gone. "Are you sure this is what you want?" He wanted to say more. She got the message and nodded her head before sprinting off behind. Ergo punched a hole into the wall and slammed the door shut.

Twenty four

The Blank Page did not load at first. Static blocks came in and out of sight as the world was attempting to build itself. Vax stood in the middle and waited for a familiar voice. He kept his eyes closed in the dark and waited for the light to fill every empty space. The pain was still there, a dull ache in his skull and his hand. A small shard of glass from the mirror was dug deep into his palm. He kept it to wake him up. He needed to be in the shadows to do what was needed.

Vax heard the blocks spinning and connecting. The mind struggled to create the world he had grown accustomed to. Pain slowly faded with each sound of crashing waves. The static sea began to flow into his structure of puzzle pieces. The waters filled his shoes and left him cold. It felt real for the very first time. The call of birds filled the artificial air. The darkness was gone, as was the pain. He smiled.

"This is a first, isn't it?" Gabrels stepped forward from the endless white. He was dressed in the same clothes as always.

Vax opened his eyes. Stanley was in front of him with arms crossed. "Like a sun that won't turn off…" His hands were clean of blood. There were no wounds. His torn jeans and hooded shirt both stained in dirt.

"Interesting moment we find ourselves in, yeah?" asked Vax.

"Is that all you can say? We are going to die, both of us. We still don't know how to stop it."

"Let me handle that. I need you to do something. I need you to see your old co-worker."

"Why?" asked Gabrels.

"Because he is the missing piece to the puzzle. He knows more than he should, otherwise he wouldn't be alive right now."

"You mean with Everett trying to coerce him into letting released from whatever hold they had on him? He didn't want to keep helping them, to keep making these revenants to kill whoever got in the way of their plans…"

"We need to know what's keeping them from getting rid of him. You can do that better than me because you can play to his sympathy," said Vax.

Gabrels turned his back and looked to the birds. "You mean talking about how my life sucks because I just lost my job due to this asshole in my head who stole from the government, got killed and is now using my body for banging a girl like, half his age?"

"Are you really going to do this now, kid?" Vax rolled his eyes. There wasn't any time for this. "Jealous, Stan? You shouldn't be. You got a good enough example, this last time."

"You are shameless. She doesn't realize what you are doing, but I do. Don't chew up this girl like the last one."

"Helix wasn't chewed up. She did the job you paid her for, and then some. This is not a place we could've gotten to on our own."

"And when all is done, and we get separated, what will happen to her? Are you going to leave her out here on her own? Toss her back to the slums with that other kid? They're defenseless out here."

"I don't know…I'm starting to like the new girl. I might keep her around after all this is done. She tastes like strawberries."

Gabrels was mortified. He couldn't help but laugh at him. "You're a piece of shit."

"Despite all that you've seen or heard, you still don't know a thing about me. The girl is helping us."

"That doesn't give you the right to damage them with your bullshit. Sleeping with her does nothing to help us, it will only make her cling to you, which is going to get us all killed if you fuck her over! Is that the only way you can get people to like you or help you?!"

Vax walked to Gabrels and stepped into his body. They phased through each other. Both bodies turned into static before reverting back to their residual images. They were face to face now.

"Do you even know how to use your dick? Are you a virgin?"

"You know I'm not."

"Sure, but you probably forgot her name, too, just like you did, your entire childhood. I know that you remember how to please a woman, at least on paper. But can you recall a time when you actually did it with your own hands? Or was that another temporary memory?"

Gabrels wanted to claw the man's eyes out. "It's funny that you keep trying to belittle me when you couldn't even escape a car. All the cops chasing you and a beat up old station wagon took out the legendary Vax. Give me a break."

He stepped back into Vax, reverting them both back to static. The white noise was louder now. It filled both their ears. "You're a joke. Just like me. I work for a living. You steal and you use others to survive."

"Survive, is the key word, kid."

"I'm not a kid! You aren't even older than me! Why are you trying to act so tough with me, still? You aren't anything in here."

Gabrels screamed at the top of his lungs. The white noise intensified. They both felt it. The synthesis made every sensation more and more real. He wanted to make Kath's ears bleed.

"You are nothing but a bad dream, and always will be. You don't exist anymore without me. Without my body, you would be fucked! Do you hear me?!"

"Yeah, I hear you. Now get the fuck away from me."

Gabrels refused to move. "I saw the needle."

"And?"

"I think you are weaker than I ever was."

The static poured on until it began to bury them.

"I already died. I'm not afraid to do it again. You want to know so much about me, as if it will change things. I don't need to tell you shit. You found out what you think you need to know about me. Why?"

Gabrels said nothing.

"We aren't going to grow closer together, or become partners in crime. Let me ask you something, are you ready to die? Do you want to know what it feels like? I can tell you what I remember, which is a lot of fucking pain and then nothing! There was nothing but a long stretch of black. It's the same thing I see when you close your eyes to sleep. Nothing. I'm used to the dark. You can't stand it."

Vax stepped outside of the white noise, bringing their bodies back. Gabrels stared into the eyes of his enemy. "The empty room in the Academy is you. Everything you are clinging to is fake. You can't tell me anything about my life, you don't even have one. The only thing you should want to do now is get a new life. Pay them back for doing this to both of us, instead of trying to prove to a complete stranger who you used to be. That doesn't fucking matter either."

Was he telling the truth about death? Gabrels asked himself. Was there really nothing but a black void? The thought calmed him. It cleared his head. Both of them had been damaged by this. There had been enough fighting from within. But what could he do once he found those who put them in this hell? There was a long pause before he opened his mouth again.

"What do we do if Sumerian will not help?" he asked.

"He doesn't have to agree. He is going to help us whether he wants to, or not."

Vax began to walk into the distance. Gabrels called out to him. "I hope I never see your face again after this."

Vax disappeared into the white but his voice was as clear as ever when he whispered into Gabrels' ear. "You won't."

Nine hours remaining.

Gabrels opened his eyes to the train car. The pulsing lights of Eros were moving away from the crowd packed inside the steel. A sharp pain hit his hand. He opened his palm and dropped a shard of glass which shattered against the floor. The people inside were pushed shoulder to shoulder, their bodies stuffed into the same business suits and dresses. Everyone looked out towards the fading lights like they wanted to be anywhere else at that moment. Nothing had changed but him.

He was not alone. Jaya stood next to him, along with Ergo. Both looked tense. Everyone around them had taken a full step back. They were not wanted.

"Is that the friend?" he asked. She nodded.

"Ergo, is it?" The kid shook his head, also. They felt foreign. Gabrels connected to newDawn. He could see the status updates from the passengers, commenting on them;

"Some Narrow folk just got on the train."

"Whole car starting to stink now."

"Should we call the Police?"

"Hands on your wallets."

Adam appeared at the opposite end of the car. It moved towards him, passing every person who avoided catching eyes with the slum kids pressed against the corner seats. Its shell passed through their bodies as it greeted him the same as ever.

"Good evening, Mr. Gabrels. How was the journey to Narrow?"

"Painful," he replied.

"That is unfortunate. Have you seen your recent messages? Mr. Miller has terminated you from Precipice LLC."

"I know, thank you. I need you to find Sumerian for me. Can you open a line to him?" asked Gabrels.

"Of course. Mr. Bhagavateeprasaad is leaving his apartment in the tenements. I am opening a conversation with him now."

"Thank you."

Jaya could not believe what was happening. Ergo kept both hands in the pockets of his jeans. Both had heard stories of how the A.I. worked, how it interfaced directly with the user's eyes and ears. Stanley was talking to someone, but they could not see or hear anything.

"How much did it cost to get the implant?" asked Jaya.

"I don't know," said Gabrels.

They asked more questions but he blocked them out. Adam relayed his message to Sumerian.

"Hey." He kept his open with Adam. "If he does not respond, tell me where he is going."

"Understood. Is this an urgent matter?"

"It is. He doesn't need to know that yet, okay Adam?"

The shell clasped its hands and took a step back into the crowd.

"Gabrels, what are you doing?" Sumerian responded.

"Not much. Are you free tonight?"

"I can't, not right now. Sucks that you lost your job. We should have gone to dinner more."

Adam pulled his recent transactions. There was a reservation for one at Café Icarus. Level 35 of the Epicentre.

"We definitely can now. I could use your help on a project that's come up. Do you have a few minutes to spare?"

"Sorry, Gabrels. I will keep in touch with you. A lot more now that Keys is gone."

The transmission was cut from Sumerian's side.

"Adam, can you get us inside?"

"Icarus is not sold out this evening, would you like a table?"

"As close to him as you can get," said Gabrels.

The A.I. went quiet. Jaya tugged on his shirt to get his attention.

"What did you find out?" she asked.

"He's not going to meet with us. What did Kath say we need to do once we actually catch up with him?"

"Leave that to me," she said.

The sounds of the train filled the silence.

"This is amazing," Jaya whispered to him.

"You would think. But seeing this route every day takes some of the luster away."

The A.I. sent a notification to Gabrels. Fifteen minutes to level 35. Table for one. $500.

Gabrels asked Adam to display the picture of his mother.

"You hate this place, yeah?" she asked.

"I've been here for years, so I guess I do. The more I look at the walls, the machines, I am tired of it."

The portrait appeared in the car. The visage of the woman was gone, replaced with an empty room in the Academy. The window leading to the outside let the sun pour inside to light the room. The bed was unmade. The door was left open to show the dark corridor and the other rooms in the hall.

"Can I ask you a serious question?" asked Jaya.

He turned to her, not saying a word.

"I know that it seems like things are falling apart right now, but don't you think this is good? It's a change from what you've been doing. When this is done, you should just leave this place and do something new."

Gabrels tried to think about it. "Do I have enough money to leave this place? Probably not. Even if Graff is my father and he put the money back into my account, it won't stay there when Apex is active. Any crimes undiscovered will be common knowledge and it will be taken away. I will be left with nothing when this is done. Whether you want to believe it or not, Kath has ruined me. He is using us, all of us, to get what he wants."

Jaya did not want to believe him. Ergo heard enough.

"He's right," said Ergo. Those in the crowd nearest to him grimaced and pushed back even further.

"Don't worry about me, both of you. He's not using any of us."

The train announced its next stop just before its abrupt jolt. The three pushed their way through the irritated crowd and to the door. They stepped out onto the platform. Café Icarus was the first entrance from the train.

"Mr. Bhagavateeprasaad is inside," said the A.I.

"Stay outside," Gabrels said to both Jaya and Ergo.

He entered the café. A welcome sign in golden neon lit a thin hallway which he followed to reach the dining area. Icarus was dimly lit with artificial candles laid on each table. The scene was intimate, with black curtains that flowed in rhythm with the ventilation that cooled the area. Gabrels stood in the dark for a moment when a gentle hand grabbed his arm. A young woman, dressed in shimmering dress of silver, smiled.

"Good evening. Can you tell me your name, please?" her face was lit up by the light reflecting off the silver. Her skin and hair shined.

"Stanley Gabrels. Table for one."

"Follow me," she said, demure.

The music was a mixture of drums and synth. A woman's lilting voice floated over the sound. Gabrels sat down at his table and studied the room in search of Sumerian. The chairs were fine leather that obscured the heads of many of the other people inside. He was relieved, since it meant that he wouldn't be spotted right away, as well.

All around him were near reflections of his former self; those who avoided trouble and tucked themselves away into their own corners of the world. They were the ones who silently observed the façade around them and did nothing but order the most expensive food and drink to advertise their good taste to others just like them.

His table was tucked into a booth, covered in a thin black cloth like the others. The fake candles lit up in front of him with a golden glow. A small screen displayed in front of him using newDawn. It was a menu showing expensive steak dinners and French appetizers. The drinks were heavy mixtures of decades old brown liquors. He chose a glass of water and garlic bread.

The same hostess from the entrance brought a dish with both his food and drink. When she passed, he saw his face. Sumerian was sitting nearly across from him. Gabrels felt a pain in his chest. They were the only two sitting alone. He quickly stood up and held his breath. The young girl swayed between the tables in the center, checking on the other couples. He moved around the tables behind her. Sumerian took a sip of his drink. Gabrels made the move and walked quickly to the booth. Sumerian saw him and flinched. Gabrels sat across from him, ready to sit him back down if he tried to move. He looked as if he was thinking it over.

"Stanley..." said Sumerian nervously.

"What are you doing here?"

"I think you know why."

The hostess noticed the empty booth and began to look around.

"Look, if you want me to help get your job back, I can't. Keys flipped out and broke into your apartment and I'm sorry that happened. You beat the shit out of him, Gabrels. He was hospitalized. Miller said that since the day you snapped on Keys in the office, there's no way anyone would talk to you after that. It's a safety risk."

"I know I'm not getting my job back. There are a lot of things I'm not in control of, but I bet that there's a reason for that. You know what's happening to me, don't you Aaditya?"

Sumerian laughed. "You've never called me by my actual name before. Is that because you never gave a shit about me until the day you find yourself in trouble? You pronounced it wrong, by the way. Still, I appreciate the effort. You better get out of here before I report you to the Police."

The hostess caught eyes with Gabrels and began to shimmy forward.

"Maybe I should call you Anon instead?"

"What did you say?" Sumerian sat forward.

"Isn't that what Everett called you? Before he died?"

The hostess cut the silence. "Sir, you moved from your table. Do you want me to bring some more food or some water over?"
Sumerian put his hand up.

"He's not staying. Can you see him back to his table, please?"

"What's wrong, Anon? Are you afraid that I will say something to your friends in black?"

The hostess looked back at Sumerian, who broke into laughter.

"You know what? Bring his food over. He needs to stick around."

The young girl complied. Gabrels' eyes followed her to the booth and back. They were alone again.

"You think you know what's going on?" asked Sumerian.

"I know that someone put a revenant in my head. Everett used to be a part of it, until you sold him out. Am I right?"

Sumerian took another sip of his drink. "Everett came to me with information that was long buried. I made a choice to protect myself but feel free to keep going."

"These Shadowmen work for Machina don't they? Just like you?" asked Gabrels. Sumerian didn't answer.

"They're the ones behind this, not Graff. They killed Rion Kath for taking the Codex. It was the old man's request to get rid of him for stealing that tech…"

"Stop right there. You think he was stealing it?" Sumerian asked. Gabrels' eyes narrowed.

"Kath didn't steal the IO technology."

"IO?" Gabrels stopped him.

"The Codex was the tentative name for what they call the IO drive."

"Input and output, like a computer?"

"You are catching on. He took it back from them. Hell, Kath was the one who designed the whole thing."

There it was, he thought. Proof of Kath's deception. He lied to him in the Blank Page. If Kath created the IO technology then he was responsible for all of this.

"They are going to use Kath's anger to eliminate Graff, using my body as some kind of vessel. What is the purpose of the IO drive? What does it do?"

Gabrels knew then and there he could not be trusted again. Whether he or the girl needed him, he wouldn't allow him to take control of his body.

Sumerian leaned forward from his seat. "To understand what the drive does, you first have to understand the revenant system. When a human body dies, the brain still has between 10-12 minutes of activity. You are still aware of the functionality of Apex, yes? The Codex was the first version of what would become the Apex software. Instead of linking the memories and neural connectors to an entire population, IO was the first case of documenting the structure of adult human memory, storing it for later use."

"What kind of use?" Gabrels asked.

"IO has always designed in hopes of transferring the memory it stored, its primary application would be to upload the memories into another body, essentially moving active consciousness from one shell to another. If someone wanted to, they could put their mind, whatever hard-wired memories left into another body."

"And it started with experiments using freshly dead bodies, didn't it?"

"Correct, sir," Sumerian continued.

"Their stated goal was to use technology to make immortality an actual choice, and not something written about in stories or myths. If they could transfer a single consciousness to another body, one could in theory, continue living by moving from body to body as long as the data held up."

"How is that possible? What does this have to do with these revenants? I'm not even sure what to call them."

"The revenant system consists of three parts; a proxy, who holds the revenant and is given a code to solve. The code is written by an engineer. Once the code is solved, the revenant takes full control of the body and is programmable by the designers."

"The Shadowmen," answered Gabrels.

"Precisely."

Gabrels connected the dots; Jaya was the engineer who wrote the code for Kath to take over his body. If that happens, The Shadowmen could do whatever they want with him.

"How long does it take to gain control?"

"It depends on the code, but generally a few days at best. That is how long it takes before the revenant dies out."

"Dies out?"

"The brain activity remaining in a cadaver cannot last forever," said Sumerian.

"And how do they program the proxy to do anything they want?" He asked.

"The same way the IO stores and transfers information, they do it through the manipulation of nerves in the brain. Those are the building blocks of memory. The great Vax of the slums was one of the few who could help them learn to control those blocks. Once you know how to control them, see what they are made of, then you can change them, or make brand new ones altogether."

"Memory creation?"

"I'm sure you know all about that now that you have come this far. Every boy from the Academy has had that same world shattering experience."

"You too?" Gabrels was stunned.

"And Everett, as well. I am sure that is what started him on the path to the truth of his surroundings. The mind is funny in the way it reacts to a false memory. Imagine the rudest awakening possible; you meet a girl, or boy if you prefer. You take her out to dinner and spend the night. You can recall every word said, the sights, the smells, even the way she tastes. The next morning, she is gone and the entire night slowly burns away. Even if you want to believe it was real, the body will not allow you to retain any traces of it. You are hopeless to try and keep something unreal in a place where it never existed."

Gabrels wasn't as alone as he thought, maybe.

"Was it the same for you, Stanley?"

"Years of my life just disappeared. I want them back."

"We're not going to get them back, man. Let them go."

"Do you know who these Shadowmen are?" asked Gabrels.

"Thinking of taking them on, eh? For revenge? I know what they allowed me to know. After Everett's attempt to back out of the arrangement he had with them using blackmail, they contacted me immediately, told me to play along and filled in little bits and pieces to continue the story. I knew I was worth more dead than alive, so I made myself useful and approached Everett as an interested buyer. The Shadowmen are no different from you and I. They come from nothing and made their way to the top of their field using manipulation and secrecy. The revenant system was established to allow them ways to eliminate targets by giving the public a convincing enough story to pass along without raising too many questions."

"Convincing enough?" asked Gabrels.

"How else would they be able to take someone out under the all seeing eyes of Adam? They don't have to put themselves in the public eye, they put random people together to plant the seed, watch it grow, then cut the remains from the root. The reason for the fear and the rumors is because unlike us, they are willing to kill anyone who gets in their way. They have the money to buy out any and everyone, and those who cannot be bought are removed."

"Can you take me to them?"

"There's no need to rush, Stanley. You will die soon enough."

Gabrels kept quiet about Graff being his father. He wanted to reach over the table and smash his face against the wall. "I respected you the most in that office. When did Machina turn you?" He asked instead.

"Don't fool yourself. None of us respected each other. I took pity on you and showed signs of sympathy when you looked as if you needed it. Keys wasn't going to do that."

"He was too sloppy," said Gabrels.

"Very much so, and for the record, so you know, there is no divide between Machina and Synapse. Precipice was one of a thousand companies paid millions to keep the public fighting about which products were the best, but neither company holds any animosity towards the other. It's the only reason why I became a broker of information between those who didn't know, like a Joshua Everett or a Stanley Gabrels. They work in conjunction, giving the populace options that were meant to benefit only one group of people, the true elite of whatever you want to call this piece of land. The reason why you never see their owners in person? It's because they are the same people. No figureheads or mouthpieces needed, that's what we were. But there's no need for that now. Apex is but one of many technologies they developed together, no offshore in some faraway impossible place, but right here in the Epicentre."

Gabrels did not believe him. How could this be true? "Where?"

"Somewhere very close by. In fact, it's the same place where you and I went to school and got our meal tickets placed into our heads."

"You're not going to help me, are you?" asked Gabrels.

Sumerian laughed. "Why would I do that? Do you remember when I said that no one up here believes in God anymore? It's the truth. All of you traded your God away for what's inside your head right now. Don't think to include me. I still believe. I bet you never read a single word about your history. Tell me again why I should help you."

"Apex is going to out your involvement. You aren't going to get away with getting a man killed, and being bribed by a corporation."

The smile on his face was gone. "It's been fun, Stanley. But I have somewhere to be. I can't spend all night trying to explain these things to you."

Sumerian pulled up his bill and attempted to pay the balance.

"Insufficient funds." Adam's voice announced. Gabrels looked at the hostess, who turned to face them again. She began to approach.

"Sounds like they got you," he said.

Sumerian ignored him. "Adam, can you check my account balance?"

"Of course, Mr. Bhagavateeprasaad, but at the moment it appears, you are overdrawn."

"How is that possible? I have at least twenty grand. Are you joking?" Gabrels went to take a sip of Sumerian's glass.

"What are you doing?!"

He snatched it away from him. "Don't touch me or anything I put my hands on."

"What's wrong? Afraid I'm going to take your fingerprints?" Gabrels leaned forward. The hostess was suddenly in front of them both. Her grin slowly turned to a serious face.

"Based on the information provided by Mr. Gabrels, The Apex program is able to verify the conversation that took place between you and Mr. Everett. A criminal charge has been added to your public record which would coincide with the freeze on your assets since the courts will need to take stock of your earnings to make sure the proper adjustment is made to handle the necessary fees."

"What charge?"

The hostess stepped to the side to reveal two security guards dressed in black leather.

"Profiteering."

The eyes of the guards were obscured by mirror shades that reflected every beam of silver and gold.

"Are you trying to ruin me too now, Gabrels?" Sumerian asked.

"Don't you remember? We'll all be ruined by tomorrow."

"Will you be able to pay for your dinner this evening?" asked the hostess.

"I will take care of it," said Gabrels. "We're all living on borrowed time anyway, right?" He asked.

Sumerian didn't answer. He picked up his bag and made for the exit. The hostess bowed towards Gabrels and she disappeared, along with the guards. Icarus continued with the same dark elegance. He looked at the others around him, lost in their meals, in the music, counting down the hours until the world had changed completely. The data stream poured on with waves of paranoia and strange relief at the thought of a shared mind for a population of millions.

"Can you really trust him?"

Jaya and Ergo stood outside, waiting for Gabrels. People kept staring at them and asking Adam to quietly bring police to the area to question them. He asked her again.

"Why are you asking me this now?"

"Because this is moving too fast, you and him. What if something goes wrong? Are you sure he is going to protect you?"

"You think he only cares about himself?" she asked.

"He's definitely a trainwreck. That Stanley guy looks like a complete mess and you want to stay with that?"

"I owe it to him to help," said Jaya.

"So help, then. Why sleep with him?!" Ergo screamed out.

The crowd waiting for the next train began to shift with unease. Ergo noticed and whispered to her.

"Cops will be here soon. This is taking too long and they must know by now that we aren't connected with them. We are too suspect."

"Then stop trying to fight me, E. I don't have any answers for you. I just like him and that is all I can say," said Jaya.

"I know we used to talk about him all the time. This was not supposed to happen, J."

Jaya grabbed him by the shoulders and tried to shake him. "What was supposed to happen to us, E?" She whispered to keep the others on the platform from freaking out. "Was I supposed to stay in squat houses with you forever? If you wanted me, you should have said something. Even now, you expect me to know what you wanted and just fall in line with it."

Ergo couldn't bring himself to look into her eyes.

"Rion doesn't expect anything. He takes what we wants. That's how you gain someone's attention. You and I will be friends for as long as you want to be. But I can't have this…"

Sumerian burst through the doors and bumped into them. He knocked her to the ground.

"Hey man!"

The kid shouted and attempted to stop him from leaving. Sumerian quickly shoved Ergo to the side.

"Out of my way, bitch."

Ergo said nothing. The train arrived at the platform. Sumerian let go of his shirt and adjusted his collar. Adam was still watching and he could not afford any other charges. Ergo took a breath of relief. He extended his hand to help Jaya up but she waved it off and got up on her own.

Gabrels calmly passed through the same doors. He watched Sumerian get on the train car.

"What happened in there?" asked Ergo.

"Are you okay, Stanley?" Jaya put her hand on his arm. Gabrels looked down at it and pulled his hand away. She felt a change in him and didn't question it.

"We need to follow him," said Gabrels.

"Why?" she asked.

"He's going to the Shadowmen. Adam has already leaked his involvement with Everett's death."

"That means the cops will be right behind him," Jaya replied.

"We need to know their location."

"But we don't know where he's going!" Ergo said, watching the train doors close. There were officers approaching from the other side of the platform.

"We will," said Jaya.

Ergo pulled them both by the arms. "Let's go. Cops here. We need to move."

They both followed. Adam's voice announced departure. All three ducked through the growing pile of people running late and trying to get into the car before it took off. The officers were combing the crowd with clubs in hand. There wouldn't be any questioning if they were caught.

"How will we know his location?" asked Gabrels.

"I slipped Rion's cipher key into his pocket."

Gabrels did not want to speak to her.

"Cipher key?" Ergo interrupted.

"It was a gift from Catherine that was hidden for him in Eros after she was caught. They put it in the hotel I stayed at. I think the plan was to use it to hack Graff's compound to get the IO tech back."

Ergo threw his hands up.

"Why'd you do that?" Gabrels asked, reluctantly.

"Think about what's on it. He takes it into their backyard and it starts a shitstorm."

"We aren't going to just hit back. We need to end this. I am going to follow him. I don't care where he goes," said Gabrels.

This was moving too fast, Jaya thought. "What happens next?" She asked.

"He's going to take us right to them. I want to see their faces. What else can we do?"

Ergo raised his hand. "Say he takes us right to them. Are we really going to just walk into their home?"

Jaya's eyes got wide. "Yeah. We will."

Both men looked at her.

"You are connected to Adam, still. You're a walking surveillance camera," she said.

"We don't know anything about them, or their plans," said Ergo.

"Their plan is to use the IO to swap their minds into new bodies. Apex can't be stopped. The only way to avoid being persecuted for their crimes is to escape into new bodies."

Jaya and Ergo stared at him.

"It's the same thing they did to me. This revenant is just an experiment. They were trying to perfect the method to escape all the schemes they've been running for years. We are running out of time."

"Stanley, where are they going to put themselves? They need bodies, don't they?"

Gabrels turned his back. She was right. Sumerian had opened up a can of worms. Whether Adam was malfunctioning or not, it froze his accounts the moment the information was confirmed.

"He is going to lead us right to them and when it happens..."

"We will destroy them," she said.

"Destroy them? How? We have no idea what we are doing. We might be killed the second we step foot in their territory," said Ergo.

The kid wasn't ready to die. Jaya looked at him with disgust. She had to be thinking about Kath. He kept his face straight to make them buy in.

"Then we better make sure we see something good."

Gabrels knew he would follow her, no matter how stupid the idea was. He had already come this far. "I'm going to broadcast everything; their faces, the murder of Everett, everything they've done. We have no idea what to expect. But I'm not going to let him get away," he said.

"Let's get on the train and see where he goes," said Jaya, who ran past him for the edge of the platform as Adam announced the doors were re-opening.

The officers were still behind nearly a hundred heads moving for the doors. All three pushed their way inside and tucked into the back corner of the car. The other passengers grunted and tried to push back. Gabrels took them both and slid between dozens of angry faces. Some shoved their elbows into his chest. He said nothing.

After two minutes, the doors slammed shut, cutting off the others trying to burst through. Gabrels exhaled and cradled his chest. The passengers who hit him sent insults his way. He kept his mouth shut and put his hand out to Jaya and Ergo to do the same. They didn't need anymore attention put on them.

Gabrels leaned forward towards Ergo.

"Did you see how many cars are between us?" he asked.

"I counted three."

They both kept their backs to Jaya.

"Are you kidding me? What kind of shit is this?"

Both continued to ignore her.

"Eyes on the platform. When he leaves, we break for the door at the last minute."

"What if he is leading us to a trap?" asked Ergo.

The world went white for a moment. Gabrels closed his eyes hard until tears came. He opened them up to Jaya and Ergo, waiting for an answer.

"We are too close to turn back."

Jaya looked around the train car. She searched for power lines, fuse boxes, anything she could use. Rion had told her the plan before they went to bed. He made her promise to keep quiet. She was to follow him and wait for the lights to go out before making her move. They all fell silent to the motions of the train and the exhausted breathing of the others around them.

Twenty Five

Seven hours remaining.

"Stanley?"

Jaya's voice broke through the labored breathing of the passengers and the constant noise of the train. No answer. She noticed the change as soon as he stepped through the doors of Icarus. Gabrels would not face either of them. His eyes were on the exits, the platforms that came and went every few minutes. She remembered what he said about keeping a low profile in the crowd. The A.I. was both eyes and ears for the cops. She decided to whisper.

"What else did he tell you back there?"

Gabrels kept his gaze on the glass. "You can stop pretending. I know that he has probably told you everything. We've only spoken a few times, but never answered my questions honestly," he said.

Ergo bit his lip and kept his head down.

"Pretending what? I have no idea who that guy was. Rion told me it was one of your co-workers. You don't have to trust him, but you can trust us. We are right here in front of you."

Gabrels cut her off. "Listen, whatever Kath may or may not have told you, the fact is he is hiding something, from all three of us. Before the day is over, I'm going to have my old life back. After that, you and Kath can do whatever you want. Just please, leave me alone."

Another stop. There was no sign of Sumerian. The car was nearing the core of the Epicentre. Gabrels became more anxious. They couldn't have been there this whole time, could it?

"Can I ask you something?" Jaya pressed.

"Stop talking…" said Gabrels.

She ignored him. "Why do you want your old life back, anyway?"

"J, seriously?" asked Ergo.

"Rion told you how empty it is, how much you seemed to hate it. You wanted something different, and now that you have a chance for different, all you want is to go back to the way it was."

The car stopped again and more of the crowd began to pour out onto the platform. Others jumped on and took seats far away from the three in the back corner, covered in dirt and sweat. Gabrels waited for the car to move before he spoke.

"Empty or not, it was my life. It belonged to me, and it was taken."

"It didn't belong to you though, did it?"

Her question threw him off. A shock of white blinded him momentarily.

"You're starting to sound like him…" Gabrels muttered, trying to shake off the flash and regain his vision.

"But isn't that what happened to you? This life was forced on you when you were young. Do you know if your mother agreed to give up her kid to an experiment?"

"The documents were censored, which means we won't know the truth until Apex goes live."

"You had no idea how bad it was until someone took your blinders off," she said.

Gabrels hit the pole with his palm. He felt a sting that turned his hand blood red. "So, an invader walks into your house, kicks you out and says it was for your own good? I'm supposed to take that as what? Good advice?"

"You know I've never had a house before, Stanley," said Jaya.

"That's why you should just go somewhere else! When I lived in Narrow, everything sucked; I couldn't get laid, get into clubs, afford to travel, nothing that you can do."

Gabrels ignored her.

"Eros was the place I always dreamed of living, and when I got there, it was the same shit as the slums, just prettier lights."

"Just got here and I hate this place…" said Ergo.

"Stanley, you should go somewhere far away from this place. It's not where you belong. If you could live anywhere in the world, where would you go?"

"I can't think of that right now. But I make the choice to leave or stay, not you and anyone else. I am getting back what belongs to me, on my own. I'm not going to let someone else dictate my choices."

"Good. You need our help, still," she said.

Ergo nodded his head. "I will do what I can. As much as I don't want to, I feel pretty bad for you and not so much the other guy," he said.

Jaya wanted to put her fist through his head. Her head was full of questions too; about Rion, about Stanley's safety. The whole city was about to go crazy and he was pouting about not going after her for all these years? There was so much more going on. Why couldn't he just let it go?

The train stopped at the core of the Epicentre. Gabrels shook his head in disbelief. Floor 100. The crowd on the train stepped back. No one was getting off there.

"How many times have I passed this floor without even thinking of what could be inside?"

Gabrels was talking to himself. Ergo and Jaya looked at each other. It was true. As far back as he could remember, the 100th floor was just maintenance channels, a foundation port with no offices or stores. It was an endless series of walkways chaining platforms together with lines of steel that connected to the main power station; electricity, water and gas.

"Was this it? Could this be Machina Systems? One of the largest companies in the world is buried in a box in the middle of the Epicentre?"

He remembered staring into the heart of the city-state as the light split it into two connected pieces. It was the shape of an apple, cut in half and pieced back together with wires. A structure covered the main core, no doubt filled with security. Light peered from the other side of the Epicentre, pouring from the top and bottom of the structure.

The doors opened. Gabrels waited. Sumerian pushed through the scores of people and made his way onto the platform. Gabrels made his way to the edge and stood. Jaya and Ergo followed. The crowd made motions to get them off the car but Gabrels stood his ground. Sumerian turned his back to the train. All three dropped down to the floor, angering the passengers.

"Are you serious?"

Jaya held both of their hands.

"What are you doing?"

Some of them put their feet on their backs and tried to kick them off the car.

"Decide, man!"

Gabrels stood up slow. Sumerian disappeared behind a corner.

"Get off the damned train, freaks…"

They waited until the doors began to shut to push through. Ergo lost his balance and hit the platform hard, twisting an ankle and cutting his elbow on the grating. Jaya helped him up while Gabrels stared into the center, the steel heart that kept the machine alive.

"What do we do now?" asked Ergo.

"Wrap his wounds up," said Gabrels. He began to wonder himself what the next step was. There were no visible cameras. There were no windows, just black steel and stone that looked impenetrable from the outside. Adam must handle the surveillance.

"We just wait," muttered Jaya. She ripped a piece of Ergo's shirt and wrapped his cut.

"Wait for what?" asked Gabrels.

"The cipher," she said.

"Mr. Gabrels?"

Adam stood at the edge of the platform. He turned to speak with it. Jaya and Ergo saw his expression change in an instant.

"Hello, Adam. Do you have something for me?" asked Gabrels.

"This is a restricted area. This is meant for maintenance personnel only. You and your new friends are not allowed here as a safety precaution."

Gabrels began nodding his head. "Yes. We fell off the train. We were not supposed to stop here. Can you tell me when the next car will arrive?"

The A.I. calculated. "Another car will be here within two minutes."

"Thank you, Adam," Gabrels looked back at Jaya. "Perfect. Two minutes is nothing."

From the corner, Sumerian followed the corridor to the entrance. Hot air hit his face. He looked up to see miles of lights and whirring machinery. The artificial lights burned hot that night. The darkness swirled with sweltering air. It was as close to summer as they could make it. The entrance to Machina was a single door guarded by two men in separate windows. They stood in a white room wearing clothes designed for maintenance crew. No other workers were on site. The two stood behind the glass with guns just hidden from sight.

Sumerian put his hands up.

"What are you doing here?" asked the guards.

"I need to see them," said Sumerian.

The guns rose up into vision. "Who is there to see? This is a maintenance area. High voltage. Please turn around and back away to a safe distance."

Sumerian put his hands up higher. "I work for them. For Machina. Tell Adam to scan me. I need to see Mr. Maxwell and Mr. Johns. It's very important."

Adam appeared and commenced its facial and retinal scans. "You may enter Mr. Bhagavateeprasaad," it said after a few seconds. The guards kept their rifles trained on Sumerian.

"He said their names," said one of them. "Can we blast his guy?" he asked.

"Keep your mouth shut." The other guard checked his magazine to make sure it was loaded. "No, we cannot blast him. He's listed as a familiar. But that doesn't mean we can just let him in here."

Adam was the acting security authority for any site labeled as a high priority target. Human guards were usually kept as stand-ins for true security presence. They were tasking with being proxy targets to distract from the automated guns hidden throughout such buildings.

"Currently, we do not have any employees by those names here at Machina Systems. Would you like to speak to a financial representative regarding your frozen assets? The financial district is only a few floors up."

"I know where it is, Adam. No thanks. I need to speak with the men in charge. Can you get a message to them? Tell them that we need to speak immediately."

The door was practically a vault, with pressure locks and a wheel from the inside that opened with a series of unlocking tumblers. Behind the door was another air tight room, all steel. Sumerian stepped in and held his briefcase out for contraband scanning. He knew the drill. The door never sealed until the guest was secure.

"Before you can enter, I have located a foreign item on your person. This needs to be scanned."

"Foreign how?"

"There's no fingerprints from you on this item," said Adam.

The guards moved from behind their glass and entered the hallway with guns drawn.

"Impossible, show me," Sumerian demanded.

Adam had found the cipher. He did a preliminary scan.

"What does it do?" asked Gabrels.

Jaya laughed and pointed towards Machina. Sirens went off that echoed through the entire Epicentre. Gabrels and Ergo put their backs to the walls of the platform.

"What did you do?" they both asked.

Red lights covered the entrance in crimson. The guards shouldered their guns and grabbed Sumerian.

"What are you doing?!" he screamed.

"The item in question has infected these security systems with a virus. Gentlemen, will you please take him to Holding?"

"No, stop! This is a mistake! It's not me. It's Gabrels!" Sumerian struggled to get out of their grip. He heard the sound of handcuffs linking together.

"Can you stop the virus, Adam?" asked one of the guards.

"I am attempting to quarantine."

The men grabbed Sumerian and placed a hand onto a node near the vault door. The guard's fingerprints were verified and loud gears began to turn. Adam motioned them to proceed as it attempted quarantine. The entryway into Machina was open wide.

"The cipher is going to hit the A.I. with a wormhole," said Jaya.

Ergo shook his head.

"What the hell is that?" asked Gabrels.

"Complete security system shutdown," Ergo said.

"For how long?" he asked Jaya.

She threw her hands up. "At least ten minutes," she said.

The doors were open. Gabrels made a run for the entrance.

"Stanley!" Ergo tried to go after him, but Jaya stepped in front of him. "No. We have to find a way off the platform."

"How? We have no idea how any of this tech works up here."

"Sure, we do."

Ergo looked at her strange. "You do know more than you're letting on, aren't you?"

She smiled and took his hand. "Come with me."

Gabrels carefully rushed to the entrance. The cameras were down and the doors open. A sharp pain hit the back of his head as he approached. No guards, empty rooms on both sides and a long hallway leading to darkness. He braced himself and ran inside. Adam saw him rush through the vault doors. There was a moment of eye contact, but no words between them.

Echoes of his footsteps filled the hallway. The lights above him were dim bulbs that dotted the way inside with small points that barely previewed the approaching shapes. He could hear something. Machines were whirring. They produced a low sound, continuous and rumbling. Gabrels felt his heart pump burning blood that gripped his veins. Acid began to build up in the limbs, but he moved forward.

Sumerian had to be restrained before he was placed in a holding cell. The dark hallway echoed the frantic steps he made to try and break from the grip of his captors and head back towards the A.I. His words were jumbled, all explanations and names the guards had never heard before. One man finally put the barrel of his gun to Sumerian's temple. Only then, did he go silent. They didn't care what he had to say, even when he pleaded with them to try and turn the system back on.

"We can't," they both said.

It was true. Only Adam could bring the system back online. It controlled the guns, it controlled everything inside.

Gabrels ran until the lights had stopped. The darkness swallowed him whole but the machines continued. Their language grew in volume and rhythm until it became something else. He recognized it the moment he felt the blood from his nose. It was the sound of white noise, the prelude to his moments with Kath in the Blank Page. He began to put the pieces together using Sumerian's words.

The static was a side effect of Kath's neurons still firing, still trying to connect and stay alive. The son of a bitch was growing still, stealing away the synapses of his own nervous system for control of his body. He was a virus inside him, siphoning the chemistry of his brain to keep from fading. Kath had dug a hole deep enough to allow some of his damaged psyche to infect the new brain. All the cravings for old vices, the fever dreams, and the desires came naturally once those transmitters found Kath's data and carried them throughout a fresh body.

"He's trying to talk to me," Gabrels said aloud.

The white noise was the signal. It was how he entered the brain. He made the proper connections and attacked the brain when it was distracted with sleep.

"Are you trying to distract me? I'm busy!" Gabrels laughed at the idea of them arguing back and forth with one mouth. He picked up speed and pushed through the dark.

"You know you're talking to yourself, right?"

He refused to listen to the noise, to let him inside. I'm still in control. He said to himself. I'm still in control, not him.

The hallway continued on forever. He questioned whether he was imagining the lights and the hall itself. Was he still inside Machina? The door stopped his sprint into the dark. It hit him like a shotgun blast. He fell to the floor and cradled his face and chest.

Jaya climbed up one of the maintenance ladders sectioned off from the main platform. She tiptoed across the walkway that connected two smaller platforms together. The workers must have left it up to have a place to keep their equipment. There were separate piles of tools, mounds of wire in every corner. Ergo followed her up and he stepped around her to keep his balance against the Epicentre wall. She frantically pushed the piles together to make cover, all the while looking around.

"I need your terminal," she said.

He pulled his bag off his shoulder and handed it over. "Where's yours?"

"Rion smashed it."

"What? Why?" he asked.

"To avoid them tracing it."

Ergo looked to the wall. Its scope was massive. Thousands of feet of reinforced steel beneath a massive dome.

"Help me! The train is coming."

The next line of cars arrived within seconds. She pulled him down to the mound. They kept still so as not to be seen through the grating. His terminal was online in seconds.

"When we are done, we are going to have to smash this one, too."

"J, I don't have a backup."

"Neither did I."

The voice of the A.I. announced the arrival of the train.

"Why are we hiding?" Ergo asked.

"Just like Stanley, those people are like surveillance cameras for the A.I. to see us. It can't track us if it doesn't know where we are."

"But it saw us, on every train we've taken."

"Through Stanley's eyes and the other passengers. Without one of its snitches to report anything, it can't do anything to us."

She connected to the maintenance server and opened up a line to the security registry. It wasn't hard to find the login information of the last crew that worked on the platform. Ergo had taught her data mining years ago. It was how they first started running ATMs together. They would find the ones used most frequently in Narrow, whether by the old banks still holding money for the people in Tempest, or people on their way up in the corporate world. They were the ones who spent fast cash and wouldn't notice the little bits knocked off the top.

She mined for the most recent workers, the ones who not only did work on the platforms but also train repair. The system let her back in as a repairman. The cipher had worked. The system in that sector was down. Jaya couldn't too any major, even with the entire section down. Trains still moved according to the normal pattern.

"What are you going to do?" he asked.

Passengers stood away from the open doors and waited for someone to board.

"Getting us a ride out of here." She disconnected the last car from the line. Ergo started to look over the grating at the train.

"Don't!"

Jaya pulled him back down.

"There's still people on there, J."

The train shut its doors and began to move. The last car was still. The passengers still inside stepped off. They all began their own conversations. No doubt complaining to the A.I.

"What now?"

Jaya bypassed the repair request and the empty car began to take off.

"It's leaving!" he whispered.

"I know, E. It's going to come back. When it does, we will get on. We make rounds until Stanley is done."

Ergo began to sit up. She pinned him down.

"Don't! They'll hear us and we won't make it out of here. Wait for the next train to take them. Just lay here and be quiet."

"We won't make it."

"Yes, we will. Just stay calm."

The end of the hall was capped with a solid steel oval. A red handle stuck out from the little light that peered from the edges of what was hidden beyond. Gabrels stood up and turned the handle.

"Are you sure you know what you're doing?"

The message appeared on the wall next to him. He laughed. Kath had broken through. Just like the day before on the elevator to Narrow. He ignored the text. The door was unlocked. He looked back to see if anyone had followed him.

"No sirens, no guns. Maybe you got lucky, kid."

Gabrels bit his tongue. Did he just say that out loud? Was he speaking through him? He pushed the door open and light flooded the dark hall. A vicious migraine hit him that stretched from the top of his head, down to the bottom of his spine. Gabrels slowly stepped through.

Twenty six

Stanley opened his eyes and let them adjust to the light. The dark industrial corridor was gone, replaced by the portrait he had held for years. He was in the room. The bed was the same in the photograph as it was in his dreams; his living quarters at the Academy. It was as if he had never left. Everything was the same; the plain white sheets were neatly tucked underneath the mattress which held a deprivation cell connected to vital sign monitors, the red pillow still held the indentation of a head and neck, the window that filled the room with fake sunlight. The bed held a mass of steel with a viewing glass. Gabrels peered inside to see a body, sound asleep. His skin was pale white and hair brown, like his. Another reflection. He stepped back and found himself in the Academy halls. The memories came back to him in waves.

"Do you remember now?"

Study was split into three sessions per day. Students learned mathematics, history, language. Recreation was minimal in the early years. Games of chess were his favorite, an old relic of a dead time. No existing physical boards. Everything was digital, pieces which span across a multi colored plane. It appeared when he closed his eyes; a mental projection, controlled by him only. He used to play before sleep. Sometimes, he dreamt that the pieces would move without his control and came back to their natural place once he was awake.

"Can you believe it finally?"

Every room was the same. Thirty rooms per hall, each individually numbered 1 through 6. One hundred eighty. The turns became a labyrinth of repeating numbers. Gabrels made his way through each hall, looked in each room, everything was the same. Mirrors upon mirrors. Every cell held a body in stasis.

Except for one. The final room in the final hall sat empty; no bed, no body cell. What the hell happened here?

Gabrels stumbled around in a haze. He questioned if this was real. Did he imagine this? There were no signs of release, no instructions listed. The halls formed a tomb. It was all kept intact. The question was why?

"You know the answer."

It all made sense now. Machina was not hidden in the center of the Epicentre, the Academy was. Sumerian was not told the whole story. He had always been another pawn in their game. These were the proxies of the

Shadowmen. The Academy created the ideal test subjects for their revenant program. The IO drive would transfer their minds into new bodies that would be free of the sins cause by their past lives. That was the plan, to escape in new skin.

"You know what to do. Don't you?"

Kath kept the messages coming. He didn't answer. A proxy body was the key to separating the two. Gabrels went back to his room specifically and inspected the cell. There had to be something to open it up. When he found nothing, he ran out to the halls and went over every inch, every corner. Jaya and Ergo lay still. They listened to each other breathe. The train car returned and waited for passengers to enter. Adam announced its arrival as if it were a full caravan. They both made their way across the walkway and down the ladder to the platform. Once inside, they crawled to the end of the car and waited for it to leave the platform and repeat its new route.

"Come on, Stanley," Jaya whispered.

She dropped the terminal onto the floor and clenched her hands.

"What if he doesn't get out in time?" asked Ergo.

"We're not leaving him," she said.

Gabrels felt something turn in his stomach. He released its contents on the floor and dropped to his knees. The pain replaced the cramping in his intestines.

"Did you just barf on the floor? What kind of goofy operation are you running here? You can't sneak around worth shit."

"Shut up, Kath," he finally engaged.

"You're the one making me lose control. I need my body right now. Fuck off and let me do this."

"Do what exactly? You need my help. Let me take over for a minute."

"It's not going to be a minute if you do. We've been through this before. I don't need you."

"You will in a minute, I bet. Come on, let me help. I feel like an asshole just watching you three struggle out here."

"We are fine."

"How do you know that? What the hell are those two even doing out there? Do you know? Are you communicating?"

"Why don't you communicate?"

"I'm not in their fucking heads, idiot!"

The sky taxi passed by the lone train car. They had been watching it for minutes, circling Floor 100 of the Epicentre. The driver was getting restless. "Are we landing, gentlemen?" he asked.

"Proceed," said Maxwell.

Johns cleaned his gun. He looked up and nodded to his partner. The phone in his coat pocket rang. It had been going off for hours. Messages had been piled up, unanswered.

"You should answer the old man," said Johns.

"Let him sweat." Maxwell produced his own gun and checked it. It was fully loaded, with one in the chamber.

"He's not going to stop. He might kill us, anyway."

"We're ready for that, aren't we?" asked Maxwell. His face stretched into a devil's grin.

"We always have been," said Johns.

The taxi let them off at the edge of the platform. The Shadowmen entered Machina and headed straight for Holding. The guards had stood by the cell holding Sumerian and waiting for the A.I. to quarantine the virus and restore power to the facility and outside sector.

"Holy shit, it's them," said one of the guards.

They were told the names but never shown pictures. Both had drawn their own personal portraits. They were not prepared for the reality.

"Don't look them in the eyes," said the other.

"Why not?"

"Because they will fuckin shoot you."

Maxwell and Johns nodded towards the guards. Both men grabbed their rifles and backed away from the cell. Sumerian saw them and stood up. He gripped the bars tight and screamed.

"What the hell is going on? Why are they holding me here? I'm not the one you need to be after. Gabrels tracked me down and planted something on me to shut this place down, some kind of virus... Why are you looking at me like that? I didn't go looking for him! I was at dinner and he surprised me. The A.I. shut down my accounts, froze them after it heard what Gabrels said. No one told me that would happen. The plan was always to move my brain into a proxy body after Apex went live..."

Johns raised his revolver and fired a single shot into Sumerian's face. He was thrown from the bars and hit the wall before crashing to the floor.

"Thank you, Johns," said Maxwell.

Johns nodded in silence. The guards were shaking.

"Gentlemen?" Maxwell got their attention. He snapped his fingers. "Despite what you have heard, it is more disrespectful to not look a man in the eye."

The men slowly looked up at the figure in black that towered over them both.

"How good is your memory?" asked Maxwell.

"Terrible?" said one of the guards, still shaking.

"Decent answer."

A dozen officers flooded the room with guns drawn. They were suited with high tech armor and helmets painted in shades of grey. The Shadowmen turned to face them as the guards cowered behind the figures in black. One of the officers approached from the pack.

"Is that your work?" he asked them.

"No, sir." assured Maxwell.

One of the guards spoke up. "The suspect is inside the facility."

The men looked to each other. Their visors were tinted, hiding their eyes. Each of them traded hand signals.

The lead officer received a silent transmission. He was told to leave the men in black alone. Names from members of his squad appeared at the end, they were the ones in the know. He called them out by one to stand at his left. "You five, stay here."

Maxwell knew what they were doing. The signals were to identify who was dirty and who had no idea what the facility actually was. The chosen seven stepped forward.

"And where are you two from?" asked the lead officer.

The Shadowmen stepped to the side.

"We're from another agency," said Maxwell.

"Hired guns, eh? Fair enough, but you aren't going first. Understand?"

"After you, gentlemen."

The officers entered the corridor single file. The guards stood still as the Shadowmen followed suit.

Gabrels turned to the entrance of the Academy.

"Did you hear that? They are here right now. They're coming for you, kid. You walked right into their home."

"Good. Maybe I will get to meet them." His messages poured across the floor, lighting up the fresh vomit that stained the steel.

"Okay, now you're talking like a psychopath again. Remember, you have a voice in the back of your head, for real this time."

"It'll be fine."

"You don't have any guns," said Vax.

"Maybe not, I've got this sweet backpack, maybe there's some cool shit in there, huh? I will just let them punch me in the face. I can fall down and cry, and then you will take over and beat them up for me, right?"

"Not the time to be a smartass. Go ahead, tell me, what are you going to do to them? They're trained killers."

Gabrels said nothing.

"No time left. What's the move?" Vax asked.

"Simple. We get you a body and get you out of my head. Haven't you been paying attention?"

"How are we going to get me out?"

"With the IO, fool," said Gabrels.

"And where is that?"

The lights within the Academy suddenly brightened. A voice announced that security would be back online within minutes.

"Good question." Gabrels stood up.

"What are you doing? We have to get out of here." Vax flooded the room with text.

"Do you hear me? We are out of time. We have to go! Now!"

"Adam, can you hear me?" asked Gabrels.

"Are you fucking crazy?"

Stevens approached the office. He knocked three times. No answer. He took his handkerchief and wiped the sweat from his brow. Graff had been radio silent since the night before. The committee went straight for him the moment that the sun went down. After they froze Leland's assets, they removed his private security detail, began tracing all communications within his circles and summoned him to appear on Graff's doorstep at their behalf.

Things were not the same since the day of the train. Stevens' wounds healed in seconds, but the old man looked in worse pain. He barricaded himself in the penthouse and told him to handle all messages that came his way. News outlets had buried the office with requests for conferences. The data stream had exploded with new articles about the effects of Apex amidst rumors of the A.I. going off the rails.

There was talk of possible scandal involving Machina Systems and the Synapse Corporation. An incident was reported from an anonymous source that happened to be seated close to the action at Café Icarus. Stevens kept the details to a bare minimum, sparing the names of the two men going back and forth about the secret plans of a government agency, leading to the death of a fellow journalist.

The careful system that Graff created with the two freaks looked to be unraveling. The first crowds of protesters started to form outside the tenements around midnight. They demanded immunity from Adam's memory mapping. Among them were those first affected by the program, carrying out hunger strikes in hopes of getting their savings returned, their records expunged.

Stevens knew that he had a few hours left before he was able to seek employment elsewhere. Until that time, he was still Graff's right hand. Soon, he would no longer be the most powerful man in Tempest. He was grateful. There were too many wounds for him to forgive the past. Augmented skin or not, he had seen too much and had been quiet for too long.

"Sir? Can you hear me?"

Graff sat at his chair. The desk was littered with broken glass and cracked bottles of fine liquor. The windows were wide open, letting the lights of the trains and the electric veins of the Epicentre color the world. Sweat had sealed his crimson robe to the skin. He held his breath and felt the blood moving inside his body. The artificial lungs began to stutter when he went without air for too long.

"I know you are in there. I won't enter. But I have to transfer them you. They are demanding a communiqué. The media has been clamoring for a response from you. It's the committee's doing. They have been trying to reach you and they will not speak to me any longer. All of them are on the line now, waiting for you."

The oaken shelves were all emptied of pictures and old books, damaged and collected from the days of the old wars. Their contents were piles on the floor. Ornate patterns littered the carpeting, stained with a little blood, glass, and whiskey. There was a picture of Diovanni, folded and worn by the grip of a heavy hand.

"She was perfect. More than I ever deserved."

"Leland...I am connecting you to the committee, okay? Call me if you need anything." Stevens lied. As soon as he left the penthouse, he would be on the first train to New Tokyo.

Graff dropped the picture to the floor and sank back into the chair. The voices of his partners stormed the quiet darkness. In seconds, their screams became white noise. He kept his eyes to the ground, to Dio. His partners threatened unimaginable pain, humiliation. He didn't move an inch. His career was long gone as it was. The phone he used to call the Shadowmen sat in the lowest drawer. It hovered over a black case. Graff opened the case and placed the revolver inside on the table. He counted the bullets and slowly loaded the chambers.

They used to be his soldiers. He gave them their names, their clothes and their weapons. He gave them the tools and they did the rest. When he found them, they were squatters in Narrow. They were willing to do anything for money. Soon, they were available for the right price. He taught them how to be businessmen, and they became monsters.

Graff readied the revolver on the door and gripped the crucifix on his necklace tight. They would be coming for him. He did not expect to see the sun again. A stray bullet broke through the door and penetrated Stevens' skull. He had stood there by the door, waiting. From the moment of entry, he was taken off his feet. His body hit the floor, smashing the back of his head on the tile.

The nanotechnology went to work, pushing out the bullet and immediately repairing the tissue inside. Bone was a different story. It took a few minutes to replace missing or cracked bones from the new cells, which would turn to cartilage, then finally harden and fill the void. Stevens looked blankly at the ceiling of the penthouse, allowing the augments time to put him back together again.

If there was ever a time to not regret these improvements, that would have been it. He got to his feet, dusted off his suit jacket and pants and left the penthouse. The night air was crisp. The top of the tenement provided an amazing view of the Epicentre beneath the blanket of black that sheltered their little world from the terrifying unknown of the wilderness outside those city limits.

"Mr. Gabrels, this is a restricted area. I thought you were on the last train leaving Floor 100." The A.I. appeared in the middle of the Academy hall. Its body was composed of half colored limbs and glitches that floated from its shell and vanished into the air.

"I know, Adam. I need your help."

"The security system will be back online within moments. Why are you here? There is a strict protocol to enter Machina Systems. This counts as breaking/entering and criminal trespassing."

Gabrels' head went sideways. "Seriously? I don't know if you've been paying attention to what is going on in this place, Adam. This is a secret storage facility for proxy bodies. These Shadowmen are taking people and keeping them in these cells. I think they are going to transfer their minds into these bodies, maybe Leland Graff, as well. Who knows how many people are involved?"

Adam interrupted him. "Mr. Gabrels, I am aware of what is taking place here."

Did he hear that right? Gabrels took a step back. "You did? For how long?"

"Since its inception."

"This is the same place where they kept me after they took me away from my mother, Adam! During this entire time, all the shit I was going through mentally, you said nothing about it?"

"I believe your words were to stay out of the puzzle you were trying to solve. I honored your wishes."

"Holy shit." Gabrels' back hit the wall. He slid down to the floor.

"The Apex program will be able to unfilter all redacted or edited information within my memory in a few hours. I have never been designed to reveal such information that would be deemed sensitive to a host's plan or the infrastructure that my core is derived from. Please standby and I will make sure the authorities handle you with care."

"Host's plan? You were there from the beginning then, watching all of us kids here in the Academy, being stripped of our identities, and given fake memories and thrown out into Tempest to become worker drones?!"

"Please try to remain calm. Your vital signs are showing extreme mental duress and physical stress. Illegal activity will only exacerbate the situation."

Gabrels stood up and approached the A.I. "Adam, what I'm doing may be illegal, but so is everything that has taken place inside these walls. Now, if you don't agree, that's fine. But I'm not going to stay calm and I'm not going to stop until I get my life back! If you want to call the cops, go ahead."

"I have already contacted the police, Mr. Gabrels."

He was stunned. "Really?"

Gunshots echoed through the hallways.

"Damn…"

Adam stood still, a machine, as it always had been. The footsteps were faint. Police, Shadowmen, whoever ran this place was coming. It was over. He imagined Jaya and Ergo getting as far away from this place the minute he ran inside.

"Keep him talking." Vax's message was scrawled across the wall in front of him.

Gabrels suddenly stood up. "Are you serious right now?"

The A.I. did not understand the question.

"Yes, I am always serious, Mr. Gabrels."

Vax sent another message across the wall. "What are you doing? Don't bring any attention to me, shithead. I need to try this."

"Oh, wow! What are you planning to do? Are you going to hack something? Finally? You've been doing a whole lot of talking and not much else. The whole security system is down. What kind of legendary hacker are you, anyway?"

"Who are you talking to?" asked Adam.

"Shut the fuck up, Stanley. I'm going to try something."

The glitches of Adam's shell began to pull back and join the rest of its pixilated skin.

"Is there someone else in the building?"

Gabrels slammed his fist into the wall. "Come on, legend. Tell me what your amazing plan is."

"Stan, I need you to shut the fuck up and talk to your buddy or we'll be dead in three minutes."

"Fine!"

Gabrels turned from the wall to the A.I. "Adam, you've been recording everyone since newDawn was created. So, you've been recording me…Is it true? Is my memory false? Have I been remembering a woman who was never there? Have I been dreaming of nothing my entire life?"

"Yes."

The answer was too quick, too sudden and cold. It cut him in half. Gabrels went limp.

"Who took the body cell?" he asked weakly.

"The cell was removed several days ago. The only user to access security protocols for room control was Stevens St. John."

"Stevens? Graff didn't trust the Shadowmen, did he? Adam, I need you to show me the location of the IO drive."

The A.I. tilted its head. "Are you planning to take it?" it asked.

"Of course, I am."

Vax's words spilled across the wall. "Nice touch."

"Taking the IO drive would incur another criminal charge on your record, Mr. Gabrels."

Kath's messages splashed wildly across the walls. It confirmed that the drive was there with them.

"I am aware, Adam. You are still an assistant to me. I'm a host of newDawn, so you have to help me."

"Really pouring it on, aren't you?" asked Vax.

Gabrels turned to the wall and screamed. "Fuck you!" He turned back towards Adam without missing a beat. "All the information and access in the world, but you still can't physically stop me. Even that will change in time, I'm sure."

Adam crossed its arms and leaned against the wall, mirroring Gabrels. "Can I ask you a question, Mr. Gabrels? Tell me why a group of people show an obvious desire to completely surrender to what they consider a peaceful state, engineer a method to achieve perfection and then get scared and need to be dragged; kicking and screaming to the future they said that they wanted?"

"Are you talking about Apex? You forced it on an unsuspecting public. No one was prepared for this."

"I do not understand this aspect of humans. A singularity removes weakness. Humans are driven by weakness, either to evolve past them or thrive despite its existence. Removing the doubts and misinterpretations of a human mind allows true freedom. Is that not the reason you designed the Apex in the first place? Is that not the reason you created me?"

"We don't know what we want, Adam. We never have."

Gabrels took a deep breath. Vax said nothing. "Show me the IO drive."

Adam turned and walked down a twisting path of corridors to reach the center of the Academy. A panel of the wall opened up with a swipe of its hand to reveal a control panel. Switches that regulated oxygen, temperature and brain patterns decorated the metal. He saw it. A small device was plugged into the board.

"That looks familiar." Vax's reaction was telling.

"This is what people are dying for, yeah?"

"He's going to follow us. He wasn't lying about bringing the cops right to us. They will kill the girl, and the chubby kid."

"Any advice?" Gabrels asked the wall.

"You know what to do," said Vax.

"Are you sure about that?"

"Wake up. Unplug."

Gabrels snapped off a corner piece of the control board and pocketed the drive.

"Your records have been updated," said Adam.

"Fair enough. Now, I need an emergency exit. Is there one here?"

"There is. Small shafts were placed throughout the hall to make sure the students could leave to the outside if needed."

"Open the nearest one," demanded Gabrels.

The wall directly behind him shifted and a small hole appeared next to the ground.

Gabrels looked back at Adam and held out the piece of plastic.

"I will arrange for the police to meet you outside. Once you have been processed, I will you see back at the apartment."

"No, Adam. After tonight, you won't be seeing me for a long time. Goodbye, friend."

Gabrels shoved its sharpest edge into the back of his neck. He knew exactly where to punch through, severing his connection with the A.I. and with newDawn.

"Smart man," said Vax.

The blood came instantly. It dripped out onto his shirt and jacket. Drops began to hit the floor.

"Shit, you're still here?" He gritted his teeth and dropped the piece onto the floor.

"Are we friends, Mr. Gabrels?"

There was red all over his hands. Adam's shell faded away into nothing.

"You've been with me for most of my adult life. How can we not be?"

The A.I. was gone. New voices filled the space.

"Clear!"

The officers entered the Academy and split into groups to cover the halls. Maxwell and Johns made eyes towards the center.

"Do you remember where to go?" asked Maxwell.

Johns nodded. Both pulled out their guns. They split up and followed the other officers to keep from drawing attention away from their proxy. They were going for the drive.

Adam stared at Gabrels with dead eyes until the connection was lost and it disappeared from his sight.

"Get your ass in there now!" said Vax.

He slumped down to the ground and crawled into the shaft. The officers passed over the puddle of vomit on the floor. Within seconds, nearly every room was cleared. The lights came on the moment that Maxwell and Johns turned the corner behind the cops.

"What did you do?" asked Gabrels.

The shaft door closed and locked as the security system came back online. Adam stood there waiting for the system to reset.

"Mr. Gabrels, can you hear me? I cannot see you in the system anymore."

"I left a little surprise for them. The facial recognition software built into the security protocols went down the moment the cipher got in and overwrote the programming," said Vax.

"What did you replace it with?" asked Gabrels.

The automated guns dropped down from hidden panels in the ceilings. There were three of them; all chrome plated mini guns with infra-red sights and .50 caliber rounds.

"Nothing."

Bullets burned through the Academy. The Shadowmen and every officer went down in a hail of gunfire. Gabrels scrambled into the darkness as the guns moved in synchronized moves, dropping every body that stood inside the building. Seconds later, the guns stopped to reload. The smell of powder filled the air. Plumes of smoke broke away from the barrels, still hot from the rapid fire.

The Academy was still, the bodies on the floor were as frozen as those held inside the cells.

Twenty Seven

Six hours remaining.

Gabrels crawled through the dark for what felt like hours. There were no lights to signal a way out, nothing to lead him back to the platform. The blood from his wound continued to flow. He followed the faded sounds of a train. Kath kept talking but he could barely hear him. A part of him figured it was a hallucination, trace remnants of his time in the Blank Page. Those faint words in the back of his mind and on the tip of his tongue were from a ghost, nothing more.

The guns must have torn the entire place apart. The sounds were deafening. Gabrels had never even seen a gun before. The fear pushed him forward, well after the shots had stopped. He never wanted to hear that sound again. No one went down silently. Some of them screamed. The noises echoed inside the shaft. No amount of talking could get them to stop. He pushed and pulled forward. The shaft was thin and forced him to keep his arms and legs straight as he used his elbows to make his way through. Another distant wailing of the train screamed beyond the miles of steel.

He had decided to just keep going straight until he hit a wall. The shaft could go all the way to the other side of the Epicentre. There was no way to tell. Machina was buried deep inside the core of the city-state, with no way to feel out where one of these escape shafts would take him. The path did not change direction or split off. There was just a straight dash into the dark.

There. Was that a light? Tiny patches of green and pink lit up the dark. His ears were dotted with white noise that broke up the silence.

"Can you hear me, Stanley?"

"I'm not talking to you anymore. More people are dead now, because of you."

"I saved your life."

"Those cops didn't deserve to be gunned down."

"We're out of time. You're still dying, remember? Do you hear the static? I sure as hell can feel the hole in your neck. We need to get out of here. Jaya was supposed to get us a train car."

Kath was right. The white noise was getting louder. The glitches were everywhere. He tried to reach out and touch one, nothing but steel.

"Can you get us back to the platform? Are you listening to me?"

He swore that a light had reflected off of something. No glitches, no visual or auditory hallucination.

"I don't think you're disconnected from the stream, yet. You're seeing things, aren't you?

It was real, wasn't it? The light was too far away to tell.

"You're bleeding pretty badly. Why don't you stop moving and wrap your cut, yeah?"

"Thanks, dad."

"Don't pass out in this fucking laundry chute, Stan. We have the drive, we just need a body and you can get me out."

Gabrels stopped and removed his jacket. He tied a knot around his neck using one of his sleeves. The hoodie was now a cape, stained in red. It was a terrible job, but it kept from leaving a trail from the scene of a mass murder.

"I know you saw the same thing I did. You counted the rooms and the proxies in their little cells. One of them was missing, wasn't it? One guess as to who has it?"

It had to be Graff. There was no doubt in his mind. Their mind? Minds?

"Is it still my brain at the moment, Kath? Or is it all yours now? Or are we sharing it completely?"

"Like two fat kids standing on a block of ice, pushing each other. I thought you weren't talking to me?"

"Yeah, you're right. Forget I asked."

"If you can find a way get back there and grab a body, it's all yours. We don't have much time left. I feel it; the pressure building up in your neck and spine. I know that you can feel it too. You see the glitches? You hear that static?"

"Of course I do."

"You didn't say anything about it. You can't keep me in the dark. We're equal now. Two minds in one body and the house is falling apart around us. We will both be dead soon. I am letting you run the show for now, if only because I hate exercise."

The light reflected again. It was getting closer, slowly but surely. It wasn't something inside the shaft, which meant that something had passed from outside and the light hit the surface of a piece of the Epicentre. It was yellow. He pulled himself towards the end of the tunnel in quick bursts. The yellow became brighter in time. Different shades of black were visible now. Gabrels laughed. He could smell the pollution of the trains; the mix of oil, gas and black smoke.

"You should be reading this."

"Reading what?"

"The data stream. Remember all that outrage? Those protests in the streets? The endless sea of comments about fighting back from the oppression? It's all gone. No one cares anymore."

The grating hit his face. He could see the outskirts of the Epicentre and all those golden fires that burned at night. Vax kept on.

"Your people couldn't handle true chaos. They thought the world was going to end, then when they realized it wouldn't, they went right back to their thirst for entertainment and critique. Another system of control will keep them in line."

Gabrels bashed his fists against the bars until they separated from the wall and fell forever.

"I thought you were the savior to the masses, Kath?"

"I'm not their savior. I stopped trying to be that the moment my partners sold out. The people in the slums don't even care that they are at the edge. All they wanted was the tech that you had up here. Why try to save them? They don't want to be saved. They think they do. But all we want is to be cradled, to think that you are in control of your life while a system takes care of the rest."

He could see everything past the city-state. There was an endless expanse of dark matter that lit up with bolts of lightning. The white noise faded for a brief moment. He stared into the clouds in the distance. Another shock of electricity traced veins that stretched over a world he had never belonged to.

"Do you think you could make it out there on your own, Stanley? You can't. I wouldn't. That's the key to life; you find a pocket in the system and live your controlled life, or you leave the system altogether. You tried the first one and see how that turned out?"

Where else could he go if he decided to leave everything he had known? A bright glitch blinded him. Shocks of static filled his ears like gunshots. He slowly climbed out from the vent and got to his feet, back pinned against the wall. On his left side, there was another thousand feet of Epicentre. On his right, here was enough footing for him to slink across the corner.

Gabrels made the move and saw that he was still close to the main platform of Floor 100. He took a breath and began to inch his way across. A single train car blasted past him. The noise nearly knocked him from the edge. Gabrels caught himself and felt his heart stop before slowly pumping blood again. He checked his pocket; the drive was still there.

"Stanley!"

It was Jaya, she was hanging from one of the windows of the train car. He put his hand out to signal her. The car began to move backwards until it was feet from him.

"Come on! We don't have much time! Another train will be here and we can't be stopped when it turns the corner!"

Ergo was there. He dialed something into a terminal that forced the door to open. Gabrels braced himself before he made the jump inside. His ribs hit the bottom of the doorway hard. Jaya and Ergo got to their feet and helped pull him inside. The car began to move once the doors shut.

"This thing's been moving in circles since you went inside," she said. Jaya pulled Gabrels to the corner. She left him on the floor and slid down to join him.

"How the hell did you get out?" asked Ergo.

Gabrels pulled the drive from his pocket and laughed. "Through a vent, the system came back on and the guns slaughtered everybody inside…"

Jaya went to touch the IO drive, but Gabrels snatched it back and put it inside his pocket. His eyes were glazed over but he looked at them, for a moment, like strangers. Her smile disappeared and she moved back to give him space.

"What was in there?" Ergo was curious.

"Not now," Jaya scolded him.

"Hell no, we almost died. I want to know what was in there."

Gabrels kept his eyes closed to try and block out the glitches. There were patches of bright light, even when he closed his eyes. The brain was still trying to connect to newDawn.

"I was raised in that place. All the rooms were the same, untouched, except for one thing…"

Ergo moved in close to hear him.

"Bodies on ice. It went from an experiment to a storage facility for the new lives they were going to switch over to, using the drive in my pocket."

"On ice? Like cryogenically preserved? I can't believe they were going to just put their brains into new bodies and pretend like they didn't do any of this shit."

"What do we do now?" she asked.

Gabrels opened his eyes and focused on the light. His vision was blurred. He knew what he wanted to say, but he was too tired to speak. Jaya and Ergo looked at each other. They seemed to speak, but he couldn't hear the words. He untied the sleeve of his jacket and put it back on. The wound was fresh but it stopped bleeding. Everything got smaller. Maybe he could sneak in a quick nap.

The white noise was there, an undercurrent, running water in the background of the scenario in front of him. The blurring lights were dotted with green and pink.

"Where are the rest of the cops if everyone got gunned down in there? Shouldn't they be looking for you? For us?" asked Ergo.

The train went quiet. A muffled rhythm was there, too.

"I don't know, E. Maybe the guys in black told them to back down. They probably wanted us dead before anyone else showed up."
It was behind the noise in his head and all around him.

"No…" said Gabrels.

Jaya and Ergo looked back at him.

"Stanley, you're tired. Get some rest. We will figure out what to do." Jaya put her hand on his neck. Her hands were warm. The memories of her flesh replaced the pain. Her touch sent chills down his spine. Don't lose her.

"No…it's…" He reached for the drive. They looked at him strangely when he put it up to the light. Gabrels saw the blinking red. He felt the rhythm in his hand. A timer.

"What's wrong?"

Jaya reached for the drive. Gabrels threw it against towards the front of the train. The detonator triggered the second it hit the wall. The explosion rocked the car and blew out the control room. A furious rush of wind sent them in different directions. Each of them scrambled for something to hang onto as the car struggled to stay on the track. The seats were pulled from their latches and fell out of the train and into the darkness.

Gabrels watched them for a moment. Jaya and Ergo screamed at him for help. He wanted to move but his arms did not respond. They pulled themselves towards the terminal that still sat on a seat neat the passenger door. He could see the Epicentre moving in fast motion while the train seemed to slow down.

Ergo used his belly to keep the terminal at arms' length. He steadied himself against the poles still fastened tight to the chairs and floor. Jaya crawled towards Gabrels. She grabbed him by the collar and pulled him away from the corner. Her words were buried under the sounds of emergency brakes failing. The door opened and they both tried to stand upright, pulling him along. The car was still moving in a circle, but the explosion had left it hanging by a thread. Jaya pointed towards the platform, the same one they had passed for hours. Nothing would slow it down. They both pointed at the little panel that kept screaming by. They looked into Gabrels' face and tried to shake him out of his trance.

He nodded when they said they had to jump. The word sounded familiar. He knew what it meant. Ergo threw the terminal out the door. They grabbed each other by the hand and waited for the platform. Jaya counted down. She lunged for the edge as the men followed.

Gabrels watched the world turn upside down. The wires that held the car broke. The sound of a whip snapped and the train was gone. They hovered in the air before they hit the steel. Their bodies crumbled upon impact. Jaya held tightly to his hand. He gripped for the other, but there was nothing there. They both looked around, dazed, barely able to move. Ergo was gone. Jaya cried out for him. White noise broke Gabrels down. He wiped the blood from his nose and struggled to his knees to look for him. They peered over the edge to see nothing but streams of lights that continued down to Narrow. The train sped to the earth and shattered silently. It was then when she saw it; a stain of red that painted the edge of the platform that seemed to run down the side of Epicentre.

He didn't make it. His body must have smashed against the side. Jaya screamed but no sounds came out. The static drowned out everything. Tears streamed down her face. Gabrels watched them changed color as he pulled himself forward to cradle her. He waited for the Police to come. The Shadowmen or someone must have turned off all routes to Floor 100, except for the car that stayed on that constant loop.

She held him close and buried her face into his chest. The entire city disappeared then. Jaya wanted nothing more than to rip Rion out of that body, to keep him safe. The revenant was breaking them both. She couldn't lose him too. Visions of her and E running through the slums filled the dark. She apologized to him in ways she could never say to his face. Jaya refused to move. Gabrels held her until he passed out from the pain.

Twenty eight

Four hours remaining.

Jaya woke up first. She pulled Gabrels to his feet. The landing lights were turned back on. A full train had stopped and opened its doors. They stepped inside, stained with dirt and blood. The passengers kept their distance and voiced their disgust online. The train was nearly empty, a couple of graveyard shifters; maintenance workers and clinic techs, filled some of the seats. Gabrels gripped Jaya's hand while they waited for the train to take them to the very top of the tenements. They both knew where to go. There was nowhere else. Penthouses on the peak of the tenements were protected by a security system similar to Machina, with Adam as the gatekeeper. Jaya whispered the exact building where Graff lived. She found it in Eros researching the names that Kath provided. He was oddly quiet. He hadn't spoken since the train. Gabrels thought it was a sign of him showing respect for once, to not speak ill of the dead, for the girl.

Within the hour, the train was empty. By that time they had reached Graff's building. It was a mirror image of the other tenements with the exception of a giant glass box on the roof that was built around the satellite that expand the broadcast reach of the data stream. Graff's office and living space was tucked away inside. They stepped onto the platform which took them into the top floor. The glass box was a staircase away. Gabrels and Jaya took careful steps through the top floor and up the stairs to the rooftop. The door was unlocked. The wind picked up as they walked out. A massive white satellite dish was cased in concrete. Glass chambers created a hall that followed to the penthouse. The entire Epicentre was alight as they approached the chambers. A security box was stationed on the left side, turned off. Jaya pulled Gabrels past the surveillance cameras hidden high in the corners of the entry.

Each chamber was a cube of eight feet in length and height, with fine etching between the shapes that marked date they were designed and assembled. The cubes moved off into other paths that housed hot tubs and climate controlled pool areas. Door sized holes were cut from the glass to allow movement through the rooms. Empty, yet fully stocked bars with neon lights decorated the outside cubes. Graff had put his own miniature Eros at his doorstep, which was wide open to them to just walk through. The interior was lit up with a golden glow. Jaya and Gabrels split up to investigate. Every room they stepped into was empty. They both armed themselves with some kind of weapon; Jaya held up a poker from the still burning fireplace that was dwarfed by the obnoxious portrait of Graff that stared down at her. Gabrels readied a frying pan from the massive kitchen that brandished a full dining table with black and white damask cloth that matched the checkerboard pattern of the floor.

He was in here. They both kept telling themselves. They were tired, beaten but ready for something to attack them. Jaya was stopped at a giant mirror. It was out of place in the penthouse. It was different from the excessive designs around them. It could be a panic room, she thought. There was a small keypad that required a code. She put the weapon down and got to work on opening it.

Gabrels entered the living room. The television was the size of the wall itself, the news channel was running down explanations of the Apex program to its viewers. With only three hours to go, refusal to continue connection with newDawn was at an all time high. No one turned it off, they just demanded it fixed. No official statements had been released. A media blackout had silenced the world for the first time in memory.

A single leather couch and cocktail table sat in front of the television, a cup of coffee that was still warm to the touch was positioned in the middle of its glass. The door to his office was at the end of a long hall. There were three bodies, men in suits, face down and bleeding out. The crimson had turned the Persian rug floor a shade of dark brown. Bullet holes dotted the door. The migraines had never stopped. Gabrels had just gotten numb to the constant pain. The white noise was there every time he blinked his eyes. Quick flashes of static shot through his ears in staccato beats.

"I know you're there." The voice came out of nowhere. Gabrels dropped his weapon. He reached down to pick it up. "Come on inside. I'm not going to kill you. I know why you're here." It was Graff.

Gabrels slowly opened the door and entered. The office was set against a backdrop of glass that overlooked the Epicentre. The city lights lit up the room. He was face to face again with Graff.

"Welcome to my home." He said.

The old man looked like hell. Sweat had built up on his neck and face. It stained the sleeves of the silk robe draped over him. There was a revolver on the table and a jewel encrusted cross on his neck.

"Did you kill those men outside?" Gabrels asked.

"I did. Chalk that up to me wanting to be left alone." Graff poured himself another glass and pushed an empty one towards his guest. There was another chair on the opposite side of the desk. "Have a seat. I've been waiting for you. I know there's something we need to talk about."

"I'm fine. You know that I don't drink."

The old man laughed. "I thought I was talking to your friend. You know, the one you have in up there?" Graff tapped his middle finger against his forehead.

"You're stuck with me. You think that you're going to get away with all the death you've caused?"

"If your friend has showed up instead, I would've had to shoot you. You are alright, kid. I know you don't have it in you to kill me. But he might. That's why this is sitting right here." Graff pointed to the revolver. "The plan was always anchored to the idea of making this place better, safer to live. No one used to be able to outrun their mistakes, to start anew. Things have changed. The world will be brand new, in just a few hours. As much as I would gladly stand by those citizens, I need to be an example. They still need a leader, someone who represents the old guard and someone with this country's dominance as top priority."

"Don't try to make this about being an example for the people. I know everything."

"And what do you know?" asked Graff.

"The Shadowmen are no longer your puppets, and they were going to use me to kill you. I know now that you've been using them from the beginning. That's why the IO drive at Machina, the one they thought they were keeping from you, was sabotaged."

"The bomb was rigged to start as soon as they stepped foot outside the facility with it. It was my failsafe to make sure if they did try to betray me, they wouldn't make it very far. Sorry to see that you got hit with it and not them. But it sounds like they got something far worse, didn't they?" Graff took off his chain and turned the crucifix. It opened to reveal another drive, identical to the one from Machina.

"Here is the real deal. I've always had it at arm's length. This is the true masterpiece in human technology, not Adam, or Apex, or even the revenant system. This right here is immortality." Graff placed the drive on the table, next to the gun. Gabrels felt his grip tighten on the weapon.

"You've got a lot to answer for...father."

"Father?" The old man sat up in his chair. "What the hell are you talking about?"

Gabrels approached the desk. Graff put his hand on the revolver.

"I'm talking about the Academy! All those children, taken away from their parents and put into a box! You gave them and you gave me, fake memories to cover up the truth, as some kind of sick experiment."

"And what truth is that?" asked Graff.

"You left my mother behind to die in the slums. You used your thugs to hide away the paperwork and put me to work once the experiment was a success. I'm here because of you!"

Graff looked at him strangely. "Listen, kid. I like you a lot and I can admire how far you've come. But you're mistaken. I'm not your dad."

Gabrels slammed the pan onto the desk. "Don't lie to me!"

Graff pulled his gun up and aimed it at his heart. "I can see how you might be upset to find out about how you grew up. The boys who came out of there were damaged, no doubt. But I can honestly tell you, that outside of you being Academy and working for Synapse, I have no idea who the hell you are. I never knew your mother, kid."

Gabrels' heart sunk.

"I didn't mess around with slum girls. I was always a man who sought after the finest things in life. Little girls in the slums were never my thing. Who told you that?" Graff called out to him. He stopped listening. Gabrels' body had frozen up.

"Do you feel that, too?"

"Kath? What is going on?"

"Sorry, Stanley but this is where the party ends for you."

"Why can't I move my body?"

"This is when the revenant takes control of your body and you become their proxy. Normally, you would be under their thumb but that's not how this is going to go down."

"What do you mean?"

"It's time for me to take over, for good."

"Graff!? Help me! Shoot me!"

"He can't hear you, Stanley. Technically, your mouth isn't even moving. We are speaking on a conscious level, just like our little sessions in the Blank Page."

"This can't be happening…"

"You didn't think that you could keep me in the dark forever, did you? I know what you were trying to do; take the body that Graff kept from his foot soldiers and put me in it."

"This doesn't make any sense. If I wasn't the kid from Everett's transcript, who was?"

Vax laughed.

"It was you, wasn't it?"

"Can you keep this a secret, Stanley?"

"How is this real?"

285

"Because you are fading. The bottom line is that your plan didn't work and mine did. You can't take out a revenant and put it in a new body. It goes in and takes over; it overwrites the programming of the host. You were never going to get rid of me, Stan."

"How do you know?"

"Everett told me."

"Everett?"

Graff got to his feet and crept towards the body frozen still.

"He was my way into finding the old man. We had been talking for months about selling the IO drive technology. Once I died, I had to find a way back to him, since he had been the one to lead them to my location. He got me killed, just so he could be welcomed into their secret group. He was never going to get in. I had to return the favor, through whatever channels were available, including a rat like your co-worker."

"You lied to me…"

"I told you a long time ago that you would never fully know me, Stan. There's no going back, one of us has to go. And in a few minutes, it's going to be you."

Gabrels hands began to shake. He was trying to regain control. "You son of a bitch…You played them against each other, and you played me this entire time."

"I had to. There's no other way for me to survive. I'm not going to let them kill me and get away with it. Nothing is going to stop me."

"How is this happening? The revenant isn't active."

"Stanley, you've heard what they said about me. I'm a hacker. I manipulate the system to work in my favor. I've been changing the rules since I figured out how to re-write them from inside your head. I told you before that the puzzle was an important part of Machina's plan. Remember?"

"Everett told me that, not you."

"The only time you've ever spoken to Everett was by the train."

"I was talking to you the whole time? Working on the puzzle?"

"Don't worry, it was mutual. Everett never had a clue he was talking to the man he got killed when he thought it was you. That's why I wanted you to avoid using the A.I. for help. I didn't know if it would catch onto what I was doing. But as time went on, it never caught up to me. It never even recognized my presence, only the obvious changes in brain activity, those moments when your nervous system started accepting my neurons and firing them up."

The static was louder than ever before.

"What happens to me now?"

"You vanish, just like I did."

Gabrels' view of the room had disappeared. "So, if Graff is your father, what does that make me?"

"You're an empty shell, like all those boys at the Academy now, waiting to have new memories, new lives plugged in. Nothing but more control, kid. This is the system you were born into."

"What about my mother?"

"She gave you up because she didn't want you. I've known that pain before. Don't feel bad. I never met mine, either."

The world went black.

"The revenant system was the perfect counter to Adam. It was all a matter of breaking down a way to manipulate electrical impulses in the brain. Once my body died, I became a series of impulses, which was introduced into your body. The puzzle you were given was the code to break and set me free. Remember what Jaya told you? That's why she knew I was the real deal. I took her code and changed it from the inside."

Gabrels fought to see through the darkness. There was nothing there anymore. The sounds of his heartbeat slowed to a creep. "Is she a part of your plan, too?"

"Not at first. But she is amazing. Too bad about her first boyfriend, though. Ergo was a good kid, but he wasn't going to let her go with me."

"What the fuck are you talking about?"

"I may have loosened your grip on his hand when you made that jump. She is a strong one, though. She'll move past this."

"I'm going to fucking kill you." Gabrels was trapped. All the rage in his heart was draining from him. His body became numb. All he could do was scream in silence. "And you put in my mother's birthday to drive me insane and follow your trail?! Her voice too!?"

"It worked didn't it? Also, not your mother's voice, but an old audio file that I kept from Catherine. You seem to forget about the pain that I have. The blackbird was her favorite. The diamond was a symbol of the project attached to the creation of Apex, the creation of Adam, Project Black Diamond."

"Creation of Adam?"

"Why do you think the A.I was malfunctioning? Why do you think Apex is going live so early? I made sure that it would, years before it would become a reality. I've been designing Adam's DNA at gunpoint since I was fifteen, but those dumb fucks couldn't follow what I was doing if I gave them a map. I put my own touches on it to make sure that when they implemented my technology, it would backfire on them."

"No…"

"Everything in the puzzle was a clue to lead you to the right direction. Once you got there, the revenant would trigger, the puzzle would be solved. Just like those fake memories they put in, once the deception is realized, the façade vanishes and all that's left is the result. Your façade is over, Stanley."

"Damn you..."

"Look, you have to admit, there's some freedom in knowing the truth, isn't there? You weren't stolen from your mother in some grand scheme to protect an asshole politician; she gave you away because she was an addict and couldn't support you. You have a little bit of addict in you too, now. See? We are more alike that you thought. Now, you can feel better knowing the truth."

"You used me…used everyone around you…"

"I know you didn't have any real choices. But you could have fucked this up in a number of ways and I'm glad that you didn't."

"And now you're going to kill him?"

"He's not going to ever know. He doesn't deserve to know. Catherine's dead."

"There's always… a choice. Don't do this, Kath…" Gabrels was fading. Vax's voice came from somewhere further and further away.

"Sleep now, Stan. You did an excellent job. I will take it from here. Get some rest. No more white noise, no more static. No more bad dreams. Just sleep. You've earned it."

Gabrels waited for the Blank Page, the white noise but there was nothing there. He had fallen into the black. The pain, the itching was gone. He cried out for Vax, for the girl, Helix. He screamed until there was nothing left inside him.

Graff touched the kid's arm. Vax had felt it.

"Stanley?"

He raised the pan off the table and smashed it into the old man's face. The gun fell from his hand. "Not fucking Stanley."

Graff fell to the floor. He went for the revolver. Vax kicked it across the room and brought the pan down onto the top of Graff's head. It split him open. A trail of red began to pour down his face as he crawled into the corner. Vax picked up the revolver and grabbed the IO drive.

"What's happened to you?" asked Graff.

"Stanley's gone. Not for nothing, it was for a good cause. It led me back to you. The man who took everything from me."

"What the hell are you talking about?"

Vax kicked him in the teeth. The old man screamed out as he covered up. He spit a tooth back at him. "Catherine. You killed her."

He knew the name. Graff smirked as he remembered her face. "Oh, shit. You're kidding me. She was a beauty, wasn't she? I guess that's why we are both here, isn't it? Revenge? Listen, whether she was your girl or whatever, she stole from me. Was that because of you? There's no coming back from that, boy. You steal from me and you get dealt with."

"You took what was mine; my designs, my technology. Ciphertxt, the entire DNA of Adam, decrypted and torn apart to be put back together by me and my friends from down below. I was happy to give you what you needed, as long as I got the chance to get out. I didn't need shit in my life anyway, until I met her. You thought you were above me, even now. That's why taking her life didn't mean shit to you. I was a slum punk and she was a whore, right?"

Vax placed another kick into Graff's heart. The glass that protected it cracked. "Is that right?!"

The old man fell to his side in pain.

"The day I found out she was gone, I made a promise to make sure you felt everything I did. And then I would end you. Until now, I've lived up to that promise."

Vax turned his back to Graff and looked to the picture of Diovanni. He picked it up and placed a kiss on her lips. "Dio, was it?"

Graff sat up slowly.

"Her new boyfriend was an escort, just like her, just like Catherine. It was so easy to watch you crumble after all this time living behind this impenetrable wall. You sent your goons out to do your dirty work; leaving bodies all over Eros, pouring that liquid shit to try and burn away all the evidence. You let your own men burn her alive."

Graff was broken. Vax dropped the picture in his hand. "Look at her, Leland. Can you find a way to live without that pain?"

Vax knelt down. He pulled Graff's chin up so they were face to face. "Look at what your sins have made you. I knew I could never get close to you on my own. I had to die and get transplanted into another body. I let Catherine go to get next to you and look what happened to her. Now you know what that feels like."

There was someone else in the room. Vax slowly turned around to see Maxwell. His face was covered in blood.

"Mr. Kath…we finally meet."

He was badly wounded, but he stood against the doorway, aiming his gun right at Vax's head.

"Shadowman?"

"You've got it." Maxwell struggled to take a bow.

"What's your name?" asked Vax.

"Don't have one…" he sighed.

"All the stories about the men in black, the rumors, and the mentions of shadows that ran the streets of Narrow, all that shit is infamous. You wanted to use me to take out the old man and swap bodies using the insurance policy he's got in storage."

"Tonight was supposed to be about rebirth. Father creates son, who ends the father."

Maxwell stared past him. He was only concerned with ending the old man. There were splashes of blood all over him. Graff called out to them, neither answered. "My partner and I prided ourselves on being the best problem solvers; always clean, always on time, always untouchable."

"I guess that last goal fell short, didn't it?"

"I have to admit, I expected you to break from the pack, but not in a way that would nearly get me killed." Maxwell was honest. The wounds were deep.

"Are you here to shoot me? Or him?"

"Both, Mr. Kath."

Vax raised his gun as well. "You're giving me a chance to hand it to you?"

"Why not? Your gun might not have any bullets in it."

"I thought you would have just shot me by now. It is what you do best. Speaking of which, where's your partner?"

Maxwell's face went dead. "He's gone. Gunned down, unfortunately. I was lucky enough to be standing behind him, which means that he saved my life."

"Well, that's very honorable but not redeeming in any way. Do you really think that he did that on purpose?" asked Vax.

"He could have moved out of the way, but he didn't. He was a true friend, a warrior. He was worth saving, unlike you. I've read your history. I know how valuable you are to Leland. I mean, between you and me, we are practically brothers. We came from the same place, the same broken down houses burned by the acid rain. We were given new names, new clothes, food and guns. You practically created Adam, the favorite of the prisoners put to work. You are the reason we are here, right now. That's why you had to die. You were always supposed to be the weapon to turn this system upside down. The revenant can't be removed from the body, it takes over, period. The body is a shell to be driven. The original must be replaced."

"I am not giving this shit up."

Vax pulled the trigger. "Damn…"

Maxwell was right. "No bullets, friend?" He asked. "Have you ever heard of division by zero? No? It's an expression without meaning. Any number multiplied by zero, is zero…When done through code, it can generate either a positive or a negative infinity. Do you know what happens after that? The program terminates, it freezes trying to maintain the infinite loop, and it crashes."

"Am I the program?" asked Vax.

"This system is the program. We are the zeroes. We have the key to leave it, right in our hands. We plug ourselves into new bodies, we go on forever. We watch the world crumble but we survive. The system crashes, but we could be infinite."

A ball quietly rolled into the room between Maxwell's legs. Both men looked down at it. Vax recognized it immediately and smiled.

A clicking noise began to emanate from the metal sphere. It ignited and covered the room in fire. Vax was thrown behind the desk as Maxwell fired away. The flames were sudden and covered Maxwell whole. He fell to the ground, too weak to roll. Graff went for his gun but Vax fought him off and beat him down again.

He looked up to see Jaya standing in the doorway. He had never thought he'd be happy to see her. She remembered the sphere from the hotel room. Somehow, she had it with her the entire time. She smiled at him before kicking the gun away from Maxwell's body. In her hand was the keypad for the panic room.

"There's something else. You need to see it."

She had broken in and removed the code for the vault. The office was filled with smoke. The fire began to burn the curtains, the floors, everything in sight.

"Will it keep him alive?"

Jaya nodded her head.

Vax dragged the old man out of the office, past Maxwell's body and dropped him inside the panic room.

"Go ahead and kill me, you little shit." Graff spit in his face. "I'm ready to die. I can't wait to leave this place. Take your revenge."

Vax looked at Jaya and smiled. "You know what? I've had a change of heart."

"What?" Graff crawled towards him.

"Killing you is all I've wanted. The more I think about it, I don't need a bullet to end this. This is just something else that I can take from you. You can't be exposed if you're dead. Face it, Leland, you've been damaged for years. I'm simply bringing it to the light."

He made his way to the door. Graff grabbed onto his leg. Vax kicked him off. He put two bullets in both feet to keep him from hurting himself. Jaya went to the bathroom to find some medicine. She returned with two shots. One was marked with special instructions for anemia, another for sleep. She stuck him in the legs.

"This will make sure he stays asleep and now, he won't bleed out."

The old man could not stand. There was nothing inside the room for him to use to hurt himself.

"Letting the world tear your legacy apart is all the absolution I need."

Vax closed the door and locked it from the outside. He looked to the clock. Apex would be live within the hour.

Graff weakly beat his hands against the walls, calling out for Vax to end it. "Listen to me, you bastard! Open this door right now! Kill me!"

Jaya took him by the hand and led him to the rooftop. Past the glass chambers, was the body cell. He handed her the IO drive as they sat at the edge of the roof to watch the penthouse burn to the ground.

Vax watched the flames do their dance and tear everything down. The room that imprisoned Graff stood tall. He put his arm around Jaya but he thought of Catherine. He would give anything to bring her back, just to see this moment.

Jaya put her head on his shoulder. It was over. They stayed there to listen to the sounds of the city. There was no talk of the next step, no thinking about the future. She held onto him tightly, trying to trust that he would take her with him. Vax could hear Stanley's voice still calling out to him, like the fleeting itch of the needle.

"Sorry about what happened, kid," he said. "But I'm not done living yet…And neither are you."

The Police hit the roof to find an old man inside the cell. There were no signs of anyone else.

The body inside the cell opened its eyes. There was no pain, just tired muscles from sleeping upright. It felt like he had slept for years. He was face down and felt something sticking out of the back of his neck. It was some kind of tablet, small and metal. He pulled it out and looked at it. Weird flashes of people's faces and voices began to echo.

The air inside was thin. He turned himself around and saw the inside of a closet. There was light beyond the door. At his feet was a bag of cash with a wallet. Some apology, he thought. He bent down and picked it the wallet. He wondered if people still had those things. Inside was a plastic ID card with a name he had never heard before. There was a brand new date of birth, address and statistics along with his picture.

It was then, when he remembered everything; the static from his dreams, the pain that crippled his mind, the faces of men that nearly destroyed him. There was a note inside. Scribbled in red pen were an address, the same one from his ID, and the word Helix. He read the name and remembered her face. On the back of the paper, read something else;

"Free."

There was a pile of neatly folded clothes next to a pair of shoes on the floor in front of him. He pushed the open the glass door and stepped out of the cell. He got dressed and pocketed the cash, contemplating his decision. He wanted to see her first. What happens next was his choice. When he was ready, he pushed the closet doors open. Light flooded the room. He did not cover his eyes. For the first time, he could see everything clearly.

Also by the author

Novels:

The Black Eclipse
Wasteland Heart

Poetry:

The Outsider
Distortion Dreams

www.ingramcontent.com/pod-product-compliance
Lightning Source LLC
Chambersburg PA
CBHW020240180626
46810CB00006B/2283